Look for More Titles by Cassandra Chandler

SCIENCE FICTION ROMANCE

Cygnian 7
NUAR
KRAL
LAR
DORN
BRON
TARN
ROM

The Department of Homeworld Security
Gray Card
Resident Alien
Business or Pleasure
Tied up in Customs
Entry Visa
Duration of Stay
Duel Citizenship
Invasive Species
Export Duty
COALITION RECKONING
Import Quarantine
Homeworld for the Holidays
Nothing to Declare
Rate of Return
Trade Secrets

—

PARANORMAL ROMANCE NOVELS

The Forbidden Knights
FORBIDDEN INSTINCT

—

PARANORMAL ROMANCE NOVELLAS

Court of the Yuletide Fae
The Yule Cat
The White Stag
The Krampus

Court of the Springtime Fae
Jack Frost
Prince Charming
The Oak King

—

URBAN FANTASY

The Blades of Janus
PACK
PROGENITOR

PARANORMAL - HORROR ROMANCE

The Summer Park Psychics
WANDERING SOUL
WHISPERING HEARTS
LINGERING TOUCH

—

COLLECTIONS

The Department of Homeworld Security
THE DEPARTMENT OF HOMEWORLD SECURITY OMNIBUS 1
THE DEPARTMENT OF HOMEWORLD SECURITY OMNIBUS 2

Progenitor

The Blades of Janus
Book Two
(Second Edition)

Cassandra Chandler

Copyright Page

Progenitor
The Blades of Janus, Book Two
Copyright © 2018, 2025 by Cassandra Chandler
Print ISBN (Second Edition): 978-1-945702-85-3
Digital ISBN (Second Edition): 978-1-945702-84-6

First eBook edition: November 2018
Second eBook edition: April 2025
First print edition: November 2018
Second print edition: April 2025
10 9 8 7 6 5 4 3 2 1

cassandra-chandler.com
P.O. Box 91
Mission, Kansas 66201

Dedication

For Tom and his many questions.

Don't miss out on any of the dark alien action.
Subscribe to Cassandra Chandler's newsletter at
https://sendfox.com/CassandraChandler

Chapter One

"This is a dead end. Let's head back to the bike." Brock projected his thoughts into Dexter's mind—which wasn't hard, since they were sharing the same brain at the moment.

"If you're bored, you can always visit one of your other replicants," Dexter thought back. *"Zach is tracking a kelpie in Europa."*

"No thanks. I'm sure you'll find a dweller to deal with eventually. Providence is crawling with them. Present company included."

"Thanks for the reminder."

Dexter's thoughts retreated. If Brock didn't know better, he'd think Dexter was sulking. At least the distance meant he'd stop bugging Brock about going back to his own body for a while. Probably.

Brock wanted to stay near town mentally as well as physically. His family was finally whole again, now that he and his dad had found Tessa. With everyone living at the ranch along with the other Blades of Janus who were assigned to Providence, it felt like home.

He was still a little tempted to hop over to Zach's body.

Watching Zach fight a kelpie would be a lot more interesting than hanging out with Dexter while he patrolled some defunct Redcap tunnels they'd discovered in Greenbriar Park.

The most interesting thing Dexter had done all night was temporarily activate his bike's flight protocols to avoid running over a possum. Tearing down the road on the alien-tech infused motorcycle was a hell of a lot better than this nighttime stroll.

"Tessa said other dwellers often move into Redcap tunnels," Brock thought. *"But I'm not noticing anything."*

"You shouldn't be trying to," Dexter projected. *"Eli says you need rest."*

"Rest isn't going to help me and you know it."

Brock's birthday was less than a week away. There was no way he'd survive it. He'd be damned if he was going to spend his last few days on Earth confined to bed in a body that barely functioned, no matter what his dad said. Especially when Brock had eight perfectly healthy replicant bodies whose minds he could piggyback on.

All part of the perks of being not-exactly-human himself.

"You've given up already," Dexter thought.

"Don't be naïve. We know what's going to happen. It's the end of another three-year cycle. The last one."

"You can't be sure."

"Come on, Dexter. I was in a coma for a week last time.

Dad barely managed to keep me alive, and you were all basically dead."

"We weren't dead."

"You didn't have any life signs," Brock thought. *"The only reason Dad knew you were still alive is that none of you vaporized. If he hadn't called in the other replicant pairs so he could monitor everyone, the Blades at your bases probably would have buried you."*

Brock wondered if his body would disappear in the glowing blue light that consumed dwellers who had died— or been killed by his Blades. After he was gone, they'd finally know once and for all just how much of a dweller he was.

His dad said every test showed that Brock was one-hundred percent human. The tests were wrong. And Brock's non-human nature was about to kill him.

"The others should be here," Dexter thought.

"Don't want them to miss the party?"

"The increase in dweller activity at our other bases is too much of a coincidence," Dexter projected. *"We should all be at the ranch to protect you."*

"You should be at your own bases helping your teams for as long as possible. I'm not worried about my safety."

"You should be. If Vaughn can finish building the stasis chambers, it'll give Eli more time to—"

"To do what?" Brock shot back. *"Dad can't fix this. It's who I am. Who we are. The sooner you can accept that,*

the sooner we can all have a little fun before—"

"Shh."

None of Brock's replicants ever shushed him. Dexter paused, cocking his head to the side as he turned in a slow circle. He stopped, staring back at the bridge they had just crossed.

"We need to gather our resources," Dexter thought.

Every time a replicant used their weird plural pronoun when talking about themselves, Brock felt a shiver in his mind, like a tuning fork had been struck and then pointed at his soul. He knew that each pair of replicants was a single entity that shared two bodies, like the one that inhabited both Dexter and Porter.

After all these years, it was still surreal to experience their existence along with them—and to know his own body had created them. Eight exact copies of Brock as he'd looked on the birthday when they... emerged. He suppressed a shudder, shielding Dexter from the revulsion Brock always felt when he remembered the process.

The replicants might not process emotions the same way humans did, but that didn't mean they didn't feel. Knowing how dedicated his replicants were to him, Brock didn't want to put that on Dexter, even if his very first copy could be kind of an ass.

Brock pushed closer to Dexter's senses, feeling a weird pressure as Dexter drew mental power from his other body, Porter, and focused his entire consciousness on this one. Back at the ranch, Brock felt Porter going dormant, frozen over his microscope and not seeing with that set of eyes anymore.

All of their brains' processing power channeled toward Dexter along the connections Brock could sense between all of them—every single replicant. Brock had to admit, it was an incredible rush.

"Getting kind of crowded in here, DP." Brock tried to project some humor along with his thought, using the combined name for the consciousness that controlled this pair of replicants—DP. Of course, DP didn't react.

Brock wasn't picking up on anything, but the Dexter replicant could detect things Brock couldn't, especially when he was using both his brains to parse through the data this body's senses fed him. Now, if Brock decided to take over Dexter's body, it would be a different matter.

Shortly after arriving at the ranch, Vaughn tried to explain her theory that Brock's mind was a hub that his replicants communicated through and used to share 'mental processing power.' Something about quantum computing. If Brock hadn't been so exhausted, it probably would have been fascinating. He had fallen asleep a few minutes into the lecture.

"Something is under the bridge." Dexter reached over his shoulders to draw both of the swords strapped to his back.

The ground on either side of the paved path had been

disturbed in several places. It didn't seem out of the ordinary to Brock.

"Looks like groundhogs," Brock thought.

"We're linking with Bradley."

Shit. Not groundhogs, then.

The pressure against Brock's mind vanished in a rush of spectacular mental energy. Dexter's thoughts surged around Brock's consciousness, faster than he could track. His vision fractured for a moment into five hexagonal sections, like he imagined a wasp might see.

The Brad replicant was sitting on a veranda going over data on one of the paper-thin tablet PCs Vaughn had designed, sipping coffee as the sun rose over the ocean on the East coast. Lee was in the weapon's room at the Caiman Beach base, putting away a wicked looking double-headed axe. Both bodies froze in what they were doing, as if someone had hit the pause button on Brock's view.

Then there were the more familiar views. Brock could see the tiny organisms Porter's eyes were staring at through his microscope as well as Dexter's view of the bridge and park.

The fifth view—the one in the middle that bridged them all—was black. Brock's eyes were closed as his true body lay in bed, a crushing weight no one could explain trapping him there.

He could hear his dad moving around the room and the

soft hum of the instruments and machines that Vaughn had coaxed back to life in the ship where Brock was staying. In the *crashed alien spaceship* buried deep beneath the ranch.

Brock's life was beyond bizarre.

His vision collapsed into a single view of the park. He felt, saw, and heard so much more than before. He could calculate the temperature by listening to the crickets, see the edges of each leaf with a crispness his own eyes could never perceive—or, rather, his own brain couldn't process. Everything around them slowed, as if time itself was no match for their combined mental acuity.

I will never get used to this. Brock kept that thought to himself, which was probably why Bradley opened with snark.

"Hey, pretty boy," Bradley projected. *"Need some help keeping that pristine body intact?"*

Sometimes, Brock really wanted to punch Bradley in the face. In both his faces.

Yeah, the Dexter and Porter pair were the only replicants who weren't covered in scars. But that was only because they hadn't lost a body fighting dwellers. Yet.

Having experienced every single 'death' along with the replicant who lost a body, as well as the hell that came afterwards when they re-grew a new one... Brock wouldn't wish that on anyone, not even the beings that had somehow spawned from him, breaking his own body in the process. He also wouldn't let his replicants wish that on each other.

They all had cold streaks. Brock did his best to watch out for those thoughts and shut them down.

"Have you ever heard me *complain about DP's appearance?"* Brock projected the thought fiercely. They could never forget that Brock didn't just endure their deaths with them—he also carried the scars of the wounds responsible. Death marks. His body was covered in them. His face...

He couldn't think about that. No matter how good he was at shielding and filtering his thoughts, he never wanted to risk the more recently created replicants sensing just how repulsed he was by his own appearance. By *their* appearances, too.

They had to know how he felt. They were too smart not to have figured that out. But they sure as hell didn't have to share his emotions on top of that.

"Apologies, progenitor," Bradley projected. *"We didn't know you were visiting DP."*

"That shouldn't make a difference." Brock didn't mind them feeling his displeasure over their comment.

Aside from the small scar that ran along their left cheekbone, the Brad and Lee replicants could easily conceal the rest of their death marks with their clothing. Brock had gained that scar when Lee was killed getting it —before Zachary had emerged, so Zach and Carey had it, too.

Those two sets had split off from Brock's body before the shit really hit the fan. They all had more scars. So many more.

Malcolm's first death had left the pair so disfigured, they couldn't be assigned a base. No amount of makeup could hide their scars, and it would be impossible to explain how the marks on their faces were identical.

Having a set of replicants freed up to travel wherever they were needed was helpful. They'd been all over the world, but Brock almost never visited them. It hurt too much to see how people reacted to them—and knowing he would have to deal with the same gasps and staring eyes if he was capable of travel.

Brock felt the hair on his own body's arms lift back at the ranch, remembering the last time he'd been brave enough to look at himself in the mirror. Even if his replicants would let him, Brock had given up on walking among humans long ago.

"You okay, Brock?" DP must be picking up on Brock's emotions. The replicants almost never used Brock's name.

"Yeah," Brock thought.

"Good, because we all need to focus." Dexter stepped off the paved trail.

Brock calmed himself, taking in the surroundings along with all the other consciousnesses linked to the Dexter body in that moment. Wind whispering through the trees, water trickling under the bridge, something moving in the earth. Something... big.

Spindly arms burst through the topsoil and reached for Dexter's legs. Dexter leapt into the air, swinging his swords as he reached the apex of his flip—upside-down. The blades flashed, reflecting the light from the lampposts along the path. A thick fluid sprayed the ground as he severed the creatures' arms at their elbows.

Even through the ground, Brock could hear the screeches of the dwellers Dexter had maimed. The loss of a couple of limbs probably wouldn't stop them. Sure enough, the ground rippled as the things pushed their way closer to the surface.

Dexter spun his swords in graceful arcs as he finished his flip, the tips of both weapons pointing at the ground. He stabbed them through the earth as he landed in a crouch.

A normal person could never have pulled off that maneuver. Dexter was far from normal.

Brock could feel Dexter drawing on all of their bodies —using the mental power of five brains, the muscle memory of five bodies. These dwellers didn't stand a chance.

More screeches came from below. Thick brown-green blood welled up around the blades as Dexter twisted their hilts. He pulled the swords with him as he stood, flicking them to the side to cut off more arms reaching for him from the ground.

Brock was about to pull back and leave Dexter to his gruesome work when a different type of scream hit his ears. Human.

"Dexter—" Brock thought.

"We know." Dexter ran toward the sound, hacking at limbs as he did, leaping over forms emerging from the earth. Time slowed again, letting Brock get a good look at the creatures.

Filthy clothes hung from their impossibly thin bodies. Their skin was coated in fine silver fur. As far as dwellers went, that wasn't so bad. It was their faces that Brock was sure he'd be having nightmares about.

The gray skin that mostly covered their eyes was wrinkled and puckered. It looked like someone had taken two clods of mud and rubbed them into their otherwise empty eye sockets. Their noses were tiny slits and oversized teeth that were jagged triangles filled their mouths, shark-like. Two tiny flaps of skin stuck out from the sides of their heads roughly where their ears should be.

"Trolls," Bradley projected.

Brock almost wished he had kept his distance from Dexter's consciousness so these things would be out of focus. He'd studied the entry on trolls in Vaughn's Dweller's Database, and knew they were ugly. Seeing them up close and clearly was much worse than the digitized files. No wonder Vaughn called them mole-people.

"Tessa warned us that other dwellers tend to move into Redcap tunnels after an infestation has been cleared," DP thought. *"Trolls were at the top of her watchlist."*

"Great," Brock projected.

Dexter leapt over a troll and hit the ground in a roll. Brock felt him calculating his inertia against his heightened strength and speed. At the end of the roll, Dexter launched off the ground, practically flying at the mass of trolls surrounding their prey. They had her on the ground and were hunched over her, punching and kicking. The woman's screams had subsided to low sobs.

"Be careful you don't hurt her," Brock thought to Dexter.

"We have *done this before,"* Dexter replied.

Brock couldn't keep himself from worrying. The writhing mass of dwellers would make it difficult for Dexter to see where his swords were landing.

A few feet from the group, Dexter skidded to a stop. He shouted, "Hey," using his voice instead of his mind.

The sound startled Brock. Dexter was one of the least chatty of the replicants. What was he doing?

Brock pushed closer to Dexter's awareness, feeling the strength in Dexter's limbs as he held both swords ready at his sides. Half a dozen of the trolls turned, sniffing the air. They stepped away from the woman, collapsing their torsos into short, squat forms rather than the long, thin creatures they'd originally appeared to be.

Dexter launched himself at them. He'd decapitated four before the others even realized what was going on. The other two who had noticed Dexter sprang at him, their bodies distending like macabre accordions.

Dexter shifted his weight to the right, then stabbed up with the sword in his left hand, skewering the troll on that side. He pivoted, pulling the weapon free and using his other blade to slash the throat of the last attacking troll in a move that was as graceful as it was brutal.

The dead dwellers started to glow with a soft blue light. It consumed them, like flame devouring paper. Even without eyes, the other trolls seemed to register it. They all turned, leaving the woman they'd been beating curled in a ball on the ground. As one, they charged at Dexter.

Looking through Dexter's eyes nearly made Brock seasick. Turns, twirls, leaps, like a violent form of ballet. It hadn't been too many years ago when Brock could perform those maneuvers himself. He remembered the rush of drawing on all of his replicants at once during battle—before they'd decided it was too dangerous for him to be in the field.

Within seconds, Dexter had killed or incapacitated every single troll. He looked around at the still forms lying on the ground, taking note of which ones weren't disintegrating yet and finishing them off.

Brock felt a snap in his mind as Bradley's consciousness disconnected. It took him a moment to adjust to Dexter's senses being muted—or at least seeming so. This was actually closer to his usual levels of perception. Brock felt Porter begin moving about his lab, working on his latest research project.

"Dexter," Brock prompted.

"Yes?"

"The woman."

"She's fine."

"Check on her, please." Brock sent the thought with a little force behind it.

Dexter headed toward her. She was huddled in a ball, arms held defensively in the air. The denim jacket she wore looked ancient and barely fit her. There were stains and tears all over it. Most looked older than this encounter. She was compact and stick-thin. Her dark hair was pulled into a tight bun. Brock caught glimpses of a shining metal collar around her neck.

"Please don't kill me," she said, her voice low and raspy.

Dexter cocked his head to the side, saying nothing. He stepped warily around the woman, studying her as if she was a threat.

"Dexter, you need to reassure her," Brock thought. *"She was just attacked."*

"Something isn't right."

The only thing Brock could see that was wrong was how Dexter was treating this woman. It was inhumane not to comfort her. Sometimes, he had to remind his replicants of how to at least pretend to be human.

"Talk to her," Brock projected.

"Who are you?" Dexter spoke in a harsh, commanding voice.

If Brock had been fully occupying a body at that moment, he would have covered his face with his hands. He didn't bother trying to hide the frustration flooding through him.

"Meg," the woman said. "I'm Meg. I won't try to hurt you, I promise. Please don't kill me."

Brock's frustration turned to confusion.

"Why is she promising not to hurt you?" Brock sent.

Brock ignored the ripple of smugness that flowed from Dexter as he pointed the tip of one sword at the woman and stepped back, giving himself more room to react.

There was a reason that DP was the only replicant set that had never experienced a death. He was the most paranoid.

"Stand," Dexter said.

Meg rose on shaking legs. Her eyes were clenched shut and her hands clasped in front of her as she was begging for her life.

"Please don't kill me," she said. "I've never hurt anyone. I swear it."

"She's a dweller," Brock sent.

"Why were the trolls attacking her then?"

Different types of dwellers seldom interacted with each other at all. The trolls had given this woman a beating. There were bruises marring her face. Blood trickled from her nose and her lip was split.

Except, as Brock observed through Dexter's eyes, the cut sealed itself. Her bruises faded and her skin absorbed the blood.

"Open your eyes," Dexter said. His voice wasn't as dispassionate as usual. He was agitated. That wasn't good.

"She said she won't hurt us," Brock sent. *"The trolls might have been attacking her because she doesn't prey on humans. We've seen it happen before."*

Meg let out a whimper. "I won't hurt you. Please…"

"Open them."

"Dexter, give her a—"

Brock's thought cut off as she opened her eyes. Light spilled out of them. They were gleaming bright gold.

Dexter raised his left sword—the one infused with silver—his arm aligned to slash her throat.

"Stop!" Brock pushed the command through their link, holding Dexter in place.

"She's a werewolf," Dexter thought. *"There must be others. We need to kill her quickly and find them before they find us."*

"I'm the omega." Meg practically screeched the words. Her hands were shaking. "I've never killed anyone. I've never even transformed. I thought the Blades only killed monsters who are a threat to humans."

"Monsters?" Brock thought.

"You're a werewolf," Dexter said. "All werewolves are threats."

Damn, Brock should have made Dexter keep his mouth shut, too.

"What about Marcus?" she said. "He's a werewolf *and* a Blade. He protects people."

Dexter's voice remained cold. "We're not recruiting."

Meg shook her head, her brow furrowed. "I don't want to be a Blade. I'm not a fighter."

"Then what do you want?" Dexter said.

"I want to be with Marcus."

That ship had sailed. Marcus was mated to Tessa, Brock's foster-sister. Their bond was the only thing keeping Tessa sane after Marcus had been forced to turn her to save her life.

"And Tessa," Meg said.

Brock's control slipped. Dexter dropped the sword in his right hand and grabbed Meg by her neck, lifting her from her feet as if she weighed nothing. She grabbed his wrist with both hands, her legs kicking wildly as she sought the ground. The collar seemed to be protecting her throat from being crushed, but it dug into her skin. Fresh blood trickled over Dexter's fingers.

"How do you know about Tessa?" Dexter said.

Brock was wondering the same. It was what had made

him slip and lose control.

Most dwellers were aware of Marcus by now, but Tessa had only been with the Blades for a few weeks. She hadn't recovered enough control since becoming infected with the werewolf parasite to go on patrol yet. No one should know about her but the Blades stationed in Providence and Brock's other replicants. How did Meg know?

"Put her down," Brock sent. *"We can find out another way."*

Dexter ignored him.

"Please," Meg gasped. "They're my… pack."

"We destroyed that pack sixteen years ago," Dexter said.

"Not all of us." She sucked in a breath, eyes widening as she spoke so fast her words blurred together. "I mean, I survived. And Marcus. I wasn't there when it happened."

"Dexter, you're scaring her," Brock thought.

"Good."

The collar around Meg's neck started to hum and snap. Dexter's hand tingled as an electric current coursed through him. Meg seemed to be getting the worst of it, though. She yelped, pinching her eyes shut as her body spasmed from the charge.

"What the hell?" Brock thought.

The current stopped, leaving a faint smell of scorched flesh in the air. Meg twitched, tears running down her cheeks.

"Interesting accessory," Dexter said.

"It helps me... control myself." Meg had to work to get enough air to speak. Between being electrocuted and Dexter's grip, it was a wonder she could speak at all.

"Shocks me," she gasped. "Please. I can't change."

Brock tried to push a command through, to get Dexter to put Meg down, but Dexter was fighting back, drawing on Porter's mind as they combined their willpower in an effort to fend Brock off.

He didn't give a shit that they were trying to protect him. They were using their link against him—the same link that had trapped Brock in a hospital bed for years.

He snapped.

"Have it your way," Brock thought.

He blasted his way into Dexter's body, knocking out the part of DP's consciousness that had been occupying it. The Porter replicant was going to have a headache for a while.

Brock took a deep breath, filling Dexter's lungs, reveling in the strength of his body. Steady legs, straight back, strong arms. Arms that were being used to hurt someone he suspected was an innocent.

He quickly lowered Meg to her feet. He kept his grip on her neck, but relaxed it, focusing all of his senses on her to detect any signs that she was about to attack. He also kept the silvered sword handy.

Her skin was warm and softer than he'd expected.

"Brock, what are you doing?" DP shouted in Brock's head, as frantic as Brock had ever heard him. *"She's dangerous. You can't let yourself be unprotected. Let me back in."*

As bizarre as it was that the replicants referred to themselves as 'we' when their consciousness was occupying both of their bodies, it was even stranger to hear them use 'me' and 'I' when they were stuck in one form. None of them understood why their speech patterns changed.

"Calm down," Brock sent.

"I don't know what will happen to you if that body is killed while you're in it. The strain could—"

"Kill me a couple of days early?"

DP didn't have a response for that.

In three days, Brock would turn thirty. He would complete another three-year cycle. He would split again. And this time, it would kill him. Probably all of them.

"Progenitor…"

"I know you're scared," Brock sent. *"I am, too. But I can handle this, and—"* He sighed. *"Can you blame me for wanting to experience more with what time I have left? To be able to feel fresh air and walk around without help?"*

He felt DP recede, but it wasn't enough. Brock put up the mental barrier he'd developed over the years—his only way of getting any privacy with four other consciousnesses tied to his own. Most of the time, he blocked them without even thinking about it. Doing so while borrowing one of their bodies was a bit trickier.

He took another deep breath and let it out slowly, enjoying the moment of quiet and being alone.

Except for the werewolf he had by the throat.

He watched her neck work as she swallowed, lips parted and eyes wide. When he smiled, she flinched.

Whatever DP thought, Brock didn't sense anything threatening about her. All he felt was the softness of her skin, a slight trembling in her frame.

His fingers—Dexter's fingers—still tingled from the collar shocking her while she'd been freaking out earlier. She'd said it helped her control herself. Knowing that she'd rather be electrocuted than hurt people, Brock couldn't bring himself to fear her at all.

"Sorry about that." He released her, and slowly sheathed his sword in one of the scabbards strapped to his back. He hoped he didn't nick Dexter's favorite jacket trying to hit the opening sewn into the black leather.

DP would be having fits if he could perceive Brock. He knew he should step away from Meg to give himself more time to react in case she attacked, but he couldn't bring himself to do so. If she decided to gut him, she wouldn't even have to stretch her arm.

"I understand," Meg said. "You're a Blade. I'm a werewolf. Of course you took action to defend yourself, but I promise you—I swear to you—I won't try to hurt you."

The words poured out of her in a flood. She was trying so hard to put him at ease. Brock reached out to gently grasp her arms, wanting to reassure her as well. The motion had been instinctual—as was her reaction. And it made his blood boil.

Her eyes screwed shut, her jaw clenched, and she turned her head, her entire body stiffening as she waited for the first blow. In that moment, he was certain of one thing. The beating from the trolls wasn't the first she'd endured.

"Meg…"

She trembled, but didn't open her eyes. It was too much. He pulled her against his chest and wrapped his arms around her.

Chapter Two

What was happening? Meg didn't understand.

One moment, the Blade had been ready to kill her. Now, he had his arms around her. And he wasn't trying to crush her or control her. He was *holding* her.

When he'd attacked, she'd been sure that he was Dexter, the coldest, most ruthless killer among the Blades. He'd killed a dozen trolls in seconds. She hadn't seen any of them land a single blow.

But with this... She wasn't sure anymore. Even the waves of malice she'd sensed from him seemed to have stopped.

She felt him move and tensed, prepared for whatever he was about to do to her. If she didn't fight back, maybe he'd take her to Marcus and Tessa.

Who was Meg kidding? She never fought back. That was her job—her place. Her alpha made sure she always remembered that.

She kept her eyes closed. It was better when she didn't see it coming.

Instead of striking her or cutting her or any number of things he could do to hurt her, he set his hand gently on the back of her head and started stroking her hair. It was kind of awkward with the bun, so he shifted his hand to her neck. What he could reach around her collar, anyway. She remembered her alpha's warning as he'd snapped it around her neck.

"This collar holds lightning magic. With it, I'll be able to see and hear everything around you. If you displease me, I'll punish you." Roy had demonstrated by activating the spell on the collar and shocking her until she'd writhed on the floor, screaming.

When he was done hurting her, he'd said, *"You must find the true head of the hydra. Get close to the Blade named Brock and stay there—by any means necessary. Gather as many of them around you as you can. It should be easy for you. They flock to helpless things. I'll take care of the rest."*

Her mind raced as she tried to think of a way to use this Blade to reach Brock. She'd already come up with a lie about the collar that would help cover any mistakes she made that Roy considered serious enough to punish her. But she needed… She needed to…

Her thoughts wouldn't stay focused. The touch of the man's hands, the warmth, the gentleness sent a tingling wave of sensation over her body unlike anything she'd ever felt. It was… nice.

"It's okay," he said. "No one's going to hurt you anymore. I won't let them."

Her stomach felt like it turned to ice at the impossibility of his promise. Her body shook violently. She tried to stop it. He might see it as a threat. He might change his mind and kill her.

But he didn't. He just held her tighter—still with such care. He pressed her head against his shoulder and whispered reassurances in her ear.

Her teeth were right next to his neck. She wasn't lying about not being able to transform, but he didn't know that. Even with human teeth, she could kill him easily with her heightened strength. He was putting himself in danger to help her feel better. No one had ever done anything like that for her before.

It had to be a trick. A cruel trick. Any second now, he would slap her or punch her or throw her to the ground. She only hoped he wouldn't laugh. It was always worse when they laughed.

"Meg, it's okay," he soothed. "I promise."

But it wasn't.

She had a job to do. A mission that would probably end with this Blade dead at her feet, along with the rest of them.

His touch was so gentle. His arms so strong.

When she'd been brought into the pack, she'd thought her wish of being part of a family was finally going to come true. She would be surrounded by people who loved her. They would hold her like this man was holding her.

With care.

Fate had a different plan for her. Fate, and a Blade named Dexter.

He had shattered her dreams, slaughtered her new family. Most of them, anyway.

Dexter would pay soon enough. She would make sure of it. All the Blades would pay. She only wished she could save this one.

Her heart started to pound as an idea formed. Maybe she *could* save him. He worked with Marcus already. After she proved herself to Roy by taking down the Blades and showing Marcus the true path, it might not be too much of a stretch to ask for this one human to be hers. With enough time, she could convince him that the curse was actually a gift. After risking so much to heal her pack, surely, she could ask—

Her collar began to hum and snap, a magical current stinging her skin. The Blade's fate had been decided. The energy would grow until it let out a shock that killed him. His scent was human, beneath strange layers of decaying leaves and grass clippings. She would survive the spell. He wouldn't. Because he had spared her, shown her mercy and kindness, he would die.

She could shove him away, tell him to run, but then her mission would be over before it even began. If she couldn't handle the death of this one man to save her pack, she'd already failed.

"It's okay," he said. "I'm not afraid of you. You don't need the collar to keep from hurting me."

She grabbed the back of his jacket in her fists and sobbed. No matter how hard she fought it, the tears kept coming. She felt like she was drowning in a huge well of emotion that she'd never been able to look at before. Not while keeping her sanity.

He held her while she cried until she felt hollowed out. Until the world seemed to spin around the two of them, alone in the universe.

Her collar hadn't built to a fatal level yet. In fact, it seemed to have gone dormant again. Why was he being spared?

Maybe the little jolts she'd received from her collar were meant as a reminder that he was the enemy. She was here to kill him and anyone else that stood in the way of her healing her pack. This man might be the key to getting her the access she needed. Of course Roy wouldn't let her ruin that chance.

The man nuzzled the side of her head briefly and she tensed again. She swore she felt him press a kiss to the top of her head. A mix of adrenaline and fear and... something else—something molten—flooded her system.

Maybe he wasn't looking for someone to beat on. Maybe he was looking for another way to use her body as an outlet. She'd done a hell of a lot worse for her pack. Seduction was absolutely on the list of methods she was willing to use to get in with the Blades so that she could take them down.

She reached up and wiped at her eyes and nose, wondering how much of a mess her outburst had made of her face. If she was going to try to seduce him, she needed to pull herself together.

"Come on." The Blade pulled back from her a bit. Apparently the nuzzling hadn't been an overture.

She ignored the sliver of herself that was disappointed. He was part of her plan, now. A tool to achieve her goal.

"Don't be scared," he said. "But if I leave this here, I'll never hear the end of it."

He slowly squatted in front of her, keeping their gazes locked while his hand went to the sharp sword lying on the ground. The blade had a slight curve and only looked like it was sharpened on one side. Her heart rate sped up again as his fingers wrapped around its grip.

"The sheath is on my back." He stood just as slowly, keeping the sword pointed at the ground. "I promise you, you're safe with me."

She nodded, then watched as he lifted the sword to his back and slid it into place.

Before, she'd been too terrified to pay attention to what he was wearing. Now that she wasn't worried that he was about to decapitate her—or worse, poison her with silver —her attention went to his gear. He was dressed all in black. His shirt and pants fit tight against his form. She doubted he was trying to show off his physique, but the outfit definitely accented his lean, muscular build. Seducing him wouldn't be a hardship at all.

His pants had several pockets, and she could see a harness under his jacket. He must have slits in the back for him to be able to wear his swords there. His hair was as black as his clothing, short, and styled away from his forehead so that it stood up in spikes. His eyebrows were straighter than she'd seen on most men, which only added to the strength of the lines of his cheekbones and jaw. And his lips... His lips were pulled in a gentle smile as he watched her ogling him.

She met his gaze, her stomach no longer ice, but doing flip-flops in her body as warmth spread through her. His eyes were dark. Darker than his clothing somehow. Darker than a starless night sky. The light from the lamps along the path didn't reflect in them.

A chill passed down her spine. How could he be so warm, yet have such cold eyes?

"I'm sorry." Meg lowered her head and looked away as soon as she realized how long she'd been staring. Roy would have back-handed her, seeing it as an assertion of dominance.

"What for?" the man asked.

She risked looking up at the Blade to find that he was still smiling at her. She stammered, trying to think of what she could say that wouldn't upset him. Coming up with nothing, she lowered her gaze again.

"Oh, right. Werewolves." He let out a soft laugh. "Don't worry, I don't see too much eye contact as a challenge." He rested his hands on her arms again. "You don't have to be sorry."

"Stop."

The word slipped out. She prayed it had been too quiet for him to hear. Of course, no gods were listening.

"Stop what?" he asked.

She wanted him to stop being kind to her. Stop talking to her in that excruciatingly gentle voice.

"You don't have to be nice to me," she said.

The corner of his mouth hitched up in a smirk that made him even more handsome. "Maybe I want to be nice to you."

She recoiled, backing away enough that he had to either let go of her or use force to keep her where she was. If he didn't let her go, it would prove that he wasn't as trusting as he seemed.

His hands dropped away from her arms.

She missed his touch instantly, but shoved that longing deep into the pit of her stomach. He had to be taunting her.

Except when she glared up at him, he was still watching her with that soft smile. His eyes had small crinkles at the sides, and there was a deep cleft between his brows. Something was bothering him. Probably this game he was playing with her.

"Nobody wants to be nice to me," she spat out.

He shrugged. "Sounds like you've been hanging out with the wrong people."

"The wrong *monsters*, you mean?"

He winced, ever so slightly, but kept smiling at her. "We call them dwellers. And they *are* people. Well, a lot of them are. Okay, some of them."

She fought the urge to laugh in his face.

Blades weren't as bad as hunters. They didn't kill every monster or fairy they met. Only *most* of them. The ones they decided deserved it. If this 'kind and gentle' man knew about her mission, he'd kill her on the spot.

She needed to use him to get back to their base. Even though he'd been nothing but kind to her, had shown her the first care that she could remember. She had to betray him. The first of many betrayals to come, she was sure.

"I'm sorry about before," he said. "Those trolls did a number on you, and…" He shook his head. "I wish we'd gotten off to a better start."

Her heart clenched. He needed to stop being kind. Again, she wondered if there might be a way to spare him. Her hopes were dashed at the next words from the man's beautiful lips.

"I'm Brock, by the way," he said.

"Brock." She forced her face to remain impassive as she swallowed hard, the collar tight around her neck.

"Tessa is my sister." He shrugged. "Well, foster-sister."

"Sister?"

Brock winced, pulling Meg from her thoughts. A small trickle of blood ran from his nose. He sniffed, then wiped it on the sleeve of his jacket and laughed.

"Are you okay?" Meg stepped closer, despite the fact that he might see it as an act of aggression. It was instinctive to reach out to him.

"Yeah, just..." He shook his head, wincing again. "Having trouble getting the troops in line. Excuse me for a moment." He put his finger to his ear and pressed it, staring off to the side. "Hey, Dex...ter. What's up?"

Dexter was here?

Meg's mouth went dry. She spun around, looking for the man who had destroyed her pack. There was no way he'd be as kind to her as Brock had been. No way Dexter would show her mercy. She didn't see, smell, or hear anyone else, though.

Brock clasped her arms firmly, pulling her against his chest. His warmth burned through her terror. He swayed a bit, as if he was having trouble staying on his feet. She crooked her head up to look into his face, just inches from hers.

He pointed at his ear and whispered, "Earpiece."

Another trickle of blood ran down his nose. Meg turned in his arms, reaching out to cradle his cheek and wipe it away with her thumb. She left her hand there, feeling the prickle of his stubble against her palm, the warmth of his skin. He stood completely still, gazing down at her with those dark eyes. He didn't even seem to be breathing, but she could feel his heartbeat pick up. Their chests were almost touching.

"By any means necessary." Roy's words echoed in her memory. She had to stay close to Brock. That didn't scare her anymore. What scared her was that she *wanted* to stay close to him.

Slowly, he reached up and wrapped his hand around her wrist. She expected him to pull her arm away, but instead, he just held on to her. He gently stroked the back of her hand with his thumb. They were standing so close she could feel his breath on her face. She could clearly discern the cinnamon of his toothpaste and the sharp, lingering aroma of his aftershave. He leaned toward her, and she rose on the tips of her toes to meet him.

Their lips were almost brushing when she heard, "Brock? Brock, are you even listening to me? Are you all right?"

The voice was desperate, shouting, and sounded exactly like his. This was Dexter? She blinked, jerking back. Brock let out a sigh as he released her hand. He stayed close enough for her to hear the other side of the conversation through his earpiece.

"I'm fine," Brock said. "But if you keep pushing me, you're going to give us both an aneurysm. Neither of us wants that, right?"

"Let. Me. In." Dexter sounded furious. Terrified, even. What could make him sound so afraid?

"I really want to make a *Three Little Pigs* joke right now," Brock said.

A new voice joined them through the earpiece—a woman's voice. "How about, 'That's Marcus's line?'"

Brock laughed. "Good one."

"Oh, hey. Ask her if she knows what a 'curator' is," the new voice said.

"Vaughn." Even through the earpiece, Meg could hear Dexter's teeth grinding together as he spoke. Whoever Vaughn was, she must not be in the same room as Dexter. Meg couldn't imagine anyone not freaking out with Dexter sounding so angry.

"You can interview her for your Dwellers Database later," Brock said.

He lifted his arms around her back. At first, she thought he was embracing her, but when she twisted around to see what he was messing with, she saw that he was tapping on a device attached to his wrist. It looked like one of the latest computer watches. The band was black, but its square face was smooth silver. For some reason, it reminded her of her collar. Brock tapped on it a few times, then put his arm around her shoulders and leaned down so their temples were pressed together. He held up his arm so the watch surface was facing them.

"Do you mind?" he asked.

She didn't know what he was talking about, but said, "No," anyway.

"Selfie!" he said.

For a brief moment, she saw their faces on the screen, cheeks nearly touching, and Brock sporting a huge grin. To her amazement, she saw that she had a bit of a smile on her lips as well. The screen turned white, and then blanked out again. Brock straightened, but didn't step away from her.

"Check your inbox, bro," he said. "Meg and I are really hitting it off."

He winked at her and she felt herself smile even more. Her cheeks felt stiff and awkward. She looked away, pressing at her cheekbone to try to relax the muscles there. She couldn't remember the last time she'd smiled, and now Brock had made it happen twice in as many minutes.

She heard Dexter's tinny voice coming from Brock's ear. "I'm getting Eli."

"Oh, come on. Don't bring him in on this." He let out a huge sigh, his smile vanishing. This time, he did take a few steps away. He braced his hands on his hips and now *he* was the one staring at the ground. His entire demeanor changed.

Who is Eli? She remembered Roy mentioning 'the true head of the hydra.' Whoever this was, it was someone Brock showed deference to.

"Yeah," he said. "No. Only a little."

She couldn't hear the other voice anymore. If she stepped closer, it might raise Brock's suspicions.

He snorted briefly, then grinned. "I wiped it on Dexter's favorite jacket, but it had to have—" His smile immediately vanished again. He started to pace, running one hand through his hair. "Give me a break, Dad."

Eli was his dad? Meg's stomach clenched. She was walking into what could have been her lifelong dream—but it had taken the form of a nightmare. Tessa was part of Meg's pack, and she had a family. Meg had never heard of a werewolf with living human relatives. Tessa had a brother *and* a father. And Meg was supposed to walk into that and destroy it.

What did Marcus think of Tessa having a family? Werewolves were supposed to only be loyal to their pack. Maybe they were planning to turn everyone?

Meg's heart began to pound. If they were already planning to turn Brock, that meant he would become part of their pack. And this time, it would be a *real* pack. No more beatings. No more rants that left her feeling like she was a worm beneath her human skin.

I was supposed to be a wolf...

She was supposed to be a lot of things. She shook herself and steeled her heart. Thinking of Brock like that wasn't going to help her mission. He was a Blade. He worked with Dexter. They were the enemy. Meg would infiltrate their base. She'd keep herself close to Brock, just as she'd been ordered. Roy would take care of the rest. Marcus would understand and forgive her once he saw how loyal Meg was to him. She would win him and Tessa over, one way or another.

"Yeah," Brock said. "Okay."

He turned back to Meg, tapping on his ear again. For a moment, his features seemed haunted by a shadow of despair that she could relate to all too well. But then he smiled, and everything else seemed to fall away around him. She wanted to smile back at him, could feel the corners of her lips start to curve. Even with everything going on around them, with the way this would most likely play out, she couldn't stop her instinctive reactions to him.

"I know it's a little soon, but my dad would like to meet you." He nodded his head in the direction of the walking trail. "I'm sure Marcus and Tessa would like to meet you, as well."

This was too perfect. Brock already trusted her enough to take her to his home. He offered her his arm, that gorgeous smile gracing his face. A surge of guilt hit her as she looped her arm into his elbow. She shook off the unwelcome feeling and focused on how to get even further past his defenses.

"I should also warn you that I have an identical brother," Brock said, leading her down the path. "He can be kind of an asshole, but... I want to say something to ameliorate that, but he's just an asshole."

Meg let out a little laugh. "I'm sure he's not that bad."

"Nine out of ten dwellers would disagree."

She froze as things clicked into place, a terrible idea taking shape. "Wait... You're not talking about Dexter, are you?"

"You've heard of him?" Brock sighed. "Of course you have. Every dweller has." He urged her to start walking again.

Dexter and Brock were brothers. Twin brothers. How the hell was she going to stay close to Brock if Dexter was involved?

"He's not always that bad," Brock said. "Okay, usually he is, but don't worry. I've got your back." He winked at her.

"Thanks." The fear turning her stomach to ice was almost displaced by another wave of guilt.

Brock had her back. Now she just had to figure out how to get close enough to stab him in his own.

Chapter Three

The dark road sped by as Brock drove toward the ranch. He thought about kicking in his bike's hovering capabilities, but Meg was already clinging to him with a near-painful grip. He doubted she'd be more relaxed if the hubcaps suddenly spread out from the tires and started emitting the weird blue light that somehow made the bike fly.

Vaughn had tried to explain how that worked as well, but Brock had fallen asleep. Again. He had a good excuse for it that time, though. He'd been in his actual body.

Borrowing Dexter, not just piggybacking on his consciousness and observing things... Brock had energy. He could breathe without pressure, could move around with ease. He felt *good* for the first time in weeks. Who could blame him for wanting more of that?

He could almost pretend that he was normal. Just him on his motorcycle with his gorgeous girl pressed to his back, her arms tight around his waist.

"Brock." Vaughn's voice echoed inside Brock's helmet.

Maybe *not* just Brock and his bike and the woman who wasn't really his girl.

He focused his gaze for a few moments on the section of his visor that activated the privacy controls for the comm system. Meg wouldn't be able to hear anything, even snugged up against him like she was.

"What do you need, Vaughn?" Brock said.

"I need you back at the ranch," she said. "Now."

In the background, Brock could hear crashing and screams. Screams he'd grown to recognize by now.

Tessa...

Brock managed to unclench his jaw enough to grind out, "How bad is it?"

"As bad as ever." Vaughn's voice was shaking. "We were in ops talking about your situation in the field and she just flipped out. There was no warning this time." After a brief pause, Vaughn said, "She almost killed me."

A surge of panic flooded Brock's system. Normally, Tessa would become increasingly agitated before an 'episode,' letting them know something was up. If they stopped having those warning signs...

"Marcus dragged her out into the hall and is trying to calm her down, but it doesn't seem to be working," Vaughn said.

"Give me a status report on everyone at the ranch."

Vaughn sighed. "As if I wouldn't have told you first off that someone else was in danger. Porter... I mean Dexter..."

"I call them DP when they're joined," Brock said.

Vaughn paused again before speaking. "I'm not touching that one."

"Could we focus please?"

"Right. 'DP' is in the lab and they have that locked down. Eli is in the ship with… well, you."

"Good." Brock could feel his heart racing. No wonder DP had stopped trying to break through and force Brock back into his body. They had enough they were dealing with back at the ranch.

"I don't want to shock her again." Vaughn's voice was thready.

"Do it if you have to," Brock said. "She'll be grateful if it saves you."

"I have another idea."

"I'm listening."

"Meg said she's part of their pack," Vaughn said. "The omega."

"She did say that." Brock didn't like where this was going.

"All that alpha and omega stuff has been discounted in actual wolf packs," Vaughn said, "but it holds true with werewolves. Tessa told me everything she knew about them so I could update their Dwellers Database entry. Right before she tried to kill me the first time."

"The point, Vaughn."

"Omegas calm the pack," she said. "I don't know how they do it, but that's their role in pack hierarchy."

"So, if I get Meg to Tessa…"

"Meg might be able to calm Tessa down."

"Hang on," Brock said. "We'll be there soon."

He locked his gaze on the section of his helmet that activated the 'enhancements' Vaughn had created. The road ahead was lit in a ghostly blue light, each leaf on the trees that crowded up along the pavement etched in startling detail. Brock saw an owl turn and look at them for a split-second before they whizzed by, leaving a streak of red-orange biosignature that he was sure Vaughn had logged somehow.

"Are you afraid of heights?" Brock shouted over his shoulder.

"No," Meg said. "Why?"

"There's an emergency back at the ranch. Hang on tight, but not so tight that you make me black out, okay?"

He felt her tense and wished his fantasy from earlier could be true. Not just for his sake, but for hers. Just the two of them, riding off into the sunset. From what he could guess, she'd been through enough, and now he was taking her into the heart of a shitstorm.

It wasn't like he could cut her loose.

All it took was the press of a button, and the wheels started to glow bright blue. He leaned his weight forward as the bike lurched up, the hubcaps separating from the wheels and fanning out on either side of them. The hovercycle made a loud *whoom* as gravity tried to pull it back to the earth, but then it bounced up and away. In the next instant, they were airborne.

"What the hell is this thing?" Meg screeched in his ear.

"Hovercycle." He craned his neck to try to smile at her before realizing his helmet made it impossible for her to see his face. He'd have to reassure her with his words. "Didn't you know? The best Blades bases have them."

Gazing around them with wide eyes, she laughed. "This is so cool."

He wished there was time to show her more, to enjoy how amazing it was that they were flying over Providence on a machine that was based on the technology in an alien spaceship. But then, they were headed toward the spaceship itself—or at least the base that was built above it.

Tessa needed him. As did the rest of his surrogate and not-so-surrogate family.

"It gets better," Brock said. "Hang on."

He flicked his gaze to several spots on his helmet's visor, just long enough to activate controls tied in with the bike. The next moment, they were hurtling through the air at an incredible speed, the city just a blur of lights beneath them. Meg let out a little yelp and clutched him tighter. He was having a little trouble breathing.

"Um, Meg?" The words came out like a whisper, using up the last of his air. Luckily, werewolf hearing was pretty keen. When he tapped her arm, she got the message.

"Oh, sorry." She loosened her grip a bit, but kept pressing her body against his back.

That was a new and... wonderful sensation. He hadn't made out with a girl since he'd snuck off to meet Becca Myers beneath the bleachers in high school. His mom had been huge on abstinence. If she'd known that he'd broken her rules back then, she would have killed him. Literally.

He felt his muscles tense as a hundred conversations tried to play through his head. They'd seemed weird at the time, but now that he knew what he was—and what his mom had been—they finally made sense. His mom was a hunter. Brock was a threat. Simple as that.

She'd known what he was and feared he would infect anyone he had intimate contact with. At least he'd found out about himself before he'd made it farther than heavy petting. If his mom had been right about him, he never would have forgiven himself for turning someone—especially with the type of dweller he was.

"Are you okay?" Meg shouted so that he could hear her over the wind rushing past them and the drone of the bike.

"Yeah," he shouted back.

Why the hell was he letting himself think about that? He only had a couple of days left. Sure, it made sense that he was nostalgic, but his parents had actually managed to give him eighteen years of a decent life. He needed to focus on what—and who—he was leaving behind. That included Meg, now.

If he could get her to integrate with Marcus and Tessa's pack, maybe it would help stabilize Tessa. The fits of rage she kept having were getting worse. Once Brock and the replicants were gone, only Marcus would be left to keep her sane. Brock wasn't sure Marcus could manage it.

This would be a good test to see if Meg was really as harmless as she was trying to make him think she was. Brock wanted to believe her, but if she was lying... Dexter needed to be around to deal with that scenario.

The ranch came into sight, a blip of pale gray in an expanse of darkness that stretched for miles. Vaughn's family liked their privacy and had the money to keep the neighbors far away. Of course, the spaceship buried in the cave system under their land probably was a motivating factor in keeping their distance.

He slowed the bike and steered toward the barn that they'd converted into a garage. The doors opened as he approached. He pressed the button to convert back to ground mode. When they were a few feet off the ground, the lights from the hubcap hover units dimmed and folded back onto the wheels. The bike hit the driveway with only a little bounce. He drove into the barn, barely slowing as they rode down the ramp that led to the *real* garage in the first sub-level below.

White walls sped past them. He braked, turning the bike in a semi-circle to dissipate more of their inertia fast enough to not smack into the wall. Luckily, the main garage was immense, holding two unmarked black vans, two other hoverbikes, and enough room for Vaughn to work on all the vehicles. Brock's maneuver left a trail of blackened rubber on the white floor. Vaughn was going to be pissed.

No one was there to greet them. Everyone must have secured themselves to ride out Tessa's latest episode. He pulled off his helmet as Meg slid from the back of the bike.

"That was amazing," Meg said.

Brock set the kickstand and jumped off the bike, then placed his helmet on the seat. "I'll give you the grand tour as soon as I can. But first, we have a situation we could use your help with."

She smiled and stepped closer. "Anything."

"Don't be so eager," he said. "I'm about to send you into the lion's den. Or werewolf's den, more like."

A boom echoed in the space as something—*someone*—hit the sealed door between the garage and the hallway that led to the other chambers in the sublevel. It had to be Tessa. Meg jumped at the sound, her full lips thinning as she pinched them together. She gripped the lapels of her jacket and pulled it tight around her body.

"Vaughn," Brock said.

"I'm here." Vaughn's light voice sounded over speakers that were embedded high in the walls of the room. The door to the upper level slid shut with an ominous clang.

Red lights blinked on either side of it, letting him know it was in full lockdown. Nothing was getting out of this room.

"What's the situation?" Brock asked.

"Bad." Vaughn paused. "I'm watching the hallway cameras. This might not be as good of an idea as I thought."

Another loud bang reverberated through the room. Brock felt the vibrations of the impact through the floor.

Shit...

"I can do this," Meg said.

She quickly pulled her jacket off and draped it over the bike. Her shirt followed. Brock's jaw went lax. He snapped it shut as soon as he realized it. He knew he should look away, but couldn't bring himself to do so.

From what he could see of her breasts, they were small and perfect, not that he had any business thinking about that at the moment. Or ever. Her skin gleamed in the lights, golden and smooth, except for one pristine bite mark on her left bicep. There were no jagged edges to any of the puncture spots. It almost looked like she'd had her arm stamped by a werewolf skull, holding completely still while it happened.

Werewolf hierarchy was determined by violence, Tessa had said. Whoever fought the hardest while being turned eventually became the alpha of the pack. There wasn't an inch of Marcus, aside from his face, that wasn't covered in bite and claw marks. Ugly scars with tears that showed where he'd been flayed trying to rip himself away or fight back.

Brock had shared Dexter's awareness when Dexter killed the werewolves who turned Marcus—Meg's pack. He'd seen the boy curled on the floor, racked with pain from the change. And Brock had seen what was left of Marcus's family. The memory of the carnage still brought up bile in the back of his throat.

Tessa had being fighting for her life—for all of their lives—when she was turned. And the only reason Marcus infected her at all was to keep her from bleeding out. She'd cut off her own arm to escape the control of the parasitic Hive Father that was trying to take over her body.

Had Meg fought back at all?

Brock couldn't imagine willingly becoming a werewolf, especially as a child. Whatever circumstances she'd been living in, it seemed impossible that joining the pack was trading up. Especially seeing as much of her as he could now.

There was no fat anywhere on her body. She looked half-starved—just bone and muscle and sinew. With how she'd reacted to him being kind to her back at the park, he doubted it was a byproduct of a high metabolism. It probably had more to do with being the pack's omega.

Did they ever give her food?

She was wearing a tattered bra with beige cotton cups

and black lace around the edges. One of the black straps of the bra had been tied in a knot to keep it in place. It looked ancient and worn.

He jumped when another boom sounded. Tessa must be throwing herself against the door. Meg walked closer to it, then looked over at Brock, a broad smile on her face and her eyes wide. She still looked scared, but also excited.

"I'm ready." She shifted her weight from one foot to the other, arms straight at her sides.

"Ready for what, exactly?" Brock asked.

"To do my job." She nodded at the door. "Let them in."

The door vibrated with another bang.

"No fucking way." DP's voice came over the comm. "Brock, get in one of the vans."

"If she's staying out here, so am I," Brock said.

Meg shook her head. "That's too dangerous. I need them to come to me."

"This isn't happening," Brock said.

"There are only two of them." Meg's voice was pleading. "I can handle it."

'Only two?' What the hell was she planning?

"Again, handle it *how?*" Brock was feeling worse about this by the moment.

A screeching sound replaced the intermittent booms.

"Vaughn?" Brock took a step closer to Meg.

"Shit," Vaughn said. "She's clawing the door with the cybernetic replacement arm I built for her."

"But you didn't make it strong enough for Tessa to get through the doors at the ranch, right?" Brock asked.

Vaughn didn't respond. She must not have thought it would be an issue when she created it—with good reason. Tessa had been fine until Brock showed up at the ranch.

Vaughn had built the garage—the entire base—to withstand all kinds of dweller attacks. Aside from what she called the 'Boom Room,' she hadn't bothered making it capable of withstanding her own tech. None of them thought it was necessary, since the Blades were the only ones on the planet who had access to her tech. At least, she always worked in kill switches. Or in this case, a shock system.

"That's enough," Brock said. "Shock her." There was nothing else to do.

"Brock..." Vaughn's voice held a pleading edge.

"She'll live—and so will we." Brock strode over to Meg, pushing her behind him. A dent had appeared in the door. "Do it. Now."

"Wait," Meg yelled.

Brock turned around. Meg's eyes were glowing bright yellow.

"You trusted me back at the park and on the bike," Meg said. "Please, can't you trust me with this? I can handle them, I swear it. They know I'm here. I have to integrate with them now. If Tessa is wounded in our first encounter, it'll ruin our chances of ever bonding. She'll see me as a rival or an enemy."

Brock looked back at the door, at the deepening dent. Meg couldn't know what she was getting herself into. But then, who was the werewolf here?

"Please, Brock." She tugged on his arm hard enough to let him feel a bit of her strength. "I'm begging you to trust me." The light from her eyes sparkled and fragmented as they filled with tears.

He cupped her cheek with his hand. "Meg..." He leaned forward, pressing his lips to hers.

He hadn't meant to kiss her, but once their lips touched, he was lost. Her softness, her strength seeped into his body. He slid his hands around her waist, reveling in the satin smoothness of her skin. She froze for a moment, but then stepped forward, pressing her body to his.

She wrapped her arms around his neck, burying her fingers in his hair. When her lips parted, he deepened the kiss, plunging his tongue into her warmth. She let out a moan. The soft sound shot through him, bringing his dick to painful life within his tight pants. Brock hadn't known that his replicants could even get erections.

"Brock." The single word dripped with threat, echoing over the comm system.

DP. His replicant. Owner of the body Brock was borrowing and using to make out with a werewolf.

He pulled back.

Meg stared up at him with unfocused eyes. She swayed

a little as Tessa hit the door hard enough to shake the floor.

"Wow, did the earth move for you, too?" Brock let out a chuckle, trying to cover for the cheesy line.

Smooth. Really smooth.

Meg glanced over at the door, then back to Brock.

"I'm sorry," she said.

"Sorry for wh—"

She ducked down, wrapping her arms around his waist and hefting him onto her shoulder. "Someone, please open the door to the closest van."

"No," Brock shouted, fighting against her hold. "No, no, no."

He heard the door click and slide open.

"Dammit, Vaughn, you are so fired," he said.

"Okay, but remember this is my house," Vaughn said. "And all the tech belongs to me. And I'm the only one who understands it or can make more or new things."

Meg tossed Brock into the van, then stepped back. He heard her say, "I'm sorry," once more   as he tried to get back on his feet. The door slid shut and clicked before he could reach it, blinking red lights along its edge letting him know he was well and truly trapped.

"Vaughn," Brock yelled, climbing to the front seat so he could at least see.

Vaughn's voice sounded from the van's internal comm system. "I didn't want to say this in front of your new girlfriend, but I also fund all of the Blades operations worldwide, so firing me really isn't an option."

"Is kicking your ass an option?"

"I don't like threats," she said. "And you're lucky Marcus didn't hear you say that. He's very protective of me, you know. And before you get any ideas, Porter has my back one hundred percent on this. I mean DP."

DP, who had stopped trying to get back into Brock's consciousness. Which meant they were planning something, waiting for the best moment to crash through his defenses and kick him back into his own body again.

Tessa's fist broke through the door, gleaming chrome and blue streaming lights humming along its surface. She widened the opening, her snarls and growls echoing in the room.

"Is Marcus even trying to control her?" Brock said.

"She's broken his neck three times. Wait... He's not moving again. Make that four." Vaughn sighed. "Werewolves heal fast, but even he's struggling to keep up."

"Shit. Meg told me she can't transform."

Vaughn was silent for a few moments, then said, "She also told you she can handle this."

"I know you hate shocking Tessa, but you have to be ready to—"

Tessa pulled her arm back through the door. Everything went still. The only sound Brock heard was his own panting breaths.

With a loud crash, Tessa kicked the door so hard it flew from its tracks, skittering across the floor. She stepped over the threshold into the garage, pulling herself up to her full height.

Reddish-brown fur covered her body. Long ears rose from the sides of her head and a muzzle dominated her face. Her eyes gleamed gold with a piercing light. Her lips peeled back from wicked-looking fangs that were three inches long. She took two steps toward Meg, fingers curling and uncurling as claws sprouted from both her 'natural' and her cybernetic hands. Vaughn had gone a little overboard trying to make Tessa's new arms match, in both forms.

How the hell did she even do that?

Tessa's nostrils flared as she sniffed the air above Meg. Brock could see everything from his elevated seat in the van. Another werewolf appeared in the doorway, staggering to the side of the frame and leaning one clawed hand against it. He rubbed his throat with his other hand and shook his head. Dark black fur covered his body.

Marcus...

Maybe this would work after all. Marcus wouldn't let Tessa hurt Meg. Right?

Meg was still smiling. Tears streamed down her face. She lifted her arms, as if offering Tessa an embrace.

"I'm here," Meg said. "It's okay now. I'm here."

Tessa reared back, letting out a howl that sounded more

like a lion than a wolf. Then she jerked her head forward, her jaws snapping shut on Meg's shoulder at the base of her neck.

Chapter Four

Pain was temporary. Pain could be overcome.

Mentally, Meg knew she would heal. Too bad her body didn't. Her nerves kept sending her warnings as Tessa bit down harder and shook her massive head. Meg ignored the screaming agony that ripped through her.

It'll be over soon.

She heard pounding off to the side. Brock was beating on the glass of the van. She couldn't hear him, but could see that he was shouting something. Heat rushed through her body, almost strong enough to distract her from the pain. The kiss they'd shared had been completely unexpected—and the best of her life. She wanted more of that, more of him. She just had to get through this first.

He started kicking at the glass. She should have explained, but there was no time. Seeing him now, she knew that if she'd tried to tell him how omegas calm their pack, he wouldn't have let her do it. He had promised no one would ever hurt her again, and she believed he would try to keep that promise. But sometimes, pain was necessary.

When she betrayed him, it was going to break her heart.

She looked away just as Marcus leapt next to Tessa. His claws sank into her arms as he tried to pry them apart. He was going to ruin everything.

Another sound joined the popping bones and ripping muscles in Meg's back. A crackling hum that was all too familiar. But her collar wasn't powering up. The sound was farther away. Tessa's arm.

"Stop," Meg screamed. "Leave her alone."

"You're fucking kidding me, right?" She barely recognized Vaughn's voice on the intercom, it was so high and tight.

"I'm okay." Meg wrapped her free arm around Tessa's neck, then leaned against her cheek.

"It's okay," Meg repeated. "I'm here."

Marcus's face was inches from hers, his breath hot in her face. His eyes were wide with panic, but as they stared at each other, his breathing calmed. Meg nodded, clamping down on the spike of pain the movement caused. She didn't want him to see her wince. The fact that he'd tried to keep his mate from hurting others at all proved to her that he was unlike any werewolf she'd ever encountered before.

This is how it was supposed to be.

Her dreams were in reach. She just had to make it through this. She could do it. Her body was already healing—around the teeth still embedded in her flesh and bones. Meg kept her cheek against Tessa's as she reached out to Marcus and squeezed his shoulder. He loosened his grip on Tessa, gripping Meg's wrist. Tessa let out a long growl.

"He's yours," Meg said. "He's yours, I know."

She pulled her hand away from Marcus and hugged Tessa's neck again. Blood trailed down Meg's other arm and back, hot and sticky. She braced herself for fresh pain as the copper-sharp scent inevitably set Tessa off again.

See me as prey. I am your prey. No other.

"I'm yours, too," Meg said. "We belong with each other."

Tessa abruptly unlatched her bite, freeing Meg without tearing her flesh any further. Meg didn't know that was even possible. She stumbled, and Tessa caught her, keeping her upright. Blue light rippled over Tessa's body. Her fur dissolved in the light, revealing lithe muscle and pale skin. The light soaked into her body, gleaming as her flesh reshaped itself into her human form.

Almost human.

Her right hand still glowed, its smooth chrome surface broken by a few lines of streaking blue. The metal faded into her arm just below her elbow, as if it and her body were one.

Meg had read a story once about a fairy with a silver arm. She wondered what kind of magic could have turned Tessa's hand into this.

"What happened?" Tessa blinked her golden eyes a few

times, the glow in them subsiding. As she noticed the wounds on Meg's shoulder, she gasped and jerked back, releasing Meg.

"Tessa." Marcus stepped to Tessa's side, also in his human form. His hair was almost as dark as Brock's, but was long enough to brush the tops of his shoulders. His bangs hung over his forehead.

Brock's features were stark and harsh compared to Marcus's rugged strength. Meg still preferred Brock's look —except when it came to the scars. Marcus was *covered* in them. His arms, his chest, his legs. Meg was sure his back was just as decorated in the compelling marks. Any injuries he sustained would have healed after he transformed. These were from his fight with the pack.

He had earned his right to be alpha after Roy was gone. He just had to claim his pack. And Tessa... Tessa seemed a perfect match for him. As they stood next to each other, their strength bared for all to see, Meg felt a surge of emotion she couldn't name. Almost happiness. Stronger than satisfaction. Was this pride? She remembered feeling something similar when she'd first been approached about joining the pack. They had picked her. She'd thought that meant she was special.

"Why didn't you shock me?" Tessa lifted her gaze to the ceiling. "Vaughn, answer me."

"I... Meg told me not to." Vaughn said, her voice small.

Meg would have to thank Vaughn later, when they

finally met. She had probably saved Meg's ability to bond with Tessa by trusting them to work it out themselves.

"Tessa, it's okay." Marcus reached out to her, but Tessa shoved him away, hard. He staggered back a few paces.

"You weren't supposed to let this happen," she screamed. "You promised me I wouldn't hurt anyone."

"You didn't hurt me." Meg wiped at the blood covering her shoulder, smearing it over her skin so it would reabsorb quicker. The bite marks had already sealed. "There's no damage, see?"

"How the fuck can you say I didn't hurt you?" Tessa said. "I *bit* you."

Meg was confused. "That was just pain. It's fine."

She stretched her arm, popping her shoulder back into its socket. Tessa winced at the sound.

"It is not fine." Tessa put her hands on her head, pulling her dark red curls back behind her shoulders. "Not fine. It'll never be fine. He's always in my head. Always."

"Was it the voice again?" Marcus asked.

"Of course it was the voice," Tessa growled. "It's always the fucking voice."

That didn't sound good. Most werewolves were turned when they were young, like Meg and Marcus. Children could adapt to the curse better. They didn't go insane as often—or as quickly, in some cases. Omegas were essential for dealing with the bursts of rage that all werewolves had. From what Meg knew, Tessa had only

Progenitor

been turned a few weeks ago, and she looked like she was in her late twenties.

"If you start to lose control again, I'll be here to help you deal with it," Meg said.

"What, like you dealt with this one?" Tessa asked.

"I'm the omega."

"The omega." Tessa shook her head, muttering as she paced back and forth. "The omega. What does that even mean? You're the one I attack when I feel a violent surge? The one I try to rip apart?"

"I heal fast," Meg said. "Faster than normal werewolves, even."

Tessa let out a laugh. "Well, great. I guess that makes it fine."

"Well—"

Tessa cut Meg off, stepping close. "I am not going to beat on you every time the fucking puppetmaster pulls my strings and tries to get me to rip the head off of someone I love."

"I'll heal. They won't." Meg would never have dreamt of talking to anyone else in her pack like this, but she was desperate for Tessa to understand. If Tessa rejected Meg's place in the pack... where would that leave Meg?

"I protect people," Meg said. "*And* the pack. I always kept them calm in places where attacks would have made us too visible." Or resulted in deaths Meg couldn't live with—like the orphanage Lydia, the previous alpha female, had wanted to target. "I can keep us off the radar of hunters or—"

"Or Blades?" The low, cold voice behind Meg seemed to freeze her blood.

She turned to see Brock leaning against the van, arms crossed over his broad chest. He was smirking, but there was no laughter in his eyes. For a moment, she thought she saw a small smear of blood under his nose. It must have been a trick of the light, because the next instant, it was gone.

"Y… Yes." Meg wasn't sure why she stammered. This was the man she'd just shared the most passionate kiss of her life with. She'd entertained fantasies of turning him, of being with him, maybe even as mates.

Looking at him now, she wasn't sure where those thoughts had come from. Yes, he was gorgeous, with his raven-black hair and epic physique. But he radiated cold, bursts of carefully contained malice breaking through. Meg took a step back. She knew a threat when she saw one. This man was glaring at her like he wanted to kill her.

Was he that mad at her for locking him in the van? She'd just wanted to be sure he was safe. It was hard enough to keep everyone from interfering. Even Marcus had tried to stop Tessa. Meg was sure Brock would try to protect her, too. At least, she *had* been.

"I helped your sister." Suddenly, Meg felt like she was making a case for her life. What had changed?

"And we appreciate that." Brock pushed off from the van, stalking over to her like a hunting cat.

Meg turned to Tessa, and said, "This is what I do. Who I am."

"No," Tessa said.

Meg's heart sank. They were rejecting her. Brock seemed to have flipped a switch and no longer gave a damn. Meg had failed in her mission. Worse than that, she felt alone in a way she hadn't felt since her pack had been destroyed. This time, there was no hope left.

"Please," Meg begged. "I can help you."

Tessa shook her head. "Not like this. Not anymore."

Meg looked up to see Marcus standing right behind her. He gripped her arms gently. What was he doing? Tessa stepped closer again. She grabbed Meg... and pulled her into a hug.

Meg was too shocked to say anything. She stammered as Tessa wrapped her arms tight around Meg. Marcus leaned into Meg's back, his arms around both of them, until the pair were enfolding her.

"No one is ever going to hurt you again," Tessa said. "Do you hear me? You're one of us, now. You're *ours*. No one will ever hurt you."

That was twice in one night someone had made that promise to her. She had believed Brock when he'd said it. And she believed Tessa now.

Meg peered out at him from between Marcus and

Tessa's arms. Brock was glaring at her, his smirk gone, along with all pretense of warmth.

Had he been lying to her? Playing with her, like some of the others in her pack used to do?

She'd thought she felt something between them. A connection unlike anything she'd ever felt. A pull as strong as a mating bond. Now, she felt nothing. Nothing but fear. This man was her enemy.

She clenched her eyes shut, remembering her mission. She was here to destroy him. To destroy all of the Blades and rescue Tessa and Marcus. It was the only way their pack would ever truly be safe again.

Meg nestled into Tessa and Marcus's embrace. This was her pack. She would do anything to protect it. Even try to seduce a man who both terrified and tantalized her.

Stay close to Brock, by any means necessary.

The trouble was, this didn't feel like the same man. At least, not since the first few moments she'd seen him, after he'd killed all of those trolls.

Maybe it was the combat situation that had changed his demeanor. Dealing with Tessa could have set him off again. Meg wanted him to change back. She wanted to see the spark in his gaze when he looked at her, to feel warmth from him instead of malice.

Then again, maybe this would make him easier to deal with. He'd certainly be easier to betray.

"If you could peel yourselves away from each other,

we'd be happy to show Meg to her room." Brock was standing right next to them. Meg couldn't smell any fear from him, no lingering arousal from their kiss. Only a strange tinge of leaf-rot.

Marcus let out a low growl.

Oh shit.

She was going to have to calm Marcus down, now. Living in a pack of werewolves was tricky enough. Adding in humans was going to keep her busy.

"It's okay," Meg said. "You need to strengthen your bond. I'll be fine."

She hadn't been with her full pack for very long before Dexter destroyed it, but Lydia and Roy had fought like this a couple of times. They'd ended by having angry sex—in front of the pack. Meg hoped that Marcus and Tessa were different in that way, too. Especially since they were already naked from the change.

"Marcus." Somehow, Brock managed to make the word into a challenge. He was just begging to get his face ripped off. Even Meg wanted to do something to him. Something violent.

She shook herself. That wasn't her place. She couldn't even transform, especially with Roy's control collar around her neck. And if Marcus looked threatening, Brock looked positively lethal. No one could be that relaxed while facing down a pack of werewolves. He was acting as if *he* was the alpha.

Marcus stepped away from her.

Meg felt as if the floor dropped away beneath her. How could Brock tell Marcus what to do without getting attacked? She glanced up at Marcus, took in how his brow furrowed and his lips curled away from his teeth. He wanted to kill Brock, but he was holding himself back. She'd never seen a werewolf with so much control over himself. Tessa was still holding on to Meg, glaring at Brock and growling low in her throat. Meg had to do something to diffuse the situation. Quickly.

"I promise, I'll be okay," Meg said. "Don't you want to be with Marcus? Alone?"

"I do." Tessa glanced over at Marcus. When their gazes met, Meg could almost feel a crackling energy between the pair. An energy she did not want to be in the middle of. She slipped out from between them and stood next to Brock.

Meg wanted that connection for herself. She'd thought she felt the beginnings of it with Brock. Now, she wanted to run away from him screaming. The hair on the back of her neck prickled as she leaned even closer to him.

That was okay. She would seduce him anyway. She *would*.

"If you need anything at all, call for us," Tessa said.

Meg nodded. Marcus and Tessa stepped through the mangled doorway, heading down what appeared to be a long hallway. As soon as Meg couldn't hear their footsteps anymore, she turned to Brock.

"Thank you for trusting me," she said.

Brock grabbed her arm. Hard. His fingers dug into her bicep.

"Let's get one thing straight," he said. "We don't trust you."

His words stung more than she expected. He had brought her to his home, let down his guard, kissed her with more passion and tenderness than she'd ever experienced. What had changed?

Maybe seeing Tessa attack Meg had shown Brock just how resilient she was. It was one thing to know Meg was a werewolf and another to see her withstand an attack like that and shrug it off. It was one of the few perks of being the pack's omega.

"I don't want to hurt anyone," she said. It was mostly true.

"Save it. The others might be suckered in by your innocent act, but we don't believe a word you've said. You're an unknown werewolf. A threat. And if you give us any excuse whatsoever, we will cut off your head or scratch you with silver and leave you to die. Do you understand?"

Her chest heaved with frightened breaths. Her mind spun, trying to reconcile this man with the one he'd seemed to be just a few short moments ago. Why did he keep calling himself 'we?' It was confusing, but at the same time, he was absolutely clear on his intentions toward her. Whatever they had shared was gone. This man would gladly kill her if she stepped out of line.

Just like Roy.

"I understand," she said.

"Good." Brock started walking toward the open doorway, jerking her along next to him.

"Brock." Vaughn's voice came over the intercom. "Brock," she repeated. "Hold on a second."

Brock didn't slow his pace. Meg stumbled, and his fingers dug in deeper. If she hadn't been a werewolf, she'd have a nasty bruise where he gripped her.

She heard a whooshing sound as a door opened in the hallway ahead of her. A woman stuck her head out and glanced down to the end of the hall, then back in the direction of the garage. Her eyes were vibrantly blue, and she had light brown hair that would brush her shoulder blades if it wasn't tied back in a ponytail. She smiled at Meg, and Meg instantly liked her, despite the fear of her current situation.

Ducking into the hall, the woman looked back over her shoulder one more time. There was a large door at the opposite end of the corridor that looked similar to the one Tessa had destroyed. The woman trotted toward them. She was so pale, it looked like she hadn't been out in the sun in a long time—not that the sun came out often in the area. The woman checked her watch quickly as she stopped in front of them.

"Sorry," she said. "Just making sure Tessa is safely upstairs, since she just tried to eat me and all. Again."

"Did you need something, Vaughn?" Brock said, in that same cold voice.

This was Vaughn? Meg smiled at her, wanting to thank her... after she was done talking to Brock.

"Yes, *Brock*." Vaughn emphasized Brock's name, which was strange. "Actually, Meg needs something."

"We're sure we can take care of Meg," Brock said.

Vaughn sighed. "Stay here for one minute." She tapped on the plain silver surface of her watch, then said, "FYI, I'm locking down all the doors for sixty seconds to make sure you don't leave."

She slipped past them, then jumped through the opening to the garage. Meg heard her mutter something about fixing the door. A few moments later, Vaughn stepped back into the hallway, Meg's shirt and jacket in hand.

"Here you go." Vaughn held them out to Meg.

Brock finally let go of Meg's arm. He stepped back, giving her room to pull her shirt over her head and shrug into her jacket. Meg noticed that he kept himself between her and Vaughn's slender frame.

"Thanks," Meg said.

"Any time." Vaughn ran her hand over her hair, smoothing down some errant locks that had escaped her ponytail. "Look, I… I'm so sorry."

"For what?" Meg asked.

"For what Tessa did to you," Vaughn said. "She had told us that omegas can calm members of the pack, but never how. I didn't know she was going to do that to you. I never would have told Brock to bring you back here if I'd known."

Meg actually laughed. She couldn't help herself.

"It's okay," Meg said.

"No, it's not," Vaughn snapped. She paused, letting out a slow breath. "Sorry. It's just been rough around here the last few weeks. We should take you to Porter to have you checked out."

"She doesn't need to be checked out," Brock said. "She's a werewolf."

A muscle in Vaughn's check started to twitch. "I don't care. She needs to be checked."

The power dynamic in the Blades was much more complex than in Meg's pack. Meg had no idea who the alpha was. Brock ordered Marcus, but Vaughn seemed to order Brock. Meg didn't know who she needed to defer to in order to keep the situation diffused.

She was supposed to stick with Brock. Siding with Vaughn against him didn't seem the way to do it.

"I'm okay," Meg said. "Really."

Vaughn sighed again. "Are you sure?"

"Omegas heal even faster than regular werewolves,"

Meg said.

"You see?" Brock said. "Everything's fine. Now, why don't you get back to work on that stasis chamber. Porter and Eli are waiting for you."

"What about Meg?" Vaughn asked.

"We'll take care of her."

"I'm sure you will," Vaughn muttered. She turned to Meg and said, "If you need anything, just ask. Okay?"

"Yeah." Meg couldn't manage more. Her throat was so tight, even without the collar. Everyone was being so kind to her—well, except Brock in the last few minutes. And she was going to have to betray them all.

Vaughn nodded, then headed back down the hall. She slipped through the open door she'd originally emerged from, and it shut behind her with a soft *whoosh*, leaving Meg alone with Brock.

"Let's get you to your room," he said.

Chapter Five

Soft voices surrounded Brock. Familiar voices, but he couldn't remember who they belonged to.

"He hasn't come around yet."

"I know."

"If he doesn't wake up—"

"He *will* wake up."

"But if he doesn't, we have to consider our options."

Brock's body felt even heavier than usual, his thoughts sluggish and strange. Glinting visions flickered across his mind. A city skyline, a view from the Eiffel tower, a small room filled with faces he knew he should recognize, but couldn't.

He forced his eyes open, letting his own senses overpower the input from his replicants. "Dad?"

"End communication." He felt someone take his hand and squeeze it. The bed dipped at his side as they sat next to him. "I'm here, son."

Brock had to blink a few times to clear his eyes. How long had it been since he'd seen the room his actual body was occupying? He avoided it as much as possible.

The ceiling was gunmetal gray, like the rest of the

surfaces on the ship. Wires hung down in the edges of his vision, a jerry-rigged system Vaughn had set up to connect the hospital bed and all its sensors to the ranch above them.

The electrodes that sent cycles of stimulation into various sections of his body were shut off. Vaughn had helped Porter and Dad create a machine that would not only keep Brock's body from atrophying but actually help Brock build muscle. They'd designed a special diet and IV cocktail to go along with it.

They were grasping at straws, trying anything that might help him survive the next split. Losing half his body mass might not be as rough when he'd put on over a hundred extra pounds of muscle, but there was a hell of a lot more to a split than the physical trauma. He still wasn't looking forward to looking like a fucking skeleton afterwards—if he survived. His body put the weight back on pretty fast, but the replicants always filled out faster. They hadn't figured out why. Yet another mystery that would probably never be answered.

Brock's dad leaned into his field of view. His blue eyes were lined with red and bloodshot, dark circles under each. Even with his thick gray and white beard, Brock could see how hollowed out his cheeks were. There wasn't much time left to worry and fret. Pretty soon, Dad would be able to take care of himself again. That was at least one small mercy about Brock's upcoming birthday.

"How are you feeling?" Dad asked.

"Okay."

"Didn't I teach you not to lie to your doctors?" Dad was quiet for a moment, then said, "Your brothers pulled a mean trick, shoving you back in your body. I didn't know they could do that."

Neither did I.

"Porter explained why they did it," Dad said. "I can't say I completely agree with them, but I know their hearts were in the right place."

"How did they do it?" Brock asked.

"They're all keeping pretty close tabs on you, even if they can't be here physically. I think it's tightened the quantum links between the entire group. From what I gathered, they all had to work together to make it happen." Dad smiled. "I understand the new girl upstairs has made quite an impression on you."

"Meg." Brock actually tried to sit up.

Dad chuckled as he gently pressed Brock back against the pillows. "I'll say she has. And that's a good thing. We need you to keep fighting. Just for a few more days, while Vaughn and I finish testing the stasis chamber."

"Even if you can suspend my biological functions, nobody knows how the quantum stuff will handle it." Yet another topic that Vaughn had gone on about, leaving Brock scratching his head. Even the replicants had trouble following the convoluted science behind their link that she had laid out for them and her theories on how the stasis chamber would affect things.

"It's our best shot." Dad squeezed Brock's hand harder. "I'm not ready to let you go."

"Dad..." Brock didn't know what to say.

His dad had already lost so much. He'd been the one to convince Brock's 'mom' to raise him instead of killing Brock when he was born. And then Dad had walked away from the real family they had started—a biological, human family—to protect Brock from a very delayed execution.

If Dad had stayed, maybe he could have saved his wife and spared Tessa from everything she went through while she was being held captive by the Hive Father—Brock's biological father. Marcus wouldn't have had to turn Tessa to save her. She wouldn't be fighting for her sanity. But Dad had seen Brock and all of the replicants as his sons. He'd sacrificed everything for them. Now, he was about to lose them all.

At first, Brock thought that being reunited with Tessa would be a blessing. With her bursts of rage becoming more frequent and harder to bring her back from, it seemed like just another loss waiting to happen. Brock wouldn't be around to help Dad through it. To help any of them. All their work building the Blades of Janus, trying to make the world a place where dwellers and humans could coexist peacefully, was about to crash and burn. When the replicants vaporized, the teams would know their leaders had been dwellers all along. There were some Blades who wouldn't take that well.

"Don't give up on me, Brock." Dad's voice was a husky whisper. "Not yet."

Brock nodded, knowing there was nothing he could say that would give true comfort. He pulled his hand free. "I'm going to rest a little while."

Dad laughed. "There you go, lying to your doctor again." He patted Brock's shoulder as he stood. "Just try not to exert yourself too much, okay?"

"Okay."

Brock closed his eyes and let out a deep breath. He felt the pull toward his closest replicants immediately, like a current that lifted him up out of his body. Lights sparked around him forming a tunnel that sucked him up to the ranch above. Everyone was sitting at the table in the dining room.

Vaughn insisted they try to gather for at least one meal a day. She always set two extra places for Brock and Dad, even though they never made it up. She brought them plates of food in the ship afterwards and stayed to keep Dad company for a while. For the millionth time, Brock was grateful Porter had discovered Vaughn and recruited her as a Blade. They owed her so much.

Dexter and Porter were at the ends of the table. Vaughn had one side to herself, sitting close to Porter and across from Marcus. Tessa was next to Dexter, of course, so he could help keep her under control if she lost it at the meal. Meg was tucked between Marcus and Tessa, the three of them crammed along one side of the table.

Brock wished his view of Meg wasn't partially blocked by Tessa. He wanted to see what it looked like when Meg let her hair down. Her bun looked as if it was pulling on her skin, making her strong cheekbones even more pronounced. He wouldn't mind the librarian or ballerina look on her if her bun didn't seem almost sadistically tight. At least she was getting decent food at the ranch. Beyond decent.

Today, the meal was a brunch spread that would have put any three-star restaurant to shame. It seemed a bit of a waste, with Tessa and Marcus's plates filled with slices of bloody meat. Meg's plate actually had an omelet, toast, biscuits and gravy, and some vegetables in what looked like a mushroom and butter sauce. If this is what Vaughn brought him, Brock might actually be able to get some real food down today, instead of just dealing with the IVs of... whatever it was Dad was pumping into Brock to keep his biomass where they needed it.

There was a little pile of something Meg had pushed aside on her plate. Brock wanted to know what it was and why she didn't like it. People seldom turned down Vaughn's cooking, unless they had special needs, like Tessa and Marcus only eating raw meat. Even then, Vaughn prepared their food so that it looked appealing.

Brock was grateful that Meg was eating at all, but it bothered him that she was wearing the same outfit she'd arrived in. They had plenty of clothes on hand that would fit her. What was going on there?

"Did you ever hang around trash bins outside of restaurants?" Tessa asked.

"Oh yeah," Meg said. "Those were the best."

"Especially when you made a racket." Tessa grinned and Meg smiled back.

"I have a feeling I'm going to regret asking this, but why trash bins?" Marcus said.

"When someone comes out to see what's making the noise and they see you, they usually feel sorry for you and give you the best kitchen scraps," Tessa said. "Sometimes they'll even make you something fresh."

Hearing Tessa talk about the time when their family was separated was always hard. She'd been through terrible ordeals. The pain and the weight of supporting his replicants hadn't been a walk in the park for Brock, but at least he'd been with their dad. It sounded like Meg had endured more than her share of suffering as well.

Meg nodded. "It works best when you're young. They stopped feeling sorry for me when I was around thirteen."

"Jesus Christ." Vaughn dropped her fork on her plate with a loud clatter, then covered her face.

"Did I say something wrong?" Meg asked.

Vaughn placed her hands carefully on the table. "My

problem isn't with what you said, but that you can say that at all. It shouldn't have happened."

"The world isn't perfect." Meg's voice was measured and low. "Human or otherwise. When the pack found me, they saved me."

She looked over at Marcus and smiled. He kept scowling.

"My experience was... very different," he said.

Meg bowed her head. "I'm sorry."

Marcus and Tessa both reached out and rested their hands on Meg's back.

"You don't have to keep apologizing." Tessa cast a look at Dexter that screamed murderous intent. She always glared at him, but this was amped up about a million times. What had Dexter done to piss her off so bad?

"We all had very different experiences with our transformations," Marcus said.

One of Tessa's eyes started to twitch.

Vaughn let out a sigh. "I'm never leaving the kitchen again. I think it's one of my new missions in life to keep you two fed."

Brock couldn't agree more. He would even add that to the list of Vaughn's permanent assignments.

"Enjoying the show?"

Brock wondered when Dexter would pick up on his presence.

"Depends on if you're going to try to trap me in my

body again," Brock projected.

"We were protecting you. You were trying to get out of the van."

"I was trying to help Meg," Brock thought.

"We took care of Meg."

Brock didn't like the timbre of Dexter's thoughts. There was more smugness to them than usual.

"What did you do?" Brock thought.

"What needed to be done, as always."

He would have to look into that, but not while Dexter was so connected to his mind. Brock could sense all the replicants' mental energy, so close that their thoughts almost felt like they were entwined. He could work with that. Leaving one part of his attention in the room, he drew himself toward the center of the energy source—his own mind. By a stroke of luck, his dad wasn't in the room with Brock's body.

"Activate monitor," Brock said.

The ceiling above the foot of his bed flickered. A screen tilted down so that he could easily see the view without having to sit up.

"Key on the werewolf known as Meg."

He was sure Porter had already given her a dehumanizing designation number, but hoped Vaughn's computer software was smart enough to figure out who Brock meant. The screen split into two views of the dining room. Both entrances were covered and he could see Meg from the different angles.

"Rewind…" How long had he been asleep? He only had three days left. He didn't want to sleep through them. "Play back footage from the garage when Meg first arrived."

He watched himself tear into the garage, spinning the hoverbike in a semi-circle as he braked. Damn, that looked cool. But what came next was not something he wanted to see again.

"Skip ahead twenty minutes. Continue to key on Meg."

The view changed to the hallway. Meg and Dexter were talking to Vaughn. The conversation seemed innocuous enough. Vaughn went back to work in her ops room and Dexter led Meg to the elevator at the end of the hall.

That was good. Brock wanted Dexter to feed her and help her settle in. But if Dexter had helped her, why was she still wearing the same ratty clothes that Brock had first seen her in? She didn't look like she'd showered or rested, either, from the deep shadows beneath her eyes and the grit that remained on her skin from being attacked at the park.

The elevator ride lasted too long. If Dexter had taken her up to the ranch, they would have already arrived. Had he taken her to the ship? No, he'd never do that. Brock's heart rate picked up. He could hear it on the machines next to his bed. He took a few breaths to calm himself. If his dad came running in, he'd interrupt Brock's search for answers.

There were only three sublevels at the ranch. The main sublevel contained ops, a couple of labs, the armory, and the infirmary. The second level had the more 'volatile' labs, plus the Boom Room for testing prototypes. Then there was sublevel 3. The pit.

On the monitor, the elevator doors opened to a gunmetal gray corridor. Holding cells lined either side. Vaughn had designed sublevel 3 to be a long rectangle, with some kind of impenetrable metal on the floors, ceilings, and exterior walls. The interior walls that separated each holding cell and the hallway were made of a clear material that was harder than ballistic glass. They could see every corner of the level from anywhere they stood.

Most of the small rooms had a bench attached to the exterior wall, and various amenities meant to handle the type of dweller being contained. Some had an electric current that would activate when the cells were prepped, creating a barrier that would shock anyone or anything that tried to escape. Others could be made to drop below freezing temperatures or had fire grates built into the floor along the walls. After the incident with the Hive Father escaping custody, they had modified a couple of the cells to be airtight.

Only one cell was meant for humanoid dwellers without specialized needs. The same one that they could use to hold human hunters if needed. It had a toilet, a sink, and a bench that was made of foamy material that would be comfortable as a bed.

Dexter grabbed Meg's arm hard enough that she winced. He half-dragged her down the hall, past the cell that might have given her some comfort. He threw Meg into the farthest cell from the elevator. She stumbled forward from the force of his push, then spun around in the center of the chamber. Dexter stepped back and sealed the room.

Brock clutched the sheets in his hands, willing himself to calm down. Werewolves needed physical proximity. Tessa had explained that they used touch and closeness to calm themselves and each other—and that being isolated could drive a werewolf insane, turning them into rogues.

Brock might be able to fool the machines, but his replicants were a different matter. He could feel DP at the edge of his mind, an irritating buzzing pushing against Brock's shields. They had to be sensing Brock's growing anger.

On the screen, Dexter said, "We don't have the resources to babysit you, and we have a patrol to finish. If you're truly as docile as you want everyone here to believe, you'll want us to make sure there aren't any unknown dangerous dwellers running around near humans."

"Of course," Meg said. "But I promise, I won't hurt

you. Or anyone."

"We know." Dexter smirked, then turned and started walking down the hallway. The overhead lights and the lights in the adjoining cells shut off as he passed them.

Meg ran toward the cell's door and pressed her hands against the glass.

"Please don't leave me in here," she shouted. "Please don't leave me alone."

The elevator doors closed. Dexter never once looked back at her.

The light from her cell reflected off the glass walls. She was isolated in a small cube floating in a sea of darkness. Minutes passed. She kept herself pressed to the door.

"Brock?"

Hearing her speak his name in that broken, tiny voice felt like a hammer to his chest. The machines started beeping again, and he didn't give a damn.

How long did she stay alone in that cell?

It was a form of torture. Dexter knew that. And he had done it in Brock's name.

"Fast-forward." Brock pushed the command out through gritted teeth.

The monitor blurred a bit. Meg stayed against the door for a long time. Then she started pacing like a caged animal. Like an *agitated* animal. She reached for the walls a few times, but then drew her hands back, as if she was afraid to touch them. Finally, she stopped in the center of the room and dropped to the floor. She hugged her knees against her chest and pressed her face to them, rocking back and forth.

Brock watched the time scroll as the screen stayed basically the same. For hours. With no outside stimulus, no way of knowing how much time was actually passing, it must have felt like so much longer to her.

Finally, lights came on in the rest of the level. Tessa and Marcus bolted down the hallway, supernaturally fast. Tessa threw herself at the door, clawing at it with her metal hand. Crackling blue energy gathered around it, and she smashed through the glass.

Holy shit.

Brock didn't know she could do that. He was pretty sure Vaughn wouldn't have known about that ability, too. The nanites she had used to fuse Tessa's cybernetic arm to her body and integrate it with her physiology might be interacting with her dwellers in unanticipated ways.

Yet another thing to worry about.

All Brock could focus on at the moment was watching his sister and her mate run into the room and wrap their arms around Meg.

Meg kept rocking. For a long time, she stayed on the floor, curled in a ball while Tessa and Marcus comforted her. Because of something Dexter had done. Something all of the replicants had allowed to happen by shoving Brock back into his body with enough force to knock him out.

Making him helpless.

As if creating them hasn't left me helpless enough.

Brock snapped.

They had used their connection against him. But they were the satellite minds. He was the central force behind them all. He let his rage build, ignoring the warning alarms from the machine at his side. The tunnel of energy linking him to all of his replicants blanked out his own body's senses, glowing bright blue this time.

Brock didn't just let it pull his mind toward the replicants upstairs—he pushed himself forward, willed himself to slam into Dexter full-force, knocking that shard of DP's consciousness into Porter's body.

Brock didn't stop there. He kept pushing, blasting his energy against DP and out along the conduits to all of his replicants' minds.

"You want to use our connection to control me?" he thought at them. *"I am the fucking link that holds us together. I am the energy source that keeps you all alive."*

Through Dexter's eyes, he saw Porter jerk in his seat. His body started to shake violently.

Marcus was first to his feet, rushing to Porter's side. Vaughn glanced back and forth between Dexter and Porter, finally settling on staring at Dexter's form. Brock was holding Dexter's body steady, hands flat on the table to stabilize him.

"What's happening?" Meg said.

"Some kind of seizure." Marcus wrapped his arms around Porter's head and shoulders, trying to hold him still.

Blood dripped from Porter's nose, eyes, and ears. Brock didn't care.

"Oh my God." Meg stood, grabbing Tessa's arm and pulling her up and away from the table.

"No, no, no," Tessa said. "It's too early. We're supposed to have two more days."

Vaughn lifted her arm and spoke into her watch. "Eli, what's happening with Brock?"

"I don't understand." Meg was glancing frantically back and forth between Dexter and Porter. She looked equally concerned. Dexter's body must be hemorrhaging, too.

Good.

Meg took a step toward him and reached out, but drew back before touching him. Even after what Dexter had done to her, she still wanted to help.

Brock's rage surged along the connection.

"We protect *dwellers,"* Brock thought. *"We're supposed to be building a better world for everyone, treating dwellers as well as we treat humans."*

"Please…" Porter said. Out loud.

The channels connecting them usually felt smooth when Brock sent or received energy from them. This time, it was like pushing through razor blades. No wonder they were resorting to their physical voice to try to reach him.

Brock didn't give a shit about the pain. He'd learned to deal with pain long ago.

"Did you listen to Meg when she said 'please?' Right before she called out my name? *She thought she could trust me, just like I thought I could trust you."*

He pushed harder.

"Eli doesn't know what's happening," Vaughn said. "But I'm getting reports from all our bases. The other pairs are having seizures, too."

"You tortured her," Brock projected. *"After she risked herself to help our family. After she suffered to ease Tessa's madness."*

"It's too soon," Tessa sobbed.

"Stop." Porter croaked out the word.

"I will fucking stop when I'm ready." Brock pushed on their minds harder, felt the pressure build in his own body, as if he was about to pop. *"I tried to teach you how to be decent human beings. To help you understand compassion. We do not torture anyone or anything. The Blades have to be better than that."*

"Brock…" Porter said.

"That is *not* what you call me." Brock snarled the words aloud. He slammed his fists on the table hard enough that the plates bounced. "That is not who I am."

Porter started choking, blood flooding from the corner of his mouth. Brock felt blood flowing down the back of his throat, warm liquid spilling from his nose and blurring his vision with red.

"Say it," Brock shouted.

"Pro… Progenitor." Porter stammered.

Brock let go of the force he'd been applying to their minds. Marcus held on to Porter as he fell forward, gasping for breath. The connection between them all felt raw and flayed. Brock slammed down his mental barriers, cutting himself off from their thoughts and shielding his own.

He wiped a hand over his face and looked at the blood on his palm. The room was spinning and his chest heaved as he fought for air. After swallowing a few times, he managed to calm his voice.

"Don't ever forget again," he said.

Chapter Six

Meg held herself perfectly still, hoping that Brock would forget she was in the room. She wanted to disappear. What she'd just witnessed... She didn't understand it, but it terrified her.

"Brock, are you okay?" Tessa took a few steps toward her brother, away from Meg.

Brock was obviously not okay. His face and neck were covered with blood. Except, while Meg watched, the blood reabsorbed into his skin. The stains on his dark T-shirt started to glow with a soft blue light, then vanished.

Her mind reeled.

He's not human. He's a dweller, too.

"Get him out of my sight." Brock bit out each word. "Everyone out!"

Vaughn was the first to move. She pulled Dexter's arm over her shoulder, grunting as Dexter rose to his feet.

"A little help here," Vaughn said.

Marcus gripped Tessa's elbow and steered her toward Vaughn. Once close enough, Marcus looped Dexter's other arm over his shoulder, and headed for the door. Meg started to follow, but Brock reached out and grabbed her wrist.

"Not you," he said.

Tessa turned toward him, but Brock said, "It's okay. They won't dare hurt Meg again after that."

What was he talking about?

Tessa looked to Meg—to *Meg*—and waited. She nodded to let Tessa know Meg was okay with being left alone with Brock, even though she was absolutely terrified.

This was her mission. Stay close to Brock by any means necessary, even if he had a Jekyll and Hyde personality. The fact that he wanted Meg to stay was a good sign. She hoped.

Tessa followed as Marcus and Vaughn half-dragged Dexter out of the room. Meg could hear them as they walked to the library, even though the carpet muffled their footfalls. She didn't hear the secret bookshelf open that Vaughn had shown her earlier, but she did hear the elevator make a soft beep when it arrived. A few seconds afterwards, Brock let out a sigh. Could he hear the elevator leave, too?

"Is Dexter going to be okay?" Meg asked.

Brock let out a short laugh. "That wasn't Dexter."

"I don't understand. Everyone's been calling him Dexter."

Brock let out a sigh, then drew her into his lap, wrapping his arms around her waist. He rested his forehead against her shoulder. She could feel the heat he was radiating even through her jacket.

"You're burning up," she said.

"It'll pass."

"We should take you to your dad. Eli's a doctor, right?"

"I'm already with my dad."

Meg didn't know what to think anymore. Nothing made sense.

"I'm really confused," she said.

He looked up at her and smiled. A real smile. Brock's smile. She couldn't believe how well she knew it already.

"I can imagine," he said.

"If that wasn't Dexter, who was it?"

"Porter."

"Porter? Who is Porter?" More frustration crept into her tone than she anticipated.

She held her breath, wondering how he'd react. After that display of... whatever it had been, she didn't know what to expect from him or what he was capable of. She only knew that he was something she'd never encountered before.

"He's... This is going to be hard to explain," Brock said. "Have you ever heard of a hydra?"

Meg's heart started to race. Roy had mentioned finding the true head of the hydra. But what did that mean?

"I read about a hydra in a mythology book once," she said. "I used to hang out in the public libraries a lot when I lived on the street."

Brock tightened his grip on her. "Whatever happens over the next few days, I want you to know one thing. You will always have a home with the Blades. Marcus and Tessa... You're right, they need you. Not like you thought, though."

He winced, pinching his eyes shut. Lines of pain were etched around his eyes. Whatever he'd done, he'd done it to protect her. Now, he was paying for it.

She ran her fingertips across his temple, then through his hair. He let out a shaky breath, and some of the tension she felt in him eased.

"It's okay," she said. "I'm good at surviving."

"Surviving isn't thriving."

"Well, yeah." She let out a little laugh before she could catch herself.

He smiled up at her again. There was no anger or malice in his eyes. The cold aloofness she'd sensed from him ever since he'd exited the van had burned away. She pressed her hand to his forehead, relieved to find it cooler. He let out another of those soft breaths.

So gorgeous...

She ran her fingertips over his cheekbone, traced his strong jaw, even dared to brush her thumb across his lips. They were just as soft and warm as she remembered. He grasped her wrist and pulled her hand away, but not before pressing a kiss against her palm.

"Meg, this is complicated." His voice was a low rasp.

"Just tell me."

"I'm not Brock. This body isn't, anyway."

Not Brock? She struggled to find an explanation that made sense.

"Are you some kind of ghost or something that possesses people?" she asked.

He looked away and shook his head. "If only it were that easy. No, I'm... I'm a hydra."

"You're a dragon?" She remembered the pictures that had gone along with the story. A huge dragon with tons of heads on long spindly necks.

He laughed. Little crinkles formed at the corners of his eyes and mouth, completing his transformation into the warm man who had already somehow made his way into her heart.

She wanted to kiss him again.

"No, I'm not a dragon," he said. "That would be really cool, though. The legends never get it quite right. It's interesting how they interpreted the 'two heads.'"

"Right. Heracles would cut off one head, and two more would grow from the stump."

"Yeah, that's not quite how it works."

Brock dropped his hand to her thigh. Warmth shot through her, pooling low in her belly and between her legs. She wasn't sure who was the seducer anymore. Except, from him, the gesture felt natural. He didn't have to try to seduce her. Everything about him drew her in.

"Unless he applied fire to it," Brock said.

Definitely not seduction talk.

"So, your weakness is fire?"

She felt a surge of panic as she remembered that Roy was listening to them, seeing everything around her. If Brock told Meg his secrets, Roy would know them, too.

Her pack needed to be healed. This was the only way. Meg had already reconnected with Tessa and Marcus. But for them to truly be whole, they had to have their vengeance on the one who had destroyed their pack in the first place. They had to kill Dexter.

She hadn't figured out why they had to go through Brock to do so. She didn't even know who Dexter was anymore. She'd thought he was the twin sitting at the other end of the table. They had *told* her he was Dexter. Which meant, they had lied. And if they'd lied about that, what else were they keeping from her?

It can't be as bad as what I'm keeping from them.

"I don't really have a weakness," Brock said. "Except for time, I guess."

"I don't understand."

He sighed, staring at her lap. Not a lascivious stare. It was like he was looking through her. His hand rubbed small circles on her back, and he kept his grip on her thigh, holding her close.

"My body is in the sublevels," he said. "Probably being

fussed over by my dad and the others, unless Porter has recovered enough to forbid Tessa from being that close to me."

"Why would he do that?"

"She keeps trying to kill me."

Meg tried to envision what he described. His real body was below them, but somehow his soul was in this one. What had happened to… whoever had been in this body originally, then?

"Who's body are you…"

"Borrowing?" Brock said. "This is the body I call Dexter."

Dexter. She was sitting in Dexter's lap. Her arms were around Dexter's shoulders. She'd lovingly traced the outline of his features.

Meg felt like she might throw up.

This 'body' had destroyed her pack. The same hands that gently held her had killed the werewolves who had promised to be her family. Hands that still sent heat streaking through her.

She shoved away from him, tumbling to the floor, but rolling up in a crouch. He tried to stand, but then swayed and sat back in his chair, hard. He was weakened. She'd never have a better chance to kill him. But what would happen to Brock?

She shouldn't be thinking of that. Shouldn't be hesitating when the chance to heal her pack was right in front of her. Her fingertips started to tingle. That had never happened before. She glanced down to see the slightest hint of a curve to her nails.

The collar started to hum.

Roy was watching. But why was he getting ready to shock her? He knew that would block this opportunity.

"I promise I won't hurt you," Brock said. "And neither will the others. What they did to you, throwing you in that cell…"

Her skin crawled thinking about it. She'd lost all sense of time while waiting for someone to find her, wondering if anyone would ever come. When Marcus and Tessa arrived, she was so far into the safe place she'd built for herself in her mind, they'd said it took them half an hour just to get her to respond to them.

"Who put me in the cell?" As if she needed to ask.

"Dexter," Brock said. "But he's learned his lesson. He knows you're off limits now."

"I feel so much better, hearing those words from *his* mouth."

"Meg, please." Brock glanced at her collar, buzzing around her neck, then held out his hand to her. Held out *Dexter's* hand to her.

She recoiled. The collar crackled.

The magic snapped into her, stinging her in bursts. She shook her head, fighting to ignore the pain. She couldn't ignore the message.

She was supposed to stay close to Brock. By any means necessary. Apparently, it didn't matter if he was using someone else's body. The only comfort she had was that he winced when she did as the collar stung her. At least Brock seemed to care about her, and that's who he was inside.

But the outside…

She rose to her feet. Her stomach churned, but she took the hand he offered and let him pull her back onto his lap. Onto Dexter's lap.

"I want you to explain," she said. "Everything. Right now."

She couldn't remember ever speaking to anyone so harshly. And for the first time in her life, she didn't care.

"I'm part of a dweller that's known as a hydra. The original body and consciousness is mine. Brock."

He held up his hand, like he was answering a roll call. It would have been a cute gesture a minute ago. Now, she fought to keep from flinching.

"When I turned eighteen, I… split," he said. "There's no other word for it. It was agonizing. Terrifying. At least my dad was there, but neither of us had any idea what was happening. A replicant emerged from my body. An exact copy. And then, the poor bastard split again. Into a right and a left replicant." He held up his right hand and then his left. "Dexter and Porter. That's what I named them."

"So, there are three of you," Meg said.

"Not exactly."

Of course, 'not exactly.' Nothing was straightforward or clear with this man. Like the way she wanted to rip out his throat and kiss him at the same time.

Except she didn't actually want to kill him at the moment. And she wasn't scared of him like she'd been before. The cold and aloof version of Brock must have been when Dexter had control of his body. Now she knew how to tell them apart.

"Dexter and Porter have two bodies, but they only have one mind between them," Brock said. "One consciousness, anyway."

"Okay. Three bodies, but two minds."

"To start with," Brock said.

She let out an exasperated sigh. "How many bodies and minds do you have now?"

"I only have my own mind, but all of our consciousnesses are linked through me. And I can borrow any of their bodies that I want."

"How many?" she insisted.

"There are eight of them. Nine counting my original body."

Nine. Nine different parts of one whole. No wonder Roy didn't want her to lash out at Dexter. What would be the point, if there were eight more versions of him walking around?

"But only four consciousnesses, aside from my own,"

Brock said. "They call me the progenitor. The origin point."

The true head of the hydra.

It was Brock. Brock's body, anyway. She hadn't found it yet, but now she knew what it was. And the truth about her mission as well.

She wasn't here to kill Dexter. She was here to kill Brock.

A shiver passed over her skin as the last bit of hope that he could be spared left her. She felt sick to her stomach, the food she'd enjoyed so much threatening to come back up.

Brock hadn't been the one to destroy her pack. He'd been nothing but kind to her. How could she betray him? Surely there was some way to kill Dexter directly. Brock was being so forthcoming. Maybe if she asked, he'd just tell her.

"My dad still can't figure out what the hell it is about my physiology," Brock said. "All the tests show me being one-hundred percent human. But I split every three years on my birthday. The last time, I nearly died. All of us did. We're pretty sure this one's going to kill me."

Tessa had been going on about having more time…

"Brock, when is your next birthday?" Meg asked.

"In two days." He let out a tight laugh. "Happy big three-o."

Roy must not know that Brock was already dying.

Meg's whole mission wasn't necessary. Relief and sadness warred within her.

"Are you sure you won't survive?" she asked.

"My body is barely hanging on as it is. I can't stand or even sit up without help." He shook his head sharply, deep furrows cutting into the skin between his eyebrows. "Even if they manage to keep my body alive, my mind can't handle the load anymore and will probably shut down. We're not sure how that will affect the replicants, but I'll be in a coma for the rest of my life, however long that is." He laughed, but the sound was joyless. "At least I only have to die one more time."

"You've died before?"

"Not me exactly. But any time the replicants die, I feel it along with them."

"I thought you said there were nine of you. If some of them have died, why are there still so many?"

"Whenever a replicant dies, the remaining 'twin' splits again. There are always two of them. Only one goes into dangerous situations at a time to make sure the other is safe and can split if their 'other half' dies."

Meg remembered Roy celebrating when he thought he'd killed Dexter. Roy had been kinder to her afterwards. But then, when they found out through the grapevine that Dexter had taken out a different pack, Roy had gone ballistic. It had been the worst beating she'd ever received. She shivered at the memory. Brock pulled her closer against his chest. Against Dexter's chest.

"Why are you telling me all this?" she said.

"Because Tessa needs you. My family needs you. When I'm gone, I need to know that they'll be okay. That my dad will be safe—and Vaughn. I don't know why, but Tessa goes after her, too. It's like Tessa just goes crazy, hearing that voice in her head. She calls it 'the puppetmaster.' Marcus says he hears a voice, too. His dweller. But he can handle it better than she can."

"It must be part of the curse," Meg said.

The furrow between Brock's eyebrows deepened. "What curse?"

"Lycanthropy. The curse of being a werewolf."

Brock chuckled. "I thought you were glad to be turned."

"I was. I am. But it's still a curse. I don't know what else to call it."

"With werewolves, we usually say that you've been 'colonized.'"

"Colonized by what?"

"Alien parasites."

The thought of little green aliens running through her system was… fairly disturbing. But so far removed from reality, she couldn't keep herself from laughing.

"I suppose they were implanted with a prober by one of those tall gray aliens with the big black eyes?" She smiled at him, but he didn't smile back.

"What Scifi fans call 'grays,' we call dopplegangers. The little shits love to mess with people, but they're relatively harmless. The Blades don't have a kill order on them."

"I've never met a doppleganger, but I've heard they're one of the most dangerous types of fairy."

"Fairy?"

"Yeah. They're part of the Unseelie court. Humans would think of them as the bad guys, but there really aren't 'good guys' among those who are born Fae. Present company excluded, of course."

"Okay, now *I'm* confused," Brock said.

"You know, the born Fae? Fairies start out magic instead of being cursed or bewitched like monsters are."

He cocked his head to the side as he stared at her. "Wait a minute. You do know that fairies aren't real, right?"

She laughed again. "Right. Like hydra and werewolves and trolls aren't real. How can you not believe?"

"I do believe those beings are real, but they aren't fairies. They're dwellers."

"You keep using that word. I've never heard it before."

His eyes widened. "You're kidding me. The pack didn't explain what you are after they turned you?"

"They did. I'm the omega."

"But did they tell you where we all came from? What dwellers are?"

"They didn't have to. I've read enough to know about

monsters and fairies."

"I don't quite know how to react to this." Brock shook his head, letting out a little laugh. "Meg, you're not a monster or a fairy or a 'cursed' human. You have been colonized by an alien parasite."

"Very funny."

He kept staring at her, his expression earnest. She could almost—*almost*—forget whose body she was sitting on.

"It's not a joke," he said. "Thousands of years ago, a spaceship crashed on Earth. It was filled with alien life forms that escaped into our ecosystem. They had to join with the native species to survive, creating hybrids."

She arched an eyebrow at him. "How is that more believable than fairies?"

"Well, for one thing, I've seen the ship myself."

"People can make things—"

"Meg. I'm on the ship right now. That's where my body is. Hundreds of feet below the Earth in a cave system beneath the ranch."

"But… Maybe Vaughn built it," Meg said.

"To do what? Trick people into thinking aliens are real? She's only let half a dozen people even go near it."

"But her inventions—"

"Come from the ship," Brock finished for her. "I mean, yeah, Vaughn is insanely brilliant, but she's the first to admit she'd never have been able to make the advances and discoveries she's come up with without using the alien tech as a baseline."

"I'm not an alien."

Roy had *told* her they were monsters. It was part of why he kept losing control. Why he needed her to keep the curse at bay.

Why he hurt her so much.

Brock lifted his arms around her and tapped on his watch. Lights appeared above the table forming a partial outline of a ship that looked like something out of a Scifi movie. Then again, the lights themselves looked like something out of a Scifi movie. The outline filled in, presenting a transparent view of the back end of a ship. It slowly rotated in front of her.

"Is this a hologram?" Meg asked.

"Something like that. It's fully interactive. Go ahead."

She reached toward the glowing blue image, cautiously touching it with her fingertips. The panel she tapped disappeared, letting her see inside the ship more clearly.

"This is so cool," she said.

"If you use both hands, you can zoom in or turn it to see better."

"Are you supposed to be showing me this?"

"No, so you better hurry up before we get caught."

She dropped her hands to her lap and turned back to him. "I don't want to get you in trouble."

"Relax. I'm the leader of the Blades, remember? Kind of like their alpha."

"You don't act like any alpha I've ever met." Her heart seemed to stutter for a moment when she realized the implications of her words. If she'd said something like that to Roy, she would have earned a beating.

Brock only laughed. "I try not to be a dick about it. Unlike Dexter."

He sneered a bit when he said the name. Was it possible he didn't like Dexter, either?

"He's a part of you," Meg said. "Isn't he?"

"Not exactly. I mean, he came from me, but each replicant consciousness has his own personality. Even the right and left bodies are a little different after each split."

"This whole concept is confusing."

"Tell me about it." Brock shook his head. "Our relationships are complicated. My dad wishes I'd see them all as brothers—like he views them as his sons—but that's not easy. I have to keep them in check." His lips pulled into a thin line and he shook his head. "I'm still furious over what they did to you."

"Don't worry about it," Meg said. "I'm fine."

"I'm glad you're fine, but it's not something I can overlook." He lifted his hand to her cheek and gently stroked her skin. "I'm so sorry."

She didn't know what to say in the face of such kindness. She was spared from trying to think of something when the image of the ship blinked out.

Brock let out a sigh, then smirked at her. "Busted."

The monitor hanging on the wall to their right flicked on. Vaughn was centered in the screen, nothing but white walls behind her, like on the level Meg had first been in when she arrived. Meg wasn't used to seeing Vaughn frown.

"Brock, we've been over this," Vaughn said. "I don't care how much you want to impress the new girl. You can't tell her about my ship to do it. Use your winning personality or something."

Brock laughed. "I'm not trying to impress her. She didn't know she's an alien hybrid."

"What?" Vaughn's eyebrows hiked up her forehead. "I thought all dwellers knew that."

"So did I," Brock said. "She doesn't even know the word 'dweller.'"

"We're not aliens." Meg clamped her lips shut, but the words were already out.

"See what I mean?" Brock gestured to Meg with the hand that wasn't wrapped around her waist.

Could Vaughn see them? But then she knew Meg was still sitting in Brock's lap. Her cheeks tingled and no doubt had turned bright red.

"I don't understand," Vaughn said.

Brock shrugged. "She thinks we're fairies."

"Fairies?" Vaughn's smile returned as she laughed. It faded as neither Brock nor Meg joined in. "Oh wait. You're serious?"

"Werewolves aren't fairies," Meg said. "We're monsters. Fairies are the ones who are *born* magic, remember?"

Brock shook his head, then turned to the monitor. "You see why I was showing her the ship?"

"Yeah." Vaughn let out a deep sigh. "I guess that means she doesn't know what a curator is."

Brock looked up at Meg.

"Sorry, I've never heard of that, either," she said. "Well, except for the ones who organize museum exhibits or art shows."

"I'm guessing dwellers mean something different when they use the word." Vaughn looked at Brock. "I'll give you a pass this time. You should bring her to ops so I can help you explain better."

"We're on our way," Brock said.

The monitor went dark again.

Brock smiled up at her. "Damn."

"What's wrong?"

"To go downstairs, I'm going to have to stop holding you like this."

Meg felt herself smile back. "There are other ways to hold people."

Taking his hand in hers, she stood, gently urging him to follow. As soon as he was on his feet, she pulled his arm over her shoulder, then wrapped her arm around his waist. Their sides were pressed together as they smiled at each other. *Held eye contact*, and smiled.

There was no dominance, no threat. Only that warmth that always seemed to fill her when he was near.

His voice had a bit of a rasp to it as he said, "Shall we?"

Chapter Seven

"Welcome to my humble abode." Vaughn greeted them with a flourish as they entered her ops center. Brock would have to thank Vaughn for the lengths she was going to, trying to make Meg feel welcome.

"You live here?" Meg asked. Her gaze quickly passed over the plain white walls, floor, and ceiling, then lingered for a moment on Vaughn's desk. It looked like a shiny chrome counter jutting out from the one wall that was 'decorated.' At least a dozen monitors of various sizes covered the space above the desk.

"I don't *actually* live here." Vaughn let out a sigh. "It just feels like it most of the time."

"It's hard to get her to leave the ops center," Brock said. "Unless she's in the kitchen."

"Hey, all it takes to lure me away from my monitors is the promise of pizza and a romcom marathon." Vaughn looked back and forth between Meg and Brock when neither responded. "Seriously?"

"You said you had a presentation?" Brock gestured to the monitors.

"I do." Vaughn pushed one of the extra black mesh

chairs over to them, then gestured for Meg to sit.

Meg gave her a small smile and sat down. Vaughn spun the chair around in a couple of quick circles. Meg let out a surprised squeal, then laughed as Vaughn wheeled her closer to the desk. Brock would totally give Vaughn a raise if she hadn't been right about being the main funding source behind the Blades. Damn, that chafed a little.

"What about me?" Brock asked. "Don't I get a ride?"

Vaughn shrugged as she sat in front of the main console. "You can get your own chair."

"Gee, thanks." Brock wheeled the last free chair over to the table and sat close to Meg.

Vaughn started typing on the smooth surface of the table, accessing command keys etched into the metal that Brock could barely see. The monitors flickered to life, showing various views of the house, the grounds outside, and a few choice feeds from security cameras scattered throughout Providence that Vaughn had tapped into.

Meg let out a gasp. "Wow, what is this thing?"

"*This* is my computer desk. And by computer desk I mean my desk which is also a computer." Vaughn pointed at a smooth square and then the etched area, saying, "Trackpad. Keyboard. And the entire desk is the CPU chassis. If you could crack it open—which only I can, because it's keyed to my DNA—you'd see that pretty much the entire interior is motherboards, processors—"

"We get it, Vaughn," Brock said. "You're super smart."

"Super-*duper* smart." Vaughn grinned at Meg.

Meg smiled back and said, "Wow."

"This is nothing." Brock leaned closer. "Remember the hoverbike we rode in on?"

Meg's smile grew. "How could I ever forget?"

"Vaughn's design."

"Seriously?" She stared at Vaughn with wide eyes.

"And lovingly built with these surprisingly soft hands." Vaughn held up her hands and wiggled her fingers. When Brock and Meg just stared at her, Vaughn added, "Okay, that was a little weird. Anyway... If you'll direct your attention to the central monitor, we can begin the show."

She typed in more commands, bringing up a video file Brock instantly recognized. It was from a recent patrol Lee had recorded to get Vaughn better data on pixies. One of their newer recruits, Rose, was running the camera. A glowing blue light whizzed across the screen a few times, darting through a field dotted with pale mushrooms. Brock had to admit, the scene did look pretty magical. He could understand Meg's confusion, even if he was still baffled by her pack lying to her about their origins.

"What is that?" Meg leaned closer, her voice breathless with wonder.

"That is a pixie," Vaughn said. "They're a type of humanoid insect. And before you become too taken with them..."

The pixie paused, pulsing a few times. Half a dozen

more lights suddenly appeared around the mushrooms, then sped right toward the camera.

The view changed wildly as Rose turned and ran away, shouting, "Ow! Fuckfuckfuckfuckfuck!" The view cut to static with occasional pops and crackles on the audio.

"Oh my God," Meg said. "Is she okay?"

Brock's heart gave a little tug at her concern for a complete stranger. "She's fine. This was filmed by a Blade named Rose. She was obsessed with pixies, so Bradley decided to play a mean trick on her and take her into the field to film some."

"Bradley?" Meg asked.

"He—they?" Vaughn shook her head. "Bradley is the replicant in charge of our base on the coast of Georgia."

"How many bases do you have?" Meg asked.

"Three," Brock said. "There's one at Caiman Beach, the Europa base near Chicago, and the Providence base here."

"We're careful that the Blades never meet the bosses of the other bases so they don't wonder why everyone in charge pretty much looks like the same set of twins," Vaughn said.

"That's only six replicants." Meg turned toward Brock. "What about the other pair?"

Brock was not ready to talk to Meg about the other pair. He said, "Mal and Colm operate freelance. They go wherever we need them."

Brock pointed to the screen, drawing Meg's attention

back to the view. At first, all that was visible was a twilit sky. Then the camera swiveled to the side as Rose got to her feet.

"Dammit, Lee," Rose said.

Off-screen, they heard Lee say, "Get Vaughn's shots before their bodies vaporize. This one's the most intact."

"Oh wow." Rose ran over to a dimly glowing form and focused the camera on the nearly dead pixie. "It kind of looks like what would have happened if dragonflies had evolved into people instead of primates."

The pixie was about seven inches tall, with six diaphanous wings sprouting from its back. Its carapace was iridescent.

"It's beautiful," Meg whispered.

"Their sting is worse than getting shocked by a stun gun," Vaughn said. "When enough of them work together, they can knock you out. And while you're unconscious, they eat you."

Meg sat back so quickly, her chair wheeled away from the desk. Brock caught her with his arm over her shoulders, then drew her back into place.

"Relax," he said. "It's just a video."

"Right." Meg nodded. "Sorry."

As they watched, the pixie began to shimmer. The blue light that always cleaned up after dead dwellers consumed its body. At that moment, Lee appeared on the screen. He was grinning, as always. From the looks of it, he'd grabbed Rose's wrist and was focusing the camera on himself. His face bounced in and out of view, thankfully.

"And that, ladies and gentlemen, is why you should never judge a dweller by its cover," he said.

"Asshole." It looked like Rose had managed to free herself from Lee's grip. Hopefully, she'd keep the camera focused on the pixies.

"If you want more footage, you'd better get it fast," Lee said.

"How's this for footage?" Rose's hand appeared in the camera's view, flipping Lee off. She had aimed it right at his face. Vaughn tapped a command and the screen froze.

Shit. Brock wasn't ready for that.

Meg's mouth dropped open and her eyes grew even wider. Lee's face was marred by a long mark that slashed along his left cheek from where a gorgon had killed Lee the year before. That had been an excruciating death.

As if that wasn't bad enough, the right side of his neck was covered in thickened red skin striated with white lines. The marks crept up slightly over his jaw and also ran down beneath the neck of his shirt. Brock's skin itched as he remembered the salamander's blast hitting Lee in the back, just over his right shoulder blade. That death had been almost as painful as the gorgon's.

Brock watched Meg closely to see how she reacted to the scars. She didn't seem disgusted, but was staring intently at Lee's neck. Her eyes started to glow faintly and she pulled her lower lip between her teeth. Maybe she was trying not to say anything. She had to be wondering why Lee looked different than Dexter and Porter.

If she saw the scars Brock carried on his real body... He didn't let himself think about that. If he had anything to do with it, she'd *never* see his real body.

The screen went black for a moment before the Dwellers Database entry for pixies appeared. One of the small creatures took up the left side of the screen, its body outlined in a computerized grid. The right side of the screen contained text commentary, scrolling rapidly as various parts of the pixie's body were either circled or highlighted.

Meg turned toward Brock. "That was another you?"

"One of my replicants," Brock said. "Their separate forms are 'Brad' and 'Lee,' but I call their consciousness 'Bradley.'"

Vaughn was still staring at the monitor, as if she could actually read the text flying over the screen. "Too bad you didn't think of the binary names before you sprouted Dexter and Porter. The others are at least a little easier to talk about."

"I wasn't thinking too clearly the first time I split." Brock glared at Vaughn, even though her attention was still on the database.

"He looks different," Meg said. "Lee."

If only she knew...

"Each pair likes to have their own look," Brock said, being purposefully obtuse. "Brad and Lee wear their hair longer and the sun has bleached it a lighter shade."

Brock leaned away from her, running his fingertips along the place where Bradley had his scar. Brock tried not to borrow replicant bodies that often. It was strange to feel the unmarred texture of Dexter's skin.

"The scar must make it easier to tell the replicants of that pair apart," she said.

Brock cleared his throat. "They both have it."

"I don't understand," Meg said.

He dropped his hand to his thigh, forcing himself not to make a fist. "Several years ago, Lee was killed by a gorgon."

Meg actually gasped. "Like Medusa?"

"You really do know your mythology," Brock said.

She shrugged. "Libraries are warm and dry. And the books gave me a place to escape to."

Brock reached out and took her hand in his. Without really thinking about it, he lifted it to his lips and pressed a gentle kiss to her palm. Vaughn cleared her throat, reminding Brock that he and Meg weren't alone, while pointedly keeping her attention on the monitors.

"If a dweller can't talk and tell us what they want to be called, we try to name them after the mythological creatures they most resemble," Vaughn said. "In this case, it was a venomous humanoid serpent. Lee was so busy watching its teeth and claws that he didn't notice its tail had a sharp edge. After it managed to slash him, he discovered that the tail was coated in a paralyzing poison, effectively 'turning him to stone.'"

"That sounds awful," Meg said.

"The poison stopped Lee's heart, but not before..." Vaughn's voice trailed off.

"Before what?" Meg asked.

Not before the gorgon had started eating. Brock shook his head hard, forcing out the memory of Lee's shared pain. Brock started talking, hoping that Meg would leave it be, distracting her with what he'd been wanting to tell her in the first place.

"I told you that when one of a pair of replicants dies, the survivor splits so there are two of them again," Brock said. "But they both bear the scar from the impact site of the death wound. In Lee's case, it was the slash to his face that let in the poison that killed him. The replicants often feel what each other feels—unfortunately, even in the case of death. When Brad saw that the scar had formed on his cheek, he knew that Lee was actually dying. After splitting again, both of them had the scar."

"This still sounds like magic." Meg shook her head. "I don't understand how the scar travels to them."

They didn't understand that, either—which made it even harder to figure out how to convince her of the truth. Maybe the only way to get her to believe was to tell her everything. Brock couldn't let her go on thinking she was a monster. And the only way he could think of to help her with that was to show her a *real* monster.

"I feel their deaths along with them," Brock said. "And I get the death marks, too."

"You?" she asked.

"Perks of being the progenitor, I guess." He forced out a laugh, but she only frowned harder. "I'm sure Vaughn will be happy to tell you all her theories about that later. For now..." Brock's throat was tight. He coughed to loosen it up, then said, "Vaughn, could you please bring up G-405's file?"

Vaughn swiveled her chair around and stared at Brock, her jaw a little lax. "Are you sure?"

"Meg is part of Marcus and Tessa's pack," Brock said. "If she's really going to be one of us, she needs to understand what she's getting into."

Meg seeing Bradley's scar and not freaking out was nice. But when she knew the truth about Brock, he doubted she would ever let him near her again.

Part of him was tempted to not tell her. He only had a few days left, anyway. He could leave it for Marcus and Tessa to explain, and maybe actually get to enjoy spending some time with Meg. But he was the leader of the Blades of Janus. It was his job to make sure everyone was ready to face the threats that inevitably came their way.

Ignorance could be deadly when facing a dweller—

especially since Meg was one of them. Some of the fairy tales had it right when it came to lethal allergies dwellers had to Earth substances. Silver and werewolves was a prime example. But there was much more misinformation than fact in the stories. In the field, that could get Meg and everyone with her killed.

Vaughn turned back toward the screens and pulled up the file. A picture of G-405 appeared in the upper-right corner of one of the side monitors. She was wearing a faded sundress, her bony hands clasped in front of her. The hollows of her cheeks hugged teeth that her lips could no longer cover. The skin around her mouth had dried out, peeling back until she was left with a macabre grimace. A few strands of long white hair were still attached to her scalp. Her skin was a uniform gray, stretched tight over her bones so that she looked like little more than a skeleton.

Meg gasped. "What is that thing?"

"She wasn't a 'thing,'" Vaughn snapped.

Meg jumped, then seemed to crumble in on herself, staring intently at the blank surface of the desk. She folded her hands in her lap, her legs clamped together and arms tight against her sides. Brock shifted closer to her in his chair and put his arm around her shoulders. She leaned into him.

"I'm sorry," Vaughn said. "I didn't mean to startle you."

"It's okay." Meg's voice shook a little. "I didn't know she was your friend."

"She lived at the ranch for months." Vaughn glared over at Brock, her eyes glittering. "All she wanted was a place to belong. She was kind and caring."

Brock tried to speak gently as he said, "That wasn't all she wanted."

"Agree to disagree." Vaughn quickly turned back to her screens and started typing again, her fingers hitting the table's surface with more force than usual. "G-405 was a ghoul—a relatively benign dweller. They're necrophages, so they're not usually a threat to the living."

"What's a necrophage?" Meg asked.

"Ghouls feed on the dead," Brock said.

"That's not so bad."

As a werewolf, Meg had undoubtedly seen a hell of a lot worse behavior from dwellers. Brock was suddenly glad that she'd been eating regular human food at the table earlier. If she had a meat aversion, that would mean she'd never eaten a human before. He suppressed a shudder at the thought.

"I've read stories about ghouls," Meg said. "They're a type of fairy."

"Actually, they're a human that's been infected with a parasite." If Brock walked her through this, maybe she'd understand. And if she needed proof... Well, that was right next door.

"G-405 was infected by a parasite that was put in her by an apex ghoul," Vaughn said. "Those dwellers call themselves 'Hive Fathers' and 'Hive Mothers.' They go around turning people into ghouls by infecting them with little maggot-creatures."

"Ew," Meg said.

Brock slid his arm from around her shoulders and leaned back in his chair. If she thought that was gross, she was probably going to freak out when she learned the rest of it. He didn't want to be touching her when she did. He didn't want to feel her revulsion.

"That's not the awful part," Vaughn said. "They use the humans they infect to gain power and wealth. Once their thralls can't pass for human anymore, the hive creature abandons them to fend for themselves. You're a werewolf. You must be able to imagine how bad that feels."

"She doesn't have to imagine it," Brock said. "She experienced it first hand when Dexter killed her pack."

Meg opened her mouth as if to say something, but then closed it, pinching her lips together tightly.

"I'm so sorry, Meg," Brock said. "If we had known you were out there—"

"Dexter would have hunted me down and killed me, too." She glared at him, her eyes glowing gold.

"You know what the pack did to Marcus's family," Brock said. "If we'd let them live, they would have kept on killing people."

"Can we just go back to the maggots," Meg said. "And how we're all 'aliens' somehow." She made sarcastic air quotes when she said the word.

"We know how." Vaughn pulled up an image of the ship on one of the side monitors. "This ship crashed here thousands of years ago. It was filled with all kinds of alien life forms—"

"That's exactly what Brock told me," Meg said. "But it's still just words."

"The hive creatures are actually made up entirely of the individual parasites that create ghouls," Brock said. "They can somehow bond to each other to make themselves look human. Clothes and everything."

"A person that's made up entirely of maggots?" Meg shivered. "That's disgusting."

"Tell me about it." Vaughn glanced over at Brock. "I mean… Sorry, man."

Brock glared at her, but the damage was already done. He'd planned to tell Meg about his origins, but had hoped to gloss over the more disturbing parts.

"I don't understand." Meg looked back and forth between them. "Why are you sorry?"

"Because my father…" Brock cleared his throat. It was probably best to get this out there anyway. "He's a Hive Father."

Meg's eyes widened and she stiffened in her seat. She didn't leap away, though, like she had when she'd found out Brock was borrowing Dexter's body. Apparently, she found Dexter worse than maggot-creatures.

"Eli is—" Meg said.

Brock couldn't even let her finish her question before jumping to respond. "No, my *biological* father is a Hive Father. Eli is the doctor who delivered me."

A little furrow appeared between her eyebrows. "Your family is really… complicated."

"Aren't all families?" Vaughn cast a strained smile at her.

"I don't remember my family from before." Meg shook her head and quickly went on. "You and Eli are the only humans here, right?"

"Uh…" Vaughn opened and closed her mouth a few times, then finally looked away.

"Yes," Brock said.

"Right." Vaughn shook her head. "All the tests say I'm one hundred percent human, just like all the tests Eli does on Brock's actual body say that he's one-hundred percent human, too. We should start a club."

"I don't understand," Meg said. "Are you a hydra, too?"

"When we threw down with Brock's biological father, he said that I'm a 'curator' after he tried to infect me and failed," Vaughn said. "Tessa and Marcus had to kill him before we could get him to tell us what a curator is and why it freaked him the hell out." Vaughn turned to face them. "Let me just emphasize this. Me being a curator, whatever the hell that is, freaked out a person made up entirely of maggots."

Brock grasped Vaughn's shoulder briefly. "We'll figure it out."

"Maybe it just means you're really smart." Meg pointed up at the monitors. "You're cataloging all these creatures. Isn't that kind of something a curator would do?"

"It is kind of like forming a collection," Brock said. "You can't gather specimens because they vaporize when they die, but you have gathered a lot of data in an easy-to-use format."

Vaughn snorted, but at least she was smiling again. "Interesting theory."

"So, was your mom a ghoul, like G-405?" Meg turned back to Brock as she asked her question.

Oh, damn.

Brock swallowed hard. "My biological mother was human."

"But she—" Meg shook her head. "The Hive Father—"

"Don't think about it too hard," Vaughn said. "Seriously, don't. It'll give you nightmares."

Meg pressed her fingers against her temples. "It's a lot easier to just believe in magic."

Vaughn and Brock both let out strained laughs.

"Is that still what you think is going on?" Brock asked.

"I—" Meg's hand lifted toward her neck, but she quickly curled her fingers into a fist and pressed it against her lap. When she spoke again, her voice was tense. "I'll believe what you tell me."

"I don't want you to just blindly listen to us," Brock said. "I want you to think for yourself. We all do."

"Agreed." Vaughn nodded her agreement. "And there is a romcom I'm going to insist we watch together as soon as possible."

"This is a lot to take in," Meg said.

"I wish we had more time, but I want you to be settled as much as possible before..." Brock let his voice trail off.

"Before you go into stasis," Vaughn said. "We're so close to finishing the test chambers."

"You made more than one?" Meg asked.

Vaughn nodded. "Just in case we decide to put Dexter and Porter in with him. Bradley and Zachary have been working on stasis chambers for their bases as well. Malcolm even made a set for their safehouse. Worst case scenario, everybody jumps in right before Brock's next split to relieve the load on his brain at least."

That wasn't Brock's worst case scenario, but he let Vaughn and the others have their dream. Brock hoped it gave everyone some comfort.

His nightmare scenario involved all of the Blades discovering they'd been following dwellers all along and disbanding. Most would go back to being hunters, and his dream of leaving behind a world where humans and dwellers could get along would be lost.

"Werewolves and pixies and ghouls may seem like part

of a fairy tale, but they're not," Brock said. "The technology is so advanced, the creatures are so... alien to our experience. We don't understand it all yet, but if we write it off as magic and stop trying to understand, we never will." He stood and offered Meg his hand. "It's time to look behind the curtain and see how the world really works."

She stared at his hand for a long moment before reaching out to grasp it. As he pulled her to her feet, he let out a breath he hadn't known he was holding. He didn't think she'd let him touch her again after finding out what he was.

Vaughn stood as well. "You can't take her to the ship. It isn't safe."

"I'm not taking her to the ship," Brock said. "I'm taking her to Porter's lab."

Chapter Eight

Meg's stomach was in knots as she walked down the hallway with Brock. Everything was white. Floors, walls, ceiling. The smooth surfaces and high-tech... *everything* made it actually feel like she was walking through a spaceship.

She shivered. Vaughn's technology was amazing, but that didn't mean Meg was an alien.

Roy had heard and seen everything in the other room. Her collar hadn't so much as buzzed. Apparently, he didn't have a problem with them telling her all these ridiculous things. Roy probably thought she would believe him no matter what the Blades said. He could see this as a test of faith.

Maybe he just doesn't care.

Her stomach felt leaden at the thought—and the ring of truth that seemed to resonate through her. Roy didn't care. But did that mean he'd been lying?

The pack had taunted her before, teased her with promises they never intended to keep. What if they had lied when they told her she was a monster? It could have been yet another cruel joke. She'd thought that was just how all packs behaved. Tessa and Marcus—everyone here —had proven that was wrong.

They could be putting on a show for Meg, gaining her trust before revealing their true natures, but they seemed so sincere. Meg didn't know what to think.

Brock paused in front of a black panel with a keypad beside it. He entered a code, then rested his hand on the smooth rectangle. Leaning forward, he stared at a small black circle. Beams of blue light shined on his eye, scanning it.

"This place doesn't seem real," she murmured.

He straightened and smiled at her. "And yet, here we are."

A section of the wall slid aside, revealing a doorway. Brock gestured for her to enter first. She took a deep breath and stepped into the room. The space appeared smaller than Vaughn's ops center at first, but only because of a large glass partition. On the other side of the window, Meg could see row after row of shelves holding shiny metal boxes.

There were large pieces of equipment, too. One table was topped by a glass chamber with gloves built into the side. Another had metal rods on each corner, with currents arcing between them, creating what looked like a box made of electricity. A machine with three mechanical arms hung from a track on the ceiling. Each arm ended in a different tool—pincers, maybe some kind of drill, and a prong whose function she couldn't guess at. It seemed like everything on this level was either chrome or that white material they made the walls, floors, and ceiling from.

More counters lined the room, with smaller pieces of equipment scattered around and monitors here and there on the walls. There were tiny shelves with petri dishes at one station, another with beakers and flasks—some empty, some containing different colored liquids and lumps of things she couldn't identify. A large metal table that could have come straight out of a morgue was pushed up against the wall at the far end of the room. There was a wheeled cart next to it, loaded with saws, scalpels, and knives.

Monsters vanished after they died. Meg knew that much. What did the Blades use that table for?

Porter was sitting on a stool, looking through an enormous microscope. He wore a white lab coat over his black clothes. His broad shoulders were hunched as he peered through the eyepieces. He straightened when they entered, then bowed his head.

"Progenitor," he said.

Brock let out a huge sigh. "Don't be a dick."

"You were pretty clear earlier about how I'm supposed to address you. Or am I not being submissive enough?" Porter glared at Meg. "You seem to have discovered a taste for it."

"Now you're being an ultra-dick," Brock said.

"I'm sorry." Meg stepped closer to Brock. "I didn't

mean to cause any trouble between you."

"You don't have to apologize to him." Brock put his arm around her, his touch as gentle as his tone was harsh.

One of the monitors flickered on, showing Vaughn's face. "Guys, could we just stay focused here?"

"Right," Porter said. "I'm supposed to stop what I'm doing to convince Meg that dwellers are aliens instead of *fairies*. It's not like I have anything more important to do, like finishing my tests of how stasis may affect Brock's physiology."

She couldn't believe Brock was making this his priority. His life was at stake. Why would he be so concerned about what she thought?

"You should keep working on the stasis chamber," Meg said. "I'm not that important."

"Yes, you are," Brock said.

No one had ever told her she was important before. Her vision blurred and she couldn't seem to breathe. She was glad for that. It helped her stop the sobs she could feel building in her chest. She stared at the ground, not wanting Porter—or Brock—to see her struggle. She had a mission. She had...

What do I really have?

A psychotic alpha who hurt her every chance he could, because she was the 'omega' and that was her job. To take his punishments, even when she'd done nothing wrong. Roy had her so twisted around, she'd always thought that was just the way the world worked. He had been lying to her all along and now he wanted her to kill the kind people who were caring for the rest of her pack—the *sane* members. Well, except for Tessa...

What exactly did Roy have planned using the collar? Meg doubted he was going to electrocute Brock through it. It took too long for the power to build. Roy wanted her to stay close to Brock. To gather everyone near her. Roy was biding his time, waiting for the best moment to strike. He wouldn't care if Meg was hurt in his attack. He wouldn't even care if she died.

She swallowed hard, the collar taking on a whole new weight in her mind, against her skin. It could relay sight and sound. Roy had demonstrated that. It could shock both Meg and those around her. What if it could do more?

She started to shake. Her skin itched and her fingertips hurt. She couldn't change. Omegas didn't change. Unless that was another lie.

"Hey." Brock's voice was achingly gentle. He pulled her against his chest, pressing her face to the strong muscles there and wrapping his arms around her.

It didn't matter that this was Dexter's body. Brock was the one hugging her, and when he held her like this, she felt safe for the first time in her life. Meg hugged him back, grabbing his shirt to keep herself from hurting him as her fingers curled into claws. The only way to really keep him safe was to leave, but she didn't think he'd let her. And she couldn't explain what was going on without giving herself away to Roy. She couldn't even write something down or try to signal them. Roy would see what she was doing, see their reactions and know something was wrong. It might push him into taking action, killing whoever was near her at the time.

She was trapped.

"It's okay," Brock said.

He rocked her side to side, soothing her with his voice, his touch. If Porter hadn't been in the room...

"We actually do have something of a time crunch," Vaughn said. "Porter, did you pull the storage chamber I requested?"

She heard Porter stand.

"I didn't have to," he said. "I've never stopped studying it."

There was something different about the way Porter was talking—beyond his tone losing some of its menace. She turned her face away from Brock's chest, but kept her arms around him.

"You keep saying, 'I,'" she said. "What happened to Dexter?"

"You're hugging him." Porter opened a compartment on the front of his microscope and pulled out a small chrome box. "Didn't Brock explain this already? That body is called 'Dexter.' This one is 'Porter.' Brock calls our merged consciousness 'DP.'"

"Which I've told him not to do," Vaughn said. When everyone turned to stare at her monitor, she added, "Because... reasons. I am not explaining it to you."

Porter went on as if Vaughn hadn't interrupted. "When I'm using both of my forms, how I perceive myself manifests in how I talk. 'We' are Dexter and Porter. When I'm condensed in just one of my bodies, shut off from my other form's senses, I use 'I.' It isn't something I do on purpose or can control."

"You seem really different, though," Meg said.

"My bodies have small variances in their personalities," Porter said. "Whichever form I'm using manifests the most strongly."

"Porter's the chatty one," Vaughn said. "I'm glad I'm recording this. It's going straight in your Dwellers Database file."

"You even have a file on Brock and his replicants?" Meg asked.

"A classified file," Porter said.

"Do you record everything that happens in the ranch or just the sublevels?" Meg glanced around the room again, but realized Vaughn could probably make cameras so small Meg would never be able to notice them. She wondered if there was a way she could use Vaughn's recordings to get a message to them.

"The ranch is covered, too," Vaughn said. "It's a security thing. But I don't watch all the feeds. I've written algorithms that tell me if there's suspicious activity anywhere, so you can shower and use the bathroom in peace."

Porter lifted the small box in his hands higher. "Now that we've sorted all of that, can we please get on with this?"

Brock tensed. He reached up and gripped Meg's arms, gently pulling her away from him. He slid his hands down to hers and held on to them, though.

"Some of the alien organisms that escaped from the ship are microscopic," Brock said. "Like the ones that colonize humans to create werewolves. Some are large creatures that either interbred to make hybrids or mixed their DNA with Earth-based life forms in ways we don't understand yet. Others act as parasites. Like my biological father."

He looked over at the box Porter held.

"You sure you want to do this?" Porter asked.

Brock nodded, then let go of Meg's hands and stepped away from her. Once again, her stomach started to tighten. What could be in there that had filled Brock with so much dread?

Meg forced herself to approach Porter, knowing Brock wouldn't let anything happen to her. Even knowing that Vaughn was watching reassured her.

"One more thing," Porter said. "No matter what, you can not tell Tessa or Marcus that we still have this specimen. They would not take it well."

Brock was sharing this with her to try to help her, even though it obviously made him profoundly uncomfortable. She'd kept secrets for and from her pack before. She could do this for him.

"I won't tell them about it," she said.

"Good." The smile Porter cast at her didn't quite reach his eyes.

Shivering slightly, she peered into the box. It was the size and shape of a shoe box, but without a lid. The sides were made up of a shiny silver metal. The open top shimmered, almost like liquid light covered it. Some kind of force field, if all their talk of aliens and spaceships was real?

"You don't have to worry about it infecting you," Porter said. "Even if it wasn't in stasis, it can't affect someone who's already colonized."

"What can't?" She squinted at the box, trying to see what he was talking about without getting closer.

Porter shifted the box to cradle it in one arm, then pointed with his now-free hand. A small white squiggle floated in the center of the box. It wasn't resting on the bottom or clinging to the side. It was just floating. One end of it was thread-thin, but it thickened in the middle to about the size of a shoelace.

"Is that a tapeworm?" she asked.

Vaughn let out a laugh, then cleared her throat. "Sorry."

"It's not a tapeworm," Porter said. "It's the last segment of the hive creature that created Brock."

Meg shook her head. "Wait... *That* was your father?"

"Yeah." Brock's voice was a low rasp.

"Actually, that *is* Brock's father," Porter said. "As we understand it, each segment of a Hive Father or Hive Mother contains all of their knowledge and experience, as well as the DNA templates needed to transform another living being. If this dweller were able to find its way into a human, it would be able to recreate the Hive Father known as Edgar Eaton."

"Oh my God..." Meg said. "Why don't you kill it?"

"Because they're trying to save me," Brock said.

"We're studying this life form as we try to build a bigger version of this stasis field." Porter lifted the box a bit.

Meg recoiled, then realized how her action must have looked to Brock. "I'm sorry," she said.

Brock gave her a sad smile. "I get it. Believe me, I get it. But that *thing* can't hurt you. That's one of the benefits of already being colonized."

"Edgar infected Tessa with a variant of his own dweller, trying to create a mate," Porter said.

Meg let out a gasp. "But you told me that when people get infected or colonized or whatever, we become the thing that infected us. How is she a werewolf if this thing had already infected her?"

"Tessa was able to contain her infection in her right forearm," Porter said. "We took this one out of her before Edgar attacked our base and activated the dwellers that he'd put in her. When he did, she cut off her own arm to keep the infection from spreading. Marcus infected her with the werewolf microorganism to stop her from bleeding out. That's why he changed her."

The room seemed to spin around Meg as she visualized everything Porter was saying. Surrounded by all this high tech equipment, seeing the creature—the *dweller*—in Porter's box, she believed them. It made too much sense to ignore.

"I think I need to sit down," she said.

Brock took her arm and led her to a stool that was tucked under one of the counters. He pulled it out and sat her on it, keeping his hands on her shoulders to steady her.

The door to the lab whooshed open and Tessa walked in. She wasn't wearing anything, and was flexing her fingers into claws and fists. Meg slid right back to her feet, pushing Brock behind her.

"Where's Marcus?" Porter asked.

"Upstairs," Tessa was looking around the room, her eyes oddly unfocused.

"Forget Marcus," Brock said. "Where are your clothes?"

"Upstairs," Tessa repeated. "I had to check on Meg. Something told me to—" Her gaze landed on the box in

Porter's arm.

"Tessa…" Porter said. He curled his arm tighter to his chest, extending his other hand as if that could fend her off.

"What is that?" Tessa said. "What *the fuck* is that?"

"Let me explain." Brock tried to step around Meg as he spoke, but she wouldn't let him.

The situation was about to go terribly wrong. She didn't want him anywhere near Tessa when it did.

"I cut off my arm!" Tessa shrieked. "I cut off my own fucking arm so I would be safe from that thing. So we would all be safe. And you kept a copy of it in the basement this whole time?"

"We need to study it to help Brock," Porter said.

"You need to destroy it," she yelled. Her eyes were glowing so brightly that gold light spilled out of them, illuminating Porter's face.

Meg leapt forward just as Tessa reached for Porter. Even though it went against everything Meg had been taught, everything she felt was right, she grabbed Tessa by her shoulders and pulled her away from Porter.

"Let me go," Tessa screamed. She ripped herself loose from Meg's grip, then turned and grabbed Meg by the neck, the metal of Tessa's hand clanging against Meg's collar.

Tessa's robotic arm started to spark. The lines of blue tracing the grooves worked into the metal grew brighter in erratic bursts. Electricity coursed into Meg, making her body convulse. Pain arced along her nerves, her neck a ring of fire. Meg could see the panic in Tessa's eyes—and the pain. The skin closest to the metal of her arm turned bright red, then started to blister.

"Vaughn, stop the shock," Brock yelled. "You're catching Meg, too."

"It isn't me!" Vaughn shouted.

"What?" Brock started toward Meg, but Porter grabbed him, pulling him back.

Brock punched Porter in the face. As soon as he was free, Brock ran toward Tessa, tackling her. Meg staggered back, gasping for breath, sickened by the smell of her own burning flesh.

"Tessa?" Brock said. "Tessa, are you all right?"

The door whooshed open and Marcus ran in. He was at least wearing pajama pants. He swayed on his feet as he looked around the room, then shook his head. Vaughn stepped through the door and helped steady him.

"Where the fuck have you been?" Brock yelled.

"Leave him be," Meg said.

She recognized that dazed look, even though she hadn't seen it in a long time. The other members of the pack would have the same vacant cast to their gazes after the alphas disciplined them.

How could Roy have reached Marcus here? And what had Roy done to Marcus?

"Help Tessa." Brock rose to his feet, then hurried to Meg's side. She hadn't even realized that she was on her knees till he crouched next to her. "Are you okay?"

She nodded. The collar felt like a brand on her neck, but she could feel her skin mending itself. She dared to reach up and shift it a bit so that it didn't heal into her flesh.

"What the hell happened?" Marcus cradled Tessa against his chest. She was breathing, but it looked like she'd been knocked out.

"I don't know." Vaughn waved her arm over Tessa's prosthetic, tapping on her watch.

"This is not giving me confidence in your stasis chambers," Brock said.

"Vaughn doesn't make mistakes." Marcus snarled the words at Brock. "Her tech has never failed us before."

"It looks like there was some sort of feedback from Meg's collar that caused a massive power surge," Vaughn said. "Where the hell did you get that thing, anyway?"

"Priorities." Brock looked like he was about to say something else, but his eyes suddenly screwed shut as he fell away from her, pressing his hands against his temples.

"Brock?" Meg grabbed Brock's elbows, helping him to his feet.

Meg heard Vaughn say, "Oh fuck," before leaping up and running from the room. She left the door to the hallway open behind her.

"What is it?" Meg shouted.

"Marcus, get Tessa and Meg out of here." Brock shoved Meg away, pushing her toward Marcus.

"What's wrong?" She tried to see what they did, but all she saw was Porter hunched over one of the counters. He was still holding onto the metal box, but... his hand was inside the chamber.

He looked up at them and smiled, his lips peeled back in an impossible grimace. All of his teeth were bared, just like Meg had seen in the image of G-405.

His head twitched from side to side at unnatural angles on his neck. "This is delicious," he said, in a voice she didn't recognize.

"Move, move, move!" Brock yelled.

Marcus leapt up, carrying Tessa. "Come on, Meg."

"I'm not leaving." She couldn't believe she was disobeying the order of a member of her pack. But there was no way she'd leave Brock alone with that... thing. "Go!"

Marcus only hesitated a moment. He nodded quickly, then ran down the hallway with Tessa. Meg would live up to the trust he was placing in her. She had to find a way to help.

"DP, get out of there," Brock yelled.

Porter let out a sputtering cough. His face turned bright red and all the veins on his forehead stood out. She could see the skin beneath his neck rippling, as if something—

lots of things—were crawling beneath his skin.

"Have to… hold him off," Porter said.

"It's too late for that form," Brock screamed. "Come back into Dexter. Please."

"The incinerator," Porter said. "I can… We can…" His voice changed again, and he said, "We can feed. Multiply." The whites of his eyes suddenly turned red as veins burst. Blood trickled out of his ears. How much more could his body take?

"Christ, I'm so sorry," Brock sobbed. He doubled over, letting out an agonized groan.

Porter made another sputtering sound as his voice changed back. "Meg. Get Brock… away."

She grabbed Brock's arm and tried to drag him toward the door. He pulled against her, gripping her shoulder painfully tight.

"Meg, stop," Brock yelled. Tears streaked his face. "Please. He's my brother."

"What can we do?" she asked. "That thing is inside of him."

"It's almost reached… my brain. You have to—" Porter's voice cut off suddenly, his eyes wide with surprise. Blue light shimmered in a line across his throat.

"What just—" Brock began.

Before he could finish his sentence, Porter's head listed forward, then fell to the ground. The stasis chamber he'd been holding clattered after it, just as his body fell. His neck ended in a blackened stump. Meg didn't even smell a drop of blood.

His wide, staring eyes looked up at them, his lips still moving. "So close…" he muttered.

Vaughn stood over the body, a line of intense blue light beaming out from her watch. She was wearing some kind of backpack with a hose coming out of it that ran down to a metal wand in her other hand. When had she even come back into the room?

She looked up at Brock and said, "I'm sorry, too." Vaughn pointed the wand at Porter as flames poured out of it.

Brock's body convulsed, then he slumped to the ground. Meg caught him as best she could, guiding him to the floor. He looked up at her and she just knew that Brock was gone.

"Dexter?" she asked.

He nodded, staring at the body. The orange light it was putting off had turned blue, then all of it just disappeared. He turned to her, and the look in his eyes made her blood run cold.

Fear. *Dexter* was afraid.

"Please, help me," he pleaded, holding her arms in a painful grip.

"I don't know what you need," she said.

Across the room, Vaughn spoke—her tone more serious than Meg had ever heard it before. "Eli, how's Brock?"

"Unconscious, but stable." Eli's voice was coming from Vaughn's watch. "When Brock's pulse spiked, I tried to call. I saw what happened through the cameras."

"Oh, Eli," Vaughn said. "I'm so sorry."

Eli's voice was like stone. "Don't be sorry. You did the right thing."

Vaughn lifted a shaking hand to her mouth. She looked like she was about to be sick, but she managed to say, "What happens now?"

"Now… you help them split," Eli said.

Dexter's face twisted from fear to terror. He pulled Meg closer, while chanting, "No. No, no, no. Please, no."

"I'm sorry, sons," Eli said. "It's going to happen. There's no stopping it. Your brothers have been through it time and again. You'll make it through, too."

Dexter looked up at Meg and whispered, "Please, help me."

Her heart started to pound. Here was her worst enemy, a man she'd dreamed about hurting, about killing. And now, the only thing she felt for him was pity.

"What do we do?" Meg said.

"Strip him completely." Eli spoke with medical detachment, but she could hear a hitch in his breath here and there. "And if he gets stuck, pull."

"What does that mean?" Vaughn asked.

"You'll know when it's time," Eli said. "Just remember that Meg is much stronger than you. You need to keep the pressure balanced, and it shouldn't take too much. And... thank you. For helping my boys."

Vaughn's watch let out a little beep. "I guess we're on our own," she said.

"Then let's get moving." Meg grabbed the bottom of Dexter's shirt and pulled it up his chest. Dexter let go of her, lifting his arms a bit to help her get it off.

As he sat back on his heels, she couldn't help but notice the rippling lines of muscle that covered his body, sleek and toned. If it weren't for how pristine and unmarred his skin was, he would be perfect. He looked like he'd never been in a single fight.

And this is the most dangerous Blade of all?

She wondered what Brock looked like. His original body. He had mentioned sharing the marks of his replicants' deaths. Meg looked closer at Dexter's neck. A line of white scar tissue circled it where there had been nothing but smooth skin before. Did Brock have the same scar now as well?

Dexter made a sound... somewhere. Deep in his torso. A sound she'd never heard anyone's body make before. Squelching.

"What was that?" Vaughn asked, her eyes wide.

Dexter started breathing more heavily. "It's starting."

Meg grabbed the fastener for his pants and quickly undid them. He fell forward onto his hands and knees. Sweat beaded on his skin, soaking his hair.

"Hurry," he said.

Vaughn unlaced Dexter's shoes and yanked them off as Meg started working Dexter's pants down past his hips.

"Dexter goes commando," Vaughn said. "I'll add that to the list of things I did not need to know about my boss. This was not in the job description." She peeled Dexter's socks off and threw them aside just as Meg finished pulling off his pants.

It was hard not to stare. She knew she should look away, but then she wouldn't be able to see if he needed her or how to help. She still wasn't sure what to do, but good God, he was gorgeous. His sculpted legs, muscular backside, the line of ribs that...

"Um, how many ribs are people supposed to have?" Vaughn asked. "Because that looks like way too many."

She was right. As Meg watched, Dexter's ribs widened and split, doubling in number. More of that awful sound accompanied it, along with cracking and pops that sounded like bones breaking. Dexter let out a horrible groan, his hands fisted on the floor and his head bowed.

"I've never died before," he ground out. "I didn't remember... the pain. Hurts so much."

He moaned as his spine split just below his neck and pulled into two lines of vertebrae, each one cracking and popping as it pulled itself away from the other. Meg dared a glance at Vaughn. She was staring with wide eyes, her mouth hanging open, shock and horror etched on her bloodless features.

"Vaughn," Meg said. "You still with me?"

Vaughn snapped her mouth shut and nodded. "I've never seen anything like this."

"It'll… get worse," Dexter grunted. He slapped at the ground near Meg, as if looking for something. She couldn't stand it. She reached out and grabbed his hand. He let out a sigh, as if that was what he'd been searching for.

"I'm so sorry." He looked up at her with eyes that each had two irises. "Please don't leave me."

"I won't," she said.

He nodded, then leaned forward again, letting out another pained groan.

"Vaughn, take his other hand," Meg said.

"Really? Now?"

"Yes, now," Meg snapped.

"Okay." Vaughn did as Meg said. *Vaughn* obeyed *Meg.*

Meg felt a strange rush of power unlike anything she'd ever felt before. Not power over Vaughn, but power *with* her. Together, they were stronger than they were alone.

Like a pack…

Before Meg could bask in that amazing revelation, Dexter let out a piercing, inhuman screech. She could hear the sound of bone grinding on bone coming from his skull, along with that horrible squelching noise.

"We have to pull," Meg said.

"Are you sure?" Vaughn looked panicked.

Honestly, Meg felt panicked as well. But she knew they had to do something. Fast.

"Pull!" she yelled.

Vaughn tightened her grip on Dexter's hand and shoulder and started to pull. Meg watched Vaughn's movements closely, matching her own strength and efforts to Vaughn's so that they pulled evenly.

Dexter's skin stretched. As they pulled, his back widened, those two spines separating, but still curved toward each other at the base of his skull. When Meg thought they couldn't shift any farther apart, she heard a loud pop at the base of his skull. He screeched again, the sound even less human.

"Meg..." Vaughn said.

"Keep pulling."

Dexter's skull started to stretch. Meg inched backwards, giving them more room to work. Two spines, two necks, two heads. Their shoulders were still fused, but then arms appeared between them, emerging from their torsos. They clawed at the floor with their free hands, crawling away from each other.

"Jesus Christ," Vaughn yelled.

"Keep pulling!"

Vaughn rose up on her heels, shimmying away from Meg. Dexter and Porter were only connected from the hips down.

"Grab them under their arms," Meg said.

"Okay." Vaughn followed her lead, grabbing Porter by his armpits to balance out where they were applying their force.

Dexter wrapped his arms around Meg. *Dexter* was embracing her.

"It's okay," Meg whispered. "I've got you."

He squeezed her tighter, panting against her neck.

"You ready, Vaughn?" Meg said.

"Ready as I'll ever be."

"Pull!"

Meg half-rose to her feet, staggering back as Dexter pulled free from Porter. Behind them, she saw Porter and Vaughn land in a pile of tangled limbs on the floor. Meg landed on her bottom, hard, Dexter splayed across her lap. Her back was against the wall, and she gladly leaned against it for support.

For a moment, they were all silent, the only sound their heavy breaths. Meg sat with Dexter resting his head on her knee, one of his arms still wrapped around her waist. She wiped at the sweat covering his brow, then ran her fingers through his hair, trying to offer what comfort she could. His arm tightened as he hugged her closer.

He swallowed hard, the muscles of his neck still corded from the strain of his split. He looked up at her and murmured, "Thank you."

Chapter Nine

Beep. Beep. Beep.

The first thing Brock heard as he floated up to consciousness was the steady hum of machinery. The voices were next.

"What if he doesn't wake up?"

"He's going to wake up. We're all still functioning."

"Maybe we can survive without him. We could maintain the Blades. Keep his legacy alive."

"He's not going anywhere. We have a plan."

"What plan?" Brock's throat hurt, a tight pain that brought the last few moments jolting back to his memory. "DP?"

His eyes snapped open as he tried to sit up. The lights above stung, dim as they were. Halos surrounded them. Everything was blurred.

"Easy there, son." Dad was right there, gripping his shoulders and pushing him back down against the bed.

"Porter…" Brock said. "Where's Porter and Dexter?"

"We're here." Dexter and Porter stepped into Brock's field of view simultaneously, flanking his bed. Unless Brock was hearing things, they'd both spoken at the same time. Damn, it was good to hear their voices.

Dad pressed a control that raised half of Brock's bed, bringing him to more of a sitting position. As Brock's view of the room improved, he saw that they had more company than he'd thought.

Tessa and Marcus were standing near the door. They both looked wrecked. They stared at Brock with wide eyes, Tessa hugging herself and Marcus keeping one arm tight around her shoulders.

"Chicken," Brock said. He hadn't meant to use his old pet name for her from when they were kids, but seeing her looking so vulnerable... It just came out.

She burst into tears and started toward him.

Dexter and Porter both drew blades faster than Brock could track. They had to be using the other replicants to move like that. Tessa jerked to a stop. For once, she didn't look like she wanted to rip off their heads.

"Stand down," Brock said.

Again, Dexter and Porter spoke simultaneously. "Abso-fucking-lutely not."

"What did you just say?" Brock couldn't believe his ears. Not just that they were speaking in unison, but that they had actually defied him. And with such a weird turn of phrase.

"We said no," they said. "Maybe you need your hearing checked."

"It's okay, Brock." Tessa stepped back into Marcus's

embrace. They were both wearing full hunting outfits, even though Tessa hadn't been cleared for the field yet—if she ever would be, with the control issues she'd been having.

She seemed to be doing okay now, though. Maybe Meg's presence was helping. Except, Meg wasn't in the room.

"Where are Meg and Vaughn?" Brock asked.

"They're upstairs," Dad said.

"You left Vaughn alone with Meg?" Brock looked over at Dexter, surprised by the show of trust.

"After what Vaughn did to Porter, we think she can take care of herself," Dexter said.

"What did she do to Porter?" All Brock remembered was feeling DP's consciousness slam into him, knocking him back into his body.

"She decapitated us," Porter said. "And then burned us with a flamethrower until our body vaporized to make sure no parasites escaped."

Holy shit.

Brock hadn't known Vaughn had that in her.

"Is she okay?" Brock asked.

"As okay as Vaughn ever is," Dexter said.

"How are you?" Tessa asked.

"I'm fine." Brock pushed all of his strength into his voice, willing them to believe him. Truthfully, he felt like he'd been hit in the head with a sledgehammer about a dozen times before being tossed onto a highway to get run over by a truck. "We can get back to business as usual."

"Business as usual?" Marcus said. "There is no business as usual. This is a clusterfuck."

"Gee, Marcus, tell us how you really feel." Brock glared at him, but Marcus didn't back down.

"I'm exhausted," he said. "Terrified."

Brock hadn't expected honesty. A wave of guilt hit him. Everyone was suffering, and it was his fault. If Brock hadn't decked Porter, he wouldn't have lost his focus enough for his hand to slip through the stasis pod's forcefield. If they hadn't been searching for a way to save Brock, they wouldn't have kept the parasite around in the first place.

If he hadn't been born, Tessa could have been raised by their parents. She could have had a normal family. She'd still be human.

"You don't know that."

Brock jerked at DP's sudden voice in his head. He'd thought he had his shields up.

"Your mother was a hunter," Zachary projected into Brock's mind. *"Hunters don't just walk away from the fight."*

"Tessa might have never even been born if you hadn't brought her parents together," Bradley added.

Damn. So, everyone was listening in.

"Don't you have anything to add, Malcolm?" Brock

thought.

"We have less than thirty-six hours to fix this."

"You're all rays of fucking sunshine," Brock projected.

"I'm so sorry," Tessa said, bringing his attention back to the room. "This is my fault."

"No," Brock said.

"It is." She glanced at Marcus, who nodded at her. "But I think I have a way to make things better. To keep me from distracting anyone from helping you."

"Why do I have a feeling I'm not going to like this?" Brock said.

"I'm dangerous," she said. "I can't control myself with this voice in my head. It's too strong. It sent me to the lab, and once I was there, it kept telling me to kill everyone. It even wanted me to kill Marcus—not just attack him. I hurt Meg again, and I promised—" Tessa's voice cut off. She shook her head sharply. "I promised I wouldn't hurt her again. I'm not going to hurt anyone again."

Brock understood where Tessa was coming from, but was afraid of where she was going with this. "We can trick out a cell for you in the pit."

She shook her head. "I tore through one of the cell walls. Vaughn doesn't even know how I managed it."

"We can deactivate your cybernetics," Brock said.

"The nanites have evolved." She lifted her arm, flexing her metal fingers. "Their programming was supposed to help them integrate with me fully, giving me absolute control and allowing me to change form completely. They're part of me now and can't be shut down unless I am."

"I already hate this idea, whatever it is," Brock said.

She ignored him and plowed on. "Put Marcus and I in the stasis chambers Vaughn prepared for Dexter and Porter."

"Absolutely not," Brock said.

"Why?" She took a step forward, and this time Dexter and Porter didn't move to intervene. They kept still, though their swords remained unsheathed.

"Vaughn and Dad need someone to test the chambers," she said. "Marcus and I regenerate. You can try them out on us with minimum risk."

"This is bullshit." Brock turned to their dad. "Tell her."

Dad was silent, but Brock could tell from the look in Dad's eyes that he didn't have an ally there.

"Oh my God," Brock said. "You're okay with this."

Dad shook his head. "I'm not okay with losing my daughter or my sons. Vaughn and I have gone over everything, with Porter's help. We think it's safe enough to try."

"'Safe enough?'" Brock said. "Come on, Dad."

"It's her choice," Dad said. "And she's made it. She just wanted to have a chance to tell you herself."

"What about Meg?" Brock asked.

Tessa shook her head. "We already talked to her. She

didn't like it, but she understood."

"How can she understand? You're risking your life." Brock knew he was grasping at straws, but he had to try to stop them from moving forward with this colossally stupid plan.

"Yes, the colossally stupid plan agreed upon by several of the most powerful minds on the planet," Bradley projected.

"Your modesty is inspiring," Brock thought back.

"We weren't just thinking of us," Bradley thought. *"Vaughn is a single entity, yet she can keep up with us. All of us. We need to do more investigating into what a curator is."*

"And to do that, we need to survive," Brock projected. *"All of us."*

"Not all. Just you." Dexter glanced over at him.

"What the hell kind of plan were you discussing when I woke up?" Brock thought.

Their silence unnerved him.

They would do anything for him. Time and again, they'd shown just how much they were willing to do for him, what they were willing to sacrifice. If they thought his life was at stake...

"Tessa and Marcus can have our stasis pods," Porter said. "It will be good to test them out before putting Brock in one, anyway."

"But then they won't be available for you," Brock said.

"When I split, if something goes wrong, we won't have an option for saving you."

Dad stepped closer and rested his hand on Brock's shoulder. "I know exactly when you were born. We'll pull Tessa and Marcus out a couple of hours before that moment. Run tests, make sure everything's all right. Then Dexter and Porter can go in, along with you."

"But that will leave you and Vaughn alone with…" Brock couldn't finish his sentence.

Tessa was right about not being able to control herself. She'd tried to kill Vaughn at least a dozen times. At this point, Brock wasn't even sure if Dad was safe with Tessa.

Porter didn't seem concerned. "Meg will be here as well."

"And suddenly you trust her," Brock said.

"We're out of options." Dexter sheathed his sword as he spoke. "And nearly out of time."

Tessa and Marcus stepped through the open doorway out into the hall. Brock's throat was too tight to say anything. Not even goodbye.

"It's gonna be okay, son." After a final squeeze, Dad let go of Brock's shoulder and followed them, along with Porter.

The door slid shut, leaving Brock alone with Dexter. As alone as he ever was when the replicants were involved.

"We're going to head upstairs when this is done," Dexter said. "You can borrow us to spend more time with

Meg if you'd like."

None of the replicants had made an offer like that in years. They were too concerned about how it would effect Brock since Malcolm had... emerged. Adding in how opposed they'd been to Brock spending any time with Meg, and he was more than a little suspicious.

"Suddenly, you're okay with that?" Brock said.

Dexter shrugged. "Death changes a person."

Brock wasn't buying it. "What are you planning? I want to know."

"Don't worry about it."

"Cut the crap, Dexter." Brock closed his eyes, pushing his consciousness out along all the tendrils that connected him with the replicants.

He felt Porter in the lab close by, consulting with Vaughn over the communicators in their watches as they made final checks on the stasis pods. Brock definitely wouldn't be trying to force anything while Porter was working on something so important. But this was important, too. Brock needed to know what they had planned, and to tell them that DP wasn't the only one who had changed from that latest death.

Lee was in his ops center with Rose, their IT person. She was sitting in front of a wall of monitors that looked almost exactly like Vaughn's. Whatever Lee had just said must have been hilarious, based on the way she was laughing. He made up an excuse about needing to check on something in the lab and headed Brad's way.

Zach was poring over screens of data in his bedroom while Carey led a sparring session at the Europa base. Carey handed the training session over to Damien, one of the senior Guards in the Blades' hierarchy, then headed to a nearby room where he could have some privacy.

Mal and Colm were making adjustments to their stasis pods in one of the many safehouses Vaughn had set up for the Blades around the globe. This one was probably in France, based on Brock's view of the Eiffel Tower when he'd connected with them all earlier. There were no windows for an amazing view here, though. It was probably the hidden panic room.

How could he have let himself get so out of touch with them all that he wasn't even sure what country Malcolm was in?

The replicants who were alone blanked out, staring at nothing while they made their minds available. The only one who remained active was Porter. Tessa and Marcus were in the pods already.

Brock felt a rush as his mind linked up with his replicants, thoughts entwining and mental energy merging together. The solution for the issue Malcolm was having with his stasis pod suddenly became obvious. Zachary recognized a pattern in the fighting technique they'd been teaching that could actually be detrimental when facing groups of subterranean dwellers. Almost as soon as he noticed the problem, a new set of exercises coalesced in his mind that would resolve the issue.

Bradley realized that Rose had been flirting with him.

"Holy shit," he thought.

Brock tried to make his thought light and teasing. *"Now you have something to live for."*

The response was a wave of darkness. Flat despair. He hadn't known his replicants could feel something like that.

"I need to know," he projected. *"What is going on?"*

The darkness continued, but images flickered across their awarenesses. They were trying to not think about whatever it was they had planned.

Brock didn't want to do this, but he had to know. He pushed, breaking through their shields so that he could see what it was they were thinking. Years of practice made it relatively easy. That and the fact that his brain was their central hub.

Brock saw Mal and Colm facing one another, drawn swords touching each others' chests right above their hearts. He flinched as they stepped forward, shoving the blades between their ribs, piercing their hearts. They fell against each other, propping each other up until both of their bodies were consumed by the blue light that claimed all dwellers after death.

The gruesome vignette was quickly followed by Zach and Carey slashing each other's throats, then Brad and Lee entering their stasis chambers and triggering a sequence that would fill the tanks with nitrogen, suffocating them.

"What the hell?" Brock projected.

"It was Malcolm's idea," Bradley thought. *"But we're all on board with it."*

"How could this possibly help anything?" Brock hadn't meant to share the thought, but connected as they were, it went through anyway.

Malcolm was the one to respond. *"Reduce the load. You were okay when it was just you and DP. Adding Bradley started your descent. Each of us emerging has accelerated your body's deterioration."*

"So, you're going to kill yourselves?" Brock thought.

"You've been convinced we're all going to die anyway," Zachary responded. *"If we determine that this is the only way to restore you—to save you—we'll gladly do it. You're our progenitor."*

They would. Brock knew it. Everything they'd ever done, they'd done for him. Because he asked them, ordered them, or forced them.

"Stop calling me that," he thought.

He felt their confusion.

"No more borrowing," he said. *"No more orders or mindblasts. I've been through so many splits with you all, so many deaths. I know the hell, the fear, the pain of it. DP was killed because I was trying to force him to do what I wanted. He had to go through that alone."*

Brock hadn't even been conscious to tell them it'd be

okay. He hadn't been able to provide what little comfort he could, as he did to the others when they died. The silence in all of the replicants' minds was deafening. It was like they were all holding their breath.

"I'm sorry," Brock thought. *"I'm sorry I've been treating you all like tools and soldiers when I should have been treating you like brothers."*

Finally, Bradley responded. *"If this is you trying to convince us to throw out our plan, we hate to tell you, but it's kind of having the opposite effect."*

Brock laughed, and could feel a sense of lightness echoed back to him. It was a momentary respite before letting them know where he stood.

"We're going to find a way out of this," he thought. *"All of us... or none of us."*

Chapter Ten

"And that is why I will be making you at least a dozen different types of eggs as soon as things settle down." Vaughn smiled over at Meg as they sat on the couch in Vaughn's living space.

Meg couldn't call the room a bedroom, even though a fair portion of it was taken up with a large bed. The room also had a kitchenette, complete with mini-fridge and a tiny stove and oven, and the nicest bathroom Meg had ever seen. She supposed the other door leading off the main room was a closet. The ceilings were lower than in the rest of the house, and the space was small, but not claustrophobic. All the dark wood paneling might be helping with that. The natural materials soothed Meg.

Exhausted as Vaughn must be, she had steered them straight to the comfy gray couch where they'd sat for the last two hours. Vaughn had wanted to share one of her favorite romantic comedies, explaining that it would help Meg understand the importance of figuring out what *she* wanted and not focusing on others' needs so much. Meg wasn't sure how well that had worked, but she had really enjoyed just relaxing and trying to think about something other than what they had just been through. When they'd first sat down, Vaughn's entire body was trembling, but she seemed to have calmed down now.

"You don't have to make me that many different types of eggs," Meg said.

"I see. So, you already know which one you prefer?"

Meg preferred steak, but she'd never tell anyone that.

"Scrambled are fine," Meg said.

Vaughn shook her head. "'Fine' isn't good enough."

"Hold on." Meg arched an eyebrow. "Do you just want to reenact that scene from the movie?"

"Maybe a little bit." Vaughn laughed, then picked up Meg's hand that was resting between them. "But that's not the only reason."

She stared at Meg, not making direct eye contact, that light smile on her lips. Vaughn's eyes were bright blue, like a robin's egg, but more vibrant. The color didn't seem entirely natural. Maybe she was wearing colored contacts.

Being able to look at her was wonderful. If Meg had stared at another member of her pack like this, they would have seen it as a claim to dominance and attacked her. Sitting next to Vaughn, Meg felt safer than she'd ever felt before—except when Brock was holding her.

"Vaughn..."

"Meg..." She said Meg's name with the same inflection, even mirroring her expression.

Meg laughed, and felt more of her own tension ease

away.

"We have now confirmed that we know each other's names." Vaughn's brow furrowed. "Actually, is Meg short for Megan?"

Meg shrugged. "I'm not sure. I sort of remember an orphanage from when I was really young, but not what they called me. The pack probably used Meg because—"

Vaughn's eyes widened. "Please don't tell me it's short for 'omega.'"

Meg looked away, feeling Vaughn's body tense next to hers. Vaughn tightened her grip on Meg's hand.

"I'm sorry," Vaughn said. "When I think about your past, I get angry. But not at you—at them. At everybody who wasn't there for you or mistreated you."

"It's okay."

"It's not okay." Vaughn let out an exasperated sigh. "And it's okay for it to… not be okay. But just so you know, I'll be calling you Megan from now on."

She chuckled, but Meg couldn't quite bring herself to join in this time. It felt horrible to be lying to Vaughn. To everyone. But confessing that Meg was here to spy on Brock and destroy the Blades didn't seem like a good idea. Especially since she wasn't even sure she could go through with it. She didn't want to hurt the Blades anymore. Not even Dexter.

What she wanted didn't matter. Roy was there, watching her, listening to everything going on around her.

If she didn't make her way back to Brock, Roy would punish her. For a moment, Meg wondered if defying Roy would be worth it.

The worst part of it all was that she *wanted* to be with Brock. Even if it meant cozying up to him while he was in Dexter's body. She'd never wanted to be close to someone the way she wanted to be close to Brock. The idea of meeting him in his real body sent a shiver through her. But that would put him in too much danger, as long as the collar was around her neck.

Meg looked around the room, searching for some distraction. Something to get her thoughts on a different path before Vaughn noticed that something was wrong. Something beyond the nightmare they'd just been through together.

A beautiful lamp cast soft light into the room. Its base was made of intricately sculpted bronze metal. There was a frame beneath it at an angle that made the glare from the glass obscure the picture. Meg reached over and picked it up so she could see better.

An image of Vaughn smiled out at her, her hands gripping the arms of a man with short reddish hair and hazel-green eyes who was standing behind her. The man had his arms wrapped around Vaughn's shoulders, holding her tight with their heads pressed together. They looked so happy.

"Who is this?" Meg asked.

"That is Tony. We met in college." Vaughn gently took the picture from Meg's hand, staring at it with a sad smile. "Once upon a time, I thought Tony was going to be the great love of my life. We were together for years. His mom had an issue with her hearing, and I even learned ASL to show him how serious I was about us."

It took Meg a moment to remember what ASL stood for. American Sign Language. One of the girls she'd hung out with for a while had taught her a little. Meg had studied more on her own at the library.

"What happened?" Meg asked.

Vaughn shrugged. "He's outdoorsy. I'm agoraphobic."

"I don't know that word."

"What, 'outdoorsy?'" Vaughn said.

Meg arched an eyebrow at her and scowled.

Vaughn just laughed. "Sorry, I couldn't resist. It sounds ridiculous, but I'm afraid of being outside. Any large, open spaces freak me out. Like 'continuous-incapacitating-panic-attacks' freak me out. That's why my room is so cozy and I love being in the sublevels so much. The ship is really my favorite place, but even crossing the cave to get to it is hard sometimes."

Meg couldn't imagine not being able to go outside. At the same time, it didn't seem like something that should have ended their relationship. It wasn't like Tony couldn't go outside by himself.

"If he didn't accept that about you, he wasn't right for

you," Meg said.

"Thanks. It was more than that, though. I was recruited by Porter right after college. He actually taught at our school while we were students." Vaughn laughed again. "All the girls were crazy about him—so mysterious and handsome."

"I can believe that." Meg smiled as well.

"I couldn't explain why I was suddenly spending time with this super hot guy. Tony would have thought I was crazy if I'd tried, talking about dwellers and aliens. And if I'd tried to show him something to prove it to him, that would have put him in danger. I couldn't even bring him to the ship, because my father hadn't told me about it yet."

There was a bitterness to Vaughn's tone when she mentioned her father. Before Meg could ask about it, Vaughn went on.

"Tony started to get jealous," Vaughn said. "I was hurt that he didn't trust me. It just kind of spiraled from there."

"I'm sorry."

"It was a long time ago."

"But you still have his picture out where you can see it all the time."

"Yeah, I do." Vaughn set the picture on the coffee table in front of them. "It's not so much about remembering him as having a reminder that there's a normal world out there. A world that's worth protecting." Vaughn shook her head and let out a hollow laugh. "Sometimes I think the others don't know why I do this. Why I work so hard for the Blades and support them with everything I have."

"Why *do* you do it?"

"Because I believe in Brock's vision. A world where dwellers and humans can coexist peacefully."

Meg had been left behind during her pack's hunts, but could smell the blood on the others when they returned. Human blood.

"Some dwellers are too dangerous to live side by side with humans," she said.

"So are some humans. And animals and any number of things." Vaughn shrugged. "There are many dangers in this world. That doesn't mean we can write off everything and everyone that's different."

She paused, staring off at nothing. It seemed to take some effort for her to swallow before she could speak again.

"What I did…" Vaughn said. "What I did to Porter… It's what all Blades have to be ready to do. We have to be ready to fight. Always."

Meg shook her head. "I don't know if I could have done what you did. I mean, I'm not supposed to—"

"To what? Fight back?" Vaughn snorted. "I bet the real reason they put that collar on you was so they could control you, not to help you control yourself. You were young when you changed, like Marcus. He handles himself just fine." Vaughn looked aside for a moment.

"That sounded wrong."

Meg laughed. "He's an alpha, though."

"Why does he get to be alpha? From what you've said, you were turned before him."

"That's not how it works. The transformation process is a kind of test to see where you fit in the pack. The longer you fight before giving up, the higher you are in the hierarchy."

Meg's heart was pounding as she wondered if Roy would think this was oversharing, but her collar stayed dormant.

"I remember Tessa saying something about that when I was interviewing her for the werewolf entry in the Dwellers Database," Vaughn said. "Something about Marcus's scars marking him as an alpha."

Meg nodded. "Any wounds he sustained after transforming would have healed. And any werewolf would recognize the marks of a turning. They're very... compelling."

"Compelling?"

"Scars in general, when we see them. They're the mark of a leader. Someone who will fight to defend who and what they see as their own."

"Just wait till you see..." A haunted look shuttered Vaughn's expression as her voice trailed off. She shook her head, all trace of mirth gone. "When I see scars, all I can think of is the pain people went through to get them.

Pointless pain, like what you put yourself through."

"Me?"

"The collar. You don't have to shock yourself to keep from hurting people."

"I don't… I don't want to talk about that," Meg said. "Is that okay?"

Vaughn let out a sigh. "Your old pack really did a number on you. Things are different for you here. When you're able to trust us, I hope you learn to trust yourself enough to let me take off that collar." She smiled and said, "And I'll stop talking about it now."

Meg didn't know what else to say, so she simply replied, "Thanks."

"Sure. I actually feel like I should be thanking you, though." Vaughn tightened her grip on Meg's hand. "Honestly, I am still super freaked out. You seemed to be, too—at least, when we first arrived. I thought we could both use the comfort of just escaping into a story for a while."

Meg nodded. "Yeah, I guess so."

"Let's watch another one," Vaughn said. "But this time, we're going to get cozy."

She grabbed the blanket from the back of the couch and spread it over their laps, scooting closer and resting her head on Meg's shoulder. Meg stiffened, not knowing what to do. Vaughn looked up at her, frowning.

"Was this a bad idea?" Vaughn asked. "In my

experience, werewolves are really affectionate with packmates. I just thought—"

"Oh no, it's fine." Tears pricked at Meg's eyes. Vaughn was claiming Meg as part of her pack, even though she was human. "Packmates are very affectionate."

Not so much with her, but with the others in the pack. Meg didn't mention that, just in case Roy was listening.

Roy would sometimes hold Meg when she was scared or after other members had needed to use her to let out their violent impulses. That was why he'd stayed with her when the others went after Marcus's family. The pack's beta had lost it earlier that day, and Meg was too freaked out to be alone after what she'd endured.

Roy had made sure no one ever crossed the line and hurt her too badly or in ways that were forbidden. Those moments of affection made the coldness and hatred she also sensed from him that much worse.

Except she knew better now. She knew his affection had always been a means to an end. Keep her in her position. Maintain the pack structure.

Feeling Marcus and Tessa hold her was different. Their touch hadn't been a reward or a way to placate her. It was genuine affection. Meg could feel how much they cared for her already through their embrace. And they were stuck in stasis tanks now. She was on her own.

Vaughn spoke again in her gentle voice. "When Marcus and I became friends, he was really affectionate. We used to watch movies, and he'd put his arm around me. I don't think he ever realized what he was doing. It led to a little… confusion on my part. But then I realized what was going on. He considers me part of his pack, and that bond goes beyond friends or even family."

After a few moments, Vaughn turned slightly, looking Meg directly in her eyes. "Megan. You're not alone. Not anymore."

Meg couldn't cry, couldn't let herself. If Roy saw, he might see that her resolve was weakening. He might decide to give up on his plan and just kill her with the collar. He might kill Vaughn, too.

The collar wasn't magic. That much Meg was certain of by now. But the level of technology that had gone into making it… It reminded her of Vaughn's creations.

Questions poured through Meg's head, making it hard to think. *Could* it shock other people? Was it a bomb? Who had made it and how?

"Megan?" Vaughn said.

"Sorry." The word came out like a reflex.

"You don't have to keep apologizing. Really. Whatever went on with you before, it's over. You're with a different pack now. A hell of lot better one."

Meg wanted to say something. To thank Vaughn, hug her. To warn her that Meg wasn't free from her other pack —that they were all in danger as long as she was with them. Her eyes filled with tears. She bit her cheek to try to keep them from overflowing, but this time, it didn't work.

"Hey, it's okay." Vaughn grasped Meg's head and pulled her close, hugging her tight. Meg clung to Vaughn, gripping her shirt to keep from hurting her with her werewolf strength, soaking in the human woman's warmth as Meg cried soundlessly onto Vaughn's shoulder.

"How did you know?" Meg whispered. "How did you know what I was thinking?"

"I've been best friends with Marcus for a long time," Vaughn said. "I don't need the pack's telepathic bond to see when you're in pain."

"What telepathic bond?"

"You know, the telepathic link transmitted through the infection vector?"

Meg pulled back so she could look up at Vaughn. "I don't understand."

Vaughn laughed, then said, "All the werewolves in one pack can communicate telepathically." She stared at Meg for a few moments. "Right?"

Her mind started spinning, memories that had never made sense surging to the surface of her thoughts. The pack had been so coordinated, both in hunting their prey and in tormenting her. Roy had written everything off as 'magic' and told her that the bond of the other packmates was beyond her reach as an omega. She remembered someone in the pack calling her 'mindblind.' She'd thought they were calling her stupid. But if the others had been linked telepathically, it would explain so much.

Including the voice in Tessa's head urging her to kill.

"Are you okay?" Vaughn said.

"I'm fine." Meg's voice was high and shrill.

If Roy was listening, he must not think Meg understood the ramifications of him having a link to Tessa and Marcus. Roy might think Meg was still so loyal that the information wouldn't make a difference.

He was wrong.

She wasn't the broken woman that Brock and Dexter had rescued from those trolls. And she was done being the omega to a dysfunctional pack. The Blades had claimed her, invited her into their hierarchy. Being with them—not just Brock—was what she wanted. She was ready to fight for it.

She would find a way to warn them all.

Chapter Eleven

Brock's awareness followed Dexter as he entered the ops center. Vaughn glanced up briefly, but then flinched before turning back to her monitors.

"How was movie night?" Dexter asked.

"It was lots of fun." Vaughn said. "I think Megan would have enjoyed it more if it'd been you, though."

"We didn't think she was that fond of us," Dexter said.

Vaughn turned back to them. "Brock?"

Dexter smirked. "Try again."

Vaughn's gaze dropped a bit and seemed to get stuck on the fresh scar that circled Dexter's neck.

"Don't worry," Dexter said. "We're going to invest in some turtlenecks."

"I'm so sorry—"

"For what? You did what had to be done. If you hadn't acted when you did…" For once, Dexter was shielding his thoughts from Brock. Brock could still feel the shiver that passed through Dexter's body. "That situation wouldn't have ended well for anyone. We're still here because of you."

"I wish there had been another way."

Dexter crossed over to Vaughn and actually reached out to clasp her shoulder. "Let us be more clear in what we're saying. Thank you."

Vaughn's eyebrows hitched up her forehead. "Are you *sure* you're Dexter?"

When Dexter laughed, Vaughn shrank back from him, holding up her hands as if to ward him off.

"Okay, now you're just freaking me out," Vaughn said.

"Death changes a person."

"I thought you'd all died dozens of times."

"The others have. Not us." Dexter straightened and paced a few steps away. "When a replicant dies, they're shut off from us until after they've split. We all know the memory of each other's pain, but that's different from going through it ourselves. Only Brock bears the pain of us all as we feel it."

Vaughn let out a breath. "Lucky guy."

"You're in a sharing mood," Brock projected.

"Like we keep saying, death changes a person."

"I was able to get a better look at Megan's collar during our time together," Vaughn said. "But I couldn't do anything more than run passive scans. It seems totally normal—"

One of the monitors flashed a series of numbers, drawing their attention. Brock recognized bits and pieces. One of Vaughn's algorithms had been tripped.

"That doesn't seem normal," Dexter said.

"It isn't." Vaughn spun her chair around so that she was facing the screen.

"Wait, the monitor, or her collar?" Dexter asked.

"Both." Vaughn started typing, her fingers flying over the surface of the table. "My scans didn't reveal anything about the collar. As in, they didn't even detect that it was there."

"That *is* odd," Dexter said.

"Yeah." Vaughn only seemed to be half paying attention. "I'm working on some modifications to the scanner in my watch that should give me better data. And now I'm going to need you to step outside."

"Why?"

"Because my algorithms are detecting odd behavior from Megan."

"Bring it up on the monitor."

"She's in the bathroom."

"We assume your algorithms wouldn't be alerting you to something if she was just… doing the regular things people do in bathrooms," Dexter said.

Vaughn twisted around in her chair so she could glare at Dexter and keep typing. "She hasn't showered or slept or anything since she arrived. I told her to take a bubble bath after the movies and get some rest."

"We appreciate your concern for her privacy," Dexter said. "Now bring up the camera view for her bathroom."

"Dexter…" Brock thought.

"If she's taking a bubble bath, her privacy will be preserved." Dexter spoke out loud so Vaughn could be part of the conversation. "Or you can blur the image. We'll even close our eyes till you tell us you're ready."

"Gee, thanks." Vaughn's tone reeked of sarcasm.

Brock's view winked out as Dexter closed his eyes. Brock hadn't thought Dexter was serious about actually doing so. Maybe dying really had changed him.

For once, Brock had been spared from experiencing a replicant's death and the split that always followed. Which meant that DP had been forced to face their first death alone. If Brock tried to talk to them about it, he was sure they'd tell him it was no big deal—that they were glad he'd been spared the experience. That only added to the guilt he felt over not being there.

After a few moments and a lot of typing, Vaughn said, "That's weird."

Dexter opened his eyes. Brock felt a wave of gooseflesh pass over his body back in the ship when he saw Meg on the central monitor. Her hair was down, slicked back against her scalp and draped over her shoulders. She was submerged in the tub and covered in thick bubbles. Vaughn had still blurred everything below her neck.

Her arms were stretched above her at an awkward angle as she leaned against the tile. Her elbows were bent, as if she was using her arms to cushion her head from the tile, but instead of that, she had her hands above her head and was wiggling her fingers.

"That looks really uncomfortable," Dexter said. "What's she doing with her hands?"

Vaughn sat up straighter. "That's ASL."

"What?"

"American Sign Language." Vaughn started typing frantically, bringing up another monitor with Meg's image. The feed rewound, and Vaughn's gaze darted back and forth between the two views. "I told her I know ASL during our movie night. She must be trying to talk to us without anyone else hearing."

Dexter leaned in closer, one hand on the back of Vaughn's chair. "Who else could be listening in?"

"I don't know, but I've initiated a full security sweep."

All of the monitors flickered, their screens rotating through multiple camera feeds, with text continuously scrolling over them. Dexter opened his thoughts to the others, drawing on their mental abilities. Brock could feel them channeling through his own mind. He didn't fight it this time. The resentment he usually felt—the invasion of his space—was gone.

"That's... different," Bradley projected.

Dexter glanced from one monitor to the next in rapid succession. *"Focus on the issue at hand."*

Data flooded Brock's mind. Coordinates, ambient temperature, lighting levels, motion records. He could see every camera feed at once, processing what they displayed along with the information Vaughn's algorithms had come up with.

"No detectable threats," Malcolm thought.

"Then why is she communicating this way?" Zachary added.

"He's watching." Vaughn's voice broke through the chorus of thought in Brock's head.

There were a hell of a lot of 'he's' watching at the moment.

"You blurred the image," Dexter said.

"No, that's what Megan is signing. Over and over again." Vaughn glanced up at Dexter. "Who is she talking about? Who is watching?"

On the monitor, Meg dropped her arms to the top of her head. She stared up at the ceiling, tears rolling from her eyes. Then she buried her face in her hands, her shoulders shaking as she cried.

"Should one of us go up there and comfort her?" Vaughn said.

"Then she'll know we really are watching her."

"She already knows we're watching her." Vaughn gestured toward the monitors. "Otherwise, she wouldn't be trying to communicate with us like this."

"Have Vaughn pull up the records from when she was alone in her room," Brock projected. *"Let's see if she's done this before."*

"Check the footage in her room from before her bath," Dexter said.

Vaughn's hands danced over the smooth surface of her desk. The monitors flashed with different images. Finally, they were left staring at a dozen screens of Meg. Meg wandering through the room. Meg sitting at the desk reading. Meg lying on the bed. Meg pulling her shirt over her head.

Brock's skin tingled with the urge to touch her. But what he wanted from her was something more. Something they could never have. He wanted to touch her with his own hands. Kiss her with his own lips. His fantasy barely had time to begin before it crumbled beneath reality. All he had to do was imagine her running her smooth fingertips over the scars that covered his ruined body.

"It looks like she did this earlier in her room." Vaughn's voice snapped Brock back to the moment. "Here are the times she was most likely trying to communicate."

The monitors had changed a bit. Meg was standing in all of them, arms stretched over her head. She was making gestures with her hands and fingers that Brock didn't understand. It looked like Vaughn had placed the feeds on a loop.

"What's she saying?" Dexter asked.

Vaughn pointed at a monitor. "In this one, it's the same as what she was just signing. 'He's watching' or 'always watching.' Here are a couple where she's saying, 'collar sensors.' It's a little hard to understand, since she's doing this all above her head instead of making the gestures in their normal locations. She's throwing in some words that she's spelling out, which helps."

Brock watched Meg form the same shapes over and over with her hands. Some were obvious, and he quickly picked out the word 'collar.' He could see that she was repeating the same letters—at least, in some of the screens.

"Here, she's spelling out 'collar hears,'" Vaughn said. "And here, 'collar sees.'"

"What about this?" Dexter pointed at the left bank of monitors, where Meg signed, 'collar,' but the letters afterwards were different.

Vaughn rolled her chair closer. "Shit."

"She's signing, 'collar shit?'" Dexter asked.

"No. 'Collar maybe bomb.'"

The room spun around Brock, his perception wavering. His instinct was to take over Dexter's body, to use it to run to Meg. But he was done using his replicants that way. He couldn't live with himself if he was the direct cause of—

"Do it," Dexter thought.

"Dexter…"

Brock felt a tug on his awareness as Dexter's consciousness left his body. Left it *empty*. Brock's mind was sucked into the space, like he was caught in a whirlpool.

"Oh shit." Vaughn jumped up to catch Dexter as his

body fell.

Brock was so disoriented, he couldn't quite remember how to make Dexter's arms and legs move. He leaned against Vaughn as Brock fully integrated with the replicant's body.

"What the hell was that?" Brock projected.

Dexter's reply was as even as always. *"An experiment."*

"We're working on ASL," Bradley thought. *"Malcolm and Zachary are helping. Fluency should be achieved in thirty minutes."*

"Thanks." Brock tamped down on the surge of guilt that flooded him just after he registered their shared response to his word. Surprise.

Damn, he'd really been taking them for granted.

"Dexter, are you okay?" Vaughn said.

"Yeah." Brock finally managed to stand. "But it's Brock now."

"It is so hard to keep track of all you guys."

"You don't know the half of it." Brock turned and started toward the door.

"Hey, wait a minute," Vaughn said. "Where are you going?"

"To help Meg."

The door didn't open when Brock approached it. He glanced up and saw that the light above blinked red, indicating a lockdown. Vaughn was already back at her desk, typing frantically when Brock turned around.

"Open the damn door," Brock said.

"Hear me out first." Vaughn spoke in level tones, quiet, but firm. Like she spoke to Marcus when talking him down from a change.

"If there's a bomb in her collar, it hasn't gone off yet," Vaughn said. "We don't know what we're dealing with. Running up there and trying to pry it off her neck might set it off."

"We can't just leave it on her."

"I know. Just give me a moment. I need to parse through all this data."

Vaughn closed her eyes, but they moved rapidly behind her lids. It looked like videos of REM sleep cycles his dad had shown Brock as a kid. The more time passed, the paler Vaughn became. Her lips pressed together tight and furrows appeared between her eyebrows.

Finally, Brock couldn't take it anymore. "Vaughn. Talk to me."

"Oh shit." Vaughn's eyes flew open, staring wide at the monitors.

"What? What shit?"

She took a deep breath, then turned to Brock. "I get that you care about Megan. We all do. But I need you to stay calm. I need you to not try to force me to open that door till we have a plan."

"Vaughn—"

"I swear by the Internet, I will not say another word until you promise me."

"Fine, I promise."

Vaughn kept glaring at him.

Brock sighed. "I mean it. If you're so freaked out that you're acting... not freaked out, I get how serious it is. I can control myself."

"You'd better, because this is bad," Vaughn said. "Really bad."

"Just tell me."

She turned back toward the monitors and pulled up several still images of Meg in her room. "Thank God I told Megan about Tony," Vaughn murmured.

"Who's Tony?"

"He's the reason I know ASL. And the reason Megan knows that I know ASL." Vaughn let out a strained laugh and shook her head. "Damn, that's clever. We are so freaking lucky that Megan knows ASL, too."

"Vaughn." Brock's patience was reaching its limits.

"If the collar is letting someone see and hear everything around her, she had to find a way to communicate without sound or leaving a trace," Vaughn said. "She couldn't write us a note or even try to signal us without risking giving herself away. The collar circles her entire neck, so she couldn't even do anything behind her back. But above her head or in the tub, especially when her hair is partially blocking the collar..."

"It's a blind spot."

Vaughn nodded, then started pointing to different loops of Meg. "The phrase she's saying the most is, 'he's watching.'"

"Who's watching?"

Vaughn pressed her lips into a thin line. Brock was pretty sure that meant she already knew—and didn't like the answer. She tapped the desk again, and another monitor started to play. This time, Brock didn't need Vaughn to translate. His replicants were feeding him the knowledge he needed to understand what Meg was spelling out.

"Puppetmaster." Brock felt all the replicants still. "The person controlling that collar is also trying to control my sister."

"It gets worse," Vaughn said.

"You know who he is?"

Vaughn pointed at a monitor where Meg was spelling out the name, 'Roy.'

"Stop drawing this out," Brock said.

"I'm trying to give you the information in small, digestible parts so that you don't run upstairs and get us all blown up."

"Vaughn."

"I'm going to tell you, I just seriously am trying to not freak you out, because I'm already freaking out, and we can't both be freaking out—"

"We're going to figure this out," Brock said. "We always do."

"I already did. I just… I don't know what to do about it."

Brock latched his foot around one of the nearby chair's legs and pulled it closer, then sat next to Vaughn. "Walk me through it."

"Okay." Vaughn turned back to the wall of monitors. "If this Roy is the puppetmaster that's been tormenting Tessa and trying to get her to kill me—and you—and he has sensors in Megan's collar, we can assume that he knows everything that happens around Megan."

"You think that's what she means by 'collar sensors?'"

"I *know* that's what she means," Vaughn said. "Here comes something that's going to make you ballistically mad. Ready?"

Brock tamped down on his temper. Instead of yelling at Vaughn to get on with it, Brock smiled at her.

"I think I liked it better when you were getting upset." Vaughn's body shook as if she'd caught a chill, but then she smiled briefly. She took a deep breath, then tapped another control on her desk. A sound recording played, taken while Brock was on patrol with Dexter when he'd first met Meg. In the footage, Dexter sounded as close to angry as he ever came.

"*We destroyed that pack sixteen years ago,*" he had said.

"*Not all of us,*" Meg had responded. "*I mean, I survived. And Marcus. I wasn't there when it happened.*"

Meg had sounded more and more panicked as she spoke, stumbling over her words in her haste to get them out. A burst of static cut off the recording. It had been the first time Brock witnessed Meg's collar shocking her. A sick feeling spread through his stomach as a terrible idea took shape in his mind.

"If Roy is using the collar to watch us, can he use it for other things?" Brock asked.

"Like blowing us all up?"

That was one thought. But Brock was stuck on another. He gripped the armrests of the chair tight, pushing down his rage so that he could form words.

"Like shock Meg," Brock said.

Vaughn didn't have to reply. The deep frown, the glinting in her eyes, the muscle twitching in her jaw—they answered clearer than anything she could have said.

"I should have noticed the pattern earlier," Vaughn said. "We could have helped her before now."

"How *are* we going to help her?" Because they *were* going to help her. And then they were going to track down this 'Roy' and skin him alive.

Brock thought of every flicker, every flinch, every shriek from Meg when the collar 'helped her control her werewolf impulses.' It wasn't helping her. It was hurting her. Torturing her. Controlling her.

Fucking puppetmaster.

"This guy is done messing with Meg—and my sister." Brock stood up and headed for the door. The light above was still red.

"There's more." Vaughn's voice shook.

When Brock turned around, he saw that Vaughn had paled even further. Her lips were bloodlessly tight and her eyes were wide. Her hands were in tight fists resting on her thighs.

After everything Vaughn had shared, this last bit of data was visibly freaking her out? Brock slowly walked back and sat down, hoping it would help put her more at ease. They sat in silence for a few moments before she spoke again.

"I know who Roy is," Vaughn said.

A million questions ran through Brock's mind. How did Vaughn know? What else had she figured out? Did she know where Roy was? How to kill him? How to make Meg safe from that damned collar?

Brock settled on asking, "Who?"

Vaughn tapped a button on her desk, and part of the recording played again. Meg saying, "*Not all of us.*"

"How many werewolves were there the night Dexter saved Marcus?" Vaughn asked.

"Five."

"An odd number."

"So?" Brock said.

"Werewolves operating alone are always rogues. Unstable and violent. We notice them immediately and take them out."

"*The point*, Vaughn."

"Tessa told us that werewolf *packs* are always even. Each werewolf has a mate to help stabilize them, like Marcus helps her."

Brock tried not to think about just how Marcus 'helped stabilize' Tessa. She was Brock's sister, after all.

"Five plus Meg is six," Brock said. "She already told us she wasn't there because omegas are non-aggressive."

"Six counting Megan. *Seven* counting Marcus."

"I don't understand."

"Megan also told us she'd just been brought into their pack right before the attack on Marcus's family. I don't think they attacked Marcus's family just for fun. I think they were looking for someone to be Megan's mate when they were of age."

Brock wanted to hit something. He wanted to hit Marcus. It didn't matter that Marcus and Meg hadn't become a mated pair. Brock still wanted to erase the concept of the two of them together from his mind. Replacing it with the thought of beating on Marcus helped.

Vaughn was only speculating, but Vaughn was Vaughn. She was probably right.

"If they were trying to even out their numbers again…" Brock said.

"Then that means there were seven werewolves in Marcus's pack when he was attacked. The five Dexter killed, Megan, and…"

Fuck.

A rush of adrenaline hit Brock so hard he felt light-headed. His muscles tensed and fluttered, wanting to move, to run, to fight. He could feel the other replicants pausing, turning their attention toward him—toward their progenitor.

This was bad. So much worse than bad.

"She said, '*Not all of us,*' and then Roy shocked her," Vaughn said. "Because Roy didn't want her telling us that we had missed one. One of the aggressive werewolves. With how much control Roy has over Tessa, he might even be the original alpha male."

Brock leapt out of his chair. He couldn't stop himself. He started pacing in the small room, his heart pounding.

"The alpha male," Brock said. "Whose mate Dexter killed sixteen years ago."

Vaughn shook her head. "I can't believe he's still alive. There's no way he's sane after losing his mate."

Brock let out a laugh. "Killing us over and over again might have helped."

"What?"

The pieces were falling into place for Brock. So many deaths he and his replicants had endured, strange behavior from rogue werewolves who seemed utterly insane, aside from their single-minded intent to kill him. One of the most painful deaths came back to him—a werewolf disemboweling Zach, screaming, 'Why won't you die? Why can't I kill you?' the whole time.

Brock's abdomen cramped at the memory of the pain, forcing him to stop pacing. He thought of the scars that lined his stomach even now—and Zachary's. One or the other of that pair of replicants had been killed by werewolves three times.

This was the werewolf who had tortured Mal for hours and then killed him by… Brock lifted his hand, his fingers shaking as he ran them over the smooth skin of Dexter's face.

"He's tried to make more." Brock dropped his arms to his sides, hands clenched into tight fists. "To rebuild his pack. But the werewolves he makes are all insane."

"If he uses the telepathic bond to try to control them, that would make sense," Vaughn said. "A pack is only as sane as their alphas. And if this *Roy* is posing as a voice in their heads, that would explain why kids don't tend to go nuts like adults do. They don't understand that the voice in their head belongs to someone else." Vaughn pressed her hands against her forehead. "Jesus, this is the guy who's been messing with Marcus since the beginning. Pretending to be his 'dweller' all along."

This one person had caused so much pain to Brock and his family. Marcus, Tessa, and all of Brock's replicants—

his *brothers*.

"Guys." Brock waited a moment, but everyone was silent. He could feel them, though. Waiting. *"I'm sorry."*

They didn't use words to respond. Instead, he felt each of their minds lightly touch on his, the connection gentler, yet more focused than ever before. He tried to send his appreciation to each of them. They hadn't asked to be created. What they were wasn't their fault. Part of Brock had been blaming them this whole time. Part that he finally knew how to let go of.

"We can use this," Vaughn said. "Once we kill Roy, we won't have as many rogue werewolves coming after you. Tessa will be able to heal and adapt."

Of course, Vaughn had figured out Roy's full impact on everyone, too. She had gone through all the records of every death Brock's replicants had experienced, cataloging everything to try to help the Blades be safer in the field.

"We can't forget about Meg," Brock said. "We need to get that collar off of her—safely. But we can't let her know what's going on. Where the hell did Roy even get it?"

"Yeah, you're not going to like what I've figured out about that, either," Vaughn said.

Brock let out a huge breath, then lifted one arm and let it drop to his side. "Go ahead."

"I had a brainstorm while we were chatting and set my machines to work on extracting data from Tessa's hand. I figured it had a much better view when she was…"

"When she was trying to strangle Meg."

"Strangle. Decapitate." Vaughn shrugged.

When Brock glared at her, Vaughn sat up straighter, then pointed at a monitor that now showed an image of Meg's collar. It was just like her views with analyses of dwellers, gridlines superimposed over its smooth surface and data scrolling along the side of the screen. Most of it read, 'inconclusive,' but a few were marked, 'match.'

"How does this help us?" Brock asked. "What are these data points matching?"

"My tech."

Brock felt like the floor had dropped out from under him. "We have a leak."

He couldn't imagine any of the Blades turning against each other or their organization. But Vaughn wouldn't be wrong about this. She was never wrong about her tech.

"It's not a one hundred percent match," Vaughn said. "Whoever made this has gone in a different direction than I would have, but the base tech is the same."

Brock shook his head. "No one else has access to the ship. The only way your tech could be reverse engineered is if one of the Blades gave it to someone. We're always careful to never leave anything behind."

"I don't know," she said. "I've read everyone's psych profiles. I keep in touch with all the Blades. I can't imagine anyone betraying us like that."

"What else could it be?"

"In all the vastness of the universe, the odds of a spaceship crashing on Earth are infinitesimal," Vaughn said. "We've kind of been making a big assumption, though."

"Which is?"

"That my ship is the only one that crashed here. That it was alone."

Oh shit.

Brock didn't have to project the thought for his replicants to pick up on it. They were all still connected. He could feel their thoughts echoing back his own.

"We need to get that collar out of here," Zachary thought.

"We need to get it off of Meg." Brock was sure to put enough force in his projection that they knew he couldn't be swayed. *"Safely."*

"How are we going to get the collar off of Meg?" Brock asked.

"I have an idea," Vaughn said. "But, again… you're not going to like it."

Chapter Twelve

Meg was just putting the last pin in her bun when someone knocked on the door. She jumped at the sound, wheeling around. Her heart pounded in her chest.

"Come in," she said.

The door swung open. Dexter—maybe—stood in the hall. She couldn't tell for sure who he was anymore. The cold malice she'd always sensed from him wasn't there. She tried to catch his scent, but the bubble bath and shampoo she'd used masked it.

"Dexter?" she asked.

"No."

She dared to hope, and said, "Brock?"

"Yeah."

Somehow, her heart actually managed to beat harder and faster. Her throat felt like it was collapsing under the weight of words she wanted to say, but couldn't.

Was he okay? Was he still himself after one of his replicants was almost taken over by that thing? Had they seen her message? Understood it?

She kept her silence. Roy was still watching. Listening.

"Can I come in?" Brock said.

"Of course."

He stepped into her room and closed the door behind him. For a few moments, he just stared at her, a slight smile on his face as he took in the black boots, matching cargo pants, and black T-shirt she'd put on.

"It suits you," he said. "Dressing like a Blade."

"I thought you might like it if I did."

"I..." He cleared his throat and looked away. When his gaze landed on the pristinely made bed, it seemed to get stuck there. "Did you have a chance to rest?"

"No, I wanted..." She didn't know how to finish her sentence. There were so many things she wanted. They cluttered her mind, made it impossible to decide what to say.

Was she imagining the heat in his gaze when their eyes met again? Her body responded as if it was real, lightning darting along her nerves in the best possible way, pooling in her belly.

"Wanted what?" he said.

"You." The word slipped out, but she didn't bother trying to correct herself this time.

He stared at her for another moment, then strode up to her, barely slowing when he reached her. He grabbed her arms and pulled her against his chest, his lips slamming down on hers. His kiss was relentless, starving, and she matched it with a hunger that shocked her. The tenderness of his previous kisses was gone. All she felt was want.

Need.

The scent of his arousal bloomed around them, filling her senses, intoxicating her. She could have him. He could be hers.

His tongue slid into her mouth, claiming her, marking her as his. She let out a moan as she rose to meet him, clawing at the back of his shirt. There was no space between them, just heat and hardness. His erection pressed against her stomach, setting off an ache deep in her belly that she couldn't wait to satisfy. She pulled his shirt loose, then tried to work her hands between them to unfasten his pants. He broke off the kiss and stepped back, gripping her arms more tightly as he held her away.

"Wait." He shook his head. "I can't."

"You don't want this?"

"I do, but—"

"Then why shouldn't we? I want you, too." She wrapped her arms around his neck and pulled him back to her.

This time, *she* kissed *him*. She couldn't believe what she was doing. She'd never initiated sex before. It felt too good to stop.

She moved her lips to his jaw, gently biting his skin. "I want you, Brock. I want you."

It wasn't even a lie. Roy would be pleased, but she didn't give a damn. She just wanted her hands on Brock, his lips on hers. She ran her tongue over the smooth flesh of his neck.

Except it wasn't smooth. Not anymore.

A chill ran down her spine as she remembered what had just happened to him. What had happened to this form, anyway.

"I can't do this." Brock's voice was barely above a whisper, but she could still hear the rasp of desire in it. "This isn't my body."

He buried his face in her neck and wrapped his arms tight around her, holding her. Just holding her.

She hugged him back. "I understand. I'm sorry, I didn't think."

"It's kind of hard to think clearly when you're near me like this," Brock said. "It's so tempting."

He pulled back from her, holding her face in his hands and studying it intently, like he was trying to memorize her features.

"I want to touch you with my own hands," Brock said. "To see you with my own eyes."

Her breath seemed to turn to ice in her chest. This was the opportunity she'd been sent here for. Get to Brock, the true head of the hydra. Help Roy get his revenge.

She felt the collar start to crackle. Roy was listening. He was probably wondering why she wasn't pushing the moment, trying to get Brock to let her come to him—to his real body.

"Dexter would never allow it," she said.

"Dexter will do as I say." There was a hardness to Brock's tone. A finality.

She remembered what Brock had done to Dexter and Porter back in the dining room. How Brock had punished them for hurting her. They had only been trying to keep Brock safe. And they were right. Meg was dangerous. She didn't want to be, but she was.

Once she was with Brock, she had no illusions about what would happen. If the collar *was* a bomb, it would detonate. Or if it was designed to shock others and not just Meg, Roy would use it to kill Brock. If she was alone with Brock, Roy would kill him, and that would destroy all of the others. It would end the Blades.

They didn't understand my message.

Her vision blurred as tears sprang to her eyes. There was only one thing she could do. She had to warn him. Roy would kill her for it. He might even take out Dexter's body as well, but not permanently. And Brock would be safe.

"There's something I have to tell you," she said.

The collar flared up, sending arcs of pain through her neck. She could feel her skin burning, but pushed aside the pain. She had to force out the words, to let him know—

"Hey, Megan." The door to her room flew open. Vaughn was holding onto the knob. She looked surprised when she saw the pair of them, Brock's shirt untucked, their arms still around each other. "Oh, sorry boss. Didn't mean to interrupt."

"It's okay," Brock said. "But knock next time."

The crackling of the collar subsided to a low buzz, but the muscles of Meg's throat were still twitching from the current. She swallowed hard, trying to regain enough control to speak.

"Sorry. I was just going to ask Megan if she wanted to keep me company while I make her that feast of eggs." Vaughn started backing out of the room. "I can see she's busy, though."

"Wait a minute." Brock stepped away from Meg and hastily tucked in his shirt. "I want to take Meg on a tour first."

"A tour?" Vaughn laughed, then looked up and down the hall. "I thought she'd already seen most of the ranch."

"I'm not talking about the ranch," Brock said. "I'm talking about the sublevels. The cave."

Vaughn's smile vanished. "I thought we agreed about this."

"She's a Blade now." Brock gestured to Meg's outfit. "Just look at her."

"Wearing the outfit doesn't mean she's automatically one of us." Vaughn quickly turned her gaze to Meg. "I mean, you *are* one of us. That doesn't mean you're ready for the cave, though."

Meg grabbed Brock's arm. "I don't want to cause any trouble. You don't have to—"

"Megan." Brock interrupted her with a force that made her step back. He had never spoken so aggressively to her. He actually took a step forward, following her retreat. "This is about what *we* want. We only have a little over a day left to us. We *will* be together for it."

"But—"

This time, he cut her off with another crushing kiss. He grabbed the back of her neck, his hand splayed over her collar, using it to keep her where he wanted her. He claimed her again, his tongue dominating hers, his free arm around her waist, pinning her to his body. He had said he wouldn't cross a line while borrowing Dexter's body, but this was just like what they'd done before.

Except it wasn't. The only 'hardness' she felt was from the planes of his chest and abdomen. He was pressing his hips to her, but it was almost like he wanted her to know that he wasn't aroused. His taste was different, and his scent had changed, too. The desire from earlier was transforming.

Into fear.

"Okay, that's enough of that," Vaughn said. "I'm leaving."

Brock ended the kiss, but kept staring into Meg's eyes intently. Had they figured it out after all? Had they seen the message she'd been trying to send them?

"No, you're not," Brock said. "We need you to take us through the decon room."

"Decon room?" Meg was struggling to catch her breath, but at least her throat was working again. Roy had turned off the current as well.

"Decontamination," Vaughn said. "Brock's immune system is weakened. We all have to go through the decon room before visiting him."

She didn't remember anyone mentioning that before, but wasn't about to bring attention to it now. Brock gripped her elbow and started leading her from the room.

"Vaughn doesn't have to go with us, does she?" Meg asked.

It was one thing to gamble with her own life and with Dexter's, knowing that he'd survive... dying. But Vaughn was human. Whatever Roy had planned, Meg didn't want Vaughn to get caught in the crossfire.

"She needs to run the decon program," Brock said.

Vaughn fell in step beside them as they headed for the library. "I'm a multi-talented gal."

She *was* talented. Talented enough that Meg was sure any 'decon program' Vaughn had made could run itself. Meg was also sure that the others had gone down to Brock's level while she and Vaughn were watching that movie. They hadn't needed any help to prepare them for seeing Brock. Meg only hoped Roy didn't figure that out.

The bookshelf that hid the door to the elevator swung open as they approached. Vaughn was already tapping on her watch. Once Meg could see inside, her panic kicked up even higher. She had to keep Vaughn out of there. It was too much to risk her life.

"Maybe we could do the eggs first," Meg said. "I'm actually kind of hungry."

"We'll deal with all our hungers soon." Brock pushed her into the elevator. He pinned her in the back corner, hands against the wall on either side of her head.

Vaughn darted in after them. "If you guys start making out again, I swear I'll let the elevator drop us to our deaths."

"Said the only human in the room." Brock smirked at Vaughn as the doors closed.

"I don't know if this is a good idea," Meg said. She was running out of time. The elevator started to descend.

"Megan." Brock hooked his finger under her chin and brought her gaze up to meet his. That strange intensity was still in his eyes. "Trust us," he said.

She nodded, wanting to trust him, wanting to believe they knew the danger they were in. But if they did, why would they be taking her to Brock's body? They should be trying to keep her away from him.

The elevator slowed sooner than Meg expected. The doors opened on a long hallway with gunmetal gray walls, floor, and ceiling. The same color as the sublevel she had learned they called 'the pit.'

She hugged herself tightly and shook her head. "I don't want to go out there."

"It's okay," Brock said.

"No." If she balked, maybe Brock would stay in the elevator with her and Vaughn would leave. Meg could quickly tell Brock everything, or try to make Roy mad enough to set off the collar. That way, Vaughn would survive.

The collar crackled to life again, but this time, Roy wasn't messing around. The charge streaked through her body, setting her nerves on fire. She felt like her teeth were about to explode. Her vision fogged as her tears turned to steam before they even had a chance to fall. Her eyes felt like they were boiling.

Brock tried to catch her when her knees buckled, but the voltage flooded into him as soon as he touched her. She felt his body start to spasm from the electricity, both of them falling to the ground.

"Shit," Vaughn yelled. "Megan, we know the collar controls you."

For a split second, Meg felt hope. But then, Vaughn said, "You have to stop trying to change."

Her hands hit the floor. She looked down the long hallway. She had to get away from them. Slamming Brock with her shoulder, she knocked him loose from her, then forced her legs to propel her out of the elevator, half-leaping from all fours.

She screamed, "Stay away from me," as she staggered down the hall.

By the time she reached the farthest end from the elevator, her skin was smoldering. She heard the whoosh of a door, and prayed it was the elevator closing as Vaughn and Brock headed for safety.

Her prayers went unanswered. Black boots appeared in what was left of her field of vision just ahead of her. She felt a shiver down her spine and somehow knew who it was.

Dexter.

"Didn't anyone ever tell you to listen to your doctor?" he said.

Strong hands grabbed her arms, dragging her into the room in front of her. Who all was there? The doors whooshed shut behind her, and she heard the clack of something being attached to her collar. The current disappeared. She stayed on all fours, surrounded by dark forms she couldn't identify.

"Jesus, look at her neck," Vaughn said.

No, no...

Vaughn was there? Meg couldn't talk, couldn't warn Vaughn to get away. Meg's throat felt like most of the flesh had been burned away.

"Focus." The coldness of the voice... That was Dexter.

"There's a lot riding on this." The same voice, but different. Was that Brock? "This will help, but we need to move fast."

She heard the *tsshh* of a spray can and felt something

hit her neck. The pain lessened.

"Porter, I don't know if I can do this," Vaughn said.

Porter was here? Porter and Dexter both?

"Then tell us what to do." Dexter's voice was right at her ear.

Meg let out a hacking cough, and somehow managed to say, "Run." The word was barely recognizable, a wheezing rasp.

"Don't try to talk, Megan," Vaughn said. "We've got you."

Meg tried to say, "No," but nothing would come out.

She could feel Vaughn doing something to the collar. Attaching things to it. Had they understood Meg's message after all?

"Everything's on, but..." Meg could feel Vaughn's hands shaking.

"But what?" Dexter said.

"We need to use this glove to feel around the metal that's against her neck," Vaughn said. "The glove is programmed to deactivate any trigger points, which should let us unsnap the collar. But there isn't room for—"

Meg screamed as a fresh source of agony hit her neck. Someone had pressed their fingers between her collar and her scorched skin. She could feel coarse fabric rubbing against her, the skin tearing away.

"What the fuck are you doing?" Vaughn yelled.

"Saving her life."

She heard a struggle, then Vaughn yelled, "Let me go."

"We can either hold you back, or treat her injuries with the analgesic spray to try to keep her pain at bay," Porter said. "It's your choice."

"Megan, I'm so sorry." Vaughn's voice was close. They were all too close. And Meg couldn't warn them of the real danger.

"It's done," Vaughn said. "That's it. It's done, it's done."

Dexter pulled his fingers out from under the collar, one final moment of fresh pain before the pulsing base-line agony was all Meg knew. Porter was there with whatever that spray was. It could barely touch the ring of fire around her neck. Her skin should be starting to heal, but the heat kept building.

"Vaughn, is the collar supposed to be pulsing red like that?" Porter asked.

"We also notice it's not detaching," Dexter said.

"Just shut up and give me a minute." Vaughn sounded panicked.

Meg felt someone grip her under her arms and was pulled against a strong chest. Dexter was kneeling behind her, holding her up so Vaughn could mess with her collar. Her vision started to clear.

Porter was standing over them, smiling benignly. "Hello, Megan," he said. "Welcome to the Boom Room, where Vaughn tries out her inventions that might blow us all right off the face of the planet."

The fog of pain began to lesson, Meg's thoughts gradually clearing. She swallowed a few times, willing moisture back into her mouth. Her tongue felt thick, but she found she could actually speak when she tried.

"Collar may be a bomb," she said.

"We're quite sure it is." Porter leaned forward, his face right next to Vaughn's. "And we'd truly appreciate it if you could get it off of our friend Megan's neck before it blows us all up."

"Not helping," Vaughn said.

She was pulling tools out of a box on the floor. It must have already been there before they'd arrived. She hadn't been carrying it on the elevator. Had they planned this all along?

The heat against Meg's neck was growing. A beeping sound started up, growing louder and faster.

"Congratulations, Vaughn," Porter said. "Looks like you were right about the collar detonating if the signal was blocked."

"Run." Meg licked her lips and spoke again. "All of you. Run."

She could feel Dexter right next to her, but she wasn't angry or afraid.

"Not without you," he said.

Meg clenched her eyes shut. She leaned her forehead against his temple. He stiffened, but then squeezed her arms, as if he was trying to reassure her. There was barely any time left between the beeps.

"I don't want you to die," she whispered. "Any of you."

"We won't," Dexter said. "Right, Vaughn?"

"Dammit." Vaughn threw down her tools and grabbed the collar, tugging on it as if she could tear it apart with her bare hands. "Ouch!"

The scent of blood hit Meg's senses, metallic and... strange. Vaughn shook her hand briefly, then grabbed the collar again. The beeping paused before making a final innocuous 'beep-boop.' Vaughn's eyebrows hiked up her forehead.

"Porter, are you seeing this?" Vaughn said.

"Yes, we are." Whatever it was, Porter didn't look happy about it. His smile was gone and deep furrows appeared between his brows.

The collar cooled. Meg heard a click. Vaughn leaned back, holding the unlocked and open collar in her hands.

Meg was free.

Chapter Thirteen

"It worked." Brock looked over at his dad and laughed. "It worked!"

"Looks like it," Dad said.

They watched the monitor above Brock's bed as Porter helped Meg to her feet and then out of the Boom Room. Dexter and Vaughn lingered for a few moments, arguing from the look of it. Dexter pointed at the ground, and Vaughn set down the collar.

As soon as Vaughn stood up, Dexter grabbed her arm and started leading her toward the door. Vaughn seemed to be struggling, craning her neck over her shoulder to keep looking at the collar, but then Dexter leaned in and said something that made Vaughn shrink away from him. She didn't tug against Dexter's hold as they left the room.

"What was that all about, I wonder?" Brock asked.

"Your guess is better than mine. I'm honestly at a loss to explain any of the choices you boys are making right now."

Dad tapped a few command buttons on Brock's bed and the monitor went dark. He sat down next to Brock and stared at him with the same bright blue eyes that Tessa used to have—before they turned gold when she became a werewolf.

"Dexter and Porter in the same room as a bomb," Dad said. "I would think after dying for the first time, they'd be even more cautious than before, not pulling a stunt like that."

"It was his choice."

"*Their*," Dad said.

To him, they would always be 'Dexter' and 'Porter.' Just like all of the other pairs were two people in his mind. Dad wanted each and every one of his sons to be counted, each life weighed individually. It was different for Brock. He'd interacted with each replicant consciousness too often in the landscape of his mind. But he had a feeling those interactions were going to be different in the time he had left.

"You seriously want me to believe that you didn't have anything to do with what just happened upstairs?" Dad said.

"Come on, Dad."

"No, you listen to me, son. I'm glad Meg got that collar off. God knows, she's suffered enough from it. And I'm glad we've taken a step to rid our family of further harm from that man, Roy."

Dad's shoulders were slumped, and dark circles shadowed his eyes. As exhausted as he must be, he still spoke fiercely when he went on. "Your brothers would do anything for you. Anything. So you tell me why all of a sudden Dexter and Porter are risking a permanent end to their lives for a woman we're pretty damned sure was sent here to kill you."

"I'm telling you, it was his idea," Brock said.

"Brock isn't lying."

Dad and Brock both turned to the doorway. Dexter was standing just outside the room.

"Dexter," Dad said. "Come on in."

Dexter stepped inside, but didn't come closer than the foot of Brock's bed.

"Thank you for keeping your word," Dexter said.

"What word?" Dad looked back and forth between them.

"We told Brock that we would take care of Meg and her collar problem, as long as Brock left our Porter body when we said to, and didn't attempt to rejoin us in any way until everything was resolved."

"I wondered why Brock was settling for the monitor instead of a front row seat," Dad said. "Why no sound?"

Dexter opened his mouth to speak, but paused for a moment. "There were things we might have needed to discuss that we didn't want you to hear. Even we need our privacy sometimes."

That was the first time Brock had heard any of the replicants say that. He thought they liked their connection. As exposed as he usually felt with them, he never conceived of them wanting privacy, too. Yet another way he'd been taking them for granted.

"I guess it wasn't as much of a risk for you, since you're all planning to kill yourselves anyway," Brock said.

Dexter's gaze snapped to Brock, casting a baleful glare at him.

"What?" Dad gasped.

"Busted." Brock just smiled.

"You're planning to do *what?*" Dad yelled.

Dexter actually flinched. Brock did, too. Dad *never* yelled.

"They were planning to kill off sets of replicants to see if reducing the load on me would help me survive tomorrow." Was his birthday really that soon? A shiver ran through Brock. He shook it off. "But now that plan is off the table."

"It never should have been on the table in the first place." Dad stalked over to Dexter. "Why didn't you ask me? Why didn't you talk to me about it?"

Dexter again started to speak, but then shut his mouth and looked away. Dad pulled him into a hug, squeezing tight enough that Brock's chest ached in sympathy. Dexter reached up and awkwardly patted Dad's back.

"We knew you'd say no," Dexter said. "And we didn't want to upset you."

"Upset me?" Dad sputtered. He leaned back, grabbing Dexter by his arms and giving him a shake.

Brock wanted to laugh, seeing the most terrifying Blade —the one that vampires and werewolves only mentioned in whispers—let a frail human push him around. But the look on Dad's face, the way his voice cracked as he spoke, chased away the thought.

"How do you think I would have felt after you were gone?" Dad said. "You're my sons."

"Eli—" Dexter said.

Dad cut him off. "You call me 'Dad,' dammit."

Yelling *and* swearing? Yeah, they'd pushed Dad way too far.

"I know you think you don't feel the way others do," Dad said. "The way *humans* do. But you're wrong. There's love in you. Love in all of you. For your brother. For your sister. And for me."

The look on Dexter's face made tears well up in Brock's eyes. Dexter's lips stayed parted, and his expression went slack. Not in the normal inscrutable way, but almost like he was awestruck. Brock wanted so desperately to peek into Dexter's mind, to see what he was feeling. But after everything he'd learned, everything they'd been through so recently, he wouldn't dare cross that line.

Dad hugged Dexter again, and this time, Dexter hugged him back. When they pulled apart, Dad looked over at Brock, and said, "I think I have an idea."

"What?" Brock asked.

Dad shook his head. "I need everyone in on this one. Dexter, check in with Porter and make sure Megan is resting comfortably in her room. Then I need him and Vaughn down here *now*."

"Meg has already recovered from all of her wounds," Dexter said. "Her healing abilities are even better than Marcus and Tessa's."

"Thank goodness for that," Dad said.

"Porter is asking her to wait for us in her room." Dexter smirked. "Vaughn is hooking her up with a 'romcom' marathon. She and Porter will be here in a few minutes."

"That'll give me time to call your brothers." Dad stretched out his arm, revealing a watch that looked just like Vaughn's.

"When did you get one of those?" Brock asked.

"It was a gift from Vaughn so I can monitor the stasis pods more closely," Dad said. "I can also use it to do this."

Several square sections of the seemingly blank wall next to Brock's bed flickered with light. Six of them. They resolved into screens with every single replicant on them.

"When did Vaughn install all of these?" Brock asked.

"They were already here," Dad said. "Vaughn was able to get them working again while you were 'resting.'" He used sarcastic air quotes to make sure Brock knew he was aware that most of those times, Brock had actually been either observing or borrowing a replicant.

"We hear there's a new plan," Brad said.

"There is." Dad glared at Brad through his screen. "And don't think you're off the hook for that lame-ass other one."

"Us?" Brad said. "Why are we the one in trouble?"

"Because you're always the one doing stupid shit," Dexter said.

Brock felt his jaw drop. He'd never heard Dexter say something like that before.

"Since when do you guys talk like this?" Brock asked.

"Since always," Brad said. "Just not when you're around."

"Show some respect." Zach and Carey wore matching glares on their identical faces.

"Please don't," Brock said. Everyone stilled to the point that Brock wondered if the monitors had frozen. "I meant it when I said I was sorry. I meant it when I said I was done borrowing you—except for that stunt Dexter pulled earlier."

"And making out with Meg using Porter's body?" Brad grinned while all but Lee seemed to try to glare at Brock through their monitors.

"We were… That was…" Brock shook his head. "I was trying to put her at ease so we could get her to the Boom Room."

Brad snickered.

"That's enough," Dad said, glaring at Brad's monitor.

"And he left as soon as we asked." Porter strode into

the room, Vaughn right behind him.

Vaughn stared at all the faces on the monitors. "Wow, it's really a party in here."

"It's a family meeting." Dad walked over to the bed and put his hand on Brock's shoulder. "I know the last few years have been hard. And the way you learned about all this… It was a shock. A trauma. I've tried to help as much as I could, but you had to come to it on your own."

"Come to what?" Brock asked.

"Understanding," Dad said. "Yourself. The others. You're finally seeing your brothers as I always have. As family."

Brock nodded, his throat too tight for words. It had taken him too long to get his head out of his ass. But reuniting with the family he'd known before his eighteenth birthday and finding Tessa… changed… He had to face it now. This was his family, strange as it was.

"This seems kind of personal," Vaughn said. "I can come back later."

"Didn't you hear Dad when you came in?" Brock said. "It's a family meeting. We need you here."

"I, uh…" her eyebrows hitched up. She cleared her throat, then said, "Thanks."

"Come here, Sis." Porter clapped his hand on Vaughn's shoulder, pulling her against his side in a hug as he cast a big smile at her.

"This is so awkward," Vaughn said. "Okay. What's

up?"

Dad walked closer to the monitors. "Brad had the brilliant idea that he and his brothers should kill themselves to reduce the load on Brock before his birthday."

"What?" Vaughn's eyebrows hiked up her forehead.

"It wasn't him." Mal spoke in a low, calm voice, as always.

Brock kept his gaze away from Mal and Colm's monitors. It was too close to looking in a mirror. Brock hadn't seen himself for so long, he could almost forget what he truly looked like—the scars that were put there by Roy.

"We came up with the plan," Colm said. "Start with the most recent pair, and reduce the load until Brock can function again."

"That's... noble, I guess," Vaughn said. "But super grim."

"If they'd come to me about it, I sure as hell would have said no." Dad glared at each monitor in turn, then at Dexter and Porter for good measure. "And we might have been able to come up with a better idea sooner."

"Which is?" Mal asked.

Dad smiled, but his gaze was fixed on Vaughn.

"Reduce the load," Dad said.

It took Vaughn about a second to mirror Dad's smile. "The stasis pods. We put them in now."

"We thought of that," Zach said. "Our link with Brock isn't something you've been able to quantify or explain. The only way to be sure—"

"Is to try," Dad said. "Your stasis pods are ready. We're all right here. The sooner we do this, the better it'll be for your brother. The better the chances that you'll all survive."

The monitors with Mal and Colm went dark.

"Oh shit," Vaughn said. "Like *now* now?"

"I guess they liked my idea." Dad turned to Brock. "Are you ready for this, son?"

"I have less than twenty-four hours till my birthday." Brock nodded. "It's now or never."

Dad nodded, already lowering the back of Brock's bed. As soon as Brock was flat, Dad started pulling off the electrodes that stimulated his muscles, probably not wanting anything to complicate things further.

Vaughn ran to the control panel next to Brock's bed and started frantically typing on it. "Sure, why not?" she said. "It's not like this wasn't already our last resort scenario. Let's just pull the trigger early." She looked up at Brock and said, "Bad metaphor."

"Let's hope." Brock smiled at Vaughn, trying to reassure her. To reassure both of them.

"Mal and Colm are in their stasis chambers," Vaughn said. She turned to look at the monitor above Brock's bed. "Wow, that was fast."

The screen now showed a split view of Malcolm's safehouse and Vaughn's ubiquitous scrolling data. Their panic room was mostly taken up with two huge shining silver cylinders with small glass windows on the front just above their faces.

"I've activated the sequence that should put them in stasis," Vaughn said. "I really hope this works. Systems nominal. Vital signs stable. Brain activity lowering. Metabolics slowing down…"

A wave of energy hit Brock like a nuclear bomb going off. His back arched up off the bed as he sucked in a huge breath. His skin felt electrified, and his limbs twitched uncontrollably.

He could hear someone yell, "Hold him down. Hold him down!" over a high ringing in his ears. The room faded in and out.

A voice said, "He's stabilizing. How are the others?"

"Uh… On the floor?"

"Vaughn! Check on them."

Vaughn. Dad. They were in the room with him. Along with Dexter and Porter.

"They're already getting up," Vaughn said. "And I'm kind of busy here handling Mal and Colm remotely. Everything seems to be working as we expected. Their biosignatures are in full stasis."

"Son?"

Brock's vision was blurred, and his ears felt like they

were stuffed with cotton. Gradually, everything came back into focus, starting with his dad's eyes.

"Are you still with us, son?"

The ringing noise stopped. The loudest thing he heard was his own breath. Brock lifted his right arm above him and made a fist. Muscles corded his forearm. Was that really his arm? It was huge. But even with the muscles, he didn't feel the heaviness that usually kept him pinned to the bed. He lowered his arm back to his side.

"Brock," Dad said. "How do you feel?"

Brock pushed himself up—pushed himself up so he was sitting, *with nobody's help*. His dad's jaw went slack, and his eyes widened so much, Brock could see the whites all around his irises.

"I feel…" Brock took a deep breath, rubbing his hand across a chest he didn't recognize.

It wasn't just that his body was twice the size he was used to after only moving around in his replicants' bodies for so long. His lungs felt expansive. His muscles receptive. He was functional.

He laughed, then said, "I feel *good*."

Chapter Fourteen

Meg paced in her room. She knew she was supposed to be resting, but how could she rest when she was finally free? She had so much to tell everyone, so much to explain.

So much to make up for.

While Porter had examined her and made sure the last of her injuries healed properly, she'd told them as much as she could. She didn't think she'd ever talked that much or that quickly. Vaughn had already figured out most of it. She'd understood Meg's message. Meg let out a shaky breath, still amazingly relieved and grateful her plan had worked.

Before she'd had a chance to properly apologize, there had been an emergency. Something must have gone very wrong for everyone to run off the way they had, leaving her alone.

She tried not to think about that. Her being alone in the large house. Marcus and Tessa in stasis. Dexter and Porter and Vaughn who knew where. Brock deep below the house with Eli.

"Brock." She slowed her steps, but her mind spun ever

faster, making up one nightmare scenario after another.

Maybe the collar had exploded after all. Maybe it had somehow compromised their systems. There could have been an emergency at another base.

Something could have gone wrong with Brock.

"Please, don't let it be him," she whispered.

If she was remembering right, he didn't have much time left. She could tell that it was night outside, even though her bedroom didn't have any windows. At least now, everyone could stop worrying about Roy and trying to integrate her with the pack. They could focus on helping Brock.

Someone was walking toward her room. She heard them even with the carpet muffling the sound, her senses hyper-aware. Two pairs of footsteps, but one heartbeat—or hearts that beat so in synch that she couldn't tell them apart. Dexter and Porter. They tapped at the door lightly.

"Megan?" one said. "Can we come in?"

"Of course," she responded.

Dexter opened the door and crossed into the room. Porter followed after him. She could tell them apart now, after being so close to Porter while Brock was borrowing him. After kissing him, too. She blushed at the memory.

She'd been kissing *Brock*. He'd just happened to be using Dexter or Porter's lips while they were doing it.

Both men were smiling now. Surely if something terrible had happened, they wouldn't be smiling.

Porter stared at the bed for a moment, still neatly made, then said, "We see you didn't get any sleep."

"I couldn't," Meg said. "Is everyone all right?"

"In a sense." Porter nodded toward the door. "Walk with us."

Meg balked. As much as she knew that she should trust them, that they'd risked their lives to help her, they still unnerved her. Why were they both together again?

"Meg," Dexter said. "Please."

She swallowed hard, and for once, there was no collar squeezing against her throat when she did. Because of *them*. She nodded and headed toward Dexter, following him as he walked down the hall. Porter fell in step beside her.

"Where is Vaughn?" Meg asked.

She had cut herself while trying to get Meg's collar off. While Porter had inspected the wound, Vaughn had been trying to say something about her blood and the collar, but Dexter had cut her off. Meg wasn't sure why.

"Vaughn is down in the ship with Eli," Porter said. "They're monitoring Malcolm and Bradley."

"Did something happen?" Meg asked.

Porter smirked. "You could say that."

Dexter let out a snort. Whatever the joke was, she wasn't in on it, but somehow, she didn't mind. Just witnessing this pair—this unique being—showing amusement in front of her felt like they were sharing something special with her. Letting their guard down.

"We want to hear more about this 'mindblindness' you mentioned earlier when you were debriefing us," Porter said. "Not just for the Dweller Database, but for our research."

Dexter glanced back at them over his shoulder. "Porter is obsessed with learning everything we can about dwellers."

"It's professional curiosity," Porter said.

Meg shook her head. "I'm confused. I thought you were the same person, but you're talking like there's two of you."

"When we occupy our individual forms, different aspects of our personality come to the forefront," Porter said. "It's quite fascinating."

"You even study yourselves, don't you?" Meg smiled at Porter, hoping that her teasing tone wouldn't upset him.

He actually laughed. "As a matter of fact, we do."

"Did Vaughn make the security updates you talked about?" Meg asked. "Roy was able to learn so much about you and the base from the collar and from Marcus and Tessa. Now that he's lost all of his access, he'll be furious. He won't be thinking straight and might come here."

She couldn't imagine Roy *not* coming to the ranch, even if he knew it was a suicide mission. He was too obsessed with killing Brock, with destroying the Blades with his own claws.

"It's under control," Dexter said.

"But we appreciate your concern," Porter added.

Dexter stopped ahead of them. He was standing to the side of a door just like the one that led to her room.

Meg paused next to him. "I don't understand. Am I moving?"

"No," Dexter said. "And neither are we."

Porter stood on the opposite side of the door, his hands clasped in front of him. "Understand that we'll do our best to preserve your privacy."

"But if we detect any threats, we will deal with them immediately... and permanently," Dexter said.

"We like you, Megan," Porter went on. "And our progenitor... Brock cares for you, deeply. Don't betray his trust."

"Or ours," Dexter added.

"I won't." She didn't understand what was going on, but she knew that she would never betray Brock. Not now that she had a choice. Not ever.

Back in the Boom Room, she'd been willing to die rather than hurt him or any of the Blades. She still was. They all felt like part of her pack.

Porter nodded toward the door. She wasn't sure what else to do, so she stepped forward. Dexter reached out and grabbed her elbow.

"And just in case we're misreading you," he said, "You should know that Brock was the very first Blade. He studied with us. He taught us, trained with us." Dexter leaned closer. "And he is every bit as deadly as we are."

Meg shrank back from him. As much as he'd said dying had changed him, she could still see a coldness in his eyes that sent a shiver through her.

Dexter smiled—a carefree expression that only made her unease worse—and let go of her arm, then stepped back to his position by the door. Both he and Porter stared ahead at the opposite wall, waiting.

Brock had told her that his body barely functioned. Why were Dexter and Porter warning her like this? Unless something had changed. Unless...

Unless Brock is on the other side of this door.

Her heart started to hammer in her chest. She took a deep breath as she gripped the doorknob, letting it out while opening the door. When she was inside, she closed it behind her. Dexter and Porter were no doubt listening with their enhanced senses, but she could at least pretend that she and Brock were alone together.

Together. We're going to really be together.

She stepped further into a room that was almost identical to hers. She walked toward the bed, but it was as untouched as her own. If Brock was here, where was he?

A deep voice came from across the room. "Vaughn, you never cease to amaze me."

She could see light spilling out from the open bathroom door, but not whoever was inside. He sounded similar to

Porter, but his voice was deeper and had a rasp to it.

"I've never been so glad that you keep clothes in all the bases that fit the whole range of our Blades. That guy Damien in Europa must have a neck like a tree trunk," the man said. "I can't believe it, but his clothes are actually a little tight."

The light switched off, leaving the bedroom lit only by a small lamp on her side of the bed. She heard footsteps approaching.

"It's weird to have all these muscles. Dad must be proud of you and Porter's work putting weight on me." The man walked out of the bathroom, his black T-shirt still above his head as he pulled it on. It was covering his face, but she could see most of his arms and his torso.

His biceps were huge, as was his massive chest. Rows of taut abs stacked themselves on his stomach. His waist was narrow, and led to muscular hips, hugged by black pants that let her know the rest of him was just as built. Big guys weren't usually her thing, but this one… Something about him made her skin tingle and her fingers ache.

Probably the scars.

He was *covered* with them. Claw marks, bites, patches of shining red burns. The skin of his abdomen looked like something had tried to dig a hole right through his body— and succeeded. There were more scars than she could count, and all of them looked absolutely lethal. This man had been through epic battles. She didn't know how anyone could have survived that kind of damage. Any pack would bow to him as alpha.

She made a choking noise. She couldn't help it. Heat blossomed deep in her belly, an explosion of arousal unlike anything she'd felt before. Guilt followed right on its heels. Where was Brock?

The man spun away from her, dragging the shirt down over his back, but not before she could see that it was just as decorated as his front.

"What are you doing here?" he demanded, his voice rough.

"Dexter and Porter brought me," she said.

"You're kidding." He let out a sigh. "Of course they did."

He ran his hand through short, spiky dark hair that was laced with patches of stark white. Then he quickly dropped his arm so that it was out of sight, blocked by his body. It was like he didn't want her seeing his skin.

But *she* wanted to see him. All of him.

She felt a pull stronger than anything she'd ever felt before. Stronger than her pull toward Brock—at least, when he'd been borrowing someone else's form. How strong would that attraction be when he was in his own body?

"They said…" They hadn't really said that Brock would be in the room, but they'd made her think so.

Even though he was huge, this man looked like he could be Brock. More than that, he *felt* like Brock. All of the other replicants she'd seen were about the same size and shape. She'd assumed Brock would match them. But he was the progenitor, as they kept saying. Maybe he was different.

"Brock?" She took a step toward him, but he turned away.

"Don't come any closer."

She hesitated, but only for a moment. Everyone here had been telling her to express herself—to *assert* herself. To be clear about what she wanted. And she'd never wanted anything as much as she wanted to be with Brock.

"I didn't want us to meet like this," he said. "I'm not ready."

"Ready…"

"For you to see."

"See what?" she asked.

"Me."

She caught a glimpse of his profile as he briefly glanced at her over his raised shoulder—the right side of his face. His eyes were as dark as Dexter and Porter's, but didn't seem to absorb the light the way theirs did.

"Brock, please. I've waited so long. I feel like I've been waiting for you forever."

"Me, too."

It's really him.

The heat building in her spread through her limbs, swept over her chest and face, made her ache to touch him and be touched. She dared to take a step closer.

"You've already shared so much of yourself with me," Meg said. "But I want more. I want to share everything about you."

It felt greedy and selfish, but it was true. He was pulling away from her, though. She had to find a way to reach him.

"If you're worried about your scars, don't be," she said. "Ever since I joined the pack, scars have become compelling. Beautiful. It's the same for all werewolves. They're the marks of what a person has endured—what they *can* endure for their survival. For their loved ones. They're a sign of strength, of your ability to lead."

"To lead?" Brock snorted. "I led the others to this. I've been so hell bent on proving that dwellers and humans can coexist, I never even thought about the cost to those around me. Because I didn't really think of them as people."

"Your replicants?"

"My brothers." He shook his head, pressing his fists against the wall. "I've been using them, justifying it by focusing on what was different about us. The way they think. They way they feel and react. The way they do whatever I want."

"Not always."

He laughed. "Yeah. They seem to be doing their own thing more and more often lately."

She took a few steps closer, but he turned away, keeping his back to her.

"Please don't," he said.

He was already cornered. She didn't want to push him farther away, so she stayed where she was, but kept trying to reach him with her words.

"Vaughn told me that she follows you because she believes in your vision," Meg said. "I do, too. All of your Blades must. Otherwise, they would just be hunters."

"Hunters." He fairly spat the word. After a pause, he said, "That's what started all this."

"I don't understand."

"My mom—the woman who raised me—she was a hunter. She was there when I was born. Eli had to convince her not to kill me, even though I seemed human. In her mind, 'the only good dweller is a dead dweller.' Jesus, if she could see her family now. Tessa a werewolf. And me…"

"You've all just done what you needed to survive."

"We could have survived other ways," he said. "Had normal lives."

"Then why didn't you?" Meg took another step closer, the soft carpet muffling her footsteps.

"I thought Mom and Tessa were alive. I split the first time when I was eighteen. We were on our way home, going to a surprise party that Tessa was cooking up for me. Probably had unicorns or ponies all over the decorations."

"Tessa and unicorns…" Meg let out a little laugh, hoping to ease some of the tension emanating from him. "That's not something I ever thought to put together."

"She was only twelve. And crazy about them." He shook his head. "We had a normal life. She had a chance to be normal. But then this happened." He looked down at his chest, the fabric of his T-shirt straining as his shoulders moved. "*I* happened. And I ripped it all away from us."

"It wasn't your fault," she said.

"Wasn't it?"

"You can't help how you were born. You didn't ask for this."

"None of us did. And yet, I'm at the center of it all. All the pain and hurt."

"Brock." Meg shook her head sharply and stepped closer. Close enough to touch him.

His shoulders were hunched up, almost touching his ears. He didn't turn toward her, but he didn't try to get farther away, either.

"Dad took me and ran, knowing Mom would kill me and DP," Brock said. "I kept thinking if we could show her that we could do good, that we could help people, that she'd be able to accept us. We could be a family again. That's why I started the Blades."

"What happened?"

"My biological father happened," Brock said. "He found them. He killed Mom and... He took Tessa. She was only sixteen and being raised by that *thing*. He called her his daughter, then tried to turn her into his mate. She won't tell us everything that happened while she was with the Hive Father, but what little I know is a worse nightmare than anything we've faced."

Brock shook his head. "And in the end, none of it really mattered. Mom wouldn't care about any of the work we've done. If she had the chance, she'd kill us all."

"You can't know that."

"I can," he said. "When she looked at me, she never saw a son. Only a monster. And now... Now, that's all I see, too."

"Brock..." Meg reached out with shaking hands that she rested on his shoulders.

He took a deep breath, then blew it out forcefully. Slowly, he turned toward her. She let her hands fall away.

As his shoulders dropped, she saw that the skin on the right side of his neck was covered in a mix of smooth red patches and raised clusters of white scar tissue that trailed up from beneath his shirt. It took her a moment to sort out that there were both burn scars and teeth marks. She wasn't sure which had happened first.

It looked like something had sunk its fangs into him and then torn out his throat. The burns ran up along his jaw, drawing her gaze to the four ragged claw marks that ran from his left temple down to his chin, streaking across the entire left side of his face.

They hadn't healed smooth or even turned back to a more normal color. Deep channels of dark red made the furrows stand out in contrast to his otherwise pale skin. One of the claw marks crossed over his left eye, which was completely white. Even the pupil was eerily clouded.

"Oh my God." The words rushed from her before she could stop them. "How did you survive?"

"It wasn't me. It was them." He paused, and when he spoke again, the rasp to his voice was more pronounced. "And they didn't."

"These are all scars from the others dying?" she said.

"Yeah." He ran his fingers along the thin line of white that circled his neck—his latest scar. "I never thought I'd have a death mark from Vaughn."

The silence between them stretched on for what felt like a long time. Meg didn't want to push him, so she waited for him to speak.

"Fire salamanders are like alpacas." Brock rubbed the burn scars on the right side of his neck. "One minute, they seem docile and harmless, and the next they're spitting napalm on you." He pointed to the ugly bite marks on both sides of his neck. "Then you've got your whacked out vampires, manticores, and…"

His fingertips barely touched the edge of the rows of scars on his face. He dropped his hand to his side and turned away, hiding the jagged wounds.

Her stomach clenched and roiled, like she was about to throw up. Some of the wounds she'd seen on his stomach before he'd turned away had similar claw marks around the edges. Including the massive scar low on his abdomen. It wasn't the scars that had her reeling, but knowing where they had come from.

"Roy did this to you," she said.

"Roy did this to Mal. And Lee and Zach. And yeah, to me, too." Brock shook his head, then said, "I've never had a name for them before now. The people—the things—that killed us." He stepped away from her, pacing in the space between her and the bed.

"It may have been their bodies that were destroyed, but I felt every death with them. Every moment of pain, of fear, of darkness." He turned toward her as he spoke, his lips curled up in a near-snarl that let her know to keep her distance, even though she wanted more than anything to reach out to him. "I've slipped into the void and back more times than I want to remember."

"I can't even imagine," she said. "And splitting afterwards."

He stopped pacing, letting out a breath that seemed to empty him. His voice was gentler when he spoke again.

"I don't feel it when they split afterwards," he said. "At least I'm spared that. Except once every three years."

"You'll split like that tomorrow?"

"It's a little different for me," he said. "But close enough."

She wanted to ask how it was different, how she could help. Before she could figure out what words to use he went on.

"I've always been there with the others when they die," he said. "And been there for them when they split. No matter how bad things were between us, I'd always tell them it'd be okay. That it would be over soon, and we'd all be there for them afterwards. The fact that DP had to go through that alone—his first split... I wasn't even conscious for his death."

"Brock..."

"I can never repay you for helping them," he said.

"You already have." She took a step closer, but he flinched and backed away. She pushed down the pain of that and tried to cover it with words. "Because of you—because of them—I'm free. I never thought I'd be able to get away from Roy or his twisted vision of my pack. I thought I'd die with that collar on... and take you with me."

"You don't have to worry about any of that anymore," Brock said. "And after tomorrow night, you won't have to worry about me, either."

"But you're better."

How *was* he better? She'd been so grateful, so surprised, to see him well. She hadn't thought to ask what had changed.

"It's only temporary," Brock said. "Malcolm and Bradley went into stasis to see if taking that load off my mind would help me regain some of my strength. But even if Zachary goes into stasis as well, there's a good chance the shock of splitting again will either kill me or put me in a coma. Permanently, this time. Every test still says I'm human, and human bodies, human minds, weren't meant to handle all of this."

Her eyes pricked, her skin itched. Her fingertips tingled.

"How long?" she asked.

"Jonathan arrives tomorrow at seven-thirty-five, sharp."

"Jonathan?"

Brock let out a small laugh that held an impossible amount of sadness. "'Jon' and 'Nathan.' I thought I should come up with a name, just in case they survive."

"Seven-thirty-five tomorrow night?" She prayed he hadn't meant the morning. They already had so little time.

"Yeah."

"That's not far away," she said. "We shouldn't waste another moment."

Chapter Fifteen

Brock didn't have anywhere to go when Meg reached for him. His back was already almost brushing the wall. He grabbed her arms as she tried to slide them around his shoulders.

"You can stay here no matter what," he said. "You're free now. This is your home."

"Thanks to you." She leaned closer to him, rising up on her tiptoes so that their lips were close enough for him to feel the warmth of her breath.

His throat felt thick. Other parts of him were following suit. The cargo pants had felt a little tight before. Now they were downright chafing.

"You don't have to do this," he said.

"I know." She pressed against his grip, forcing his arms down to his sides. For all her talk of not being like other werewolves, she definitely had their strength. "I want to. I want *you*."

He released his hold on her and she stepped even closer, her breasts brushing against his chest. She held his gaze as she started to lift his shirt.

"Meg."

"You've all been telling me to figure out what I want for myself. To be okay seeking it out."

"Yes."

The corner of her lips pulled up in a tiny smile. "Right now, I want you to lift your arms."

He let out a laugh, then complied. Part of him wanted to close his eyes, to not see the look on her face when she saw his chest. But he had to watch. He had to see her reaction.

She pulled his shirt up and over his head, then tossed it on the floor. Her eyes widened, the golden glow brightening enough to make his own sting. Her hand shook as she reached toward him and gently traced an old set of claw marks on his left pectoral muscle. Lots of different dweller types liked to dig out people's hearts.

"You're beautiful." She lowered her hand, the backs of her fingers dusting against the scars that covered his abdomen.

Her touch was feather-light, but sent a jolt through him that made gooseflesh rise along his arms. His dick responded as well, pulsing in time with his heartbeat.

If he went off in his pants, he'd never forgive himself. But he hadn't been touched like this... ever.

"Meg, there's something else you need to know," he said.

She laughed. "After all that? What more could there be?"

"This is a little more mundane, I guess," he said.

She unbuttoned his pants, then slowly drew down the zipper. "I can't imagine anything about you being mundane."

The pulsing in his dick turned to a deep, pounding throb. She hadn't even touched him, and he was already set to fire. What would happen when her hands wrapped around his shaft? Or he pressed himself to her heat? Thinking about that only made the throbbing worse. He had to distract himself.

"I need to slow down." He gripped her arms lightly, brushing his thumbs over her smooth skin.

"But we don't have much time."

"I know, but…" He let out a deep sigh. "I haven't done this before."

"Done what?"

He stared at her, one eyebrow arched. After a few moments, her eyes widened and her mouth dropped open.

"Oh," she said. "Oh, wow."

He tried to lighten the mood, but failed miserably. "It's not like anyone's been beating down the door to be with me."

Unless they're trying to kill me, anyway.

He kept that thought to himself.

She let out a light laugh. "We travel in very different circles. *Every* werewolf would want to mate with you."

"I don't travel at all," he said. "I've been bedridden for

the better part of three years."

"And yet you look like this?" She gestured to his chest and arms.

"That's all Vaughn, Porter, and Dad. They had me hooked up to some sort of electrodes that stimulated my muscles, as well as IVs and a special diet to make me put on weight."

"Why?" Meg asked.

"Because I'll lose half of it when I split."

"I don't understand. Dexter and Porter didn't... shrink. Why would you?"

"We don't know," Brock said. "Just like we don't know why my blood doesn't vaporize when it's removed from my body and theirs does. Or why every test they've run shows me as one-hundred percent human, when I'm most certainly not." Brock actually chuckled. "Ask Vaughn to tell you her theories about quantum cellular... something. Especially if you need help falling asleep."

Meg laughed, a broad smile brightening her face. She lifted her hand to Brock's intact cheek.

"Are you sure you want to do this with me?" she asked. "I mean, there are other women who would—"

"I don't want anyone else." He pulled her against his chest and leaned closer. "I want you. Only you."

She wrapped her arms around his waist as he kissed her, rising up on her toes to respond in kind. She was so warm and real. He couldn't believe he was holding her with *his* body, feeling her with his own senses.

He wanted more.

He slid his tongue along her lips, never pausing as she opened herself to him. He let out a groan as he thrust into her mouth, imagining how it would feel to delve into her in other ways. Her fingers curled against his back, exploring him as much as he was exploring her. He pressed his hips against hers, and even through their clothes, he could feel her heat.

The bed was only a few steps away. He backed her toward it, but when they reached it, she turned so that he was the one at its edge. He broke off their kiss, panting as he grabbed her shirt and pulled it off. All of that dark, shining hair was loose around her shoulders. He never wanted her to wear it up again. He buried his fingers in it, pulling her face back to his for another searing kiss.

He kissed a line along the silken skin of her neck, then hooked his thumbs under her sports bra and drew it up and over her head, tossing it away. He wanted to touch her, to taste her, to feel her breasts crushed against his chest, to take them in his mouth.

His dick sent him a steady stream of encouragement, each thought making the pressure build. He grabbed a handful of her hair and pulled her head to the side, raking his teeth gently over her neck. She let out a moan that sent a pulse through him, threatening to send him over the edge.

"Meg…"

He murmured her name against her neck before sliding down to sit before her, trailing kisses along her collarbone and over her breast. He sucked her nipple into his mouth, running his tongue over it in quick circles that made her gasp. She buried her fingers in his hair, pressing his head to her harder. He cupped her other breast in his left hand while he reached behind and squeezed her ass with his right.

She brought her knees up onto the bed on either side of him, straddling him. The friction of her hips clamped around his, his dick pressing against her core, sent pulsing waves of pleasure through his body.

"This isn't… slowing down," she gasped.

He released her breast just long enough to say, "I know," then shifted to the other side. Between kisses and sucking on her, he said, "I want you so bad. But I want to last for you."

Her voice was breathless as she said, "It doesn't matter. Once won't be enough anyway."

She tightened her grip on his hair and pulled him away from her chest, then shoved him back on the bed. She ran her nails along his chest as she slid down his body. When she reached the waistband of his boxer-briefs, she pulled them off, along with his pants. He hadn't put on shoes or socks after his shower, so she had him naked in seconds. She paused for a moment, her eyes glowing ever brighter as she stared at his legs and his dick. Her gazed flicked to his as she licked her lips.

"Meg…" Brock lifted himself on his elbows just as she dropped to her knees. "I won't last a second if you—"

His words turned into a grunt as she leaned forward and ran her tongue along his shaft. The pulsing intensified, arcs of pleasure rocketing through his body. She didn't give him a chance to catch his breath. As soon as she reached the tip of his dick, she wrapped her mouth around his crown, tightening her lips and swirling her tongue around it.

"Shit!" The first throb hit him deep in his belly.

She moved in time with it, mouth sliding down over his shaft, lips tight. She gripped him in her hand and started pumping him, all while she sucked on him, hard, pulling on the pulse that reverberated in his bones, a pleasure that vibrated deep as a split.

His eyes clenched shut and his head flew back against the mattress. His hips bucked up against her, but she kept taking him in, swallowing everything he had to give. Her tongue swirled around him, her lips pressed tight. Her hand kept moving even when he finally started to come down, his body sinking into the mattress. The room seemed to be spinning when he opened his eyes. He could barely catch his breath.

Meg climbed onto the bed next to him. Naked. He hadn't noticed her stripping, after the mind-bending ride she'd taken him on.

"I said I wanted to last," he panted.

She trailed her fingernails along the inside of his thigh, sending waves of gooseflesh down his legs and over his torso. "And now, you will," she said.

As his body calmed, his resolve grew. He would spend every moment he had left with her, giving her the same pleasure she gave him, making her feel as welcome and loved as he could.

Damn, he thought. *If only we had more time. This could have been love.*

It might already be.

"Slide up for me." He was still close enough to the edge of the bed that his feet were on the floor.

Meg shimmied up till her head rested on the pillows. Brock rolled to his side, gripping her legs and spreading them apart. Her dark curls glistened. He could feel his dick already start to stir again as he imagined sliding into her and feeling her stretch around him.

He pressed a kiss against the side of her knee, then up along the inside of her thigh. He listened for cues to what she liked, hitches in her breath, little moans of pleasure. Raking his teeth over her soft skin had her writhing beneath him.

He pinned her legs to the bed as he reached his goal, stroking her in a long lick. Her back arched off the bed when he reached her clit, sucking the tight flesh and pinching it between his lips. When her breath came in little gasps, he released her, but only to delve into her with his tongue.

"Brock," she moaned.

His dick had hardened again. He pressed himself against the mattress, desperate to plunge into her, but wanting to give her this pleasure first. He returned to her clit, flicking his tongue over it, quickening his pace. She was so wet, heat radiating from her that he could lose himself in.

He pressed a finger to her core and she took him in easily. He added another, and a third, thrusting inside of her as he increased the pressure with his mouth. For a moment, her back arched, her breath held, and she was still. Then her hips thrust against him, her sheath pulsing around his fingers as she screamed his name.

She was so strong he had to rise to his knees, pinning her legs to the bed as he kept his hand moving within her. He pressed his thumb to her clit, not willing to let up on the pleasure he was giving her.

Finally, she stilled. She looked up at him with eyes gleaming gold and said, "More."

Brock lowered himself on top of her, reaching between them to line himself up with her core. Her flesh was unbelievably soft and slick as he pressed himself into her. Her sheath was still pulsing from her orgasm, so tight around him as his dick stretched her. He drove into her, burying himself as deep in her heat as he could. He hadn't known anything could feel so good.

"Meg…" He moaned her name against the soft flesh of her neck.

Slowly, he pulled back, savoring every inch of friction, every shock of pleasure that pulsed through him from the movement. When he was almost all the way out, he drove himself back in, hard. He felt a throbbing build deep within him again, but wasn't ready for this to be over.

Tingling streaks of energy spread along his nerves, lighting them up. His skin hummed, his muscles sang. Every part of him felt alive in a way beyond anything he'd ever experienced.

He moved his hips faster, sliding in and out, landing harder each time. Meg rose to meet each thrust, rocking her hips against his. She ran her nails along his back, tracing his scars, gasping as the force of his thrusts increased. She wrapped her legs around his thighs, digging her fingers into his ass as her eyes rolled shut.

Pressure was building deep inside of him. He wanted this to last forever, but he could already feel the energy starting to cascade.

She tensed for a brief moment, then her core started pulsing again, each throb pulling against him, coaxing everything from him that he had to give. He pounded into her, losing all sense of time and place as the pressure released in a blast of ecstasy centered on where they were joined.

Like a thousand fuses lit at once, a wave of pleasure swept along his limbs, through his body, his mind, every part of him. He felt himself spilling into her as her orgasm kept going on, drawing him further and further into his own bliss. He threw his head back and let out a hoarse scream as the force of it hit him, burying himself as deeply as he could in her heat, pinning her to the bed with his body.

Sweat dripped from his chest onto hers. Her eyes were still shut, but he could see golden light along the seam of her eyelids. She let out a contented sigh, running her legs along his as she stretched them straight, her hands still stroking his back.

"Meg."

Sluggishly, she opened her eyes, blinking up at him with a soft smile. He knew what he wanted to say, but couldn't get the words out. It had more to do with their impossible timing than the way his lungs heaved, pulling in breath after breath. From the look in her eyes, he wondered if she understood, though. Maybe even felt the same longing.

He brushed her dark hair away from her face, cradling her cheeks in his hands, then leaned down to kiss her— gently, but thoroughly. When he pulled back, he left their foreheads touching.

"I'm glad we found each other," he said.

She smiled up at him. "Me, too."

Chapter Sixteen

The sun had risen. Meg could sense it beyond the walls of Brock's bedroom. She knew they'd slept for a little while, after talking and making love all night. She wasn't sure how much time had passed, though.

Or how much they had left.

Someone knocked. She slipped from the bed and grabbed Brock's T-shirt, pulling it over her head as she walked to the door.

"Coming." She spoke loud enough that Brock should be able to hear her from the bathroom.

Dexter stood in the hallway, holding a tray with two covered plates and a large bottle of water. He avoided her gaze, and his cheeks looked a little pink.

Still giddy from everything that had happened, she actually dared to say, "Dexter, are you blushing?"

He glared at her briefly before pushing past her into the room. "We can't help our biological response to…" He shook his head.

"Wait, Brock said you guys were giving us our privacy."

"As much as we can. We're finding it difficult to block

out everything during certain... extreme moments."

"Oh." She was sure her face had turned redder than Dexter's. "You could have mentioned something."

"Don't worry about it. We didn't want to disturb either of you." Dexter set the tray down on the table nearest the door. "We also want to be sure Brock is at full strength for tonight."

"Is that code for 'let him sleep?'" She made a half-hearted attempt at a laugh, but Dexter didn't join in.

"That's our way of saying take a break long enough to eat and drink something. We wouldn't take this away from him."

Dexter stepped closer, way into her comfort zone. She stepped back reflexively. He actually winced as she did.

"I'm sorry," she said. "I didn't mean to—"

This time, he did laugh. "Hurt our feelings? Don't worry about it. We deserve that and worse for how we treated you when you arrived."

"You were worried about Brock," she said. "And you were right. When I arrived... I was a threat to him. To you. But I hope we can move past it."

Dexter snorted. "Great. We can be besties for..." He looked at his watch, and his smirk faded.

"How long?"

"Just under five hours."

Meg's vision blurred, gold light refracting in the tears filling her eyes as a wave of despair hit her. "We should get Brock into the stasis chamber. Isn't that the plan?"

"Soon. You should know that we're not sure how it will affect him. Or us. Vaughn and Eli are running some final tests."

Meg glanced past him into the hallway. "And Porter?"

"Is with them."

"It means a lot to me that you trust me so much," Meg said.

"We're down to the wire, here. The last hours of the Blades of Janus as we know it."

A new instinct rose in her, one that called her to reach out to him. She stepped closer this time, gently resting her hand on his arm.

"You're going to figure this out," she said. "Brock will be okay. All of you will."

"We appreciate the thought, but no one knows that for sure. Even if Brock survives, even if we aren't incapacitated from him going into stasis…" Dexter shook his head. "You told us you were sent to find 'the head of the hydra.' Brock isn't our head, much as he likes to think so. He's our heart. Without him to help guide us, to help us be human—"

She reached up and laid her hand against Dexter's cheek. His eyes widened and he sucked in a breath.

"It's okay to *not* be human," she said. "We don't need to be human to be good people. That's a choice we all get to make."

He smiled at her softly, gripping her wrist much like Brock had done when he'd been borrowing Dexter when they'd first met.

"Am I interrupting something?" Brock stood in the doorway to the bathroom, glaring at them.

She tried to move away, but Dexter held on to her hand. He squeezed it tight before letting go and turning toward Brock.

"As you're so fond of telling us, don't be a dick," Dexter said. "We and Meg were sharing a poignant moment. We're family, now, after all."

Dexter looked back at her, and something in his expression made her wonder about that. There was warmth in his gaze, but it didn't seem familial. Dexter shook his head briefly, as if he was trying to clear it, then walked to the door.

"We'll be outside if you need us," he said. "Eat something."

He closed the door with a soft 'click.'

Brock stayed where he was. "That was new."

"He didn't mean anything by it." Meg grabbed the tray and carried it to the bed, wanting to change the subject. There was one piece of information she had to share first, though.

No more secrets.

"Dexter said he and the others are having some trouble blocking you," she said. "That's probably all you're seeing."

"They didn't mention anything to me."

"He said they didn't want to disturb us, which I'm grateful for." She crawled onto the bed, awkwardly reaching the middle of it before setting down the tray. "He was blushing when he came in."

As she'd hoped, Brock laughed.

"Dexter blushing?" He shook his head. "Damn, I wish I'd seen that."

"Well, come eat something with me, and then we can see if we can make enough mental noise to bother the neighbors again."

"How can I resist an offer like that?" Brock finally smiled, then strode toward her.

He was wearing a pair of black pajama bottoms that hugged his hips and showcased the lines of his abdomen that flowed down past his waistband. Everywhere she looked on him, all she saw was muscle, sinew, and all that history carved into his flesh.

"Meg," he said. "Your eyes are glowing."

She stopped herself from apologizing and said, "Oh," instead.

"If you keep looking at me like that, I'm going to want to wait a while to eat."

She smiled, curling up next to the trays. "Then I'll stare at the food. I'm sure Vaughn has made us something special."

It might be Brock's last meal.

Pushing aside the thought, she opened the trays.

The smell hit her first. Blood. Fresh meat, piled high on a plate. She gasped and jerked back.

"What's wrong?" Brock asked.

"I'm not supposed to." She shook her head hard.

"Not supposed to what? Eat meat?" He laughed. "You're a werewolf."

"I know, but I was never allowed—"

He let out a frustrated sigh. "Those bastards. I knew they were starving you."

"Omegas aren't supposed to eat meat," she said. "Not like this."

"How many things did Roy tell you that you now know were lies?"

Her shoulders slumped. "Everything?"

Brock picked up a fork and handed it to her, then stretched next to the tray. Her gaze swept over him again, the rise and fall of his broad back, his long legs reaching past the edge of the bed. He watched her ogling him, then let out a sigh.

"Meg," he said. "Eat."

She took a deep breath, then stabbed one of the thin slices of meat and brought it to her lips. It smelled so good. Her mouth was watering. Still, she couldn't quite bring herself to eat it.

"What if it changes me?" she said, holding the fork

farther away. "What if it triggers something?"

"Like you putting on a few pounds?" He shrugged. "Sounds good to me."

"Brock..."

He reached out and ran his hand along her arm. "You're the most beautiful woman I've ever seen."

She felt her eyes widen at the compliment. No one had ever said anything like that to her before.

"But it's pretty damn obvious your body is not getting the nourishment it needs," he said. "And if you're worried your first bite of steak is going to make you go crazy, well..." He picked up a fork and pointed it at her. "I'm prepared to defend myself."

She laughed, shaking her head. "How is it you can make me laugh even when I'm terrified?"

Brock sat up, dropping his fork back on the tray, then took her free hand in his. "You don't have to be scared anymore. I know you'd never hurt me."

"Never."

He laughed again, but it was a darker sound than before. "You know, the stasis chamber's not a sure thing. Maybe I should let you bite me. Then we could be werewolves together."

"Brock, don't—"

"I'm sorry." He shook his head. "I keep bringing up things we shouldn't be thinking about right now. Please. Eat."

Her eyes filled with tears again, but she blinked them away. They had less than five hours left. The least she could do was honor this simple request.

She took a bite, chewing quickly. The taste had barely hit her before she swallowed.

"Oh my God," she said. She stabbed another bite and shoved it into her mouth.

Her nerve endings came alive, gooseflesh spreading over her arms and back. Her stomach cramped painfully, making a loud growling sound. She gripped her abdomen with her free hand and managed, "Sorry," around another mouthful. She couldn't eat fast enough.

Brock laughed and leaned back, hands in the air. "No worries. Except maybe that you'll still be hungry after you finish that huge plate. You're welcome to mine."

She glanced at his plate, laden with eggs, biscuits, gravy, and vegetables. A day ago, it would have been a delicious feast to her. Now, it smelled like ashes.

"No thanks," she mumbled, finishing the last of the meat.

He smiled, closing his eyes for a moment. When he opened them, he said, "Dexter's bringing you more."

"You could have just called out to him, you know," she said.

"Where's the fun in that? This way, I can give him a hard time about blushing earlier."

"You really are an obnoxious older brother, aren't

you?"

Brock laughed, then shook his head. "I guess I am. How do you feel?"

She paused, letting the feelings of well-being soak in. Her stomach didn't hurt. Her muscles didn't ache. She felt energized, powerful. She hadn't even been aware of how awful she'd felt before having this to compare it to.

No wonder Roy had forbidden her from eating meat like the others did. If this was how she could have been feeling all along, she might not have put up with the crap they kept giving her.

"Meg?" Brock reached over to her, running his hand along her arm.

Her skin prickled, all the hairs standing on end. Her muscles rippled, sending a shiver through her.

"Are you all right?" He sat up, obviously concerned.

"I'm fine. Better than ever, actually." She laughed, but it didn't seem to reassure him.

Dexter knocked on the door again. At least, she guessed it was him.

"I'll get it." She jumped up from the bed... and landed in front of the door. "Whoa."

The door opened just as Brock reached her side. Dexter stood in front of them, holding another plate heaped with sliced meat.

"Everything okay in here?" he said.

"Fine." Meg grabbed the plate and started picking up

pieces and dropping them into her mouth.

"Brock?" Dexter said.

"I think we can tell Vaughn we found her favorite food." Brock's voice didn't match the levity of his words.

They were both silent as she finished the plate, but they exchanged looks that let her know they were communicating. It didn't bother her in the slightest, even knowing that they were probably talking—thinking— about her. She used the time to think about them, too. To really look at them and see both how different and alike they were.

Same height, but radically different builds. Dexter looked younger, somehow. It was more than just that he lacked the scars. His body didn't show the wear and tear that Brock had been through. All of the replicants' deaths had taken their toll on him.

She couldn't even say they had the same eyes. Brock's glittered in the lamplight. Dexter's were a flat black, as if they sucked in the light. Neither of them said anything as she stared at them. Dexter glanced at Brock suddenly, and Brock shook his head.

"I know you've been talking this whole time," Meg said.

Dexter glanced at Brock then looked back to her. "We were just comparing notes."

"What kind of notes?" She handed the plate back to him.

Dexter only smirked. "Go wash your hands."

"Excuse me?" she said.

"It's Vaughn's rule." Dexter crossed to the bed and picked up her other empty plate. "As she says, 'Not everyone at the ranch is gifted with a dweller's immune system.'"

"Come on." Brock put his hands on her shoulders and turned her around, nudging her toward the bathroom.

"And make sure Brock eats, too." Dexter closed the door, leaving them alone again.

"What is going on?" Meg asked.

"Just humor me," Brock said.

"I know you guys were talking about me." She let him steer her to the other room.

"It was all good."

She arched an eyebrow, her instincts telling her that he was keeping something from her.

"Really?" she said.

"Okay, almost all." Brock shrugged. "Dexter has a few concerns."

When they were in front of the sink, Brock turned on the water. She went ahead and washed her hands, flicking the excess water away as he grabbed a towel. She took it and dried her hands.

"What kind of concerns?" she said.

"Mostly about that." Brock pointed at the mirror.

Meg glanced over at it and gasped. "Oh my God."

She lifted her arm, just to make sure that the reflection she was looking at was her own. The bones that had stuck out from her limbs on the few occasions when she had a chance to see herself in a mirror were hidden beneath layers of muscle. Her cheeks weren't hollowed out anymore and the dark circles under her eyes were gone.

"This has to be a trick," she said.

Brock shook his head. "I checked in with Dad and Vaughn through Porter and everyone agreed. It's your dweller physiology finally getting what it needed."

She leaned forward to see herself more closely, not that she needed to with how clear everything appeared to her eyes. Even her senses seemed stronger.

"What is Dexter worried about?" she said.

"There may be a reason omegas aren't allowed to eat meat. Dexter and the others are a bit concerned that the changes go deeper than your appearance. Like how you leapt across the room earlier." Brock moved behind her and wrapped his arms around her. "Don't think I didn't notice the surprise on your face. Personally, I think your pack starved you just because they were all assholes."

"Me, too," she said. "But Dexter's right. When the pack turned me, it made me stronger. But this feels different. What if I can't control it?" Her stomach flooded with icy panic. "What if Roy can link with me now?"

"We'll handle it." Brock nuzzled her ear.

"I don't want to put you in danger. Or anyone here."

"We're Blades," he said. "We're always in danger. And the thought of losing you is worse than anything Roy can throw at me."

"Brock..."

"I mean it."

He pressed a kiss against her neck, then slowly looked up at their reflection. He winced before his gaze locked on to her.

"I told you, you're the most beautiful woman I've ever seen," he said. "You sure you want to be stuck with a guy... A guy who looks like me?"

She reached up and ran her fingertips along his forehead and cheek, tracing the lines Roy had etched there.

"Not stuck," she said. "I get to choose now, remember? And I choose you."

Chapter Seventeen

Why had fate brought Meg to Brock now? Whether he was stuck in a stasis pod or dead, the result would be the same for him. And for Meg. They only had four hours left. Less, depending on when the others called him down.

"I can't believe how much better I feel." Meg laughed, taking him by the hand and leading him back toward the bed.

"I can't believe your pack never fed you what you needed to thrive."

Her smile fell and she looked away. "There were a couple of times that they offered, but I refused. They said that was part of what made me a perfect omega."

"I don't understand."

"The meat they offered..." She shivered, hugging herself tight.

Oh shit.

After all the years Marcus had been a Blade, and now watching Tessa, Brock had forgotten what most werewolves were like. What they ate.

"I've been out of the field too long," he said. "I'm sorry to bring up bad memories."

"It's in the past now. Once we find Roy, it'll be over for good. Right?"

"Yeah," Brock said. "I only wish I could be there to see it."

"You might."

"I've always been honest with you, Meg. I'm not going to start lying now."

She reached out to him, sliding her arms around his waist and pressing her cheek against his chest. He wrapped his arms around her and held her tight. His chest felt over-full. There was a rightness to them being together that he couldn't explain.

"It seems so unfair to have met you now," he said. "I mean, I'm grateful. And I think it'll work out for the best for everyone in the long run. I guess I'm being selfish. I want more time with you."

"If that's selfish, then I'm in the club."

"I don't want you to be sad after I go," he said.

"You're not going anywhere."

"Okay, I don't want you to sit outside my stasis chamber, waiting for me to wake up. Dad and the others have no idea what they're going to do or what will happen afterwards. I know they'll keep working on a solution, but they may never find one."

She leaned back, her eyes glittering as she looked up at him. "Brock—"

"I don't want you to waste your life waiting for me."

"I will wait for you forever."

"That's what I'm afraid of," he said. "I want you to be happy, Meg. Tessa said it's normal for werewolves to bond quickly. If what you're feeling for me is half as strong as what I feel for you..."

She reached up to cradle his face in her hands, then pulled him down for a kiss. He pressed her against him, relearning her body as he explored the new curves, wishing he'd be around to see her fully healed and integrated with her pack.

Her eyes were still closed when he broke off the kiss, staring down at her dark lashes, memorizing her face just in case he was able to dream in stasis.

"I love you." He whispered the words without thinking.

His breath caught, stuck in his chest as he wondered how she would respond.

Her lips curved into a soft smile. "I love you..." Her eyes opened, glowing gold. "Too."

A furrow appeared between her brows. She leaned back, and said, "Too," again.

"What?"

"Two. Brock, you have two irises."

"Most people do."

"In each eye."

Two irises? That was impossible. That only happened right before—

The first wave of pain crashed into him. It would have

dropped him to the floor if Meg hadn't been right there to catch him. He heard a loud crash in the hall, followed by a scream from his own lips at a sharp, unexpected agony in the center of his chest. He felt something pierce him, all the way through to his back.

"Dexter, help!" Meg yelled.

Brock clutched at his chest, reaching out for his brothers. All he found was darkness.

He looked down, trying to fight through the double-vision of trying to process input from the new pair of eyes forming inside his own. Blue light escaped between his fingers. When he took his hand away, a new scar glowed right above his heart.

"Someone died," he said. "Oh shit, someone died!"

"What? Who?"

"I don't know. The replicant goes offline when they—" His muscles cramped, making him arc his back as he cried out again.

Meg helped him to the floor. "What do I do?"

"Check Dexter."

Brock curled up on his side, his body shaking as he tried to breathe through the pain. Meg ran to the door. He heard her gasp, then run out into the hallway. In a few moments, she was back at his side.

"I can hear his heartbeat, but it's faint," she said. "I think he hit his head when he fell. And his eyes…"

"Are open. They look dead." Brock grunted, his guts

twisting. "One of them *is*."

"But he'll split, right? The replicant who died?"

"Don't know."

A loud cracking cut him off, his bones popping as they expanded. He tried not to scream, but failed.

"Vaughn! Eli!" Meg yelled.

He felt her pull his pajama pants off, and for a brief moment, was almost grateful she'd been through a split with DP. But he couldn't wish this on anyone. Not splits and sure as hell not an emergence.

"Stomach," he said.

"Oh God…" Meg stared at his abdomen, her eyes wide with terror. He could only imagine what she was seeing.

"Over. On stomach. Help." Each word cost him, using energy he needed to save.

She grabbed his shoulders and waist and rolled him over. Her werewolf strength was really coming in handy. Drawing on what strength of his own he had left, he pulled himself up to all fours.

Meg supported him as best she could, one arm around his shoulders and another gripping his hip. He didn't know how she was holding on to him with all the writhing and rippling he could feel under his skin.

Pressure and pain. Everywhere. His body was too full, muscles slipping over each other, bones sliding and cracking, pulling apart.

It wouldn't be long now. He felt like he was going to

explode. Maybe this time he would. He would almost welcome it. Anything to stop the pain.

But Meg was here. He didn't want her to go through that. She couldn't watch him die.

"Jonathan," Brock gasped.

"Please, tell me how I can help."

"Back of my head," he said. "Grab my hair."

He felt her fingers run over his scalp, her gentle touch a momentary reprieve. Then she firmly gripped a handful.

She gasped. "It's changing."

What was changing?

"It's turning white," she said.

Just another type of scar. He'd deal with it later. If he made it through this.

"Brock…"

"Pull," he gasped.

Her hands were shaking, but she did. He screamed again, his vision cycling between blue, red, and black. His skull cracked, his brain on fire as he was pulled in two.

He leaned forward, but could see the wall opposite him as well as the floor. He couldn't feel Meg's touch anymore. She was holding on to Jonathan now.

At least the pain in Brock's head had lessened. The rest of his body was another matter.

This part Brock knew. He grabbed the carpet and used it to help pull himself forward.

The pressure on his back, in his guts suddenly let up.

He felt his body lift from the ground for a moment, then heard Meg say, "Sorry."

He felt her doing something above him and dared to focus his attention through the other set of eyes— Jonathan's eyes. She had moved between them and was holding Jonathan around his chest. She gently put her foot on Brock's back, careful not to step on his spine.

Then she stood, pulling Jonathan with her.

Brock let out a final shriek as their hips and legs separated, a sound echoed by his newest brother. But then, the pain was gone. He'd never gone through an emergence so quickly.

He lay on the carpet, panting. Through both sets of eyes, he watched Meg gently help Jonathan to the floor.

She turned to Brock, eyes glowing painfully bright. Her cheeks were wet and her lashes clumped together, but she let out a laugh.

"You're still here." She leaned over and started kissing his face, his shoulders, his head, crying and laughing the whole time.

He wished he could feel her relief.

His vision was still flickering. Blue, red, black. Blue, red, black.

The blue, he was used to. The red had happened during the last split. The black... The black was new. And it was lasting longer with each cycle.

Brock managed to roll to his side. He could see himself

through Jonathan's eyes, his mind processing the data from both of their senses in a mental split-screen view. There was a lot more white in Brock's hair, but it was still mostly dark. As dark as the circles that shadowed Brock's eyes. His skin had an unhealthy gray pallor and waxy cast to it. Brock wasn't nearly as gaunt as he'd been after the other splits, though. He almost looked the same.

Jonathan... Jonathan didn't.

He was bigger than the rest of them. Almost as big as Brock had been before the split. A side-effect of their methods for helping Brock put on weight? Or a complication from his latest split?

The same scars covered Jonathan's body and face, but his hair was completely white. Jonathan ran his hand over his chest, staring down at the newest death mark.

"Can you hear me?" Brock projected.

"Understand... Not... Happening..." Jonathan's thoughts were fractured, disjointed. It was like each word was ripped from a screaming screen of static in his mind. *"What... Who..."*

"You are Jonathan. And I am Brock."

Jonathan cocked his head to the side. *"Progenitor?"*

"No. Brother." Brock lifted his arm toward Jonathan, but his strength gave out.

Meg must have noticed what he was doing, because she took Jonathan's hand and brought it to Brock's, squeezing them lightly. She knelt between them, running her fingers through Brock's hair. Her touch soothed him more than anything. She reached out to Jonathan. He flinched away from her.

"She'll help you," Brock thought. *"Trust her. I wish I could do more."*

He pulled his awareness back. The darkness was claiming him more, his hearing cutting out along with his vision.

He heard Meg say, "It's okay. I'm a friend."

As he forced his eyes open, she gently cupped Jonathan's cheek. Jonathan's lips parted and his eyes widened. Brock wasn't sure what Jonathan was feeling. He couldn't reach Jonathan anymore.

Which meant Jonathan's split was about to happen.

"Help him," Brock said.

Meg looked back to Brock. "I will."

His eyes drifted shut, and he didn't have the strength to open them again. He had to hold on long enough for Jonathan to split. Surely whoever had lost a replicant body had already completed theirs. He prayed they were all safe, getting to their stasis pods.

What was going to happen here, though? They didn't have enough stasis pods for everyone. Brock was supposed to be in stasis before he split. And they would have to take Tessa and Marcus out to put DP or Jonathan in.

Brock wasn't ready to go. He wanted to stay, to help.

He had to make sure everyone was taken care of. That they were safe.

Brock heard his dad's voice.

"Dexter, can you hear me?" Dad sounded far away, but had to be out in the hall.

Everything was foggy. Brock felt like he was drifting outside of his body.

"Eli." Meg's voice was louder, desperate and close. "In here."

"What…" Dad said. "Oh my God. What happened?"

Meg sounded wrecked. "He split."

"Sweet Jesus," Dad said.

Brock felt fingers at his throat above his pulse point. That had to be Dad.

"He wasn't due to split for hours." Dad continued his exam, hands flying over Brock's body. "How long has it been?"

"Only minutes," Meg said.

"And his brother?" Dad asked.

"Jonathan," Meg said. "Is he supposed to look different?"

"He is what he is."

"He hasn't said anything yet. Is that normal?" she asked.

Dad's touch disappeared. "Brock is stable. I'll check on —"

An earsplitting screech reached Brock even through the

haze surrounding him.

"No, Jonathan!" Meg yelled.

What the hell was happening? Brock wanted to open his eyes, to rise up and help the others, but he couldn't.

"It's all right," Dad said. "I'm here to help. Jonathan, stop."

When she spoke, it sounded like Meg was using her heightened strength—and reaching her limits. "He's your dad."

Jesus, what was Jonathan trying to do?

Another inhuman screech pierced Brock's ears. He winced, and even that small movement exhausted him further.

"He's splitting," Dad said. "He needs help."

"Stay back." Meg spoke more firmly than Brock had ever heard. "He'll hurt you."

Brock's heart picked up from its sluggish beat. His skin prickled. He felt his dad hook his arms under Brock's shoulders, dragging him across the room, just like the night of Brock's first split. Dad held him, hugging him close to his chest, propped up against the wall, no doubt. But this time, Brock could feel warm drops hit his shoulder.

Dad hadn't cried the first time.

"Stay with me, son," Dad whispered. "Christ, we're going to need you to deal with this."

There were more crashing sounds and shrieks. Meg was

yelling something... Something Brock couldn't understand.

No one would come to help her.

No one was left.

The room grew still. Brock couldn't feel his dad's arms around him anymore.

Blue, red, black. Blue, red, black... white.

Like the light he sometimes glimpsed when one of his brothers died.

"Brock? Brock?" Meg's voice grew more agitated, but was also fading. "Please don't go."

Chapter Eighteen

Rows of beds. Soft beeps. The *whoosh* of machines breathing for everyone in the room.

Everyone except her.

Meg sat curled in a ball, hugging her knees tight to her chest. She was in the farthest corner from the door, not because she was scared, but because it was the closest place to Brock's bed. From her seat on the floor, she could see the wires trailing down from the heads of everyone's beds. Dexter, Porter, Jon, Nathan, and Brock's.

The door to the infirmary opened.

"Meg?" Eli called. "Are you in here, honey?"

Fresh tears welled in her eyes at the endearment. She put her head on her knees and tried to cry quietly, hoping he would leave.

There was a small room right next to her with a bed for when any medical staff needed to sleep but wanted to be near their patients. She could crawl into it, but Eli would see the door open.

"I checked the footage and no one has been in or out since you left." Vaughn's voice. Meg didn't catch her scent. Vaughn must be talking to Eli through their watches.

"She has to still be in there," Vaughn said.

Eli's footsteps sounded from the far side of the room, paused, then headed her direction. She sniffed and wiped at her eyes and nose. Eli saw her as he rounded the foot of Brock's bed.

"Sweetie…" Eli walked over and squatted beside her, putting one arm over her shoulders.

"Did you find her?" Vaughn sounded strung out—and why wouldn't she? She'd been working nonstop for the last two days running everything, doing damage control, and trying to keep all the Blades calm when their leaders suddenly went missing or collapsed or… worse.

"Yeah, she's in the infirmary," Eli said. "Looks like there's a blind spot on the camera feed."

"Great." Vaughn sighed. "The only access route into the infirmary is covered. I'll add tweaking the camera positions to my list so we have a better interior view, but it's a low priority for now."

Eli's watch made a beeping sound that Meg knew meant Vaughn had ended their communication. She hadn't even said goodbye or asked how Meg or the others were doing. That was a bad sign. Meg needed to pull herself together. She needed to help.

"I'm sorry," she said, wiping her eyes again. "You don't need to check on me. You should focus on them."

"There's no need to be sorry. And I've already done all I can do for them." Eli sat down on the floor beside her, keeping his arm around her shoulders.

"How are they?" she asked.

Maybe Brock's vitals had changed. Maybe Eli had figured something out.

She knew before he said anything that her hopes were unfounded. The defeat in his tone was heart-breaking.

"Well, the younger boys are stable," Eli said.

She loved how he talked about them, how he so obviously cared, even with as terrifying as Jon and Nathan had been during their split. If they hadn't blacked out when Brock did, she wasn't sure what would have happened.

The replicants were strong. Stronger than a normal human. And she was the only fighter they had left.

If Roy showed up, they were screwed.

"All of them are still unresponsive. Brock—" Eli paused for a moment, then cleared his throat before he went on. "Brock's vitals are weakening. Vaughn is working with Damien to move the stasis pods from Europa since Zach's only using the one."

"I'm sorry about Carey," Meg said.

"I haven't given up on him yet. Or any of my boys. We'll see what happens when Zach comes out of stasis and Brock is back on his feet. Zach will probably split, and then we'll have Carey back."

Eli spoke with such conviction, but there was an edge of tension to his tone. She wondered if he really believed they would ever figure out how to help Brock—or any of the others.

"Vaughn never told me what happened to Carey," Meg said. "Just that Damien was really mad."

Eli let out a puff of breath. "Mad doesn't begin to cover it. Carey and Damien have always been close. When Brock's split started and all the boys lost their link, they went catatonic. Carey and Damien were sparring... with swords."

"Oh my God."

Eli pulled his lower lip between his teeth, making his gray beard bristle out. He released it with a sigh.

"Hell of a thing," Eli said. "Finding out about your best friend that way."

Meg didn't know what to say to that, so she kept silent. After a little while, Eli spoke again.

"We should have brought Damien in before now," Eli said. "He's a good man. People look up to him. He's agreed not to tell the other Blades anything till he gets a chance to talk to us here, but how he takes this might make or break us going forward."

The thought of Brock's legacy being lost on top of everything else was just too much. She had to keep her focus on saving the man behind it.

"You're still planning to put Brock in stasis?" she asked.

"Yeah. Vaughn's working like crazy to try to get two

more stasis pods built for Jon and Nathan before Damien gets here. "

"What about Tessa and Marcus?"

"We'll figure out what to do with them when the pods are ready," Eli said. "But we need to get Brock into one as soon as possible. It'll be safest for him and everyone else if his brothers are in stasis before him. All Porter's testing at least told us that."

"What if Roy gets here first?"

Eli smiled at her. "We don't even know he'll come."

"He'll come."

"Well, then he's in for a surprise. Vaughn has the grounds wired up with all kinds of defenses. Roy won't make it into the ranch. And if he does, it'll be even worse for him. We're safe here."

She hoped Eli was right.

They sat leaning against the wall, staring at Brock's still form on his bed.

After a moment, Meg said, "What was Brock's mother like?"

Eli pondered her question before replying. "I didn't know her that long, but she seemed sweet. She was concerned for her baby and only spoke of him through the delivery. Wanted us to name him 'Brock' after the hunter who was killed helping her get to us."

Meg's stomach sank, imagining that scene. But that hadn't been what she wanted to know.

"I actually meant the other woman," she said. "Your wife."

"Oh." Eli tensed. "She was... a hard woman. Strong and passionate."

"I don't mean to bring up bad memories."

"It's okay. Just been a while since I spoke of her." He was quiet for a bit, then said, "I was a county medical examiner when we met. I kept seeing her at crime scenes —this woman with dark red hair and piercing blue eyes." He laughed softly. "A lot like Tessa's."

"Brock told me he started the Blades to show her that dwellers and humans can get along," Meg said.

"I'm glad he's admitting that now." Eli let out a deeper laugh. "When he first named the Blades, he kept saying, 'It's pronounced Yah-nus, Dad. Like the Roman God with two faces.' And he had a point about that fitting since Dexter and Porter are... what they are."

"But you think he had another reason for the name?"

Eli smirked at her. "His mom's name was Janice."

Meg laughed. She couldn't believe it, but she did. "You're kidding."

"Nope." Eli shook his head. "I don't know what he expected from her if they'd ever met after he manifested."

"She was his mom."

"She was a hunter," Eli said. "Through and through."

"But she raised him."

"Jan... She knew I worked the weird cases. She *let* me

see her at those crime scenes. Then one day, I caught her in my morgue, all tricked out with weapons. She tried to get me to leave, but I wouldn't. I demanded an explanation. Then something burst out of one of the cold chambers, all spindly legs and tentacles and—" He shivered. "I never did find out what it was called. She killed it with a flame thrower. Triggered the sprinkler system. After it had vaporized, we just stared at each other for a minute, dripping wet." He chuckled. "Then she offered to buy me a drink."

Meg rested the side of her head on her knees, watching Eli's face as he remembered.

"You probably needed it," she said.

"Yeah. But more than that..." Eli's voice took on a wistful tone. "She was the most beautiful woman I'd ever seen. So in command of herself, fearless. I was smitten. I helped her out with cases. She called them 'hunts.' Then one night, she brought Brock's mother to me."

The lines around his eyes deepened. He started chewing on his lower lip again, hard enough Meg was afraid he'd draw blood.

His voice was just above a whisper when he went on. "Katey was four months pregnant and at full term. Scared. Terrified. And she just wanted her baby to have a chance. Jan was standing by with a bone saw."

"Oh my God."

"I kept telling myself it was for the mother. In case she

turned—which she did. After she died on the table. But not before bringing Brock into the world. This perfect little boy, born in a morgue."

"Katey died delivering Brock?"

"She died because Edgar killed her," Eli said. "He knew she'd turn, with what he did to her. He'd already infected her with enough of his dwellers to turn her into a Hive Mother."

Eli shook his head sharply. "Jan managed to get Katey into the incinerator. Then Jan turned to me and looked at the baby in my arms."

"She couldn't have been thinking—"

"I don't know. I don't want to know. I asked her to marry me right on the spot. We weren't even dating, but I was already crazy about her. I told her we could give Brock a chance, a family. And if he ever manifested... Well, we'd deal with it then."

"Jan must have really loved you."

Eli glanced over at her, surprise plain on his features. "How do you figure?"

"If she was really as hardcore as you and Brock have both told me, the only way she would have taken you up on your offer was if she wanted to."

Eli was quiet again for a few moments, then said, "Maybe so."

"Thank you for sharing this with me. It helps me feel closer to him. To Brock."

"I'm the one who should thank you," Eli said. "I've never seen Brock as happy—as alive—as he's been since he met you."

"I wish I could do more."

Eli snorted. "Don't we all? Even with everything I've learned about humans and dwellers, I never could figure out what it was about him that was different. Every single test I've ever run shows Brock being completely human."

Meg shook her head. "But he can't be."

"I know. Vaughn and Porter were working on this theory that Brock builds up quantum energy till he has enough to split. That would explain why he's weakest right after a split and gets stronger as time passes."

Hope surged through Meg, strong enough to make her skin tingle. She remembered Brock mentioning quantum... something earlier.

She sat up straighter, and said, "That's great. If he just needs energy, can't you find a way to give that to him?"

"Even if we could figure out exactly what kind of energy he's processing and a way to channel it into him safely, it wouldn't matter. His body *is human*. It's not meant to process whatever the hell has been going on with him the last twelve years. The only way to save him is to stop the cycle. And I'm afraid we might be too late for that."

Eli gestured across the room. "Jon and Nathan, they didn't come out right. Normally, the new brothers look and act exactly like Brock at the time they emerge. They have the same body weight, match in every detail. Jon and Nathan are as big as Brock was before the split. Their hair, the way they were acting. This split is different. And watching Brock's vitals slip…" Eli shook his head. "We have to face the facts in front of us. Brock can't handle the stress of this. His body is failing. It's only a matter of time. And when he goes, the others will too. All my boys."

"They're not going to die," Meg said.

Eli looked over at her and rested his hand on her knee. "You'll have a home here no matter what—"

She smacked his hand away and stood. "Brock is not going to die."

Eli stared up her, almost like he was a little awestruck. No one had ever looked at Meg that way before. She held her ground, hands fisted at her sides. Her nails were digging into her palms.

"I won't give up on him," she said. "And neither should you."

"You're right." Eli nodded, then rose to his feet stiffly. "I better get back to Vaughn. I don't know that much about engineering, but I'm helping her as I can."

"Do you need me?" Meg asked.

"I think the best thing you can do is stay here with Brock. Keep an eye on them all."

"I will."

"Thank you." He headed to the door, casting one last

glance at her over his shoulder before leaving.

When he was gone, she said, "I'm not giving up on you. Any of you."

There had to be something she could do. She sat on the bed next to Brock and picked up his hand. Blood smeared his skin.

She gasped, but then saw that it was coming from her palm. She stretched out her fingers. Her nails had lengthened and curved. Like claws.

How many lies had Roy told her? Was anything he'd said true?

The wounds on her palm closed as she watched them. The blood on Brock's hand vaporized in a soft blue light. If only she could give Brock her healing abilities. Her strength. She'd do anything for him, anything to save him.

She leaned over him, brushing her fingertips across his forehead and cheek, careful not to scratch him with the claws that wouldn't seem to go away. Her fingers had darkened as well.

"The stasis chamber's not a sure thing. Maybe I should let you bite me. Then we could be werewolves together."

Brock's words rang out in her mind. He had to have been joking. Hadn't he?

She looked over at the monitor, watched the slow beat of his heart. There must be sensors built into the bed, feeding data to Vaughn's algorithms. They would alert her if something changed with Brock.

If Brock changed.

Meg jumped up from the bed, unable to believe what she was contemplating. She didn't even know if she could change herself, let alone someone else. And if she did transform, would Roy finally have access to her mind?

So what if he did?

Alphas weren't alphas forever. There were constant power struggles within packs, werewolves struggling for a higher position. She knew that eventually a pair would have challenged Roy and Lydia.

Brock kept his replicants in check, which was a much bigger deal than she'd realized. Jonathan's freakout when he emerged had scared the crap out of her, and it had only started *after* Brock lost consciousness. No matter what other dynamics were going on among the Blades, Brock was their leader. He just… wasn't a dick about it.

She smiled as she remembered him schooling Dexter on his behavior. Brock was an alpha trapped in a human body. A dying human body. What if she could do something about that?

She didn't know where the cameras were, but she knew there was a blind spot behind Brock's bed. The bottom half of the door to the side room fell in that space. Before she could think herself out of it, she walked to the door and opened it. She left it open when she stepped into the small room.

The lights stayed off, probably on a manual control so

that people using the room to rest weren't disturbed. She hoped there weren't infrared cameras or anything monitoring the place. Vaughn was sure to find out what Meg was up to eventually, but she didn't need much time to go forward with her insane and desperate plan to save Brock the only way she knew how.

She was going to turn him.

Chapter Nineteen

Brock's guts were on fire. He'd already split. Couldn't he have at least a little bit of time without excruciating pain?

He was supposed to be dead, anyway. He prayed this wasn't what death was like. His skin was burning. His brain felt like it was melting in his skull.

He forced his eyes open. The room was bathed in flickering lights. Blue, red, gold. Blue, red, gold. He pinched his eyes shut, but the strobe-effect continued. He couldn't think.

Instinctively, he shielded his eyes, wincing at the arcs of pain that radiated out from his arm. Something wet and cold covered his skin. The sharp, metallic scent that hit him was unmistakably blood.

His stomach churned. More pain. New pain.

It wasn't a split. His bones didn't feel like they were stretching. No muscles were sliding against each other in ways they were never meant to. The unbearable pressure wasn't there.

He felt like he was melting. What was happening?

He reached out to the link connecting him to his

replicants. A strange buzzing surrounded his mind. They were cut off.

Rolling onto his side, he saw Meg sitting on the floor. Naked. She was hugging her knees tight to her chest.

"Meg?"

She smiled at him, but then let out a sob that shook her entire body. Her eyes gleamed like flashlights, reflecting off the tears coating her cheeks. Blood trickled from the corner of her mouth.

"I'm so sorry," she said.

What was she apologizing for that she looked so wrecked? And the blood... The blood on her mouth wasn't vaporizing. It was human.

Shit.

Brock tried to push himself up. "Dad? Vaughn?"

"They're not here," she said.

What had happened to them? What had she done?

One of the machines near the bed started beeping. The room was spinning. Brock let his head drop, hoping it would help.

He was bleeding. Bite marks lined his forearm, a neat row of serrated holes that seeped red. The sheet beneath him was stained in a clear outline of a clawed hand. A werewolf's print, made in blood.

"Shit," he said.

Roy must have found them. But then why was Brock still alive?

He groaned as another wave of pain hit him. The cloth of the hospital gown he was wearing felt like sandpaper. Brock slid to his feet, tearing it off and throwing it on the floor. Meg was next to him in an instant. She reached out, grabbing his elbow to help stabilize him, but he shook her off.

"Where's my dad?"

Brock looked out over the row of beds in the room. They were in the infirmary. Dexter and Porter were in the closest beds, and Jon and Nathan were beyond them. The machines next to them all started beeping loudly.

"Probably on his way," Meg said.

Brock's heart was pounding. He could feel the blood pumping through his veins, see the pulses in the throats of the helpless forms lying before him. It would be so easy to rip them apart.

What the fuck?

"What's happening to me?" Brock said. His lips curled back from his teeth in a snarl. He couldn't stop it.

"I'm sorry."

"What did you do?" he roared.

"I saved you." Meg's voice was small, but he could hear it perfectly, along with her heart pounding in her chest.

He looked at his arm. The wounds were starting to heal.

"Jesus... You bit me," he yelled.

Was this Roy's idea of revenge? Turn Brock into a

werewolf so that Roy could torture him for longer? Maybe get inside Brock's head and twist it around like he'd been doing to Tessa, trying to get him to hurt the people he loved?

People like Meg.

Brock loved her, and she'd done this to him. She'd bitten him, which meant she could transform.

And that meant she'd lied.

He clamped down on his muscles, fighting the urge to pick up his bed and throw it across the room. A surge of energy pulsed through him. He felt strong enough to actually do it.

"Was this the plan all along?" Brock said. "Get close to me so you could infect me?"

"No! I'd never transformed before." Meg stepped closer. "I didn't even know I could. I was desperate to save you. Please tell me I've saved you."

"What do you—" His muscles cramped, a much more familiar pain. But it wasn't nearly as intense as a split. Each wave of pain left power in its wake. He felt strong. Alive. He rode each wave, trying to control what was happening to him, how his body was trying to change.

If Roy thought this would be a way to get revenge, he was wrong. *Dead* wrong.

Brock would show him. Roy had handed Brock everything he needed to get his *own* revenge for all the pain Roy had caused Brock and his family. He only hoped his brothers would be okay without him.

He blew out a breath and let go, dropping to all fours. The burning in his muscles released, the pain in his guts settling into a steady burn that radiated out through his limbs. Brock breathed through it. He'd been through so much worse.

Blue light rippled over his body with each pulse of energy. His arms darkened, thick fur sprouting everywhere he could see. When the next wave surged over his body, he didn't fight it.

He felt another energy—more familiar—like something crawling up his neck under his skin. The new energy burned along after it, consuming it. The crawling settled in his brain, a last stand of what he had been as his body remade itself. Brock couldn't believe he was rooting for the werewolf parasite, willing it to win over his Hive nature. His brain was on fire. His face burned as his nose and mouth lengthened.

He felt something seeping from his ears. His left eye was a ball of molten agony. He slammed his fist down on the floor, over and over again, then raked his claws along the metal, peeling it up.

Blue, red, gold. Blue, red, gold.

The world settled into a uniform red. Brock could see the outline of his claw marks on the floor in minute detail. His breath was loud, deafening in his ears. He shook his head, then lifted it to scent the air in the room.

Meat was in front of him. Tainted meat, but it would do. He stood. The room was smaller than he remembered. So was the woman standing in front of him.

"Brock?" she said.

He growled as he turned away from her—toward the meat lying still on the beds in the room. Annoying beeps came from the monitors mounted on the walls above them.

"No, no. Brock!"

The woman grabbed his elbow and pulled. Brock snarled, jerking his arm from her grip with enough force to send her flying across the room. She skidded to a stop a dozen feet away. He laughed as he walked toward her. She scrambled to her feet, glaring up at him with glowing gold eyes. Beautiful eyes.

She was bared for him. Long legs, trim build, perfect breasts. He remembered sinking into her heat, using his other form to twine with hers for hours. He would enjoy her again, after they ate. There was plenty of meat to share.

"I can't let you do this." The woman shook her head from side to side, her face elongating, fur emerging from her skin as waves of blue energy pulsed over her body. Claws sprouted from her fingertips, her ears lengthened to tall points on either side of her head. She rose up on the balls of her feet as her legs changed shape.

Brock laughed again, wondering what she hoped to accomplish. Her other form was much more distracting.

She leapt at him, fangs bared. She must want to play before they ate. He let her push him back a few paces. She wasn't even using her claws.

The door to the room opened. Fresh meat stepped in. Good meat.

Brock grabbed the woman by the neck and lifted her from the ground. They couldn't let this meat get away while they were distracted with their fun. She grabbed his arm, finally digging her claws in.

This pain was familiar. Insignificant. He didn't bother to try to get her to stop.

"Put her down," the meat yelled.

Brock was surprised enough to pause. Did this meat really think Brock would obey him?

His skin crawled along the back of his neck. He *knew* this meat.

"Vaughn, shock Tessa with enough voltage to take down Marcus, too," the meat said.

"What?" Another voice sounded in the room. Brock growled, looking all around to try to find its source.

"Why?" the voice said. "They're both right here in their stasis chambers."

The voice was Vaughn. Meat with a name.

Curator.

A shiver passed down Brock's spine that he didn't understand.

The meat at the door stared at them. Brock could smell

his fear.

"There are two werewolves in the infirmary," the meat said.

"Holy shit." Vaughn sounded panicked.

Appropriate.

"That's not Tessa and Marcus," Vaughn said. "Get out of there, Eli."

Eli...

"I can't." Eli glanced at the beds holding the tainted meat.

Sons. His sons. My brothers.

Brock shook his head, trying to get his thoughts to make sense. That damn buzzing was louder, static energy pushing on his mind. He reinforced his shields, blocking it out completely.

"Brock's gone and," Eli's voice hitched, "there's blood on his sheets."

"If he were dead, the others would be, too," Vaughn said. "Their vital signs are stabilizing, though. I'm running the footage for the room. Just don't move. I don't know why the big one isn't attacking, but let's not provoke— Oh, no. Oh, no, no, no."

Brock could hear Vaughn hit something wherever she was hiding.

"Goddammit, Megan." Vaughn bit out each word. "What were you thinking?"

Brock growled. Meg. The wolf he held was Meg. She

was *his*. And no one spoke to her that way.

But he was mad at her. Furious. He couldn't remember why.

"Meg?" Eli said. He looked back at the empty bed, then to Brock. "Brock? Oh my God. Is that you?"

Eli dared to take a step closer—even smiled. "Son."

Brock roared at him. Eli froze.

None of this made sense. Brock flexed his hand and heard the woman make a choking sound. He dropped her to the ground, trying to sort through his thoughts.

That was Meg. He was Brock. Eli was his dad, and the men on the beds were his brothers.

Then why did he still want to kill them all?

Brock grabbed his hospital bed and lifted it over his head. Alarms sounded from the machines. He threw the bed at the wall, delighting at the crashing sounds it made as it shattered to pieces.

Better.

He grabbed the monitor that had been next to the bed and tore it off the wall, then smashed it on the floor. Someone tackled him around his waist. He struck them, feeling his elbow connect with a strong, furred body. Meg. Was she betraying him after all?

She grabbed his leg and pulled, knocking him off his feet with her ridiculous move. Brock almost laughed. She was still holding on to his calf, leaving herself wide open for the kick he launched at her shoulder. She flew across the room, yelping as she slammed into the wall. The moment her feet hit the ground, she leapt back up, keeping herself between Brock and the others with her arms outstretched.

She was protecting them. But she'd bitten Brock. Turned him, without his permission.

I was unconscious. How could she have asked?

He shook his head again. If she'd been sent to kill him, they might at least have taught her how to fight. Her attacks were ludicrous.

"Get them out," Meg yelled, her voice raspier, deeper than usual. "I'll handle Brock."

She thought she could handle him? He let out a rumbling laugh.

"Meg, I can't—" Eli said.

"Just do it!" she roared.

Eli flinched, then grabbed the nearest bed and started pushing it out of the room. Meg's lips peeled back from her teeth. She snarled, running forward and grabbing Brock around his waist again. This time, she lifted him from the ground.

He was surprised by her strength for long enough that she'd made it into the small side room before he recovered enough to react. He struck her shoulders just hard enough to force her to release him. She hit the ground and rolled to the side, scrambling for the door. She slammed it shut and somehow managed to lock it with her clawed hand, then turned to face him.

"Alone at last," he growled.

"I don't want to hurt you, Brock."

He laughed. "I don't want to hurt you, either. But I do want to hurt them."

"You'll learn to handle it," she said. "I can help you."

"I've had enough of your help."

He took a step forward, and she moved to block the door. He could hear Eli in the other room, the sound of wheels squeaking against the floor.

Vaughn's voice was muffled through the door. "I'm locking down the infirmary."

Brock heard a distant beep, and knew he was trapped. They both were. Meg must have understood as well, because she loosened her stance, standing straighter. Did she think this meant she was safe?

She's just relieved that they are.

Brock let out a low growl. He was tired of being trapped. He wanted to be free. Even more, he wanted to break something. The only thing in the room was a puny bed. And her.

He grabbed her arms, pinning them to her sides as he lifted her from the ground. She didn't try to escape, didn't try to defend herself in any way. Pathetic omega.

No.

He shook his head again. The movement made the room spin. He stumbled to the wall, slamming her against it.

"Please, Brock," she said.

Blue light swept over her, consuming her fur as her face and limbs shrank back to their normal size and shape. What was she doing? He could hurt her so much more easily in her human form. Without even meaning to.

Shit, have I been trying *to hurt her?*

No. He'd pulled all of his hits, lessened every strike, but still...

"I know the violence you feel," she said. "The urges. Being mindblind doesn't make me stupid. But it's okay." She swallowed hard, but her voice still broke. "I'm here now."

He'd heard those words before. Meg had said the same thing to Tessa when Meg had offered herself up to appease Tessa's uncontrollable rage.

He wouldn't use Meg that way. Ever.

The fact that her pack had taken her reassurance as an invitation to hurt her made his skin crawl. He wanted to make them all pay, but Dexter had already taken care of that. The only one left was Roy.

Roy would pay soon enough.

Brock's hands flexed at the thought, and Meg winced. He quickly released her, but couldn't bring himself to move away. His chest vibrated with a low growl that wouldn't stop. Meg reached between them, gently running her trembling fingertips over the scars on his face. Her touch sent a jolt of energy through him—this gentle touch on a place that had been ravaged by madness.

There had to be another way.

He pressed his hands against the wall on either side of her head, raking his claws along the metal.

Not enough.

He punched the smooth surface, sending pain lancing through his fist and all the way up into his shoulder.

Better.

Meg grabbed him, hugging his arm. "Don't."

She didn't betray me. She saved me.

She transformed. For the first time, she transformed. And she pushed herself to do so for him. Because she loved him.

Brock let out a breath, releasing as much of the new energy as he could. He felt the strength and power coil within him, even as his new form evaporated like a weight falling away. Meg's eyes were huge as she stared at him, her breath coming fast. He could hear her heart pounding in her chest. She still looked afraid. He wasn't sure she shouldn't be.

"Brock..."

He grabbed the nape of her neck and pulled her against him, crushing his lips to hers.

Chapter Twenty

Brock's fingers twined in her hair as he pinned Meg to the wall. The metal was cold, but the heat he was putting off more than warmed her. He drove his tongue into her mouth, demanding, dominating. She did her best to match him, wanting...

Wanting him. This. Nothing else mattered.

He grabbed her thigh, lifting it to wrap her leg around his waist, pulling her head to the side at the same time so he could latch on to her neck. He shifted his mouth to her shoulder and raked his teeth over her skin, hard. She gasped, her belly filling with molten need.

The night before, he'd been passionate as they made love. This... This was something more.

He released her hair, but only so he could grab her breast, kneading it, rubbing his palm over her nipple until she cried out. Her core ached for him, arcs of pleasure already speeding along her nerves in anticipation of feeling him inside of her.

Her cry caught his attention, bringing his lips back to hers, where he could swallow her moans as he ground his dick against her. He reached down for her other leg and lifted her from the ground. She wrapped her legs around his waist, pulling him tight against her, not holding back as she'd had to last night.

He was as strong as she was now. Stronger. He was healthy and... intense, but he would adjust.

We can be together.

She burrowed her fingers in his hair, grabbing a fistful and deepening their kiss, pouring all of her passion into him. He paused for a moment, then let out a growl, thrusting his tongue into her mouth more forcefully. He rocked his hips back, centering his dick at her core and pressing against her. The ache between her legs intensified, a steady stream of tingling energy spreading from deep in her belly.

She wriggled her hips, trying to pull him in, desperate to feel him part her flesh. Her sheath was already pulsing, all of her senses focused on his hot skin pressing so close to where she wanted him. He shifted his lips to her neck, his grip on her thighs tightening, holding her still. Then he plunged into her, burying himself deep.

She screamed from the pleasure of it. Her nerves pulsed, her skin felt electrified as the climax tore through her.

Brock didn't pause. He kept her pinned to the wall, pounding into her, lips latched onto her neck, hands tight on her legs. The throbbing in her core kept on, squeezing against the impossible hardness of his shaft. Each thrust drew out more pleasure, saturating her body with his heat, with his need for her.

"Meg!" He shouted her name, throwing his head back as his eyes pinched shut and his hands gripped her even harder.

She felt him pulsing deep inside, spilling himself into her. Finally, his thrusts slowed. With one final stroke, he buried himself as deep as he could.

His chest pressed against hers, their hips joined, her arms around his shoulders. He kept kissing her neck, his breath quick and hot against her skin. He rocked against her slowly, even though she could feel him softening inside of her.

"I need more," he said.

"Yes." She did, too. Needed him, wanted him.

She dropped one hand as far as she could reach down his back, then raked her nails up along his spine. He sucked in a breath, pushing against her harder.

"You love me." He said the words right next to her ear. Somehow, it sounded like a question and a command at once.

"I do," she said. "I love you."

A tremor swept through him. He nuzzled the side of her head.

"I love you, too." He leaned back, gazing at her with one eye that gleamed gold and one that was still all-white, with bits of fragmented brilliant blue sparking from its pupil.

She rested her hand against his cheeks, wondering if there were any more surprises in store from his transformation. His demeanor was different. There was a current of danger surrounding him that she hadn't felt before.

"Brock…"

He gripped her wrist and pulled her hand away from the right side of his face, but only to press a kiss against her palm. That loving gesture hadn't changed.

"Mate," he said.

Her heart started to pound. He was claiming her. As his mate. She'd always longed for a mate. Having it be Brock seemed beyond anything she'd dreamed.

"This doesn't feel real," she whispered.

He pulled her legs from around his waist. Her knees were weak. She wondered if they would even hold her up. He steered her toward the small bed, helping her sit, then he knelt in front of her.

"Does this feel real?" He leaned forward and took one of her breasts into his mouth, swirling his tongue around it in firm circles.

Her back arched away from the wall as she gasped. He grasped her other breast, flicking the tip of his thumb over her nipple. His touch was gentler—and more maddening— than when he'd grabbed her against the wall.

He looked up at her, smirking, just long enough to say,

"Answer me," before bending his head to her other breast.

Heat was pooling between her legs again. This time, her entire body thrummed with it, as if he'd primed her senses for what was to come.

He ran his nails along her ribs, fingers curled like claws. "Answer me."

"What?" She couldn't remember his question. "Answer what?"

"Does this feel real?"

This time, he dropped his head between her legs, his tongue sliding between the folds of her flesh. She gasped, burying her fingers in his hair. With his elbow, he pinned her right thigh to the bed. He pushed her other leg aside and held it there with his broad shoulders, spreading her before him. He slid his fingers into her, deep.

"Brock," she cried. Pleasure radiated out from her core, pulsing through her body.

"Answer me."

"Yes." It felt real and amazing and—

He lowered his lips to her again, sucking her clitoris, flicking his tongue over it as his fingers kept pumping in and out.

"Yes," she repeated, she wasn't sure how many times. Her nerves were on fire, heat building where he touched her. "Please."

He spread his fingers, stretching her as he thrust them in and out, faster and faster. He increased the pressure on her clit until the pleasure he was stoking built to a white-hot explosion of bliss.

Her back arched, her fingers pulled on his hair as her hips bucked against him. She screamed his name as he held her down, relentless in his stimulation, tongue still swirling, fingers pumping. Her core clenched against him, a steady beat that slowed along with his movements as her body settled back to the bed. He smirked up at her as he backed away, eyebrows dark over those mesmerizing eyes.

She ran her hand along his cheek, and said, "Mate."

If anything, his expression darkened, the possessiveness there sending another thrill through her body.

"Yes," he said.

He pulled her to her feet and spun her around. He reached in front of her and grabbed the bed, flinging it out of the way as if it weighed nothing. Grabbing her wrists, he brought her hands up to the wall, his chest flush against her back.

"I'm going to be demanding as a mate," he said, his lips against her ear.

"What—" She gasped as he nipped her ear. "What will you want?"

He dropped his grip to her hips, lifting her to the balls of her feet. His dick pressed her core, lighting sparks along nerves she'd thought couldn't take or give any more.

"This," he said. He buried himself deep in one smooth stroke.

Hands firm on her hips, he slammed into her, over and over, his hips hitting her ass each time he landed. Her fingers curled against the wall, clawing at its smooth surface. She'd never felt so alive, so desired, so… free.

He slid one hand around her belly, helping her balance as the force of his strokes nearly lifted her from her feet. His other hand found her clit, his fingers running over it in deft circles. The stimulation turned the sparks to lightning, crackling through her in sharp bursts, arcing out through her skin. Her muscles felt electrified with a pleasure so intense she thought she might black out.

She cried out again, core throbbing around his dick, coaxing him to join her. She felt him hesitate for a fraction of a breath, and then he grabbed her hips again, pummeling into her. His dick pulsed within her, filling her with his seed. He thrust in deep and held himself there, pulling her hips against his, fingers tight against her skin. She listened to their heavy breath, their hearts beating in sync. The throbbing in her core ebbed as he slid from her. He kept his arms around her, holding her against his chest, gently stroking her breast as he nuzzled her neck.

"If that's what you're going to demand, I'm more than willing to—" Her sentence was cut off by a distant explosion.

The floor shook beneath them and alarms sounded. A flashing light cast everything in an orange glow.

"What's happening?" she said.

"I don't know." Brock stepped away from her, looking all around. He pointed at the pile of her clothes that she'd tucked into the corner of the room when she'd snuck in to transform. "Get dressed."

She grabbed her shirt and pulled it on. Brock picked up her pants, taking her hand in his and leading her into the infirmary. He tossed the clothes to her and started picking through the wreckage of his hospital bed, finally pulling out the gown he'd been wearing. It looked more like a robe than the hospital gowns she was used to seeing. The charcoal gray fabric opened in the front and was thicker and held together with a belt. It was also long enough to reach his knees.

"We have to find the others," he said.

"Where would they go?" Meg finished fastening her pants, then followed him to the door.

"The safest place is the ship. There's no way into it except the hatch. Most of it is buried under rock from the crash. That's where the stasis pods are, as well. Ops is two rooms down. We can check it on the way."

She glanced up at the lights above the door, both relieved and further terrified that they were dark. Meg's heart caught in her throat when they stepped into the hallway. The four beds that had held Dexter, Porter, Jon, and Nathan were crammed together at the end of the hall in front of the elevator, empty. Two of them were on their sides. A line of blood streaked across the wall, heading toward the ops room.

"Shit," Brock said. "Dad. Dad!"

She followed Brock as he ran toward ops. The scanner let out a strangled beep and flashed red when he touched it. He lifted his hand. His palm was covered in blood. Only Vaughn or Eli's blood wouldn't have vaporized.

"No..." Brock pressed the keys, entering code after code, but each time, the scanner reacted the same.

Meg rested her hand on his shoulder, trying to give him what comfort she could. There was nothing else she could do. She hated feeling so helpless.

"No. No," he yelled. He slammed his palm against the door. "Dad."

"It doesn't recognize you."

They both turned at the smooth, low voice coming from down the hall. Dexter stood in front of the open door to Porter's lab.

Brock let out a laugh. "Dexter, you're okay."

"I guess that's a matter of perspective." Dexter glared at Meg.

Meg's stomach sank. Dexter was using 'I.' She'd thought he only did that when Brock was borrowing one of his bodies. She could feel Brock tense beside her.

"Is Porter okay?" she asked.

"Okay?" Dexter let out a harsh laugh. "He's alive, if that's what you mean."

Brock took a step toward him, and Dexter jerked back.

"What's wrong?" Brock said.

"We're diminished." For a moment, Dexter looked lost. He stared vacantly at the floor in front of him and shook his head. His voice was tight when he continued. "We can't feel you anymore. Or hear the others. Porter and I can barely sense each other."

Meg couldn't imagine what that was like for them. How alone they must feel. Brock hesitated, then continued forward. Dexter held his ground. It looked like he was readying himself for an attack.

"Brock," Meg warned.

As soon as he was close enough, Brock reached out and grasped Dexter's shoulders. He pulled him into a hug.

"I'm so sorry," Brock said.

Dexter lifted his arms out to his sides as if he didn't know what to do. Then he wrapped them around Brock, hugging him back. Meg could see Dexter's face, the wonder in his expression, the fear. After a few moments, they separated.

"It's better than the alternative, I guess." Dexter's signature smirk was back, but there were lines of strain around his eyes.

"I wholeheartedly agree," Brock said. "We'll figure this out."

Dexter's smile faded. "You should know that Carey is gone."

"What?" Brock gasped.

Meg stepped forward, not reaching out to Brock physically, but letting her proximity calm him.

"There was an accident," Dexter said. "With all of us circling the drain, Dad and Vaughn decided they couldn't wait to see if Zach would split before putting him in stasis. Damien was able to get Zach stabilized with Vaughn's help."

"Jesus." Brock ran his hand through his hair.

"We're going to have to handle Damien carefully when he arrives," Dexter said. "This wasn't the best way for him to find out he's been working with dwellers all along."

"When he arrives?" Brock asked.

Dexter nodded. "He's insisting on coming to the ranch. Vaughn was able to convince him not to tell the other Blades yet, but Damien wants to know everything."

"Vaughn told me the stasis chambers are self-contained and mobile," Meg said. "Damien is bringing Zach here so we can help him. Eli is hopeful Zach will split once he emerges."

"Is Dad okay?" Brock asked. "What happened to Jonathan?"

Dexter shook his head. "Jon and Nathan are having trouble adapting. When we all woke up in the hall, they went berserk. We managed to get them into the lab and subdued them. Porter doesn't know how long the sedating agent will work, though."

"What about Dad?" Brock said.

Meg was as worried as Brock sounded. Dexter seemed to be hedging, purposefully avoiding giving an answer.

He paused for another moment, then said, "Nathan broke his nose and wrist."

Brock hissed in a breath, his shoulders hunching. His fingers curled at his sides and his nails lengthened. "I'll kill them."

Meg put her hands on Brock's shoulders and gently urged them down.

"They're confused," she said. "They need your guidance, like the others did."

"How am I supposed to do that when our link has been severed?" Brock snapped.

She recoiled from his harsh tone, but he caught her arms before she could step away, keeping her close.

"I'm sorry," Brock said. "I guess I'm having trouble adapting, too."

Meg nodded. "We're going to figure this out."

"We'd better do it fast," Dexter said. "Because Jon and Nathan aren't our only problems."

Chapter Twenty-One

The lab was a wreck. Broken glass littered the counters, several of the cabinet doors were off their hinges, and the floor still had scorch marks on it from where Vaughn must have used the flamethrower on Porter's body. Jon and Nathan were propped up against the wall farthest from the door.

Brock herded Meg away from the glass. He wished he'd waited long enough for her to put on shoes.

"Love what you've done with the place," Brock said.

"Watch the sass." Dad's voice had a thick nasal twang to it.

Brock didn't know if he was more relieved or furious when Dad stepped into view. His nose was covered in bandages, but it didn't mask the bruising on his cheeks and under his eyes. He was cradling his right hand against his chest. It was wrapped in a makeshift splint—strips of cloth that held two metal bars in place on either side of his wrist.

"Dad." Brock felt frozen in place. His eyes were tingling, probably glowing. He didn't want to scare his dad, but he was so happy to see him in one piece, and he knew werewolves' eyes glowed when they felt heightened emotions.

Dad walked to Brock and looked him over. Brock's left eye made a few electric popping sounds. Motes of blue energy floated in front of his field of view.

What the hell am I?

"I'll be damned," Dad said.

He laughed, then wrapped his arms around Brock, squeezing hard. Brock hugged him back, but not too tight. Werewolf strength was going to take some getting used to. He rested his head against Dad's shoulder.

"I'm so glad you're okay," Dad said. He leaned over to reach out to Meg, pulling her into the hug and murmuring, "Thank you. Thank you for saving my sons."

Brock felt Meg tense, her shoulders trembling. He pulled back enough to kiss the top of her head.

"This is all quite touching, but you should know that Jon and Nathan are coming around." Porter's tone was dry. "And there's a fire in sublevel 2."

"The Boom Room?" Brock asked.

Porter nodded. "Looks like Meg was right about the collar having an explosive in it."

"Is Vaughn still working on the stasis chambers?" Brock asked. He stepped away from Meg and his dad.

"I assume so," Porter said.

Brock felt a chill shoot down his spine hearing Porter use 'I' referring to himself, just like when Dexter had earlier. They were handling the change incredibly well, all things considered. Brock wasn't sure what the long-term ramifications would be. He had more immediate concerns.

"None of us has had a chance to tell her about what happened yet," Porter said.

"What?" Brock's stomach seemed to turn to ice. "No one's checked in with her?"

"We've *all* been a little busy." Dexter looked pointedly between Brock and Meg.

Dammit. While he'd been... distracted, everyone around him had been in danger. But then, before Meg had helped Brock settle down, he'd *been* one of the dangers.

"What set off the bomb?" Brock asked.

"I'm not sure." Porter finally seemed to start sharing some of Brock's agitation.

"Check on Vaughn," Brock said. "Now. I'll take care of Jon and Nathan."

Brock turned toward the rousing twins, watching them carefully as they stumbled to their feet. Dexter stood behind Brock, holding a spray bottle of what Brock hoped was whatever they'd used to sedate the new pair in the first place.

"Meg, keep Dad safe," Brock said.

"I will."

He heard them move away, but didn't turn to look. His gaze was locked on the twins'. Well, on one of them at a time.

There'd always been a fighter and a talker—not that

both replicants weren't equally deadly in battle. Normally, Brock could tell which was which by looking at them. The fighters always had a readiness about them, even when they were 'relaxing.' The way they stood, the way they constantly surveyed their environment.

Both replicants in this pair looked like they would love nothing more than to rip out Brock's throat with their fingers. Brock walked right up to them. They stiffened, as if they hadn't expected him to be so bold. Or maybe so reckless.

Damn, had he really been that big when he split? He didn't understand how all three of them had kept so much mass. Even he was bigger than he'd expected. It was just another weird thing about the latest split.

My last split…

The pain was over for him. If he died again, that would be it. He wouldn't have to experience death with anyone else, or know that it wouldn't be his last.

Brock reached out for the link. Buzzing static was in the way, flocking to his thoughts the moment he let down his shields. He quickly snapped them back in place.

Just because he wouldn't feel their deaths—or the splits that he hoped would still come after—that didn't mean he wouldn't go through it with them, be there for them. They needed him, like he needed them. They were family.

Now, we're pack.

His chest tingled as a growl vibrated deep in his throat.

"You want to throw down with me," Brock said. "I know."

The corners of their noses twitched, like they were barely suppressing a snarl. Brock stepped closer, getting right in their faces.

"I don't need a link to know you," Brock said. "It doesn't matter what else I am. I'm still your progenitor. And you will do as I fucking say."

Meg stepped forward, her touch light on his arm. She reached out to Nathan the same way. Jon and Nathan both looked to her, the malice leaving their gazes.

"You should listen to him," Meg said. "Brock cares about you. He can help you."

They might not be linked, but their actions echoed each other perfectly. So did their expressions—and Brock didn't like it. He shifted his weight so that he was between Meg and the pair.

"That doesn't mean I won't kick your asses when you need it," he said.

The corners of their mouths twitched into little proto-smirks.

Behind them, Dad said, "Oh my God."

At the same time, Porter said, "Holy shit."

Brock stepped back from Jon and Nathan before turning so he could keep an eye on them while also seeing what Dad and Porter were upset about. Porter was sitting on a stool in front of a monitor with Dad hovering over his shoulder, partly blocking the view. All Brock could make out was a bunch of wriggling brown... somethings.

"What the hell is that?" Brock asked.

Dad turned around, his face ashen around the bandages. "Trolls. Hundreds of them. Thousands, maybe."

"Where?" Brock's skin was crawling. The monitor was completely filled with the writhing things. What were they doing?

"They tunneled through the walls of the cave." Porter's voice sounded strained. "This is supposed to be a view of the ship."

Brock's skin felt electrified, his fingertips tingling and his teeth aching. He pushed against the change, focusing on what needed to be done—in his *human* form.

"Did you reach Vaughn?" Brock asked.

Porter shook his head. "No response. The feeds from inside the ship have been cut off. I have no idea how."

Brock dug his fingers into his palm. He had to keep it together. Tessa was in there. And Vaughn and Marcus.

"Ops," Brock bellowed. "Porter, get Meg and Dad to ops now. I want every monitor fired up with live feeds and footage starting ten minutes before the blast. There's no way it's a coincidence."

Porter stood and walked Dad out of the room. Meg lingered, though. Brock wasn't surprised.

"I'll hit the armory." Dexter was already heading for the door. "Get us all real clothes, weapons."

"Take the twins with you," Brock said.

Dexter paused. "You sure that's a good idea?"

"Yeah." Brock turned toward Jon and Nathan, and said, "Our family—your family—is in danger. We need you. Are you with us?"

Jon and Nathan stared at him for a moment. At least this time they didn't seem to be challenging him. They turned to the door and headed out into the hallway.

"I'll take that as a 'yes,'" Dexter said.

Brock wished he could send Dexter a silent warning to watch his back. Instead, Brock nodded his head toward the hall and said, "Be careful. And grab me a set of Marcus's spare clothes, would you?"

"Built for a werewolf on the go." Dexter smirked. "On my way."

Brock turned to Meg. She was staring at the monitor.

"There are so many of them," she said. "Are we really supposed to be able to see the ship?"

"The view's never been that great, but Vaughn has cameras hooked up to constantly monitor the area. The ship is mostly buried. *Was* mostly buried, anyway."

He leaned closer to the screen. The trolls were covering every surface, clawing frantically. Some of them were actually killing each other in their frenzy to…

"They're digging out the ship." Brock grabbed Meg's hand and pulled her from the room. Porter had left the door to ops open. Brock paused before entering. "Porter, update my security readings. I need to be able to access everything."

"On it." Porter entered the necessary commands, one of the monitors changing to a view of what must be Brock's official picture. For once, Brock didn't flinch when he saw his face.

He put his hand on the biometric scanner, then leaned forward to update his optical record. Getting locked out of a system or area he needed to get to could be fatal with the scale of the attack they were facing. The scanners beeped and flashed green.

"Meg, too," Porter said. "Vaughn created a record for Meg already. She just hadn't enabled it, yet."

Brock stepped aside so Meg could copy what he'd done. He glanced into ops. Seeing Porter at Vaughn's station was just wrong. The moment the scanner indicated it was done reading Meg's data, Brock put his arm around her and ushered her into the next room. They stopped in front of the monitors.

"They're digging out the ship," Brock said.

"I came to the same conclusion." Porter nodded toward a monitor showing previous footage.

Silver metal gleamed in the lights they constantly kept on in the cave. The fins on the back of the ship were dark green, and instead of the round rocket-thrusters Brock had expected when he first saw the ship, there were huge, flat black panels that Vaughn said would serve the same purpose.

"That's it?" Meg sounded surprised. "From the hologram I saw back in the dining room, I just thought it'd be more…"

"It's a lot more impressive on the inside," Porter said. "Only the back of the ship was ever exposed. Since we couldn't access parts of the ship, Vaughn had to extrapolate what she thought the rest of it was like."

"There's a hatch here that we use for access." Brock pointed to the hatch. "It's nearly invisible if you don't know to look for it and it only opens for Vaughn."

"How are we going to get in?" Meg asked.

"We'll figure that out after we get these things cleared from the area." Brock watched the monitor carefully as the first trolls appeared. "When was the blast?"

"Seconds before they showed up," Porter said. "The first dust you see falling from the cave's roof is from the explosion. Then, this happened."

Trolls started dropping through the camera's field of view. The first ones to hit the ground let out hideous screeches. Some died instantly, but others writhed on the ground, twitching broken limbs. The next wave had a softer landing. They were falling faster than the dead could vaporize, until the floor of the cavern was completely covered.

"What would make them do that?" Meg said.

She turned away from the monitor, burying her face

against Brock's chest. He wrapped his arms around her, but kept his focus on the screen. Tried to, anyway.

The camera cut out.

"What happened?" Brock asked.

Meg glanced over her shoulder. He led her closer to Porter, till they were standing right behind him.

"Just a minute." Porter tapped a few commands and a different view appeared on the monitor. "They took out all the cameras. We only have one left."

"The one on the elevator tube," Brock said.

Dexter, Jon, and Nathan filed into the room. The newest twins stood along the far wall, stances wide and arms loose at their sides. They were decked out with swords, stun weapons, and what looked like grenade belts crossing their huge chests. In the full Blades gear, they looked damn imposing, but Brock didn't let himself feel the slightest bit of intimidation. Showing any weakness would probably lead to another fight, and they didn't have time for that.

He forced himself to feel pride instead. This was his pack. If Roy ever dared to show his face, it'd be Brock's turn to rip it off. And that would be if Roy was lucky. Jon and Nathan didn't look like they'd be that gentle.

Brock smiled at them, his teeth bared.

They smiled back.

"Nice to see you three are coming to an understanding." Dexter stretched out his arm and flicked his wrist, extending the wand of one of Vaughn's flamethrowers. He checked it over, then retracted it. "Do we have a plan?"

"They only took out the cameras mounted on the cave walls," Brock said.

Porter cocked his head to the side. The familiar gesture helped Brock feel a little bit better.

"The camera is embedded in the elevator shaft," Porter said. "They can't claw through the metal."

"And if they can't get through the composite Vaughn designed based on the ship, there's no way they can get through the real thing." Brock reached out and squeezed Porter's shoulder. "We have a little time."

"Don't count on it." Dexter pointed at the monitor he was watching. "The collar blew the Boom Room and took out the entire second sublevel. This isn't just trolls expanding their territory. It's a calculated attack, and whoever's behind it has access to technology that can breach Vaughn's inventions. We don't know what else they can do."

"As if we don't know who's behind it." Brock felt his shoulders hunch, his spine cracking and popping as he fought the urge to change. It was a hell of a lot easier than trying to hold off a split or control someone else's body remotely.

"Roy," Dexter said.

Porter shook his head. "I've never heard of a dweller using another group like this. And the scale of it is unprecedented. How is he controlling the trolls?"

"How is he blocking the signal from the ship?" Dexter's tone made it clear he wasn't looking for an answer. "And how did he get his hands on the tech that took out the Boom Room and let him spy on us?"

When Brock had calmed himself, he said, "Those are questions for another time. We know what he can do. Let's show him what *we* can do."

He turned to Jon and Nathan. "We were connected when you first emerged. I know you understand words, even if you're not talking. The others knew everything I did when they formed, including how to fight. Are you ready for this?"

Jon grinned and pulled one of the grenades from its holster. He looked pointedly at the monitor still showing the elevator-cam's view of the ship.

"Nice," Brock said. He wasn't sure how the link worked, whether his replicants were formed with all of his knowledge or... downloaded it through their link after emerging. With them not talking, he'd been worried. Honestly, he still was.

"This is my fault." Meg's voice trembled. "I'm the reason everyone is in danger. I brought the collar. Roy sent me here to destroy you."

"Meg—" Brock started to speak, but Dexter cut him off.

"You're right," Dexter said.

Brock snarled as he stepped toward Dexter. "What the fuck is wrong with you?"

Meg moved between them, one hand on Brock's chest, holding him back. "Brock, no."

"Roy did send Meg here to destroy us." Dexter looked at Meg as he continued. "And you fought off his brainwashing and the fear of what he'd do to you if you helped us. You trusted us when we took off your collar. Even tried to protect us. And then you had the guts to save Brock."

Dexter shrugged one shoulder, smirking as always. "And you helped 'stabilize' him afterwards. Which couldn't have been easy, with him being such an annoying prick."

Meg actually laughed.

"Language," Dad said.

Dexter's grin widened. Brock was going to have to thank Dexter later—after they'd all made it out of this. And after Brock kicked Dexter's ass for that 'annoying' crack.

Dad walked over to them and put his good hand on Meg's shoulder. "Brock's vitals were fading and we were scared to death of what the shock of going into stasis would do to him. They were slipping away from me, my sons. And you brought them back."

Meg let out a choked laugh, her eyes filled with tears. She rested her hand on Dad's, smiling.

"You're all so sweet," she said. "But I wasn't looking to be reassured."

Jon and Nathan both took a step away from the wall, eyes locked on her. She nodded toward them.

"I led Roy here," she said. "He used me to learn what he needed to attack you. To destroy part of your—of *our*—home."

"And?" Dexter said.

Her lips curled back from her sharpening teeth, her eyes glowing bright. "And now I'm going to make him pay."

Chapter Twenty-Two

Standing behind Nathan at the base of the emergency access shaft for the cave, Meg had trouble believing how much her life had changed. She was part of a pack that was unlike anything she'd imagined, yet was beyond anything she'd ever wished for—and she was mated to the leader of the Blades.

She glanced over at Brock in his full uniform. His clothing smelled faintly of Marcus, but Brock's scent was already working into the fabric. The black material strained to hold Brock's form, showing off his physique. He wore a pair of swords strapped to his back and the pockets of his cargo pants looked like they all held surprises.

Her outfit was similar, and had a bit of Tessa's scent. They hadn't given Meg equipment, though. From what she'd seen of the gadgets they had geared up with, she wouldn't know how to use them anyway.

She would learn.

The life she wanted was within reach. She just had to survive fighting off a couple thousand trolls to have it.

I can do this. We *can do this.*

Dexter tapped his watch a few times, then held up his arm so everyone could see the holographic display coming out of it. The image showed the other side of the door, highlighting the trolls' heat signatures. Most of the cave was red.

The others had been vague about the plan before heading out. Even without their link, they all seemed to operate on the same wavelength. It was probably a side effect of sharing their thoughts for so long.

Brock had insisted that Porter stay in ops with Eli to protect him and to monitor the situation. Meg had worried that Brock would try to get her to stay behind as well, but he hadn't mentioned it. She was glad he was taking her bloodthirsty promise of retribution seriously.

Now that she was moments away from her first real fight, she wondered if she'd done the right thing. Not because she was scared, even though she was. She was inexperienced. She didn't want anyone getting hurt trying to protect her or because she messed up.

"How are we going to get past them?" Meg asked.

"We're not getting past them," Dexter said. "We're taking them out."

"All of them?" Her voice rose higher than she wanted. She worried that the trolls might have heard her, but the others didn't seem concerned. The small stairwell they were in was probably soundproofed.

"Yes, all of them." Dexter pulled off the grenade belt he

was wearing. When he nodded to the others, Jon and Nathan did the same, then handed theirs to Dexter.

"You didn't think we'd only bring swords to a bomb-fight, did you?" Dexter asked.

Meg arched an eyebrow at him.

"Like bringing a knife to a gunfight?" Dexter sighed. "Nevermind. I blame any lame banter on my not having access to all those extra brains."

Meg patted Dexter's back. "It's okay. At least you're still pretty."

Brock snorted loudly. Huge grins spread across the new twins' faces. Even Dexter laughed.

It was strange to her that they could be laughing before going into a situation that was likely to get them all killed. Meg felt a sort of giddy anticipation, along with the strongest sense of camaraderie she'd ever experienced. Even if they didn't survive, she'd go down fighting, with her pack at her side. Which reminded her...

"Shouldn't I have a weapon?" Meg asked.

Brock shook his head. "You're not trained. It's best for you to use your natural weapons and trust your dweller instincts."

"You want me to change," she said.

"That's the best option," Brock said. "But only if you need to. I'm hoping we can get into the ship without that happening."

"What about you?" she asked.

He grinned at her. "Whoever is behind this can't know that I've been colonized. I'm going to do my best to keep that as a surprise." He stepped closer to her, cupping her elbows gently.

"If this is the point where you tell me I don't have to go out there—" she began.

Brock laughed. "I have a feeling insulting you like that would be more dangerous than stepping out into the cave alone and unarmed. No, I just wanted to do this."

He leaned in and kissed her.

Heat pooled in her belly, fire racing along her limbs. She buried her fingers in his hair and held him close. Before things could escalate, someone cleared their throat. Loudly. They broke off the kiss. Dexter was staring at them.

"Actually, this is the point when we chuck a couple dozen of Vaughn's little toys into the cave and let them incinerate every bit of organic matter outside of the ship." He held up the belts of grenades and jiggled them.

"How are they going to clear out the whole cave?" she asked.

"They've been programmed to detonate on split-second delays," Dexter said. "The first one to go will distribute the others through the cave."

"Will we be safe in here?" The door looked sturdy, but she still wondered.

Dexter smirked at her. "As long as the seals hold."

"Great," she said. "What about the others? We don't know for sure where Vaughn, Tessa, and Marcus are."

"We still haven't heard from them." Porter's voice sounded through her earpiece. "But I'm sure they're in the ship. It would've been too risky for Vaughn to wake them up from stasis. And if she left the ship…"

Meg didn't need Porter to finish his sentence to know what he was thinking. If Vaughn had left the ship, she was already dead.

From everything they'd told Meg, the ship was the safest place to be. There was no way anyone could have made it inside. Somehow, the thought didn't comfort her.

Brock stepped away and took the belts. "I'll get them as close to the ship as I can."

"We'll be monitoring the results and let you know when it's clear…er," Porter said.

Dexter gripped Meg's elbow a lot more gently than he had the first night she'd arrived. He steered her to one of the corners of the room along the same wall that held the door. It seemed like they didn't have as much faith in the seals holding as they were letting on.

"Brock," she said.

Brock smiled at her. "Just a precaution. But, if you don't mind…"

He looked at Jon and Nathan and spun his finger in a circle. The pair headed toward Meg and Dexter.

"One more thing," Brock said. "We don't know if any

of you will still split so… nobody die, okay?"

"Let's hear it for our fearless leader," Porter said.

Dexter laughed. "A rousing speech if ever I've heard one."

Meg's nerves skyrocketed. "This is going to work, right?"

"It should take out most of them," Dexter said. "We'll be able to handle the rest."

She would have been more reassured if he didn't push her back against the wall and then stand close right in front of her. Jon and Nathan put their arms on either side of Meg and Dexter, further shielding her—with their bodies.

"Brock," she growled his name through gritted teeth.

"Everything will be fine," Brock said. She heard a click, then he said, "Grenades are active."

"Three," Porter said.

She felt the air shift as the door opened, but couldn't see past the wall of man-flesh trapping her against the wall.

"Two." Porter's count continued.

The door slammed shut. Brock's scent was closer suddenly. She glanced up to see a look of surprise on both Jon and Nathan's faces as Brock shielded their bodies with his as best he could.

"One."

Dexter smiled at her and mouthed, "Boom."

The noise reached her first—a string of explosions that

made her ears sting. Then the shockwave arrived, thumping against her internal organs. She staggered forward as the wall shook behind her. She and Dexter held on to each other, struggling to keep their balance. Brock, Jon, and Nathan were clustered close by, holding each other upright.

"What the hell was that?" Brock said. "I thought those were all thermal grenades."

Dexter smirked. "I threw in a couple of concussive grenades, just in case. You're not the only one who likes surprises."

Brock's eyes glowed brighter, his lips curling back from his teeth. He took a step toward Dexter, but Meg intercepted him.

"Save it for out there," she said.

Brock drew the two swords strapped to his back. Dexter released the wand for his flamethrower into his left hand, drawing one of his swords with his right.

"You planning on joining us?" Dexter asked, looking at Jon and Nathan.

They glanced at each other, then drew their weapons.

"Swords are best against trolls," Brock said. "Cut off their limbs if they grab you from the ground and leave Dexter to burn whatever's left in their tunnels. For kills, decapitation only. Last thing we need is some flaming trolls running around trying to set us on fire. Meg, stay near me."

She nodded, feeling helpless. Again. She was sick of it.

"Hang on a minute." She shook her hands, then took a deep breath and let it out, focusing her attention.

Just my hands. Just my fingers.

She willed her claws to push out of her fingers, her nails lengthening, sharpening. Her fingertips tingled. She held them up to see, smiling at the result.

"That's my girl." Brock was smiling at her, a feral gleam adding to the gold and blue glow of his eyes. She smiled back.

"FYI, most of the trolls were incinerated by the blasts," Porter said. "I'm still reading several dozen heat signatures, though. They must have been shielded by the ship."

"Can't you see them?" Brock asked.

"The topography of the cave has changed," Porter said. "And before you blame Dexter, it wasn't the concussion grenades. The trolls have been redecorating. The camera angle from the elevator is low and can't see over their rubble piles."

"Great," Brock said.

Porter went on. "They'll pick up on your location quickly once you're in the cave. You're going to have to fight your way through."

"Vaughn told me Blades always have to be ready to fight," Meg said. "I'm ready."

"Then let's not keep the trolls waiting." Dexter opened

the door.

They hurried out into the cave. Meg was surprised at how well-lit the area was.

"Why didn't they take out the lights?" she whispered. "Trolls hate light."

"I think it's coming from the ship," Brock said. "Vaughn had it set up so the running lights were on. I don't remember them being this bright before, though."

Dexter reached the top of the nearest pile of loose rocks and dirt in front of them and stopped short.

"What the fuck?" He turned back to them. "The lights are brighter now because most of them were blocked."

Meg scrambled to his side, along with Brock and the others. They all stood still, staring down at the cave before them—at the ship that *filled* it.

The tailpiece she'd seen on the monitors was only one of three. An identical section of thrusters was just opposite it, and an even bigger section sat centered above those two. The ship stretched on, at least as long as two football fields and twice as wide. Blue, green, and gold lights pulsed along its every surface like fireflies on crack, along with steady white lights that illuminated the cave as well as if the sun was shining overhead.

"I thought you said it was buried," she said.

"It was." Brock's voice was barely above a whisper.

"Our uninvited guests have been busy," Dexter said.

Jon pointed toward the side of the ship with his sword.

At the very front, a jagged tear cut through the bottom of the ship.

"Oh shit," Brock said. "The hull has a breach."

It only took Meg a moment to realize why he was so panicked.

"They can get inside," she yelled.

Brock was already moving. He leapt down from the hill, breaking into a run the moment his feet hit the ground. Meg tried to follow after, but the loose rocks made her stumble. Nathan caught her flailing arm and righted her. They slid down the side of the rubble together.

As soon as she was on stable ground, she tore after Brock, letting herself run as fast as she could. She'd never cut loose before. The rocks blurred around her. She skidded to a stop beside Brock, reaching the breach right when he did. They both looked back to see Dexter, Jon, and Nathan far behind. Dozens of trolls started pouring out from under the ship.

"We've got this," Dexter yelled. "Go on." He lit a flare and waved it over his head, screaming, "Come and get us."

"Brock," Meg said.

Brock looked torn. He glanced between the opening above them that led into the ship and back to his brothers, then shook his head sharply. The trolls had surrounded the others. Bursts of flame and flashes of gleaming metal were all Meg could see of the trio.

"Porter, monitor heat signatures in the cave and let me

know if they're in trouble," Brock said.

"It won't be easy to tell them apart from the trolls, but I'll do my best." Porter's honesty was hardly reassuring.

Brock reached out to Meg. "Come on."

She took his hand and nodded. They leapt up to the opening together, landing inside the belly of the ship.

Chapter Twenty-Three

Brock had never been in this section of the ship. No one had walked these halls in thousands of years—except for Roy, probably. Vaughn's diagrams barely covered an eighth of the actual ship's size. She'd said she had to extrapolate based on the parts she could reach, but this...

She'd be so excited to see this.

Brock's jaw felt like it was about to cramp from how hard he was grinding his teeth together. Vaughn *would* be excited to see this. They were going to find her, and she would be fine when they did.

"Where are the stasis chambers?" Meg asked.

"Other end of the ship."

Brock took her hand in his to lead her deeper into the ship, but she froze in place, pulling him to a stop.

"What is it?" he asked.

"The scent. You were right. It's Roy."

Brock took a few short breaths through his nose. It took him a moment, but he finally picked out what must be Roy's scent, acrid and musky. Brock wanted to shake his head to get the smell out—as if that would work—but they needed to be able to track Roy through the ship.

"Then let's go kick his ass," Brock said.

Meg nodded, but her lips were pulled in a thin line and her brow was furrowed.

"Are you ready for this?" he asked.

"I am. I just... Roy scares me."

Brock leaned in, smiling in a way that showed all his teeth. "And I scare Roy."

She actually laughed. "That's true. You always have."

Brock nipped her neck, then kissed it. She sucked in a breath, but pulled away.

"If you start touching me like that, I'm going to forget we're in a life-or-death situation," she said.

"Werewolf libidos are so much more intense than I realized. Now I get why Marcus and Tessa are always running off together." He shuddered and shook his head. "And thinking of that has effectively extinguished the moment."

"I've never been happier to be mindblind," she said. "I don't want their 'activities' to interfere with ours."

"Me either."

Meg's smile faded. "But wait. Are you mindblind, too? If Roy can read you, he'll know we're coming."

"I haven't heard any thoughts but my own."

Brock couldn't believe how much that bothered him. How lonely it felt. He'd dreamt of having his mind to himself without having to extend any effort. Now that his dream had come true, he almost wished he had the link back. He missed it.

"I suppose you do have a lot of practice keeping people out of your head," she said.

"I do."

Keeping up his shields was second nature. What if he was blocking Roy without realizing it? When Brock had tried to reach out to his replicants, he'd felt a kind of buzzing. Could that have been his new dweller nature trying to establish a link with Roy, Marcus, and Tessa?

If it was a new link emerging and Roy tried to fuck with Brock's mind through it, he'd be in for a shock. After dealing with his replicants for so long, Brock could do a hell of a lot more than block other people's thoughts.

His lips peeled away from his teeth in a broad grin. This was going to be fun.

"Come on." He tugged on Meg's hand, stepping through the only open door and pulling her after him. "Let's give Roy something to *really* be afraid of."

They were standing in a long corridor. There were walls spaced periodically through it that had large openings they could easily step through. Brock bet that those could be sealed in the event of hull breaches. Why were they all standing open now?

The corridor itself was gunmetal gray, with clear walls on either side. Every dozen or so feet, there was a large rectangle etched into the wall, made of the same transparent material. Even without the access panels attached to the wall next to them, it was obvious they were doors. The rooms beyond, though…

Each was small, with clear walls separating them. The only solid metal walls were opposite the doors, letting them see into every corner. Some rooms had benches built into the walls, varying in sizes. A couple even had basins and what could be toilets.

"Is it just me, or does this kind of look like the pit?" Brock asked.

Meg's eyes were wide and glowing. Her grip on his hand would have broken it if she hadn't turned him. She was so close that she kept bumping into him as they walked.

Yeah, she saw the resemblance. He squeezed her hand, trying to reassure her.

"These could be security panels," he said. "If they were meant for palm prints, whatever ran this ship had much longer fingers than humans."

"They could be designed for a variety of life forms," Meg murmured.

"Yeah."

They reached a corridor that bisected the hallway. Roy's scent clearly led left.

"This ship is huge," Meg said. "Roy could ambush us easily."

"We don't have time to get lost. We have to follow his scent."

"Too bad the hatch won't open for us," Meg said. "We could have ambushed him, maybe."

"You're right, the hatch won't open for anyone but Vaughn." Brock's heart felt a little lighter.

"You say that like it's a good thing."

"It is. Vaughn explored every inch of the ship she could. She knew there were some parts that she couldn't get access to, but didn't realize how much was out of her reach."

"And that makes you happy because…"

"Because, Vaughn could never get from the sections she's been working in to these. Which means that if Roy thinks he's going to get to Vaughn—or Tessa and Marcus —by going this way, he's wrong. If Vaughn couldn't get through, no one can."

"I hope you're right."

Brock hoped so, too.

"The interior doors will open to anyone, though?" she asked.

"In the section I used to live in, yes. They don't have digital code panels, but the ship already had biometric scanners for reading palm prints next to several of the doors. Vaughn programmed them to recognize us after she managed to hack into the system."

"Then how did Roy make it into this corridor? The first thing we did was cross through an open door."

The relief Brock felt vanished in a fresh wave of dread.

Where the hell had Roy gotten access to this kind of tech?

Even if there was another ship, as Vaughn had theorized, there still had to be someone to figure out how things worked and make the gadgets and controls Roy was using. Another ship was useless without another Vaughn.

Brock shivered at the thought.

"We're going to figure that all out later," Brock said. "After we take care of Roy."

Brock picked up the pace, running as quickly as he could through the maze of hallways without losing Roy's scent. They hadn't made it far when they turned a corner and both skidded to a stop.

One of the cell walls in front of them had been smashed. Clear pebbles were strewn over the floor. The cell itself was triple the size of most of the others they'd passed.

What chilled the blood in Brock's veins were the enormous claw marks covering the floor, ceiling, and transparent wall of the opposite chamber. It looked like something had broken out of its cell and gone berserk in the hallway, scratching everything in reach. The thing had to have been as big as a T-rex.

There were scorch marks on the metal as well as claw marks—some on the wall of the creature's chamber, but most out in the hall on the floor and ceiling. The dispersal pattern seemed similar to some of the Blades' plasma weapons.

The hatch that led to the next section of corridor had been stretched and crushed, deep finger marks bent into the metal where something had pushed it apart. Brock and Meg walked forward slowly, staring up into a giant hole in the ceiling. From what he could see, the level above was all white metal, like the main sublevel of the ranch.

What the hell could have done that? And was it still in the ship?

It couldn't be. The ship had crashed thousands of years ago. Nothing could have survived that long. At least, he hoped not.

Edgar—his biological father—had said that he was one of the original passengers on the ship. Brock had thought it was a ploy to make Edgar seem more powerful. It had to be.

Whatever had done that damage must have died long ago, whether it was trapped on the ship or managed to escaped into Earth's ecosystem like the other organisms that created dwellers.

Just one more thing to worry about.

"I really don't like this," Meg said.

"Neither do I. You're better at tracking scents than I am. Are you picking up anything?"

She shook her head. "Only Roy."

"Let me know if that changes."

They started to run again. Brock could feel his heart pounding in his chest, his senses hypervigilant.

"Wait." Meg slowed, then headed back to a small open door they had run past. It was barely more than human-sized. "The trail goes in here."

They entered the small room. Lights flashed bright blue on the wall in a weird script. Below them, a trap door in the floor stood open.

"Blue is good, right?" Meg said.

It felt more like a warning to Brock. "For us, maybe. For the aliens that built this ship? I don't know."

He stood above the large open square in the floor and looked down. The area beneath him was gunmetal gray.

"If Roy can open the doors, he can get to the section where Vaughn was working," Brock said.

He didn't bother with the ladder that led down from the hole. It was only about a twenty foot drop, and he'd seen werewolves clear more. He tucked his elbows to his sides and jumped through the trap door, landing in a crouch below. Wires hung from the ceiling, and he could feel the familiar vibration of the engines nearby.

As soon as he stood and stepped out of the way, Meg landed next to him. She stayed close to the floor, glancing all around for a moment before standing. Brock pulled her against his side, wrapping his arms around her for a quick hug.

"I won't let anything happen to you," Brock said. "Remember?"

She let out a breath through pursed lips. "I know. I

just… There's a lot I'm trying to sort through. I was with Roy for so long, just the two of us."

For a moment, Brock wondered if she was having second thoughts about killing Roy. That would be a big problem, because Brock was really looking forward to ripping Roy's head off. Her next words reassured him and made him more determined than ever to make Roy pay.

Her voice was small as she said, "I don't know how to not be afraid of him."

Brock held her tighter. "We get through this, and you'll never have to be afraid of him again. Just focus on what you're moving toward, not what you're running away from."

She let out a short laugh, clutching the back of his shirt. "How do you always know exactly what I need to hear?"

He leaned back and hooked his finger under her chin, lifting her gaze to his. "I'm your mate, remember?"

"If you kiss me, I won't be able to stop us this time," she said. Her eyes were glowing bright.

Brock laughed. "Then let's get this over with."

They held each other's hands as they followed the trail of Roy's scent. It didn't take long before they stepped through an open door that led into a section of the ship Brock recognized.

"Dammit, he made it through." Brock hurried toward the room that held the stasis chambers.

Meg pulled against his hand briefly, pausing in front of

an open door. He glanced into the room and froze.

"Your scent," she said. "It's strongest here."

"This was my room."

It *had* been, anyway. Roy had destroyed it.

The bed was in pieces, fragments of the plastic frame littering the floor and embedded in the machinery that had been tracking Brock's vitals. It looked like Roy had stabbed the equipment with metal he'd snapped off from the bed. The mattress was shredded, bits of foam scattered everywhere. Dad's chair had been crushed like a soda can somebody stepped on.

Brock took a deep breath through his nose. "I don't smell any blood."

Meg sniffed, then nodded. "Neither do I."

"He came here first. And this had to have made a hell of a lot of noise."

Meg smiled. "Vaughn knew he was coming."

Brock nodded. "Let's go."

The stasis chamber room was around another corner. Now that Brock had a better idea of the ship's design, he was pretty sure this labyrinthine section of the ship was part of the engine room. The door to the chamber was shut. Brock didn't let that reassure him. Roy's scent led straight to the door.

Brock had purposely avoided this room. He'd figured he would be spending enough time in the pods within to last a lifetime. Now, he wished he'd checked it out. He paused, closing his eyes as he took a few deep breaths, willing his body to calm.

"Are you okay?" Meg asked.

"Yes. Just focusing. We don't know what's on the other side of that door."

He reached into one of the pockets of his cargo pants and pulled out what would probably be their best weapon —a pair of sunglasses that Vaughn had designed for Marcus to keep people from seeing the glow of his eyes. Surprise could always turn the tide of battle.

Brock put on the glasses. "And now, neither will Roy. Open the door."

"How?"

"Just place your palm on the rectangle." He nodded toward the biometric scanner.

"I have access to the ship?"

"You're a Blade now."

She cast a somber look at him and nodded. "I won't betray your trust."

Brock smiled at her. "I know."

She only hesitated for a moment before reaching out to the scanner. The door opened with a soft *whoosh*. Brock stepped through. He felt Meg follow, staying close behind him.

Roy was standing with his back to the door. Naked.

He was smaller than Brock expected. Tall and lanky, but corded with muscles. Pale scars peppered his back and legs—claw marks from his transformation. Roy turned toward them slowly, his eyes already glowing bright gold. He had pale brown hair that brushed his shoulders. His lips peeled away from his teeth in a snarl.

Brock really hoped Vaughn's glasses were working, because from the way his own eyes were tingling, they must be as bright as Roy's. Something deep in his gut told Brock to rip off Roy's head in response to the challenge of his stare. Brock pushed it away.

He recognized this man. He remembered...

He remembered Roy disemboweling him, digging out his heart, ripping off his face. How many other deaths was Roy responsible for?

"Another replicant," Roy snarled. "How many times do I have to fucking kill you before you *stay dead?*"

The only reason the replicants had been killed was that Roy had caught them off guard. He always had something up his sleeve—even when he was naked. He stepped aside, revealing Tessa standing behind him.

Oh shit.

She stared at Brock over Roy's shoulder, her expression dazed. Behind her, five huge stasis pods lined the wall. Well, four and a half. Vaughn had been busy. Parts for the fifth one were stacked on the floor.

The doors to the pods were mostly chrome, with a small window where the person's face would be. Brock could see Marcus suspended in one of the chambers. Blue lights shimmered in vertical lines all around him and his hair was floating around his face as if he was in zero-G.

Only one of the pods was open, revealing the dense white cushioning that lined the inside of the chamber. It must have been Tessa's. How the hell had Roy managed to bring her out of it?

Vaughn, Dad, and Porter weren't sure how the pods would affect the people in them. Otherwise, they would have put Brock in one weeks ago. Porter and Dad were supposed to carefully monitor Marcus and Tessa as they woke up. No wonder Tessa looked so disoriented. That and the fact that Roy was probably fucking with her mind again. It was time for Brock to dish out some of the same.

"You must be Roy." Brock smiled. "It's such a pleasure to meet you *face to face*."

He fought to keep himself from growling out the last words.

"Brock?" Tessa sounded half-asleep, but the ghost of a smile played over her lips.

Roy's sneer faded. He grabbed Tessa's shoulder as she took a stumbling step forward, then wrapped his arm around her waist.

"Is he really, love?" Roy asked.

"My brother," Tessa mumbled.

Roy put his lips right against her ear and whispered, "He is not your pack. I am."

Brock's skin started to crawl. He could feel his claws

trying to extend, his teeth sharpening. He used every ounce of self-control to keep his shoulders from bunching.

No tells. No werewolf body language. No changing.

Yet.

With Tessa in the picture, surprise was their only advantage. She could do a hell of a lot of damage with her cybernetic hand. Why had Roy left Marcus in stasis, though?

Roy kissed the side of Tessa's head, and said, "Go take care of the curator for me."

The curator? Vaughn was there?

Brock felt the buzzing push against his mind, like the room was thick with static. Tessa winced, then turned toward one of the empty stasis chambers. She gripped the side of it with her cybernetic arm and pulled, but nothing happened.

"Break the window," Roy said. "Just like you did to that prison cell where they held our omega."

Roy had seen that? Of course he had. He didn't even need Meg's collar. He'd been linked to Marcus and Tessa. Feeding her violent urges, telling her to kill.

The fact that Roy had left Marcus in his stasis chamber made Brock wonder about how Roy actually used his telepathic link to control his pack. It was possible that he had power over them because he was the alpha. Or it could be because they didn't actually know what was going on. If he was tricking them—deceiving them, like he'd deceived Meg—maybe Brock could get through to Tessa. Roy seemed more a manipulator than a leader.

Even without a link, Roy had twisted Meg's self-perception into a knot that had taken everyone's help to untangle. How much worse would it be hearing him whisper his thoughts in their own minds?

"Brock," Roy said. "I thought you were dying."

Brock shrugged, feigning a casual demeanor. "I got over it."

Tessa started pounding on the glass window of the stasis chamber where Vaughn was presumably hiding. Brock expected Vaughn to shock Tessa any second. She didn't. Or she couldn't.

The thought tested the limits of Brock's control. Carey might already be gone. Brock wasn't about to lose anyone else. His muscles cramped with the need to change, to tear through Roy's skull and dig out the brain he was using against Brock's family. Against *Brock's* pack.

Roy wasn't the alpha anymore. He just didn't know it yet.

"You can come out now, Meg," Roy said. "I know you're there."

Brock felt Meg's hands on his back, trembling as she grabbed the fabric of his shirt and held on. She stepped closer, her heat seeping into him.

"I'm not mad." Roy's tone had become cloyingly sweet. "I'm proud of you. You've done so well. Come to me and I'll reward you." He held out his arms as if he expected her to run into his embrace.

Meg moved out from behind Brock. He could see her body shaking, her eyes wide and skin pale. She took a step toward Roy.

"Meg," Brock said. "You don't have to obey him anymore. You get to choose, remember?"

Roy laughed. "You don't understand us at all, *traitor*. Meg follows the natural order. Dwellers do not turn on each other. We work together. And werewolves always follow their alpha—even mindblind little bitches like this one."

It was too much.

Brock lowered his head. The reflected glow from his eyes obscured his vision. The sound of Tessa pounding on the window covered Brock's spine popping.

"You think I don't understand being a leader?" Brock unbuckled his weapon's harness, letting the sheathed swords slide down his back. He held them out to Meg and smiled at her when she took them. "It's not just about control. It's about worthiness to lead."

"You think you're more worthy than me?" Roy said.

"I *know* I am." Brock laughed. "I get why you left Marcus in the chamber. Pack hierarchy is based on how hard you fight when you're turned? Even he has more scars than you."

Roy growled.

Perfect. He was as easy to bait as Brock expected.

"You're a fucking coward," Brock said. "Preying on the people you were supposed to protect."

"Like you've been using your replicants?" Roy said.

The words stung. Brock didn't let them push him over the edge, though.

"Yeah, I used to control my brothers to get them to do what I wanted," Brock said. "But at least I have the excuse that I was trying to help them fit in with society. To teach them how to help people and not hurt them."

"You made them kill other dwellers," Roy said.

Brock nodded. "Hunters, too. *Human* hunters—if they were killing dwellers indiscriminately. And I didn't just mess with my brothers' heads. When I wanted to, I would override control of their body. Use it as my own. It's a neat trick, once you learn how to do it. It has a price tag, though."

Brock reached up and tore off his shirt, tossing the shredded fabric on the floor. Roy's eyes widened as he took in the scars that covered Brock's torso. Brock just chuckled as he kicked off his shoes.

"All these years, I've acted as judge, jury, and executioner," Brock said. "That's who I was. Who I've always been. As to *what* I am? Well, not even I am sure of that anymore. But I promise you one thing."

Brock reached up and pulled off his glasses. Blue and gold light reflected back at him from their surface, casting his hand in an eerie green glow. He tossed the shades aside as he looked up at Roy and smiled, running his tongue over his lengthening fangs.

"I am not the easy target you expected," Brock said.

Chapter Twenty-Four

"What the hell did you do, Meg?" Roy's eyes blazed with fury.

Meg had seen that look too many times to mistake it. Always right before a beating.

That wasn't what scared her, though. Brock was with her. He'd do anything to protect her. Anything. And *that* was absolutely terrifying.

She wouldn't let him die for her.

Roy vs. Brock was a no brainer. Brock would win. But adding Tessa to the mix changed everything.

Brock would pull his punches. And between Tessa's cybernetic arm and Roy's influence over her, Brock wouldn't stand a chance.

Communications were cut off. Without being able to warn the others, Roy could kill Vaughn, wake up Marcus and use Tessa to get him to comply. Three werewolves against the three replicants outside… She wasn't sure who would win. She had to protect her pack—her real pack. And she had an idea of how to do it.

Brock wasn't going to like it, though.

"You told me to stay close to Brock by any means

necessary," Meg said.

"So you turned him?" Roy yelled. "You're the fucking omega. You don't get to turn people. How did you even —"

"I didn't," Meg said. "There's no way an omega could turn the head of a hydra."

"Then explain this abomination." Roy gestured toward Brock.

"Brock split again," Meg said. "He made two new replicants. I was able to infect this version of him right afterwards."

It was a misleading truth that she knew Roy would take the way he wanted to.

"What the hell are you talking about?" Brock said.

Meg took another step closer to Roy, even though every part of her was screaming to stay near Brock. She knew it was what Roy would expect, and she needed him off guard.

"Another fucking replicant," Roy said.

"Meg, what are you doing?" Brock turned to Roy. "I *am* Brock."

Meg shook her head. "I know you believe that." She turned back to Roy. "He's confused. He'll make a great fighter for the pack, but right now, we need to get to Brock before the others can move him to safety. I can help you get to him."

"Stop it," Brock said.

Roy's lips curled away from his teeth. He'd never doubted her word before. Why didn't he believe her now?

"You've been keeping secrets from me." Roy pointed at Brock. "You can transform. You say that you're mindblind, that you can't hear the pack, but maybe you're just not letting us in."

"I only transformed to change him, and I'm not even sure I could do it again." Desperation laced her voice. "Please, Roy."

The corner of his mouth twitched up in a smile.

That was the issue. She wasn't acting enough like the omega.

Ducking her head, she took another step forward, hunching her shoulders. "I was only trying to help. Please don't be mad."

Her stomach churned hard enough to raise bile to the back of her throat. Had she really acted like this? For years?

Brock tried to reach out to her, but she leapt away. Toward Roy. The look on Brock's face broke her heart.

"You'll understand soon," she said, praying it was true. "When you find your place in the pack."

When she looked up at Roy, he was smiling. Hope fluttered in her chest, a bittersweet contrast to the pain she knew she'd just caused the man she loved.

"You wouldn't lie to me, would you, Meg?" Roy said. "After everything I've done for you, how I saved you and gave you a home and a family, you wouldn't lie."

"Never." She forced her face into the closest semblance to adoration she could manage, remembering how she used to look at Roy. It was nauseating to think of, but she had to convince him she was earnest.

"Meg, you don't have to do this," Brock said.

She ignored him, along with the ache in her chest.

"If we don't go quickly, Brock will get away," she said. "You sent me here to heal our pack, remember?"

"I did." Roy nodded. He reached out and gently stroked the side of Meg's head. "Tessa, change of plan."

Tessa stopped banging on the stasis chamber and turned around. Blue light rippled over her body as fur sprouted from her skin. Her joints popped and cracked, muscles rippling as the change swept over her. The thin gown she'd been wearing tore and floated to the ground at her feet.

"Kill this one," he said, nodding toward Brock.

"What?" Meg yelled. "No, he's one of us."

Roy grabbed her hair and yanked her close. "I choose who joins our pack. Not you."

"Let her go," Brock yelled.

The change swept over Brock so quickly. Meg was amazed at his mastery of his new form. In one smooth movement, Brock tore his pants away and leapt toward Roy, fur sprouting over his body.

Brock's claws glanced off of the metal of Tessa's arm. She was already in front of them, moving faster than Meg could track.

"An alpha never fights alone." Roy smiled.

"Do they fight at all?" Brock said. "Or just hide behind others?"

Roy snorted. "That's Brock's specialty. But he's run out of places to hide. Cut off the true head, and you kill the hydra. It'll be interesting to see if you go with them. Tessa can have some fun with you until we find out."

Tessa slashed and snapped at Brock, forcing him to retreat. He was holding back even more than Meg had feared he would.

"Don't," Meg screamed. "Please, he's one of us now. He's pack."

"For all his talk of worthiness, this *thing* is unfit to join our pack." Roy tightened his grip on her hair, dragging her toward the door. "We're leaving. We need to reach Brock before his little roaches can stick him in some other hole where we'll never find him."

A sob tore through Meg as Roy picked her up and threw her over his shoulder, carrying her from the room. The last she saw of Brock was him blocking a vicious swipe from Tessa's natural claws, opening four lines of blood along his forearm.

Meg couldn't help him like this. She had a plan, and it was a good one—she hoped. For it to work, she had to pull herself together. The sooner she did, the sooner everyone would be safe. She just hoped it would work.

"We're going the wrong way," she said, sniffing and wiping her eyes to clear them. "We need to get outside."

Roy threw her to the ground, hard, then pressed his hand on one of the palm scanners. A hatch opened that led out to the cave.

"I know what I'm doing," he snarled. "Never second guess me again."

She wouldn't have a chance to. In a few minutes, he'd be dead. She scrambled to her feet and followed him out of the ship.

No trolls lurched up from the ground to attack them. She couldn't hear any fighting nearby. That was bad. For her plan to work, she needed help.

An alpha never fights alone.

The view to the elevator was blocked by mounds of dirt, but Roy must have known which direction it lay in. He started heading toward it.

Jon, Nathan, and Dexter must already be in the ship. They'd find Brock and Tessa and hopefully save them both. Meg just had to keep Roy busy until then, maybe loosen his hold on Tessa by distracting him. Meg also couldn't let him reach the sublevels where Porter and Eli were.

Once they were in sight of the elevator, the camera would pick them up. Porter could lock the elevator doors or trap them inside. At least, she was pretty sure he could.

Roy veered off toward the emergency stairs. Her plan

was starting to seem like less of a good idea.

"It's this way." Meg pointed to the elevator.

"Don't be stupid," Roy said. "We're not getting in a tiny metal box filled with cameras and microphones that other Blades have full control over."

"But that's how they took Brock away. I'm sure of it. There's no way he could have taken the stairs. And we need to follow his scent."

"I thought you knew where they were taking him."

"I do. I mean, I know the whole base, but I just think the elevator is the best idea."

Roy stopped, then slowly turned toward her. "Are you trying to betray me, Meg? Because, that might be something I have a hard time forgiving."

She couldn't bring herself to lie. The words stuck in her throat.

"I wouldn't betray my pack," she said.

"Your pack is me."

"What about Tessa and Marcus?"

Roy stalked toward her, his lips curled up in a snarl. "If it wasn't for Marcus, our pack wouldn't have been decimated in the first place. And Tessa is a freak, contaminated with curator technology."

"I don't understand."

"You're not supposed to understand," he roared. "You're supposed to *obey*. Only those who know their place belong in my pack."

Her blood seemed to freeze in her veins. "You're going to kill them, too. Marcus and Tessa."

"They think themselves an alpha pair. I've seen it in their thoughts."

"And what about me?" Meg said.

"You need to learn your place again." Roy sneered at her. "I'll be more than happy to remind you again and again as soon as we've finished the Blades once and for all."

A stone rolled down one of the mounds of dirt behind Roy. It could have been a coincidence. It could have been a troll. But Meg had a feeling it wasn't.

"I already know my place," she said, straightening her shoulders and standing tall. She held his gaze, eyes glowing bright enough to cast his features in golden light. "And you're right. Marcus and Tessa are not the alpha pair."

As she expected, Roy snarled and lunged at her.

"You bitch," he yelled.

Meg dodged away, spinning past his grasp. The hill was at her back.

"I never really had a place in your pack," Meg said. "But I've found another. This is *my* pack, and I am mated to their alpha. I am mated to Brock."

"You lied to me," Roy said.

"Careful," she snarled. "An alpha never fights alone."

She heard more rocks skittering down the hill behind

her. Lots of them. And she didn't need to see the pair of warriors at her side to know they were there. She could feel Jon and Nathan flanking her.

"You think you're an alpha?" Roy said. "You weak, pathetic—"

She heard metal rasp against metal as the twins drew their swords. Cocking her head to the side, she said, "You were saying?"

Roy glowered at them, his shoulders hunching as claws sprouted from his fingertips. His gaze flicked to the ship, and Meg knew he was trying to get Tessa to come to him.

Finally, after all this time, Meg saw him for what he truly was. A coward.

She had pushed him. She wanted to push him. Because she knew just what it would take to send him over the edge, bringing all of his attention here. If he had to make an effort to reach Tessa, she was still busy at the ship. Brock was still alive. Meg intended to keep it that way.

"These are my packmates, Jon and Nathan," Meg said. She gestured toward the third man standing in front of the hill and smiled, baring her sharpening teeth. "And this is my *friend*, Dexter."

Dexter's voice was as smooth as melting butter. "I believe you've been looking for me," he said.

Roy's eyes widened till she could see the whites all around them. The change tore through him, his wolf form bursting through in a flash of blue light. She actually felt the energy of his transformation hit her, like the shockwave from the explosion earlier.

Roy leapt at Dexter, swiping at Meg as he did. She was surprised Roy could divide his attention once Dexter was brought into the mix. Luckily, Nathan was there, pulling her out of harm's way. He held her against his chest, his arms a cage that both protected and trapped her.

"Help them," she said.

Nathan didn't budge. Maybe she wasn't quite the alpha she thought she was.

"Please, Nathan." She rested her hands on his chest and looked up into his dark and white eyes. He only held her tighter.

How could she convince him to join the fight? The scent of blood hit her nose, tinged with fallen leaves. She looked over her shoulder and saw blood dripping from a gash in Dexter's shirt. Roy was using the terrain to his advantage, leaping over the replicants, just out of reach of their blades, and dashing in with his heightened speed to strike at them.

Jon was a split-second too late lifting his sword to block Roy's attack. Roy's claws raked him across his stomach. Dexter was breathing heavily. Meg didn't understand. Dexter had defeated the entire pack single-handedly.

Except not really.

His might have been the only replicant body in the

room, but he was probably using the link to draw on the others, like Brock had explained the night Meg arrived. And now, Dexter didn't have that link to help him. The replicants' skill was incredible, but as Dexter had said, he was diminished.

It had never occurred to her in her wildest fantasies that in a fight with a single werewolf, Dexter might lose. Her plan was going to get him killed. It might just get *all* of them killed. Everything hinged on Dexter being able to kill Roy.

If the replicants couldn't do it for her, she would do it herself. She tried to push away from Nathan, but he held on tight. This was not happening. She would not stand by and watch them die.

"Let me go," she said.

Nathan didn't budge. If anything, he tightened his grip again, hugging her closer against his chest, like he was trying to protect her.

"Your brothers need you," she said. "If Roy kills them, he'll come for you, and then me. If you really want to keep me safe, you'll let me fight to protect myself and all the people I love," she said. "We're pack. All of us. Let me fight with you."

He opened his mouth as if he was about to say something, but then shut it again.

"I don't want to hurt you," she snarled, letting the change flow over her. "But I can *make* you let me go."

She pushed against him with her fur-covered arms, not using even half her strength. Nathan's eyes widened, but he let go of her and stepped back. He glanced at the fight, then stared at her, gaze moving up and down her wolf form.

Reaching over his shoulder, he drew a blade.

Chapter Twenty-Five

"Tessa, this isn't you." Brock dodged another swipe of Tessa's claws. Her left set didn't worry him as much as the right. He'd seen what her cybernetic arm could do, and those claws looked absolutely wicked.

"Roy is the puppetmaster," he said. "He's been messing with your mind all this time. But you can fight him. I know you can."

He ducked, making her punch land on the wall instead of his face. Sparks flew where the metal connected with the bulkhead. Her hand made a series of garbled beeping noises and was dented all across her knuckles.

For a moment, he thought he might have lucked out. If that hand stopped working, it would be a lot easier to incapacitate her without hurting her—or pushing the limits of his new werewolf healing abilities.

She lifted her arm, staring at the odd angles her fingers protruded in. More sparks crackled as she wiggled them, snapping them back into place. The chrome started to smooth itself, the dents in her knuckles popping back out.

"Self-healing?" Brock said. "Really, Vaughn?"

This wasn't going to work. Brock had to try something

else, and he only had one idea remaining.

"I didn't want to do this," he said.

He focused his thoughts. The buzzing grew louder as he brought it more into the center of his awareness, gathering energy just as he had with the link between his replicants.

This had better work.

The lighting in the room took on an odd blue cast. He didn't let that distract him. Reaching out to the annoying buzz surrounding him, he imagined it as a tangible energy, then tore it open. He let his consciousness pour into the stream, filling it, overpowering it.

First step, tell Roy to fuck off.

Brock pushed against the current of energy that had been trying to break into his mind. He let his anger fuel his attack, like he'd done to the replicants after they put Meg in the pit. It amplified the mental energy he sent along the corridor.

For a moment, he was out in the cave. Dexter swung a blade at him, but he ducked in plenty of time, then lashed out with claws, laughing as they parted Dexter's flesh. Blood rained down on the stone beneath his feet.

Another opponent crashed into him, lifting him off the ground. Furred, clawed, and with teeth that were sinking deep into his arm. He let out a howl of pain, then grabbed the smaller werewolf by her neck, twisting until it snapped. Her body went limp and she fell to the ground.

"Oh shit," Brock shouted in his mind. *"Meg? Meg!"*

He lashed out at Roy, blasting him with every ounce of energy he could.

"You fucking bastard," he yelled.

Roy screamed, grabbing his head and digging his claws into his own scalp. Brock felt a searing wave of agony spear through his gut as someone impaled him through his back. The tip of a blade burst through his belly.

At first, Brock hoped it was infused with silver. But when Roy dropped to his knees, he grabbed Meg's limp form and lifted her, pulling her toward the gleaming metal sticking out of him.

"I won't die alone." Roy's thought dripped with hate and malice.

Brock had to stop him.

Another pain—a closer pain—burned across Brock's neck and torso. His awareness snapped back to the room where his actual body was.

Tessa had recovered and was still obeying Roy's command. Her teeth were embedded in Brock's neck, her clawed hand shoved all the way through his abdomen. She shook him with her jaws, tearing more of the flesh on his throat.

Brock blocked out the pain. Dying and splitting, enduring the pain of his replicants, dealing with his own body—he had years of practice. He had to get to Meg.

"Tessa." Brock could still feel the tether of energy connecting her to Roy. The shithead wasn't dead yet.

Brock sent energy along that mental corridor, letting his consciousness fully connect with Roy and Tessa's.

"Tessa, let me go," Brock thought. *"I'm your brother."*

"My brother is dead. Everyone is." Her thoughts were wild, almost incoherent. It was no wonder, with what Brock could pick up from Roy.

He was sending her revolting images of Tessa killing Brock—and their dad. And... feeding on them. Brock's own stomach churned from the visions.

"This isn't real," Brock projected. *"Roy is sending you these images."*

"Roy?"

"The previous alpha."

"Alpha..." Her thoughts began to dull. *"We have to obey the alpha."*

"I am the alpha now." Brock sent the words with force. He didn't want to, but he felt her slipping away. Dammit, he didn't have time for this.

But that only left him with one option.

"Brock is weak." Roy's voice whispered in Tessa's mind. *"He doesn't deserve you. You've almost killed him. What kind of alpha is that?"*

"Tessa, please don't make me do this," Brock thought.

She had been so messed up by being colonized by Edgar, and now Roy's mental control. Puppetmasters getting into her head and under her skin. What would she think of Brock if he used his true power to stop her?

Roy's presence faded a bit. Either his body was dying or he was retreating. Either way, Brock could sense his fear.

"Marcus is alpha," Tessa thought. Her teeth tightened around Brock's throat.

If Brock didn't do something soon, she really would kill him—and it would destroy her. He knew if she ever snapped out of Roy's control, knowing she'd killed Brock would destroy any sanity she had left.

Meg needed him. The Blades needed him.

He had to act.

"I am alpha." Brock intensified the connection, shoving her consciousness to the side, like body-slamming her mind. He sent energy along her nerves, willing her limbs and jaws to obey him.

"How... What are you doing?" Tessa thought.

"I'm saving us both."

He carefully unlatched her teeth from his neck. The less damage he had to heal, the sooner he could get outside and help Meg and the others. Even waiting a few seconds felt like hours. When his throat was healed enough that he thought he wasn't at risk of dying from that trauma, he slowly pulled her arm out of his stomach.

Tessa's biological hand rested on his chest. He could feel their bodies breathing in synch, sharing the pain. For Brock, it was nothing. For Tessa... She hadn't experienced pain like this before.

"I'm so sorry," Brock thought. He tried to shield her from the worst of it, but knew his pain had to be passing on to her.

He felt her fighting against his control. She wanted to jerk her arm back. Honestly, so did he. But his body would heal faster if she didn't disembowel him.

Damn, his eyes were freaky while he was doing this. He was used to the golden glow of his right eye from being around werewolves. The crackling, sparking blue light that kept flickering out of his left eye was new, though.

He pulled her arm out slowly, giving his body a chance to seal itself and heal, keeping his insides in place as his body knitted back together.

"I didn't mean to." Her thoughts were disjointed. He could sense her shying away from the reality of what she had done—and what had been done to her.

The moment her arm was out, he released his control of her. She fell backwards, retching. Blue light pulsed over her body as her fur retracted and her muscles and bones shifted to her human form.

Brock shoved himself to his feet, shaking off a wave of disorientation at being back in his own body—and only his own body. In a raspy growl he said, "We have to go."

He ran toward the back hatch, following Meg's scent as much as memory. The door was hanging open. The smell of blood hit him as he leapt out into the cave. Tessa landed next to him.

Dexter was on the ground, cradling Meg in his lap. She'd reverted to her human form, but she hadn't vaporized.

Silver poisoning takes time to kill a werewolf.

Brock pushed the thought away. She would be okay. She had to be. Dexter looked up at him, his expression somber.

"Meg…" Brock took a step forward.

"She'll be okay," Dexter said. "Nathan grabbed the blade and broke it off before it could touch her. If we'd been linked, he would have known that I could have pulled it out in time."

If Dexter believed that, why did he look like someone had just died?

"Is Nathan okay?" Brock asked. "And Jon?"

"Nathan lost some fingers, but they're already growing back." Dexter nodded his head to his right, glancing at something behind Brock and Tessa. "He's keeping them busy. I didn't think it was safe to try to stop them on my own."

The scent of blood thickened. Werewolf blood. Brock could hear flesh ripping, the sickening squelch of flesh hitting the stone ground. He was familiar with the sound.

"Oh my God." Tessa was staring over Brock's shoulder. She covered her mouth, stumbling toward Dexter and Meg.

Brock didn't bother to look. He knew what he'd see. The link with Roy was still active. Silver poisoning did take a while to kill a werewolf. So did being torn apart, one tiny bit of flesh at a time.

Brock could still sense Roy. He was still alive and conscious—barely. And Jon and Nathan, what they were doing to him…

They hadn't turned out right. But at the moment, Brock couldn't let himself think about that. Meg needed him.

He walked over to her, letting the energy of the change wash over him, returning him to his new not-quite-human form, and dropped to his knees beside his mate.

Chapter Twenty-Six

Meg's neck hurt. Not like the pain she'd felt from her collar. This was new. Her bones ached and her muscles throbbed. She tilted her head to the side, wincing as nerves twanged across her tendons.

"Ow," she said.

"What's the matter, never had your neck broken before?"

That smooth voice and snark...

"Dexter?" she asked, opening her eyes.

He was smiling at her. Holding her in his arms. She was lying across his lap. She tried to sit up, fast, to move away. Instinct and conditioning were hard to fight. But other hands grabbed her and held her in place.

"Easy."

She knew that voice, too. That scent.

"Brock." She looked up at him, her chest filling with relief and joy and so many other emotions, she couldn't begin to name them all.

He was smiling, too, and Tessa was staring down at Meg from over his shoulder. But Tessa wasn't smiling. Her lips were pulled in a worried frown, her brow was furrowed, and her eyes were filled with tears that gleamed in the golden light cast from her eyes.

"Tessa." Meg smiled and sat up, more slowly this time. "Are you okay?"

Tessa shook her head, but laughed. "I'm not the one who just had her neck broken."

Meg reached up and touched the front of her throat. That's right, Roy had broken her neck during the fight.

She looked over at Dexter. "Are you okay?"

He laughed, lifting his shirt. The skin on his side had already healed. There weren't even any scars.

"We hydra are a hardy sort," he said.

Porter's voice sounded from the area of the elevator shaft. "It's good to know our regeneration is intact, though I'd rather have found out under more controlled circumstances."

Meg leaned forward, hoping to see him, but no one was there. It must be coming from a speaker.

"Did Vaughn get the communications back up?" she asked.

"Not inside the ship," Brock said.

He lifted her to her feet, not stopping till she was pressed against his chest. He wrapped his arms around her, holding her tight. For a moment, she let herself rest there, leaning against him, feeling his strength, his warmth, his love. He kissed the top of her head.

"I was so scared," he said.

Meg smiled. "I wasn't."

He pulled away, looking down at her with a puzzled expression. She only laughed.

"Alphas don't get scared." More quietly, she added, "I knew you'd come for me."

Brock laughed, then gave her another hug.

Jon and Nathan approached. She wasn't sure what they'd been doing until she noticed the dark red staining their arms up to their elbows. She swallowed hard.

"Thank you," she said.

The blood started to glow. Both men lifted their arms in unison, twisting their hands from front to back and watching as the blue light vaporized, every last trace that Roy had ever existed vanishing.

"I can't believe it," Meg said. "He's finally gone."

Dexter rose to his feet. "About fucking time."

"We're free." Meg smiled at Tessa, but Tessa didn't smile back. In fact, if anything, she looked more upset than ever before. Saner, yes, but more troubled.

"What's wrong?" Meg asked.

"I'll explain later." Brock hugged her closer. Tessa glared at him briefly, then quickly looked down at her feet, her shoulders hunched.

"Porter, get down here with Dad," Tessa said. "I want Marcus out of his stasis chamber."

"We'll be there shortly," Porter said.

She turned and walked toward the ship. Brock

followed, pulling Meg along with him.

"I want to make sure Vaughn's okay," Brock said. "You three wait for Porter and Dad, just in case we missed any trolls."

Dexter let out an indignant snort. "We didn't miss any trolls. But don't worry, we'll keep Eli safe."

Brock paused. He stared at Dexter for a few long moments. Finally, Dexter let out a sigh.

"Fine." Dexter smirked. "We'll keep *Dad* safe."

"There you go." Brock headed for the ship again.

When they were inside, Meg said, "Did you get a chance to explain what was going on to Tessa? About the voice and how she can control herself now?"

"If Brock lets me," Tessa snapped.

"You know I had no other choice," Brock said.

Tessa wheeled around, snarling at him. "That doesn't make it any better."

"I feel like I'm missing something," Meg said.

"It turns out I still have at least some of my hydra abilities," Brock said. "Only with the pack instead of my replicants."

"That's amazing." Meg didn't understand why it was upsetting Tessa so much.

"See if you still think so the first time he takes over your body and makes you do what he wants," Tessa said.

"Dammit," he yelled. "That's not fair and you know it."

Tessa flinched away from him.

Meg could only imagine how awful that must have been for her, after everything she'd been through. To have her own brother take over control at that level.

"How could you have done that?" Meg asked. "She's your sister."

"Yeah, she is," he said. "And you're my mate. Roy was about to kill you, from what I saw, and Tessa was in the process of killing me. If I hadn't stopped her, Roy might have survived. Tessa was barely hanging on to her sanity as it was. Forgive me if I was wrong in thinking that killing her brother would send her over the edge. I know if the circumstances were reversed, it sure as hell would have broken me."

"Just forget it," Tessa said.

Brock dropped Meg's hand and took a menacing step forward. "No, I can't forget it. I feel like absolute shit that I had to do that. I'd also do it again in a heartbeat and expect you to do the same and more to protect our pack. There are too many of us for me to look after myself."

"You can't handle four wolves?" Tessa snorted.

"Four wolves, ten replicants, and a shit-ton of human Blades, including our Dad," Brock said.

Meg needed a way to diffuse the situation. A non-violent way. She waited a beat, just for effect, then said, "And also Vaughn." Both of them turned toward her. Meg shrugged. "She deserves her own category."

"Curator?" Brock said.

"I was thinking 'IT gal.'" Meg smiled at him.

Tessa laughed. A moment later, so did Brock.

"Who ever heard of a werewolf pack with an IT gal?" Tessa said.

"Hey, it's the new millennium." Brock shrugged. "We need to adapt to changing times."

Tessa nodded, still smiling, though it was subdued. Meg would take what she could get.

During their movie night, Vaughn talked about how effective humor was in helping Marcus in the field and for coping with their bizarre lives in general. Meg was so glad that had worked.

"Speaking of which, we should go let her know she's safe now," Meg said. "I'm not as good at telling jokes."

"You did great." Tessa reached for Meg's hand and squeezed it. She held on as they walked to the stasis chamber room.

Tessa went to Marcus's pod while Brock led Meg to another one. It looked empty to her, but she could smell Vaughn's scent leading toward it.

"How do we let her know she can come out?" Meg asked.

Brock slapped the glass a couple of times, then rested his hand on it. He pressed his face against the glass, peering inside.

"I think I can see her," he said. "She's curled up at the bottom."

"Can she hear us?" Meg asked.

"I don't think— Uh-oh."

"What 'uh-oh?'" Tessa said, joining them.

"She saw me and I think she's freaking out." Brock pointed at his face. "It's probably the eyes."

"They are really freaky," Tessa said.

Meg tried to pull herself up so she could see down through the window. "Give me a boost. I'll talk to her."

Tessa gestured toward the stasis chamber. "She can't hear you."

"She doesn't have to." Meg waited for Brock to kneel down in front of her, one leg bent so that she could stand on it and look inside the chamber.

Vaughn's arms were braced against the sides of the cylinder. Meg could see her chest heaving. Her eyes were wide. Meg smiled at her. It felt incredibly lame, but she didn't know what else to do. Then she waved.

"Wow, why didn't I think of that?" Tessa said. "Waving —the universal language of, 'we're no longer trying to kill you.'"

"Shut up, Chicken," Brock said.

"Shut up yourself, Bock-Bock."

Meg laughed and they both glared at her.

"Sorry," Meg said. "Sibling rivalry isn't something I've experienced in a pack before." She glanced at Tessa. "But seriously, don't poke the alpha."

Meg turned her attention back to Vaughn and pressed

her hand against the glass, this time making the Scifi 'V'-shaped salute Vaughn had taught her. Vaughn did a little double-take. Now that Meg had her attention, Meg started trying to sign. The angle was awkward, as was trying to balance on Brock's leg.

"You're safe," she signed. "Everyone's safe."

Vaughn didn't look convinced. She signed back, "What the fuck with those eyes?"

Meg laughed.

"What's funny?" Tessa asked. "Is she making jokes? Because if she's making jokes, I'll stop freaking out."

Meg glanced over briefly. "Don't worry." She turned back to Vaughn and signed, "I bit Brock."

Vaughn stared at her for a moment, then replied, "Kinky."

Meg laughed again.

"Okay, I'm both mad and relieved," Tessa said. "What's she saying?"

Meg ignored Tessa this time.

"Please come out," Meg signed.

"You're sure it's safe?" Vaughn asked.

"Promise."

Vaughn slowly rose within the chamber. Meg jumped down from her odd perch.

"Give her some space," Meg said.

Brock and Tessa did as she asked. They did as *Meg* asked. A jolt of exhilaration shot through her. This was her pack, and she'd do anything to protect it.

The door to the stasis chamber opened a bit and Vaughn peered out at Meg.

"You're sure it's safe?" Vaughn said.

"Yes, I'm—" Meg forgot what she was about to say when she could see Vaughn better. Her skin was gray in the darkness within the chamber, but there were white lines offsetting shaded clusters in a scale-like pattern. Meg shook her head. The stress of everything must be playing tricks on her senses.

Vaughn stepped into the light. Her skin was pink, if paler than usual, and there was nothing off about her at all. No lines, no clusters of... whatever that had been. Definitely just the stress making Meg see things. Or maybe probably... Their lives were so weird.

Vaughn lurched back when she noticed Tessa.

"It's okay," Meg said. "She won't try to hurt you anymore."

"It was never Tessa trying to hurt you in the first place," Brock growled.

"Whoa." Vaughn ran her hands over her hair as she stared at Brock. "That is... That is freaky. Sorry, but..."

"Yeah." Brock laughed. "Porter's going to put me through a ton of tests. He'll be so happy."

"You might even say, he'll be beside himself with joy," Meg said.

Brock groaned.

Vaughn reached out and rested her hand on Meg's shoulder. "I've never been more proud."

Meg laughed, then threw her arms around Vaughn's shoulders.

"I'm so glad you're okay," Meg said.

"Me too." Vaughn hugged Meg back, then pulled away far enough to look over at Brock. "What happened to the crazy werewolf that ran in here screaming, 'curator?' Because that guy was super fantastic."

"He's dead," Brock said.

Tessa added, "Jon and Nathan tore him apart."

"Gross," Vaughn said. "And awesome. Couldn't have happened to a shittier guy. I'll have to send Jon and Nathan a 'Thank You' card or something. I can send it along with the 'In Sympathy' for you." She nodded toward Brock.

"'In Sympathy?'" Brock asked.

"Yeah, you poor, poor bastard." Vaughn shook her head and spoke solemnly. "You're right—Porter's going to run every test he knows on you, and then come up with about a thousand more."

When Vaughn grinned, everyone laughed.

"Porter will have to wait." Meg stepped away from Vaughn so that she could wrap her arm around Brock's waist. "We have a lot of work to do."

"I kind of want to get out of here," Vaughn said. "I'm already agoraphobic. If this experience makes me claustrophobic, too, I have no idea how I'll handle that."

"We can head up to the ranch, *after* we get Marcus out of stasis," Meg said.

It was getting easier for her to tell others what she wanted. Especially now that she knew what she wanted for herself and for her loved ones.

She smiled at Tessa and Brock. "We want our pack together again."

Chapter Twenty-Seven

The living room had never been so full. Dad was sitting in one of the leather reading chairs, pulled up as close as Tessa would let him be. She still didn't trust herself, and after seeing the thoughts that Roy had been feeding her, Brock couldn't blame her.

Tessa and Marcus were on the couch. Marcus had his arm around her and they were also holding hands. Brock would bet they were communicating through their link as well. Vaughn was sitting on the other side of Marcus, her arms draped across the couch and her head hanging back, showing her exhaustion.

Jon was standing by the door that led to the rest of the ranch and Nathan was by the sliding doors to the back yard. They seemed relaxed to the casual observer, but Brock noted their wide stances and the way their gazes swept the room at regular intervals.

With Marcus around, Brock was a lot more comfortable being near Tessa. But he wouldn't be turning his back on either of his newest replicants anytime soon.

Porter was in another reading chair, holding one of Vaughn's tablet computers on his lap and scrolling through data. Not much had changed there. But Dexter was hovering over Porter, arms crossed, staring down at him as if he could drill a hole into the back of Porter's head with his eyes.

Was Dexter trying to reestablish a link? If so, he was either failing miserably or Porter was doing a great job not showing signs that they were also communicating silently.

With all the other seats taken, that left Brock in the overstuffed, oversized chair—with Meg sitting in his lap. He wasn't about to complain.

Vaughn let out a loud groan. "Let's never do that again, okay?"

"Agreed." Porter didn't look up from his tablet when he spoke.

"So, this isn't normal for you guys, right?" Meg asked. "I mean, I imagine you have a lot going on, but please tell me life as a Blade isn't always this exciting."

"This is definitely not your typical Thursday," Vaughn said.

Meg looked down at Brock. "Is it Thursday?"

He laughed.

"I have no idea," Brock said. "I just woke up from a coma, remember?"

She wrapped her arms around his head and hugged it against her chest. "Don't remind me."

"I hate to ask this," Dad said, "but is it really over? I mean, can we at least get a little break to…"

His voice trailed off and he looked to Tessa. She reached out to him and he gripped her hand tight, leaning forward to kiss the back of it. He didn't seem to give a damn that it was her metal one.

"There's a long road ahead." Brock turned to Porter. "I'm guessing part of what's keeping you occupied is figuring out the damage in sublevel 2."

Porter nodded. "We're not in imminent danger of structural collapse or anything, but that level is toast. From what I can determine—which I must point out isn't as much as usual, with only this one brain to work with— none of the other levels were affected."

Vaughn lifted her head so she could glare at Porter. "I did design the place to withstand all kinds of attacks. There's enough rock between each level to keep them all contained. And that's in addition to the layers of materials meant to keep out the diggers, which I apparently should have built around the whole freaking cave." She sighed and shook her head. "I'm going to have to build another room around the entire ship now, complete with defense systems. Hell, it'll be a hangar at this point. That thing's huge."

"Language," Dad said.

Vaughn's eyebrows rose and her mouth dropped open. She snapped it shut, trying—and failing—to suppress a smile.

Dexter smirked at her. "Don't act like you're not

thrilled at the idea of building a hangar around the ship."

"I'd rather be *exploring* it," she said.

"Let's get the hangar built first," Brock said. "It'll be safer that way."

Vaughn shrugged. "I guess building the new hangar and repairing sublevel 2 will be fun. But you try coming up with a plausible reason to reallocate several factories toward making the materials we'll need and getting them all shipped here without raising too much suspicion."

"I'm sure you'll think of something," Porter said.

"I always do." Vaughn squeezed Marcus's shoulder. "At least we'll have plenty of manpower here. And woman-power." She nodded toward Meg, who beamed back at Vaughn.

"Between replicants and werewolves, with your heightened strength, we should barely need to use my heavy machinery," Vaughn continued. "And working on a project with Damien will be a good way to show him that there's nothing to worry about from us."

"And what's going to show us that we have nothing to worry about from him?" Porter finally set aside his tablet.

"Damien's a good guy," Vaughn said.

"We know." Dexter stepped forward, resting his arm on the back of Porter's chair. "And that's precisely the problem."

"I don't follow," Vaughn said.

Brock spoke up. "He has a reputation among the

Blades. Damien is very highly regarded. If he decides we're dangerous or that the Blades were founded as a trick to get hunters off the streets—"

"He won't." Vaughn bristled, leaning forward with her hands resting on her thighs. "Damien doesn't make snap judgments about people. He's fair and reasonable and smart enough to figure out that we're doing all that we do for the right reasons."

Dexter smirked. "Gee, Vaughn, tell us how you really feel."

Vaughn's face turned pink as she glared at Dexter. Before Dexter could say anything else, Dad held up a hand and said, "Knock it off," sharply.

Porter chuckled. "You're in trouble."

"Shut up," Dexter said.

Hearing those two talk to each other might be weird for the others in the room, but it was downright surreal for Brock. The replicant pairs had barely acknowledged each other's existence before. They hadn't needed to, because they *shared* it. Seeing them interact was like watching someone talking to themselves. No, it was worse. It was like seeing two body parts suddenly start talking to each other.

Brock suppressed a shiver. He'd get used to it in time. They all would. But they had some things to overcome first. He didn't like the way Marcus was looking at him. He didn't like the way Tessa was *not* looking at him. And he sure as hell didn't like how Jon and Nathan kept staring at Meg.

At the same time, he was grateful for his problems. Problems were part of being alive—a reminder that he would be around to fix them.

He knew he'd work things out with Marcus and Tessa. Jon and Nathan... Well, they would all work together to figure out whatever was going on with them and get them the help they needed to adjust. They also needed to figure out who or what had made Meg's collar and how Roy had managed to gather and control all those trolls. Brock would never believe Roy could have managed that attack on his own.

Vaughn was undoubtedly already planning out repairs for the ranch and ways of making the ship more secure. And working as a team or a pack—whatever they wanted to call it—working as a *family*, Brock was sure they would be able to open up to the other Blades without alienating them.

His family was intact. Brock was determined to keep the Blades that way, too. And that gave him the first problem for him to focus on.

He turned to Vaughn and said, "When does Damien arrive?"

—

Thank you so much for reading *Progenitor*, the second novel in *The Blades of Janus* series! Brock and his replicants have always fascinated me. I was so excited to delve deeper into what makes them work. I'm even more excited to move forward with this series and see how their newfound autonomy affects them all, and the rest of the Blades!

Readers have been in love with Vaughn since the very beginning of these adventures—and that includes me. I like to say that she's my imaginary best friend and even have a "Vaughn is my Copilot" T-shirt that I wear all the time (I'm on my second one—the first disintegrated, I wore it so much!). The question I'm asked most often for this series is, "What the heck is a curator?" Well, you'll finally get the answers you seek in Vaughn's story! Read on for a sneak peek at the third *Blades of Janus* novel, *Perihelion*.

Perihelion

The Blades of Janus
Book Three

Gold eyes means werewolf.

Chapter One

"Huh." Damien glanced at the high-tech display on the van's main console for the seventh time. Another red blip had appeared on the screen, but vanished so quickly he wondered if he'd imagined it.

It was probably nothing. He didn't know how the scanners in the vehicle worked, but doubted they could analyze every animal he passed and check them for characteristics that might mark them as something unnatural—especially with how fast he was driving down the dark highway.

Most people labeled the creatures they couldn't understand as fairies or monsters. Blades called them dwellers. Damien wasn't sure why, but went along with it. He'd been going along with a lot of things, all while not knowing his bosses—his friends—were lying to him. No, not really lying. But they were keeping important truths hidden.

Bringing his mind back to his current situation, he had to consider the possibility that he might be hallucinating. Being awake for forty-eight hours was a lot, even for him.

He hadn't reached the most dangerous part of his journey —the Providence base for the Blades of Janus, otherwise known as the ranch. It wasn't the place that was the threat but the people living there. If they even *were* people.

A blue light flashed on the dashboard, letting him know someone was trying to contact him.

Speak of the dweller, Damien thought.

Damien only paused a moment before activating the comm link. There was no sense putting off the inevitable.

"Yeah," he said.

"Hey, Damien." Vaughn's cheery voice filled the van. "How's it going?"

A frisson rocketed down his spine at the sound of her voice. It always did.

"Fine," he said.

"Cool." There was a brief pause before she continued. "It looks like you're about half an hour out."

Damien didn't bother responding. He'd thought he was farther away, but she knew the area better. And the tech. And more about everything in general. She was an absolute genius.

Vaughn had designed the sleek van that Damien was driving, along with all of its high-tech components—some of which Damien hadn't even figured out how to use. He'd been a member of the Blades of Janus for five years and was still learning what all the buttons did.

"I just wondered if you have any questions I can

answer before you get here," she said.

Damien looked at the rear view mirror. Soft blue and white lights blinked along the sides of the two stasis pods that took up the sizable space. In the dim light that illuminated the back of the van, his gaze lingered on the pod behind the driver's seat. The pod that was empty.

Damien only had one question that really mattered. Too bad he didn't have the guts to ask it.

"You still there?" Vaughn asked.

"Yeah."

"Cool. Comms have been a little glitchy."

Damien focused on what he could see of the road ahead, occasionally glancing at the overland display that fed him data about his route and its surroundings. He hadn't been surprised by a single curve while driving into the mountainous region around the ranch, even with only his headlights to see by.

"I've been meaning to ask..." Vaughn said. "Are you one of those people who doesn't talk much, or is it that you like silence? Because if it's the first, we'll get along great when we finally meet in person. And if it's the second, you're going to hate me."

Damien let out a little snort before he could stop himself. He heard an answering chuckle from her. The only good part of all this mess was that he was finally getting a chance to meet her in person and put a face with that sultry voice.

"There's hope for us yet." She cleared her throat, then said, "And by that I mean—"

The red blip appeared on the display again. It lingered this time, letting Damien know it wasn't his imagination.

"Are you seeing that?" he asked.

"Seeing what?"

"Red blip. Northwest quadrant."

Vaughn was silent for a few moments. "Okay, that's weird."

"What is?"

"My data feeds aren't picking it up, but I can see it in the sensor logs from the van," she said. "It looks like a kind of sensory echo. I don't know how else to describe it. The scanners are detecting something, but they're... I don't know. Reflecting off of it. They can't get any data."

That didn't sound good.

"The anomalous readings only started a few minutes ago," she continued. "But there are a lot of them. It could be a glitch in the van's sensors. We've been seeing a lot of those the last few days. I'm going to dispatch a team to meet up with you and escort you to the ranch just in case."

Damien's skin prickled into goose flesh. He did not want an escort. Not from the ranch.

From his days as a hunter, Damien was used to going into situations where he wasn't sure who to trust. He *wasn't* used to not knowing who was human.

"They're en route," Vaughn said. "Should intercept you

in three minutes."

"I thought I was thirty minutes out."

"We have… alternate transportation here."

Damien stifled another snort. With Vaughn being at the Providence base, these Blades probably used teleportation devices to get around. Or maybe some kind of portable wormhole generators. The vans, cars, and motorcycles—not to mention the weapons and holding systems—she designed for all the Blades bases had always seemed so far ahead of what everybody else was using, it was like they were straight out of a sci-fi movie. And if that was the stuff she shared, he had to wonder what kind of tech she was keeping to herself.

That wasn't the most immediate question on his mind, though.

"Who?" Damien asked.

"Dexter, Tessa, and Marcus," Vaughn said.

The only unknown on the list was Tessa. Marcus had a good reputation among the Blades. He was one of the most effective Guards when it came to taking out dangerous dwellers. Dexter… Dexter was a fucking legend. The Blades received training on how to put dwellers at ease if there wasn't a kill order on their species. They only took out dwellers who were too dangerous to coexist with humans—the ones that were using humans as breeding material or a food source or just for sick entertainment.

Damien's stomach clenched at his memories of

dwellers who used humans for all three. He shoved away the thoughts. Now was not the time for a trip down memory lane. He couldn't lose focus.

Dexter was one of Damien's heroes, and Damien was about to meet him. Dwellers feared Dexter so much, there was a special sub-unit just on how to handle it if Dexter's name came up while in the field. Dwellers were terrified of him. Damien had always used Marcus and Dexter as inspiration. Train harder, fight better, and maybe he'd come close to hitting their numbers. With what had happened to Carey, Damien wondered if there had ever been a chance he could approach the other men's skill.

After all, Damien was only human.

His grip tightened on the steering wheel as thoughts of his past failures threatened to push their way into his mind. He couldn't afford the distraction. Not with Zach helpless in that stasis pod. Not with the chance of getting Carey back.

"Um, apparently the roster's been changed." Vaughn's voice was tight. "Dexter's benched."

Who the fuck could bench Dexter?

She let out a sigh that had become familiar. She'd made similar sounds a lot while talking Damien through the process of getting Zach into his stasis pod.

"Brock and Megan are with Tessa and Marcus instead," Vaughn said.

Damien had never heard of either of them. He didn't

bother asking who they were. It was more important to know *what* he'd be dealing with.

"Classification?" Damien said.

There was a pause before Vaughn asked, "What do you mean?"

"You gave me the 'who,'" he said. "Tell me the 'what.'"

When Vaughn spoke, her voice was colder than he had ever heard it. "The four of them are a fully stable... pack."

That little pause in her response set his stomach to churning again. A pack. All four of them were dwellers then. Was anyone at the Providence base human?

"Lots of dwellers run in packs," Damien said, praying they weren't what he feared they were.

The next pause was even longer before she spoke again. "Werewolves."

Bile rose in the back of his throat. The prickling in his skin intensified painfully and his heart rate picked up.

Werewolves? Motherfucking werewolves?

"I know what you're thinking," she said.

He seriously doubted that.

"I've..." she cleared her throat. "I've read your file."

His jaw clenched painfully.

So she got to know all of his secrets, but he barely knew anything about her? Hell, he didn't even know her first name. Damien hated the power disparity. If she knew about his past, then she knew... She knew that when it mattered most, he had failed. Just like with Carey.

Damien's head swirled as a mix of terror and rage swept through him. His heart was pounding so fast that his chest hurt. He felt like his skull was in a vise that was quickly tightening, threatening to make him black out. He took a deep breath and let it out slow and quiet.

Vaughn wasn't the enemy. She was an ally. And if she knew about Damien's background, she also knew that he would never stop trying to be better. Never stop trying to make the world safer for everyone. For the past few years, that meant working with the Blades. After checking out what was really going on at the ranch... Damien wasn't sure what his future held.

"Damien?" Vaughn said. "Are you still with me?"

Her voice brought him back from the edge, like it had in countless battles. He still couldn't form words to reply. All he managed was a grunt. That must have been good enough for her. She went on, her tone more subdued.

"The pack is made up of two mated pairs," she said. "And they're *Blades*. Marcus was one of the first Guards ever. He's been fighting for peace between humans and dwellers for twelve years—ever since he was colonized."

No wonder Marcus was so effective as a Guard. He had parasites living in his body that made him into a killing machine—and something out of a storybook nightmare. Damien wasn't entirely sure how it all worked, but he knew that much.

"Brock is the guy who founded the Blades of Janus," Vaughn said.

Damien was still trying to wrap his head around *werewolves* on the way to *help* him. He couldn't even look at 'founder' and 'werewolf' in the same sentence. What the fuck kind of organization had he signed up with?

The Blades had one order for dealing with werewolves. *Run.*

They weren't even supposed to try to engage with them. They were too dangerous and powerful. Werewolves were deadly, insane, and violent. Damien's time as a hunter backed up the Blades' 'run and report' policy as the only way to survive an encounter. And he had only become a hunter originally because...

His chest constricted painfully—almost like his heart was trying to eject itself through his mouth. More bile rose as those memories threatened to surface. Memories that would lead to him running over any fucking werewolves that tried to 'escort him safely' to the ranch.

Carey. Think of Carey.

Repeating the mantra helped him shove the memories back down. Carey might have been a dweller—a surprise Damien was still working to process—but he was also Damien's mentor and best friend. And it was Damien's fault that Carey was dead. Or gone. Or... whatever the hell he was. Still, things at the ranch were worse than Damien feared. Much worse.

"Our founder…" Damien swallowed hard, almost choking on the words, "is a werewolf."

"Kind of," Vaughn said.

Damien ran one hand down his face. He wanted to blow out a breath, but knew she would hear. He didn't want to let any of them know how bad this was getting under his skin—even if Vaughn had read his fucking file.

"Care to elaborate?" he clipped.

"He only became a werewolf recently, and before that…" she let out a deep sigh. "It's a long story, and one that's better told in person."

A soft *whump-whump-whump* noise broke into the conversation. Damien leaned over the steering wheel so he could look up at the source of the sound. A dark silhouette hovered above him, two blue circles glowing brightly on each side of it. The… whatever the hell it was… flew in front of the van. In the headlights, he could see that it was a motorcycle. Four circular lights spun around it parallel to the ground, two on each side near where the wheels must be.

Holy shit.

Two figures were riding the bike. The person on the back—a woman—looked over her shoulder at him, her dark hair whipping behind her wildly. He hadn't had a chance to fully digest the idea of flying motorcycles when his headlights caught in the woman's eyes, gleaming back at him. Gleaming gold.

Werewolves…

She had long black hair that fanned out around her head from the buffeting wind. Her features were oddly familiar. He could see in the light that she had olive-hued skin—just like his. Just like Tammie's.

Shove it down. Shove it down.

Seconds before the bike hit the ground, the blue lights on either side folded along the midline, snapping onto the wheels. It didn't slow—barely even bounced—as it touched down on the pavement.

"Keeping the best toys in Providence?" he forced out.

"Cutting down on unauthorized air traffic," Vaughn replied.

Damien couldn't believe he had to suppress a chuckle. He looked at the screen that showed him the road behind the van. Another bike just like the first was tailing him. There were no headlights to catch those wolves' eyes, but it didn't matter. They were glowing gold on their own. Just like that, the lightness Vaughn had introduced into the moment vanished.

What the hell am I driving into?

"I'm gonna need more than that," Damien said.

"Let's just say I have access to certain technology that has proven very enlightening to reverse-engineer."

He snorted, desperate to distract himself with the most outlandish thing he could think of. "You have a spaceship in the basement or something?"

She laughed, but it sounded forced. "Not in the basement." She cleared her throat. "It's in a cavern beneath the sublevels."

Damien's mind just kind of... stopped at that.

"A spaceship." He said it out loud more to process it than anything else.

"In the sublevels," she said.

"So, what? You guys are aliens or something?"

Vaughn laughed again. It started out more natural than her previous one, but faded oddly.

"Not me," she said. "I don't think so, anyway. But dwellers are."

"Dwellers... are aliens," Damien said.

Yeah, that sounded as crazy out loud as it did in his head.

"This whole conversation would go over better in person," she said. "I probably should have waited... But I'll answer all your questions when you get to the ranch. I haven't seen a blip in a bit. That doesn't mean we should let down our—"

The sound of screaming metal cut off her transmission as something rammed into the side of the van. The vehicle fishtailed, the whole thing rocking back and forth ominously. Damien cut the wheel to the right, trying not to tumble down the mountainside. He managed to stay on the road, but the van tilted over. Somehow, the glass of his window didn't shatter as the side of the vehicle hit the pavement. It skidded a hundred feet to a stop. The seatbelt kept him mostly against his chair, but cut into his chest and side painfully as he dangled from it.

As soon as the van stopped moving, Damien hit the release for the belt. Nothing happened. He drew the short knife he kept in his right boot and sliced through the thick fabric, catching himself on his elbow as he landed against the door. The lights were on in the van, dim as they were. The stasis chambers were still attached to the walls, but Damien didn't know how long they'd stay that way—or if Zach had been jostled in the crash.

Zach's chamber had been on the side that was hit. If it fell, he could be injured. Damien wouldn't let that happen. Not after what had happened to Carey. Not after what Damien had done.

Climbing over the seat, Damien made it into the back section of the van just as something pulled off the doors. He held up his pathetic knife, ready to defend Zach from whatever the fuck this was.

Gold eyes stared at him from a pale face surrounded by dark red hair. Her features were delicate, gorgeous even, but there was something unhinged about her eyes that went beyond their unnatural color.

Gold eyes means werewolf.

Damien's heart was pounding in his chest. He tried to calm himself to seem less like prey. Again, fury and terror battled within him in equal measures. Part of him *wanted* her to attack.

The woman held the crumpled remains of the door with a chrome hand that was streaked with glowing blue light. The metal continued up her arm to just below her elbow, fading into her flesh.

'What the hell?' Damien thought for the hundredth time.

She stepped aside so that the man next to her could jump into the back of the van. He had black hair that brushed his shoulders and matched the all-black ensembles that the Blades wore. The tight T-shirt and cargo pants outlined his muscular form. Lines of white scar tissue criss-crossed his arms—rows of claw marks, jagged bites. Damien had only seen scars like that on the toughest, craziest werewolves in Vaughn's Dwellers Database.

For some reason, the guy was wearing thick-framed glasses. Werewolves wouldn't need the help. Becoming infected should have fixed any vision issues he had. The lenses obscured his eyes, but Damien didn't need to see their color to know this guy was a wolf, too.

"You okay?" the wolf said.

Damien wasn't sure how to respond. He felt something sticky and wet trickling down the side of his head. If it was blood, it could set them off.

The wolf sighed, then said, "You need to leave."

Damien bit back the obscenity on the tip of his tongue. He widened his stance and shifted the knife in his grip.

The werewolf held up his hands. "We're here to help. I'm Marcus."

Marcus? This *is Marcus?*

"The red-head is my mate, Tessa," Marcus said.

Tessa peered around the side of the opening and waved with her non-metal hand. "I'm staying put till the testosterone thins out in there. But you might want to hurry, with an unknown nasty running around. Oh, and here." She messed with her ear for a moment, then threw something to Marcus.

He caught it easily, then opened his palm so that Damien could see what he held. An earpiece.

"Vaughn wants to talk to you," Marcus said.

Damien held his ground. Every instinct he had told him to prepare to fight. But fighting these two was a death sentence.

"Maybe Damien's worried about werewolf cooties," Tessa said.

Marcus closed his eyes and let out a sigh that sounded a lot like Vaughn's when she was frustrated. When Marcus opened his eyes again, he tilted his head back toward Tessa.

"Damien is one of our top Guards," Marcus said. "He knows there's no such thing as werewolf cooties."

"Does he also know he needs to get his ass out of the van before Brock and Meg tip it back over?" Tessa said.

"What about Zach?" Damien straightened a bit,

glancing at the stasis chamber.

He could see Zach's still form through the clear window built into the top of the chamber. However Zach was strapped in, he didn't seem to have moved at all during the crash. Vaughn had said the stasis chamber actually made a zero-G environment. Damien hadn't said anything, but part of him didn't really believe her at the time, even with how Zach's hair was floating around his face. After what she had just told him, it didn't seem so far-fetched.

"We aren't going to let anything happen to him," Marcus said. "But we need room to work—and that means we need you out of the van. Please."

A polite werewolf. If Damien hadn't witnessed it himself, he never would have believed it. He held out his hand, focusing all his energy on keeping it from shaking. Marcus dropped the earpiece onto Damien's palm.

Now for the hard part. Walking past a werewolf in the cramped space.

Damien put the earpiece into place as he carefully headed toward the back of the van, skirting the empty stasis chamber by walking on the van's wall. His heart was pounding against his chest in a punishing beat. He breathed a little easier when he heard Vaughn's voice in his ear.

"Damien? Damien, can you hear me?" she said.

"Yeah, I can hear you." He glared at Tessa as he

reached the opening where the back door had been and jumped down onto the pavement.

She stepped in front of him, blocking his way. Her eyes brightened.

Maybe there was a reason Tessa hadn't been mentioned before. She didn't seem as 'polite' as Marcus.

"We have a problem?" Damien asked.

Showing weakness didn't seem like a good idea, so he held his ground. Tessa's lips pulled back from her teeth. Her canines were growing longer. Sharper.

Shit.

Yeah. They had a problem. Well, *he* did, anyway.

The light cast from the inside of the van dimmed briefly Something blurred next to her, then Marcus was at her side.

"Tessa, calm down." Marcus grabbed her arm and pulled her away from Damien, but not before her fingers had lengthened into claws—even the metal ones.

"What's going on?" Vaughn asked.

Damien ignored the voice in his ear. He needed his full attention on the werewolf who was glaring at him like she wanted to rip out his throat with her teeth. Maybe he'd get that fight after all. And finally a release from living in this world of blood and chaos.

"What's taking you guys so long?"

Damien jumped at the new voice right next to him. He backed away from the people surrounding the van. The pack of werewolves and…

"Holy shit." The words slipped out before he could stop them.

Vaughn had said that Brock was 'kind of' a werewolf. Damien was pretty sure that's who he was looking at. Brock had black hair with streaks of stark white running through it. He was thick with muscle—almost as big as Damien, and Damien always got crap from the other Blades about being the biggest Guard.

Four jagged lines ran down Brock's face, starting at his hairline above his left eye, crossing his nose, and running down to his chin. It looked like something had practically ripped off his face. The wounds hadn't healed right and the scars were still dark red, even though the wounds seemed to be sealed.

His right eye glowed gold, like the other three werewolves surrounding Damien. But his left eye was entirely white—except for a gleaming blue pupil that sparked and crackled like a live wire. Tiny motes of energy continuously emerged from it, fizzing out when they were a few inches from his face with quiet 'pops.'

Brock just stared at Damien for a few moments, then turned back to the van.

"Everybody in position," Brock said. "Let's get my brothers home."

"Wait, 'brothers?'" Damien started forward, but balked when Brock leaned down and wedged his hands under the van. The dark-haired woman joined him, sliding her slender hands beneath the vehicle. She must be Meg. Inside, Tessa and Marcus had braced themselves against the stasis chambers. Damien hadn't even seen them move, they were so fast.

"I'll explain when you get to the ranch," Vaughn said. "Right now, we have to get all of you out of there. We still don't know what attacked or if it's coming back."

"On three." Brock nodded to the woman crouched next to him. "One, two, three."

The two wolves lifted the enormous van as if it was made of balsa wood. It crashed onto its wheels and rocked on its suspension a few times before settling. Brock headed for the opening in the back of the van while the woman Damien assumed was Brock's mate walked up to him. Her hands were held in front of her, fingers interlaced.

Damien's heart felt like it stilled for a moment before starting that punishing beat again. The big eyes, high cheekbones, the shape of her chin and lips… She looked just like he imagined Tammie would have—if she'd lived long enough to grow up.

If something like *this* hadn't killed her.

The *wolf* said, "Hi, I'm Meg. Or Megan, if you'd like. That's what Vaughn calls me. It's nice to meet you."

Her build was slight, but muscled. He didn't dare underestimate her.

"I'd offer to shake your hand, but I don't think you'd like that very much." She cast a warm smile at him. If he didn't know what she was, he might almost be starting to like her.

"I do have some unsolicited advice, but it's really important." She took a step closer.

He jerked back, wanting to keep at least some distance between them. As if that would make a difference if she went for him. She actually winced, like it hurt her feelings that he didn't trust her. What the hell kind of pack was this?

"Nobody's going to hurt you," she said. "We're here to help. But it would maybe be a good idea to not make so much eye contact with the others." She cast a chagrined smile at him and half-shrugged. "It's you know... a werewolf thing."

He *didn't* know. Because he wasn't a fucking werewolf.

"Damien, you have to chill." Vaughn's voice sounded in his ear. He was surprised at how much it reassured him.

"I've opened a private channel for us," she said. "Eventually, I'll teach you how to subvocalize so you can talk to me without the others hearing."

Of course she would.

"Listen, we've all been through a lot in the last couple of days," Vaughn said. "And Tessa is still recovering from... a lot of things."

Damien's gaze flicked to that metal arm of hers. Had

she lost the original before, after, or during her being turned into a werewolf? Any of those scenarios was a nightmare.

"Just ease up on the eye contact," Vaughn said. "And try to give them a break. We could all use one right about now."

Damien snorted. Tessa glanced over at him, and this time, he stared at her chin. He'd still be able to track what she was doing, and maybe this way he'd avoid a fight there was no way he'd survive.

Two people had now given Damien hope that Carey could somehow be restored. Damien had no idea how that would work, but he hung onto the possibility as tight as he could. There was so much blood on his hands already. If there was any chance he could wipe this stain away, he had to do everything in his power to make it happen.

"The stasis pod is intact." Marcus hopped down from the back of the van. He pulled off the glasses and tossed them to Damien. "Vaughn wants you to wear these, just in case I have to change."

The idea of Marcus transforming made Damien's heart pick up again. His skin joined the party, electric gooseflesh of the most unpleasant kind skittering over his body.

Damien wasn't surprised Marcus's eyes were gold. He *was* surprised they weren't glowing like Tessa's. She was shifting her weight from one foot to the other, eyeing the trees around them, obviously spooked. She cast a meaningful look at Marcus, and he shook his head.

"Use your words, Tessa," Brock said.

"How about these words—fuck you." She flipped Brock off for good measure.

Who the hell was the alpha here? From what Damien knew about dwellers, the alpha of a werewolf pack would skin any member who showed such disrespect. There was something familiar in the way Tessa was ripping on Brock, though. A dynamic Damien could almost remember.

Brock's boots crunched on loose gravel as he jumped down from inside the van. He shook his head and laughed.

"You'll have to excuse Tessa's manners," Brock said. "Little sisters can be a pain in the ass."

"Sister?" Damien said.

Brock shrugged. "Foster sister. We grew up together."

Damien's stomach lurched.

Yeah, that was the dynamic he was picking up on. The way Tessa was picking at Brock was just like—

Damien shook his head sharply. He couldn't let himself think about his past, especially with Tammie's werewolf-doppelgänger standing nearby. It was done. Dead and buried, like his entire fucking family. He had to stay in the moment, remember the fight. It was the only thing that kept him going.

"Nobody subvocalizes or uses the mental link while Damien's with us," Brock said. "It's rude."

Brock smirked at Damien. Damn, those freaky eyes…

Megan picked up the door Tessa had ripped off the van and walked past Damien with it, shifting it in her grip as she passed.

"Sorry," she said, smiling at him.

A pack of considerate werewolves. As if Damien's life wasn't bizarre enough already.

"Let's load up and get the van moving again before our uninvited guest decides to come back," Brock said.

Damien wasn't sure which he should be more afraid of —whatever had attacked the van, or the group who claimed to be protecting him. He glanced into the gaping hole in the back of the vehicle, catching sight of the stasis pods.

None of it mattered. He had to get Zach to Vaughn. Get Zach to Vaughn and somehow they might be able to get Carey back. That was Damien's mission. If he had to work with a pack of werewolves to do it... He would get it done.

—

Check out my website to see where you can get *Perihelion* now! I'd love to keep in touch. Join my newsletter to get sneak peeks and behind-the-scenes insight into my many worlds, and check out other ways to join my community on my website at cassandra-chandler.com/community. I really want to know what *you* think. If you enjoyed this book, please consider leaving a review at your favorite book review site. I'd really appreciate it—reviews help readers and authors alike! Thank you for reading *Progenitor!*

Cassandra Chandler

About the Author

USA Today Bestselling author Cassandra Chandler uses her vivid imagination to make the world more interesting, spawning the ideas she turns into her captivating Science Fiction Romances and enthralling Paranormal and Urban Fantasy Romances. Fast-paced and funny, lighthearted or filled with suspense, her stories will introduce you to characters you'll fall in love with and worlds you long to explore.

www.ingramcontent.com/pod-product-compliance
Lightning Source LLC
Chambersburg PA
CBHW072255020726
47501CB00002B/268